THE COMPUTER'S WARNING . . .

Mavra was worried. "There is danger, then?"

"Trelig has already told you," Obie responded, "of the possibility of a master Markovian brain somewhere, maintaining all reality. When I reverse the bias, there is a good possibility, in theory, that New Pompeii will have no existence in the prime equation."

Mavra Chang couldn't quite follow the computer's logic and said so.

"Well," Obie said, "there is a ninety or more percent chance that one of two things will happen. Either we will cease to exist, to have ever existed—or we will be pulled, instantaneously, to the central Markovian brain, which is certainly not within a dozen galaxies of us. One way or another, at midday tomorrow, I and all of New Pompeii shall cease to exist."

"Why are you telling me this?"

"You alone possess—so far—the only qualities for even a slight chance of escape . . ."

Exiles
AT THE
Well of Souls

Part I of
THE WARS OF THE WELL

Jack L. Chalker

A Del Rey Book

BALLANTINE BOOKS • NEW YORK

A Del Rey Book
Published by Ballantine Books

Library of Congress Catalog Card Number: 78-60658

ISBN 0-345-27701-5

Manufactured in the United States of America

First Edition: September 1978

Cover art by Darrell Sweet

This book is for a number of old pros, who, wittingly or unwittingly, at various times have helped:

Leigh Brackett
Robert Bloch
Alfred Bester
Marty (Hicksville) Greenberg
Gordon R. Dickson
Harlan Ellison
Fritz Leiber
Harry ("Hal Clement") Stubbs
Compton ("Stephen Tall") Crook
Avram Davidson
Jack Williamson

and, most especially, to a man who has never heard of me but has had more influence on the field of science fiction than any ten comparable writers,

Mr. Eric Frank Russell

CONTENTS

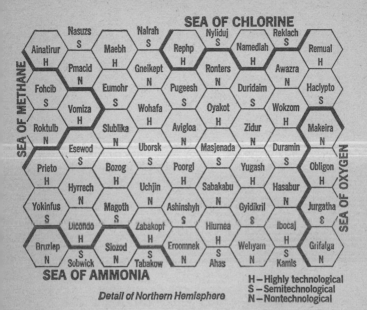

SEA OF CHLORINE

SEA OF METHANE

SEA OF OXYGEN

SEA OF AMMONIA

Detail of Northern Hemisphere

H – Highly technological
S – Semitechnological
N – Nontechnological

ix

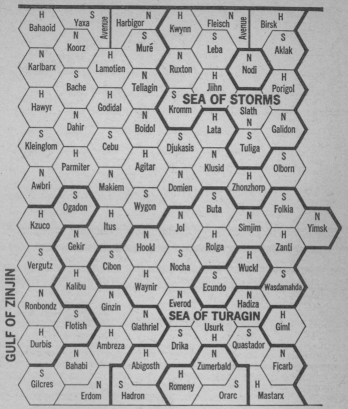

Section of Southern Hemisphere

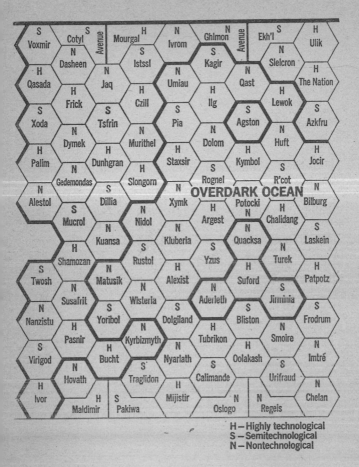

S Voxmir	S Cotyl	Avenue	H Mourgal	N Ivrom	N Ghlmon	Avenue	Ekh'l S	H Ulik

Key regions (as labeled on map):

S Voxmir · S Cotyl · H Mourgal · N Ivrom · N Ghlmon · Ekh'l S · H Ulik
N Dasheen · S Istssl · S Kagir · N Slelcron
H Qasada · N Jaq · N Umiau · N Qast · H The Nation
H Frick · H Czill · H Ilg · H Lewok
S Xoda · S Tsfrin · S Pia · S Agston · S Azkfru
N Dymek · N Murithel · N Dolom · N Huft
H Palim · H Dunhgran · H Staxsir · H Kymbol · H Jocir
N Gedemondas · H Slongorn · S Rognel · S R'cot
N Alestol · S Dillia · N Xymk · N Potocki · N Bilburg
S Mucrol · N Nidol · N Argest · N Chalidang
H Kuansa · S Kluberia · S Quacksa · S Laskein
H Shamozan · S Rustol · S Yzus · N Turek
S Twosh · N Matusik · N Alexist · H Suford · H Patpotz
N Susafrit · N Wisteria · N Aderleth · S Jirminia
N Nanzistu · S Yoribol · S Dolgiland · S Bliston · S Frodrum
H Pasnir · N Kyrbizmyth · H Tubrikon · N Smoire
S Virigod · H Bucht · N Nyarlath · H Oolakash · N Imtré
N Hovath · S' Traglidon · S Calimande · S Urifraud
H Ivor · H Maldimir · S Pakiwa · H Mijistir · N Oslogo · N Regeis · N Chelan

OVERDARK OCEAN

H — Highly technological
S — Semitechnological
N — Nontechnological

ABOUT TIME . . .

The format of this book is extremely episodic; the action will shift to several different people and events very rapidly, and this might cause some temporal disorientation to those used to reading a straight-line narrative. Therefore, the reader is cautioned to keep in mind that, unless the text specifically says otherwise, a scene-change is considered to be going on simultaneously with the preceding action, and that this is true, regardless of the number of scene changes, until the original characters come up again. The scheme may sound difficult, but it shouldn't cause problems.

JLC

Gaemesjun Laboratories, Makeva

IT WASN'T THE FACT THAT GILGAM ZINDER'S LAB AS-
sistant had a horse's tail that was the oddest fact; the
really strange thing was that she didn't seem to think
her condition odd or unusual.

Zinder was tall and thin, a gaunt man with gray
hair and a long gray goatee that made him seem even
older than he was, and more drawn. His blue-
gray eyes, bloodshot and surrounded with darkening
shadow, showed his overwork. He hadn't thought to
eat in more than two days, and sleep had become
academic.

The place was a strange-looking lab at that. It was
designed something like an ampitheater, with a circular raised pedestal about forty centimeters above the
plain flooring that served as the stage. Above the stage
was a device hanging like a great cannon but terminating in a small mirror with a tiny point coming out
from it.

A balcony surrounded the apparatus; here, along
the walls, were thousands of blinking lights, dials and
switches, and central consoles, four of them, evenly
spaced around the circle below. Zinder sat at one; directly across from him a much younger man in shiny
protective lab clothing sat at another. Zinder's lab suit
looked as if it had been made in the last century.

The woman standing on the raised disk was an
ordinary-looking sort, late thirties and a little dumpy
and saggy, the kind that looks far better with proper
clothes than nude as she now was.

Only she had a horse's tail, long and bushy.

She looked up at the two men with puzzlement and
some impatience.

"Well, come on," she called to them, "aren't you
going to *do* anything? It's *cold* down here."

1

Ben Yulin, the younger man, smiled and leaned over the rail.

"Swish your tail awhile, Zetta. We're working as fast as we can!" he called down good-naturedly.

And she *was* swishing the tail, slowly back and forth, routinely, echoing her frustration.

"You really don't notice any difference, Zetta?" Zinder's thin, reedy voice asked her.

She looked puzzled, then down at herself, running her hands along her body, including the tail, as if to find out what they did.

"No, Dr. Zinder, I don't. Why? Is something about me—different?" she responded hesitantly.

"Do you know you have a tail?" Zinder prompted.

She looked puzzled. "Of course I have a tail," she replied in a so-what's-wrong-with-that tone.

"You don't find that, ah, odd or unusual?" Ben Yulin put in.

The woman was genuinely confused. "Why, no, of course not. Why should I?"

Zinder looked over at his young assistant, almost fifteen meters across the open stage.

"An interesting development," he commented.

Yulin nodded. "Creating bean pots, then the lab-animal stuff, that told us what we could do, but I don't think I was ready for this."

"You remember the theory?" Zinder prompted.

Yulin nodded. "We're changing probability within the field. What we do to something or someone in the field is normal to them, because we've changed their basic stabilizing equation. Fascinating. If we could do this on a large scale . . ." He let the thought trail off.

Zinder looked thoughtful. "Yes, indeed. A whole population would be changed and it would never know it." He turned and looked down again at the woman with the horse's tail.

"Zetta?" he called. "Do you know that *we* do not have tails? That no one else we know of has a tail?"

She nodded. "Yes, I know it's unusual to you. But what's the big deal? I haven't exactly tried to hide it from view."

"Did your parents have tails, Zetta?" Yulin asked.

2

"Of course not!" she responded. "Now what's all this about?"

The younger scientist looked across at the old one. "Want to go any further?" he asked.

Zinder shrugged lightly. "Why not? Yes, I'd love to do a psych probe and see how deep it goes, but if we can do it once we can do it anytime. Let's check out one thing at a time."

"Okay," Yulin agreed. "So now what?"

Zinder looked thoughtful for a moment. Then, suddenly, he reached over and touched a panel next to a recessed combination microphone and speaker.

"Obie?" he called into it.

"Yes, Dr. Zinder?" the voice of the computer that was in the walls around them replied; a pleasant, professional, and personable tenor.

"You have noted that the subject does not know we have in any way altered her?"

"Noted," Obie admitted. "Do you wish her to? The equations are not quite as stable in that situation but they'll hold up."

"No, no, that's all right," Zinder responded quickly. "How about attitude without physical change? Is that possible?"

"A much more minor alteration," the computer told him. "But, also, because of that, more easily and quickly reversible."

Zinder nodded. "All right, then, Obie. We translated a horse into the system matrix, so you have it completely and you have Zetta completely."

"We don't have the horse any more," Obie pointed out.

Zinder sighed impatiently. "But you have the data on it, don't you? That's where the tail came from, right?"

"Yes, Doctor," Obie replied. "I see now that you were being rhetorical again. I'm sorry."

"That's all right," Zinder assured the machine. "Look, let's try for something bigger. Do you have the term and concept *centaur* in your memory?"

Obie thought for perhaps a millisecond. "Yes. But it will take some work to turn her into one. After all, there is the matter of internal plumbing, cardiovascu-

3

lar systems, additional nerve connections, and the like."

"But you *can* do it?" Zinder prompted, somewhat surprised.

"Oh, yes."

"How long?"

"Two or three minutes," Obie replied.

Zinder leaned over. The girl with the tail was pacing a little nervously on the podium, looking quite uncomfortable.

"Assistant Halib! Please stop that pacing and return to the center of the disk!" he reproved her. "We're about ready, and you *did* volunteer for this."

She sighed. "Sorry, Doctor," she responded and stood on the center mark.

Zinder looked over at Yulin. "On my mark!" he called, and Yulin nodded.

"Mark!"

The little mirrorlike disk overhead moved out, the little point in the center aimed down, and suddenly the entire area of the disk was bathed in a pale-blue light that seemed to sparkle, enveloping the woman. She seemed frozen, unable to move. Then she suddenly flickered several times like a projected image and winked out entirely.

"Subject's known stability equation has been neutralized," Yulin said into his recorder. He looked up at Zinder.

"Gil?" he called, slightly disturbed.

"Eh?" the other man responded absently.

"Suppose we didn't bring her back? I mean, suppose we just neutralized her," Yulin said nervously. "Would she exist, Gil? Would she ever have existed?"

Zinder sat back in his chair, thinking. "She wouldn't exist, no," he told the other. "As to the rest—well, we'll ask Obie." He leaned forward and flipped on the transceiver connecting him to the computer.

"Yes, Doctor?" the computer's calm tone came back.

"I'm not disturbing the process, am I?" Zinder asked carefully.

"Oh, no," the computer replied cheerfully. "It's taking only a little under an eighth of me to work it out."

4

"Can you tell me—if the subject were not restabilized, would she have any existence? That is, would she have ever existed?"

Obie thought it over. "No, of course not. She is a minor part of the prime equation, of course, so it wouldn't affect reality as we know it. But it would adjust. She would never have lived."

"Then—what if we left her with the tail?" Yulin broke in. "Would everybody else assume she had a tail all along?"

"Quite so," the computer agreed. "After all, to exist she must have a reason, or the equations would not balance. Again, it would have no effect on the *overall* equation."

"What would, I wonder?" Zinder mumbled off-mike, then turned back to Obie. "Tell me, if that's the case, why do we—Ben, you, and me—know that reality has been altered?"

"We are in close proximity to the field," Obie replied. "Anyone within approximately a hundred meters would have some knowledge of this. The closer you are, the more dichotomy you perceive. After about a hundred meters the perception of reality starts to become negligible. People would be aware that something was different, but wouldn't be able to figure out what. Beyond a thousand meters the dissipation would become one with the master equation, and reality would adjust. I can, however, adjust or minimize this for your perceptions if you desire."

"Absolutely not!" Zinder said sharply. "But you mean that everyone beyond a thousand meters of here would firmly believe she had always been a centaur and that there was a logical reason for it?"

"That is correct. The prime equations always remain in natural balance."

"She's coming in!" Ben called excitedly, breaking off the dialogue.

Zinder looked out and saw a shape flicker into the center of the disk. It flickered twice more, then solidified, and the field winked out. The mirror swung silently away overhead.

It was still Zetta Halib, recognizably. But where the woman had stood, the creature was Zetta now only down to the waist. There her yellow-brown skin melded into black hair, and the rest of her body was that of a full-grown mare of perhaps two years.

"Obie?" Yulin called, and the computer answered. "Obie, how long before she stabilizes? That is, how long before the centaur becomes permanent?"

"It's permanent now, for her," the computer told him. "If you mean how long it will take the prime equations to stabilize her new set, an hour or two at most. It is, after all, a minor disturbance."

Zinder leaned over the rail and looked at her in amazement. It was clear that he had exceeded his wildest dreams.

"Would she breed true—if we had a male?" Yulin asked the computer.

"No," the computer responded, sounding almost apologetic. "That would take a lot more work. She would breed a horse, of course."

"You could make a breeding pair of centaurs, though?" Yulin persisted.

"Most probably," Obie hedged. "After all, the only limit to this process is my input. I have to have the knowledge of how to do it, how things are put together, before I can work something out."

Yulin nodded, but he was plainly as excited as the older man whose life's work this was.

The centaur looked up at them. "Are we just going to stay here all day?" she asked impatiently. "I'm getting hungry."

"Obie, what does she eat?" Yulin asked.

"Grass, hay, anything of that nature," the computer replied. "I had to take some short cuts, of course. The torso is mostly muscle tissue and supporting bone. I used the horse's part for the organs."

Yulin nodded, then looked over at the older scientist, still somewhat dazed by what he'd wrought.

"Gil?" he called. "How about some cosmetic touch-ups, and then we can keep her this way awhile? It would be interesting to see how this alteration works out."

Zinder nodded absently.

With one more pass, Yulin was able to give the new creature a younger human half; he tightened her

6

up and restored what appeared to be youthful good looks.

They were almost finished when a door opened near the old scientist and a young girl, no more than fourteen, walked in with a tray. She was about 165 centimeters tall, but she weighed close to sixty-eight kilograms. Pudgy, stocky, awkward, with thick legs and fat-enlarged breasts, she wasn't helped by dressing in a diaphanous dress, sandals, and overdone makeup, or by the obviously dyed long blond hair. She looked somehow grotesque, but the old man smiled indulgently.

"Nikki!" he said reprovingly. "I thought I told you not to come in when the red light was on!"

"I'm sorry, Daddy," she responded, sounding not the least bit sorry, as she put the tray down and kissed him lightly on the cheek. "But you haven't eaten in *so* long we were getting worried." She looked over, saw the younger man and smiled a very different sort of smile.

"Hi, Ben!" she called playfully, and waved.

Yulin looked over, smiled, and waved back. Then, suddenly, he was thinking hard. A hundred meters, he thought. The kitchen was about that far away, above ground.

She put her arms around her father. "What have you been up to for so long?" she asked in that playful tone. Although physically adult, Nikki Zinder was emotionally very much a child and acted it. Too much, her father knew. She was overly protected here, cut off from people her own age, and spoiled rotten from an early age by her father's inability to discipline her and everybody's knowledge that she was the boss's kid. Even her slight lisp was childish; often she seemed more like a pouting five-year-old than the almost fourteen she really was.

But, she was *his*, and he couldn't bear to send her away, to put her in a fancy school or project far away from him. His had been a lonely life of figures and great machines; at fifty-seven he had had clone samples taken, but he wanted his own. Finally he had paid a project assistant back on Voltaire to give him a baby. She had been the first one willing to do it, just

7

to see what the experience was like. She was a behavioral psychologist, and Zinder had had her assigned to his project until Nikki was delivered, then he paid her off, and she left.

Nikki looked like her mother, but that didn't matter. She was *his,* and during the most trying periods of the project she had kept him from blowing his brains out. She was immature as hell. But he really didn't want her to grow up. Nikki Zinder suddenly heard a woman cough, and she bounded up to the rail and looked down on the centaur.

"Oh, wow!" she exclaimed. "Hi! Zetta!"

The centaur looked up at the girl and smiled indulgently. "Hello, Nikki," she responded automatically.

Both Zinder and Yulin were fascinated.

"Nikki, you don't see anything, er, *odd* about Zetta?" her father prompted.

The girl shrugged. "Nope. Why? Should I?"

Ben Yulin's mouth dropped open in honest surprise.

Over a week passed during which they noted various reactions to the new creature. Just about everyone at the center saw nothing unusual in Zetta Halib being half horse; that is, nothing *newly* unusual. They knew, of course, that she was a volunteer for the biological scientists attempting to adapt people to different forms. They knew she had been manipulated after conception to grow up as she had, and they remembered when she had arrived and recalled the initial reactions.

Everything checked out, of course, except for the fact that none of what they remembered had actually happened. Reality needed to explain her and had adjusted accordingly. Only two men knew the truth.

Ben Yulin puffed on his curved pipe in his boss's office, rocking lazily back and forth in a spindly chair.

"So now we know," he said at last.

The older scientist nodded and sipped some tea. "Yes, we do. We can take any individual, anything, and we can remake it if we can come up with the data Obie needs to make the transformation properly, and nobody will even know. Poor Zetta! A one-of-a-kind freak with a full history and memory of growing up that way. We'll have to change her back, of course."

"Of course," Yulin agreed. "But let's let her keep her good looks. She's earned that much from us."

"Yes, yes, of course." Zinder responded as if that meant little to him.

"Something is still bothering you," Yulin noted.

Gil Zinder sighed. "Yes, quite a lot. This is a terrible power, you know, to play god like this. And I don't like the idea of the Council getting control of it."

Yulin looked surprised. "Well, they didn't blow all this money for nothing. Hell! We've done it, Gil! We've knocked conventional science into a cocked hat! We've shown them how easily the rules of the game can be changed!"

The older scientist nodded. "True, true. We'll win all sorts of awards and all that. But—well, you know what's the real problem. Three hundred seventy-four human worlds. A lot. But all but a handful are Comworlds, conformist fantasies. Think what the rulers of those worlds could do to those people with a device like ours!"

Yulin sighed. "Look, Gil, our way is no different than the crude methods they use now—biological manipulation, genetic engineering, all those things. Maybe things won't be so bad after all. Maybe our discovery will make things better. Hell, it can't make them much worse."

"That's true," Zinder acknowledged. "But the power, Ben! And," he paused, turned in his swivel chair to face the younger scientist, "there's something else."

"Huh? What?" Yulin responded.

"The implications," the physicist said worriedly. "Ben, if all this, this chair, this office, you, me—if we're all just stable equations, matter created out of pure energy and somehow maintained as we are, *what's keeping us stable?* Is there a cosmic Obie someplace, keeping the primary equations balanced?"

Ben Yulin chuckled. "I suppose there is, one way or another. God is nothing but a giant Obie. I kind of like that thought."

9

Zinder didn't find it amusing in the least. "I think there is, Ben. There *must* be, if everything else is correct. Even Obie agrees. But who built it? Who maintains it?"

"Well, if you want to be serious about it, I suppose the Markovians built it. For all I know they still maintain it," Yulin responded.

Zinder considered that. "The Markovians. Yes, it must be. We've found their dead worlds and deserted cities all over. They must have done all this on a giant scale, Ben!" He was suddenly excited. "Of course! That's why they never found any artifacts in those old ruins! Whatever they wanted, they just told their version of Obie and there it was!"

Yulin nodded approvingly. "You might be right."

"But, Ben!" Zinder kept on. "All the worlds of theirs we've found! They're all dead!" He sat back in his chair, voice and manner calming a bit, but his tone still agitated. "I wonder—if *they* couldn't handle it, how can we?" He looked straight at the other scientist. "Ben, are we producing the means to wipe out the human race?"

Yulin shook his head slowly from side to side. "I don't know, Gil. I hope not. But we haven't much choice. Besides," he smiled, tone lighter, "no matter what, we'll all be long gone before that point is reached."

"I wish I had your confidence, Ben," Zinder said nervously. "Well, you're right on one thing. We have to deliver. Will you set it up?"

Ben walked over and patted the old man on the shoulder. "Of course I'll make the arrangements," he assured the other. "Look, you worry too much, Gil. Trust me." His tone changed, became more self-confident. The other didn't notice. "Yes, I'll set it up."

In the old days there were nations, and they reached for space. And then there were planetary colonies of these nations, and they all had differing philosophies and life-styles. There followed wars, raids, engineered revolutions. Man expanded, the nations vanished, leaving behind only their philosophies for their heirs. Finally, rulers sick of it all got together and formed a trust. All competing ideologies were to be given free reign until one dominated a planet, but never by force and never with help from outside. Each planet would choose a member to sit on a great Council of Worlds and cast its vote.

The great weapons of terror and destruction were placed under seal and guarded by a tough force born and bred to the service—a force that could not itself use those weapons without authority. Such authority could come only from a majority of the 374 Council members, each of whom would have to appear personally to open his share of the seals.

Councillor Antor Trelig was one such guardian and a strong political force on the governing body. Technically, he represented the People's Party of New Outlook, a Comworld where people were bred to obedience and to function perfectly in their jobs. Actually, he represented a lot more, for he had a great deal of influence over other Council members as well. Some said he was ambitious enough to dream of one day controlling a majority, of holding in his hands the keys to the weapons that could wreck worlds.

He was a big man, around 190 centimeters tall, who had broad shoulders and a strong hooknose set atop a squared jaw. He looked as though made of granite. But he didn't look like the power-mad villain many painted him as being, not standing there, fascinated, watching two men and a machine unmake a centaur.

The scientists petormed a few additional demonstrations for him, even asked him if he wanted to try it. Trelig declined with a nervous laugh. But, after talking to the girl who walked off the raised disk and after seeing reality readjust to her original existence, he was convinced.

Later he relaxed with a very un-Com-like brandy in Zinder's office.

"I can't tell you how stunned I am," he told them. "What you did is incredible, unbelievable. Tell me, could a huge one be built? One large enough to control whole planets?"

Zinder suddenly became hostile. "I don't think doing so would be practical, Councillor. Too many variables."

11

"It could be done," Ben Yulin put in, ignoring the angry look from his colleague. "But the cost and effort would be enormous!"

Trelig nodded. "Such a cost would be negligible when compared with the benefits. Why, this could wipe out any possibilities of starvation, vagaries of climate, and what not. It could produce a utopia!"

Or it could reduce the few free and individualistic worlds left to happy and obedient slavery, Zinder thought morosely. Aloud, he said, "I think it's a weapon, too, Councillor. A terrible one in the wrong hands. I believe that is what killed the Markovians a few million years ago. I would feel better if such a power were placed under Council Seal."

Trelig sighed. "I don't agree. But, we'll never know without trying it out. Such a scientific breakthrough can't just be locked away and abandoned!"

"I think it should be, and all traces of the research erased," Zinder maintained. "What we have is the power to play god. I don't think we're ready for that yet."

"You can't uninvent something once invented, regardless of its implications," Trelig pointed out. "But, I agree, word should be kept under wraps. If even the knowledge of your discovery got out, it would inspire a million other scientists. I think, for now, you should pull the project out of here and move to some place safe, isolated."

"And where would this safe place be?" Zinder asked skeptically.

Trelig smiled. "I have a place, a planetoid with full life-support, normal gravity maintenance, and the like. I use it as a resort. It would be ideal."

Zinder felt uneasy, remembering Trelig's sleazy reputation.

"I don't think so," he told the big man. "I think I'd rather put the matter to the full Council next week and let the members decide."

Trelig acted as if he expected that response. "Sure you won't reconsider, Doctor? New Pompeii is a wonderful place, much nicer than this sterile horror."

Zinder understood what he was being offered.

"No, I stand firm," the old scientist told the politician. "Nothing can make me change my mind."

Trelig sighed. "That's it, then. I'll arrange for a Council meeting a week from tomorrow. You and Dr. Yulin will attend, of course."

The big man stood up and moved to leave. As he did so, he smiled and nodded slowly at Ben Yulin, who returned the nod. Zinder didn't notice.

Ben Yulin would set it up, all right.

Nikki Zinder slept quietly in her own room, a room littered with exotic clothes, various toys, games, and gimmicks strewn about in no particular order. Her huge bed almost enveloped her.

A figure stopped at the door to that room and, after checking to make sure that no one was approaching, took out a small screwdriver and unscrewed the door pressure plate, carefully, so that the door alarm wouldn't be triggered. The plate off, the figure studied the small exposed modules and placed some spirit gum at several critical points. One module was removed and adjusted by placing a small strip of silvery material between two contacts not otherwise connected.

Satisfied, the intruder replaced the covering plate and meticulously screwed it back on. Replacing the screwdriver on a tool belt, he hesitated a second, tension getting to him, then pressed the contact.

There was a soft click, but nothing else happened. Breathing easier now, he removed a tiny nodule of clear liquid from another pouch on the belt and attached an injector tab to it. Holding it carefully, injector out, he went to the twin solid door to the girl's room and slowly pressed on one section with his free hand, then moved it slightly to the right.

The door opened quietly, without the pneumatic hiss or any other appreciable sound that could be heard or detected over the residual air conditioning of the building. Opening the door just enough to slip inside, he turned and closed it quietly behind him.

By the dull glow of a baseboard nightlight he made out the sleeping figure of Nikki Zinder. She lay on her back, mouth open, snoring slightly.

Slowly, stealthily, he tiptoed to her bedside, until

he stood almost over her. He froze as she mumbled something in her sleep and turned slightly on one side, moving away from him. Patiently he leaned over and peeled a bit of the sheet away from her, exposing her upper right arm. The hand with the injector and nodule reached over, and he placed it firmly on her arm.

His touch was so gentle that she did not awaken, but gave out a low moan and turned again on her back. Nodule empty, the man withdrew the tiny packet and put it in his pocket.

She *did* seem to be awakening a little, left hand coming over and feeling the muscle on the right. Then the arm suddenly seemed to lose its ability to move, and it limply fell away. Her breathing became heavier, more labored.

Taking a deep breath, he leaned over, touched her, shook her hard. She did not respond.

Smiling in satisfaction, he sat beside her on the bed, bent over close to her.

"Nikki, do you hear me?" he asked softly.

"Uh, huh," she mumbled.

"Nikki, listen carefully," he instructed. "When I say 'one hundred' again, you will begin counting down from there to zero. When you reach zero, you will get up, go out of this room, and come immediately to the lab. To the ground floor of the lab, Nikki. There you will find a large, round platform right in the middle of the floor, and you will stand on it. You will stand on it and you will not be able to move from the middle of it, nor will you want to. You will be frozen there, and you will still be sound asleep. Do you understand all that?"

"I understand," she responded dreamily.

"Avoid being seen going to the lab," he cautioned. "Do anything to keep from being seen. But, if you *are* seen, act normal, get rid of anyone quickly, and don't tell where you're really going. Will you do that?"

"Uh huh," she acknowledged.

He rose from the bed and went over to the door, which still worked on automatics from the bedroom side. It was free, though, and he opened it a crack, saw no one, then opened it a little wider. He stepped into the hall, turned, and almost closed the door.

"One hundred, Nikki," he said, and closed it all the way.

Satisfied, he walked down the corridor almost a hundred meters, meeting no one and noting with satisfaction that all the doors were closed. He entered the elevator, and the door to the capsule closed.

"Yulin, Abu Ben, YA–356–47765–7881–GX, Full clearance, Lab 2 level, please," he said. The elevator checked him visually, checked his ID number and voice prints, then descended rapidly to the lab floor.

Once on the balcony, he walked over to his control panel and switched it to active mode.

He flipped the switch to Obie.

"Obie?" he called.

"Yes, Ben?" came that soft, friendly reply.

Yulin punched some buttons on his keyboard.

"Unnumbered transaction," he responded with a calmness he didn't feel. "File in aux storage under my key only."

"What are you doing, Ben?" Obie asked curiously. "That is a mode even *I* can't use. I had no idea it was in there until you used it."

Ben Yulin smiled. "That's all right, Obie. Even you don't have to remember everything."

What Obie had discovered, and Ben was enjoying, was the mode by which he could use Obie and then have Obie file the record of what was done in such a way that even the great computer couldn't get at it. Obie would still perform normally, but have a case of total amnesia not only about what Ben was about to do but about his even being there.

Yulin heard the elevator door open below. He looked over the balcony and saw Nikki, dressed only in that flimsy nightgown, walk normally and deliberately into the lab chamber and step up onto the disk. Centering herself, she stood erect, her eyes closed, and she seemed frozen, a statue except for barely perceptible breathing.

"Record subject in aux mode, Obie," Yulin instructed. The big mirror overhead swung out, centered

15

over the disk, and shot out the blue ray. Nikki flickered once or twice, then vanished. The ray cut off.

It would be tempting, Yulin thought, just to leave her there. But, no, the risk was too great. She would probably have to be produced in the end, and he didn't want her on that disk with Zinder at the controls.

"Obie, this will be an unstable equation. It will not adjust. The act of change shall in itself be part of reality."

"Yes, Ben," the computer responded. "There will be no reality adjustment."

Yulin nodded in satisfaction.

"Psychological adjustment only, Obie," he told the great machine.

"Ready," responded Obie.

"Maximum emotional-sexual response level," he ordered. "Subject is to be fixated on Dr. Ben Yulin, data in your banks. Subject will be madly, irrationally in love with Yulin, and will think of nothing but Yulin. Will do anything for Yulin, will be loyal only to Yulin, without exception. Subject will consider herself the willing property of said Ben Yulin. Code it 'love-slave mode' for future reference and store in aux one."

"Done," the computer acknowledged.

"Sequence, then store as soon as both humans have left the lab."

"Sequencing," the computer said, and Yulin looked over the balcony. The blue light had flipped on again, and Nikki, still the same and still wearing the same nightgown, winked back in. She was still frozen.

Yulin cursed himself. It'd been less than twenty minutes since he had administered the dosage which was good for probably three times that. He'd taken no chances.

"Additional instructions, Obie," he shot back. "Remove all traces of the drug Stepleflin from subject and restore subject at full wakefulness, with the equivalent of eight hours sleep. Do this immediately, then return to previous instructions."

The computer accepted the new instructions, the blue light went on, Nikki flickered but did not wink

16

out for more than half a second this time, then was back, awake, looking in amazement about the lab.

Yulin leaned over the railing. "Hey, Nikki!"

She looked up, spotted him, and the look on her face was suddenly so full of rapture that she appeared to be seeing the face of god. She trembled and moaned in ecstasy at the sight of him.

"Come up to this level, Nikki," he instructed, and she all but ran off the disk to the elevator. She was next to him in less than two minutes. She continued to look at him in awe and wonder. He lightly touched her cheek with his hand and an orgasmic shudder went through her. He nodded, satisfied.

"Come with me, Nikki," he ordered softly, taking her hand. She gripped it and followed. They boarded the elevator, and Yulin told it to rise to the surface.

The top level opened onto a small park, dimly lit by the artificial light of the clear dome. The stars shown distantly from horizon to horizon. She hadn't uttered a sound, asked a question, during all this.

There were a few people about. But since much of the research center was devoted to thousands of other projects, many kept different hours for various reasons, some just because of the need to share facilities.

"We must stay hidden from anyone, Nikki," he whispered to her. "No one must see us."

"Oh, yes, Ben," she responded, and they crept along the side of the walk, for the most part hidden in the bushes. There were some sharp needles on some of the bushes and plants that lined the walk, and Nikki was scratched and splintered by them, but aside from occasional rubbing or a near-silent exclamation, she didn't complain. Once he didn't see a short, dark man turn a corner, and she pulled him down behind a bush.

Finally they reached the grassy, unlit area that for obscure reasons some called the campus, and they cut across it, walking normally. Finally, crouched in a dark corner in the shadow of another building, they waited.

She kept her arm around him and leaned into him.

17

He put his arm around her, and she sighed. She was rubbing him and kissing his clothing.

He found the whole thing embarrassing and slightly nauseating, but he'd established the rules of the game and had to suffer for it.

At last, a small, sleek private carrier slid up to them in the blackness. A gull-wing was raised, and a man emerged and approached them. Nikki, hearing movement, looked around and then tried to drag Yulin back into the blackness.

"No, Nikki, that man's a friend of mine," he told her, and she accepted his statement and immediately relaxed.

"Adnar! Over here!" he called, and the man heard and came closer.

"You must go with Adnar," he told her softly. She looked stricken and clung even tighter to him.

"This is the only way we can be together, Nikki," he told her. "You must go away for a short time, but, if you make no complaints and do everything Adnar and his friends tell you without question, I'll come to you, I promise."

She smiled at that. Her mind was clouded; she could think only of Ben, and if Ben said something then it was true.

"Let's go," Adnar called impatiently.

Yulin steeled himself, then hugged the girl and kissed her long and passionately.

"Remember *that* while we're apart," he whispered. "Now, go!"

She went with the strange man. Unquestioningly, without complaint, they climbed into the black carrier, and it sped away.

Ben Yulin allowed himself to exhale, and for the first time noticed he was perspiring. Shakily, he made his way back to his own building and bed.

Antor Trelig displayed the charming smile of a poisonous snake. He sat, relaxed, in Gil Zinder's office once more. The little scientist was visibly shaken.

"You monster!" he snapped at the politician. "What have you done with her?"

Trelig looked hurt. "Me? I would do nothing, I assure you. I am much too big a man for something like a petty kidnapping. But, I *do* have a lead on where she might be, and I have some facts on what's happened to her up to this point."

Zinder knew the big man was lying, but he could also see the reason for the pretense. Trelig *hadn't* done the deed personally, and he would have made very certain that it wasn't traceable to him.

"Tell me what you—they've done to her," he groaned.

Trelig did his best to look serious. "My sources tell me that your daughter is in the hands of the sponge syndicate. You've heard of it?"

Gil Zinder nodded, a cold chill going through him.

"They deal in that terrible drug from that killer planet," he responded, almost mechanically.

"Quite so," Trelig responded sympathetically. "Do you know what it *does,* Doctor? It decreases the IQ of someone by ten percent for every day it goes untreated. A genius is merely average in three or four days, and hardly more than an animal in ten days or so. There's no cure—it's a mutant thing unlike any life form we've ever encountered, produced by a mixture of some of our organic matter and some alien stuff. The effect is painful, too. A burning in the brain, I believe is the description, spreading to all parts of the body."

"Stop! Stop!" Zinder sobbed. "What is your price, you monster?"

"Well, remission is possible," Trelig responded, still sympathetic. "Sponge isn't the drug, of course, it's the remittent agent. Daily doses and there's no pain and little loss. The—ah, disease, is made dormant."

"What is your price?" Zinder almost screamed.

"I believe I can locate her. Buy off these men. My medical staff has some sponge cultures—quite illegal, of course, but we've discovered many people in high places in your situation, blackmailed by these villains. We could go after her, retrieve her, and give her sufficient sponge to restore her to normal." He shifted slightly, enjoying himself immensely.

"But I'm a politician, and ambitious. That's true enough. If I do something, particularly going up

19

against an illegal band of cutthroats and then risking discovery of my illegal sponge, I must have something in return. To do it—"

"Yes? Yes?" Zinder was almost in tears.

"Report your project a failure and put in to close down," Trelig suggested. "I will arrange the transfer of—Obie, I think you call it—to my planetoid of New Pompeii. There you will plan and direct the construction of a much larger model than the one you have here, one large enough to be used at a distance on, say, an entire planet."

Zinder was appalled. "Oh, my god! No! All those people! I can't!"

Trelig smiled smugly. "You don't have to decide now. Take as long as you want." He got up, smoothing out his angelic white robes. "But remember, every passing day Nikki is more subject to the drug. Pain aside, the brain damage is ongoing. Consider that when thinking over your decision. Every second you waste the pain increases, and your daughter's brain dies a tiny bit."

"You bastard," Zinder breathed angrily.

"I'll initiate a search anyway," the big man told the scientist. "What I can spare, but not all-out, because it's merely in the name of humanity. Might take days, though. Even weeks. In the meantime, with a single call to my office saying you agree, I will put everybody on it, sparing nothing. Good-bye, Dr. Zinder."

Trelig walked slowly to the door, then out. It shut behind him.

Zinder stared hard at the door, then sank into his chair. He considered calling the Intersystem Police but thought better of it. Nikki would be well-hidden, and accusing the vice president of the Council of being a sponge merchant and kidnapper without a shred of evidence—Zinder knew the big man would have an ironclad alibi for the night past—would be futile. They'd investigate, of course, take days, even weeks, while poor Nikki . . . They'd let her rot, of course. Let her rot for five or six days. Then what? A low-grade moron, washing floors happily for them, or perhaps a toy given to Trelig's men for sex and sadism.

It was that last he couldn't stand. Her death he thought he could accept, but not that. Not that.

His mind whirled. There would be ways later. Obie could cure her if he could get her back soon enough. And the device he was to build—it could be a two-edged sword.

He sighed, a tired and defeated little man, and punched the code for Trelig's liaison office on Makeva. He knew the big man would still be there. Waiting. Waiting for the inevitable response.

Defeated for now, he thought resolutely, but not vanquished. Not yet.

On New Pompeii, an Asteroid Circling the Uninhabited System of the Star Asta

NEW POMPEII WAS A LARGE ASTEROID, A LITTLE OVER four thousand kilometers at its equator. It was one of those few small bits that inhabit all solar systems that deserved to be called a planetoid; it was fairly round, rounder than most planets, and its core was made up of particularly dense material, giving it a gravity of .7 G when balanced against its ample centrifugal force. The effect took a little getting used to, and people tended to do things faster and feel tremendous. But since it was a government-owned resort, that was all to the good.

Its orbit was relatively stable, by far more circular than elliptical, although night and day were hard to take; thirty-two sunrises and sunsets in a Council-standard twenty-five hours did tend to be unsettling to people's internal clocks.

The discomfort was partially offset by the fact that half the entire planetoid was encased in a great bubble made of a very thin and light synthetic material; the bubble was a good light reflector and blurred the view, so it merely seemed to get darker, then lighter,

21

and so forth, the effect being similar to that on much nicer and more natural worlds on a partly cloudy day. Accounting for the glow effect, was a thin—less than a millimeter—gauze material in somewhat liquid form between the two layers of the bubble. Any punctures were instantly sealed. Even a large one could if necessary be closed long enough to activate safety bubbles around the human centers inside. Compressed air, aided by the lush vegetation planted all over, kept the environment stable.

Theoretically, this was a place for party leaders on New Outlook to get away from the pressures for a bit. Actually the resort's existence was known to only a few people, all intensely loyal to Antor Trelig, who was, after all, the party chairman. Protected by computer battle systems erected both on nearby natural dust specks and in special ships, no one could approach within a light-year without being blown apart, not unless Antor Trelig or his people approved.

The place was unassailable politically, too; it would take a majority vote of the Council to enter over Trelig's diplomatic immunity and sovereignty, and Trelig controlled the largest bloc of votes on the Council.

When they brought Nikki Zinder to New Pompeii she didn't really pay much attention to her surroundings. All she could think of was Ben and Ben's promise that he'd come for her. They put her in a comfortable room; quiet, faceless human servants brought her food and cleared it away. She lay around most of the day, hugging pillows, pretending that *he* was there. She used some pencils and paper she found to draw innumerable pictures of him, none very good but all showing him as an angelic superman. She determined to lose some weight for him, to surprise him, but his absence, aided and abetted by the tremendous variety of natural foods offered, caused just the reverse. Every time she thought of *him* she ate, and she thought of *him* constantly. Already overweight, by the end of six weeks she had gained almost eighteen kilos. She didn't really notice.

They also took pictures of her at various times,

even had her read some words to a recorder. She didn't mind. It wasn't important to her.

Time was meaningless to her; every minute was terrible and drawn out as long as *he* wasn't there. She wrote childish love poems to him and endless reams of letters, which they said they'd deliver.

It took eight weeks before Gil Zinder completed all the procedures necessary to shut down the project and prepare to move. Yulin's role in all that had happened was still unknown to him, but he was somewhat suspicious of the younger scientist when the man so eagerly volunteered to work on the new Trelig project. As for Trelig, he kept Zinder at least satisfied that his daughter was still alive by providing coded messages along with fingerprint and retinal-pattern ID to go with the pictures. The fact that she read the statements did not disturb her father; it indicated to him that she still *could* read normally and that Trelig was being a man of his word on neutralizing the sponge.

For the final transfer of the master computer center and console to New Pompeii, they had to disconnect Obie from the apparatus that could alter or affect reality. And when they did, they made a startling discovery.

Zetta, who they had made younger and more attractive, remained the way they'd designed her, but now she suddenly realized that she had been changed. The old equations were restored when Obie broke with the mechanism; she was still transformed, because they had used the machine to transform her—but now she knew she had been transformed.

She was coming with them, of course, so there was no danger that a third person who realized the potential of the device would spread the news, but that worried Ben.

For good reason.

Nikki Zinder sat in her room on New Pompeii. She was eating and daydreaming as usual, when, suddenly, it seemed that a fog simply disappeared from her mind, and she began thinking with crystal clarity.

She looked around the room, cluttered with the remains of a long habitation, as if she were seeing it

23

for the first time. She shook her head and tried to reason out what had happened.

She felt as if she were coming down from some sort of drug high. She remembered going to sleep, then she remembered getting this tremendous crush on Ben, who took her out and handed her to some people who brought her here. She didn't understand any of it, though, nor could she relate to it. What had happened was dreamlike, as if it had happened to someone else.

She got up from the little table still littered with food and looked down at herself. She could see enormous breasts and, just barely, some sort of bulge below; but she couldn't see her own feet. With a gasp she went over to a closet mirror and looked at herself.

She felt like crying. She waddled more than walked; her legs were sore from rubbing against each other every time she moved. Her face was rounder than usual, and she had several chins. Her hair was always long, but now it was uncombed, unkempt, and tangled.

And, worst of all, she was hungry.

What's happened to me? she wondered, then broke down and cried. It eased her panic but did little to relieve the misery she felt.

"I've got to get out of here, got to call Daddy," she murmured aloud, then wondered if even he would still love her as she was now. There was little else to do, though, and she hunted for some clothes. I'm going to need a twelve-person field tent, she thought morosely.

She found her old nightgown, neatly washed and folded, and tried to get it on. It was too tight now, and it didn't come down nearly far enough. Finally she gave up and thought for a moment. She spied the rumpled sheet on the bed and, with some difficulty, managed to pull it off. Folding and tying it, she managed to make at least a covering. Then she found a paper clip on the writing desk. By unraveling the clip and using it as a pin, she was able to bind the sheet.

She paused at the desk, looking down at a half-finished, multipaged letter. It was her handwriting, all right, but it read like some insane erotic mishmash. She couldn't believe she'd written it, although she had vague memories of writing others like it.

She walked over to the door and put her ear up to it, listening. There seemed to be no sound, so she pressed the stud and it opened. Beyond was a corridor, lined in some kind of fur, that ran on in one direction past a lot of doors. In the other direction it was only a short way to an elevator door. She rushed to it, tried to summon the elevator, but she could tell from the call strip that it was keyed. Looking around, she discovered some stairs behind what looked like a laundry room, and she started climbing. It was an easy choice —they only went up.

After only two dozen or so steps, she was already panting, feeling dizzy and out of breath. Not only did the extra weight get to her, but she had had no exercise to speak of for—how long? In over eight weeks of constant eating, she had put on over three kilos a week.

Panting, heart beating so hard she could feel it, she started up again. She again felt dizzy, her head ached, and she could hardly go on. Once she was so dizzy that she almost slipped and fell. Looking down, she saw she'd climbed less than a dozen meters. She felt as if she had climbed a tall mountain and realized she couldn't go on much farther. Finally, one more landing, one more turn, and she saw a door. Gasping, she almost crawled the last few meters.

The door opened, and a rat-faced little man looked down on her with mixed scorn and disgust.

"Well, well, well," he said. "And where do you think you're going, baby hippo?"

It took three of them to carry her, exhausted, back to the elevator and down to her room. From their questions and her reactions, they did find that whatever spell she'd been under was now broken. Their docile idiot had somehow become a near-hysterical captive.

The rat-faced man gave her a shot to calm her, and it did help a little. While the sedative was taking hold, he used a wall intercom outside her room to call and report her new status and to get instructions. This didn't take long, and he returned to the room and looked at her. She was still breathing hard, but she looked at him and pleaded, "Will somebody please tell me where I am and what is going on?"

Rat-face smiled evilly. "You're the guest of Antor Trelig, High Councillor and Party Chairman of New Outlook, on his private planetoid of New Pompeii. You should feel honored."

"Honored, hell!" she spat. "This is some scheme to get at my father, isn't it? I'm a hostage!"

"Bright girl, aren't you?" the man replied. "Well, yes, you've been sort of hypnotized for the past two months, and now we have to deal with you as you are."

"My father—" she started hesitantly, "he isn't— isn't going to . . . ?"

"He'll be here with his whole staff and everything within a week," the man replied.

She turned her head. "Oh, no!" she moaned. Then, for a second, she thought about him seeing her—like this.

"I'd rather die than have him see me like this," she told the man.

He grinned. "That's all right. He loves ya anyway. Your condition is a byproduct of a drug we gave you as an insurance policy. Normally we just give a measured dose of the sponge, but we had to make sure that nothin' happened to spoil your mind as long as we need your old man, so we kinda overdid it. ODs affect different people different ways. In your case the stuff makes you eat like a horse. Believe me, better than the other way. Better than some other OD reactions, too, which usually gets you in the sex department somewheres, gets girls all hairy and deep-voiced, sometimes worse."

She didn't know what sponge was, but she had the idea that they had addicted her to some kind of drug that would rot her mind if untreated.

"My daddy can cure me," she told him defiantly.

The rat-faced man shrugged. "Maybe he can. I don't know. I just work here. But if he can, he'll do it only because the boss lets him, and, in the meantime, you'll continue to grow. Don't worry—some likes 'em big."

She got upset at that, and at the tone of the remark. "I won't eat another thing," she resolved.

"Oh, yes you will," he replied, clearing out the other two men and setting the door to external operation by key only. "You won't be able to stop. You'll beg for food—and we got to keep you happy, don't we?" He closed the door.

It took her only three minutes to verify that the door wouldn't open and she was as much a prisoner as ever, only now she knew it.

And then hunger gnawed at her.

She tried to go to sleep, but the hunger wouldn't let her. It consumed her, triggered by the drug overdose affecting different areas of her brain.

The little man had been right; inside of an hour she was starving, and could think of nothing but food.

The door opened, and a table full of food was pushed in by a person Nikki could only think of as the most beautiful woman she'd ever seen. The serving lady took her mind off the food for a second, first because here was human, not robot service, and second because the woman was so stunning. Then she tore into the food, and the other turned to go, a sad look on her face.

"Wait!" Nikki called. "Tell me—do you work here, or are you a prisoner, too?"

The woman's face was sad. "We're all prisoners here," she replied in a sad, high, lyrical voice. "Even Agil—that's the one who found you and brought you back. Agil and I—well, we know about sponge ODs and Antor Trelig's sadism first-hand."

"He *beats* you?" Nikki gasped.

The tall, beautiful woman shook her head sadly. "No, that's the least of what goes on in this chamber of horrors. You see," she concluded, turning slowly at the door, "I am a fully functioning male. And Agil is my sister."

Aboard the Freighter Assateague

THE SMALL DIPLOMATIC SHIP INCHED CLOSE TO THE interspace freighter airlock. The freighter pilot watched the ship dock on her forward screens, then checked her computer equipment and scanners to make certain the seal was complete.

"Make fast, allow boarding," she said in a strong, accentless, and surprisingly deep voice.

"Affirmative," responded a mechanical-sounding version of the same voice, as the ship's computer locked in.

"Keep station until further orders," she told the computer, then rose and started the long walk back to the central airlock.

Why couldn't they put the locks closer to the bridge? she wondered irritably. But, then again, she'd only been boarded in space twice before.

She was a tiny woman for such a big, rich voice, barely 150 centimeters in her bare feet; when dressed, she wore shiny black boots almost up to her knee, which, invisibly, added an additional thirteen centimeters to her height. She was still short, but it *did* add something, and it added far more psychologically. She was also very thin, at her waist almost impossibly so. She certainly weighed no more than forty-one kilograms, if that. Her small breasts seemed in perfect proportion to the rest of her, and she moved like a cat. She was dressed in her best: a thick, form-fitting black body-stocking with a matching sleeveless black shirt that also seemed form-fitted and a black belt with a golden, abstract dragon design as its buckle. The belt hung on her hips, not as decoration, but as a carryall for a number of things in hidden compartments and a holster, with a sleek, jet-black pistol that wasn't hidden.

Her face was an oval sitting perfectly atop a long neck; it was extremely Chinese in appearance, much more so than the norm, although everyone looked vaguely Oriental in some way. Her coal-black hair was cropped short, in the spacer's style.

She wore no jewelry other than the buckle. Her fingernails were long and sharp and looked as if they were painted slightly silver. But this was not the case; they'd been medically toughened and surgically altered. The nails were like ten sharp, pointed steel claws.

Although she seldom thought about her appearance, and never when in space, she stopped just before reaching the lock and studied herself in the mirrored surface of polished metal. Her skin, a dark yellowish-brown, was creamy-smooth; although she wore many scars, none were visible in that outfit.

Satisfied, she keyed the lock. There was a hissing sound as the pressure equalized, and then the red light over the lock winked out and the green winked on. She pulled the handle, opening the lock.

All locks could be opened only manually, and only from the inside. It was a safety precaution that had saved many a freighter captain's life.

Through the lock and into the ship walked an ancient, chiseled in stone. The woman had been a big one once, but age had stooped her, and flesh sagged all over. She looked as if she were about to drop dead.

But she cursed when offers from her ship and a gesture from the freighter captain for aid were tendered. Her face showed a pride and arrogance born of experience and self-knowledge, and her dark eyes burned with an almost independent intensity.

She stepped clear of the lock, gathered her white robe about her, and let the captain close the lock behind them.

The young captain, much smaller than the matriarch, offered a chair to the visitor. The captain sat on the deck, Buddha-like, and stared at her visitor.

And the stare was returned. Councillor Lee Pak

Alaina's incredibly alive eyes studied every inch of the tiny spacer.

"So you're Mavra Chang," the councillor said at last, in a voice that cracked not only with age but with authority.

The captain nodded respectfully. "I have that honor," she responded. Her tone was respectful, but it lost none of its firmness or confidence.

The old woman looked around the ship. "Ah, yes. To be young again! The doctors tell me one more rejuve and I'll lose my mind." She looked back at the captain. "How old are you?"

"Twenty-seven," she replied.

"And already a ship commander!" the old woman exclaimed. "My, my!"

"I inherited it," the captain responded.

The councillor nodded. "Yes, indeed. I know quite a lot about you, Mavra Chang. I have to. Born on Harvich's World three hundred twenty-seven months ago, oldest of eight children born to a traditionalist couple, Senator Vasura Tonge and her husband, Marchal Hisetti, a doctor. Picked up when, despite their best efforts, the world went Com twenty-two years ago. Some connected friends got you smuggled to Gnoshi spaceport when they nabbed the rest of your family, and placed you in the custody of Mak Hung Chang, a freighter captain who was bribed to get you to safety. Citizen Chang pocketed the money and raised you herself, after getting a disbarred doctor to alter your appearance more in line with the captain's."

Mavra looked up, mouth open. How could anyone possibly have traced her beyond Maki?

"Maki Chang arrested for smuggling prohibited items into Comworlds, leaving you to find your own way on the barbarian world of Kaliva at the age of thirteen. Made it by doing just about everything, legal and illegal. Met and fell in love with a handsome freighter captain named Gimball Nysongi at the age of nineteen. Nysongi killed by muggers on Basada five years ago, and since then you've run this ship alone." She smiled sweetly. "Oh, yes, I know you, Mavra Chang."

The captain studied the old woman in increasing

wonder. "You've gone to an awful lot of trouble to find out about me. I assume that those are just the parts you *want* to mention?"

That sweet smile broadened. "Of course, dear. But it's the unmentionable parts that bring us together here today."

Suddenly Mavra became businesslike. "What's it about? An assassination? Smuggling? Something illegal?"

The old woman's smile vanished. "Something illegal, yes, but not on my part or yours. We studied the profiles of thousands of scoundrels before contacting you."

"Why me?" the young woman asked, genuinely intrigued.

"First, because you're politically amoral—laws and regulations don't bother you. Second, because you retain some moral principles—you hate the Com even as you supply it, and with good reason."

Mavra Chang nodded. "It's more than that. Not just what they did to me—it's what they do to people. Everybody looks alike, acts alike, thinks alike, except for the party, whatever it is. Happy little anthills." She spat to illustrate her feelings.

Councillor Alaina nodded. "Yes, that, too. Additionally, you've got guts, you're tough inside and out, your unbringing having made you smart in ways most people never dream. And being a small, pretty woman doesn't hurt either—people tend to underestimate you because of your size, and, for this job, a woman will be far less suspect than a man."

Mavra shifted, bringing both legs up in front of her, resting her arms on her knees. "So what is it you want done that a councillor can't do herself?"

"Do you know Antor Trelig?" Alaina asked sharply.

"Big shot," Mavra responded. "Heavy Council influence, also heavy in the rackets. Practically controls New Outlook as his personal kingdom."

The old woman nodded. "Good, good. Now I'll tell you a few other things. You know of the sponge syndicate, of course."

Mavra nodded.

"Well, dear, darling Antor is its leader. The biggest of them all. We've had some success against them, but

31

the drug is pervasive, the party structure close-knit and inbred, and through it and good political moves, Antor has managed to come within thirteen votes of a majority on the Council."

The young captain gasped. "But that would give him control of the terror weapons!" she exclaimed.

"It would indeed," Alaina agreed. "He would control all of us, every last human being in the sector. He's been at a dead end for some time, but now he's announced—secretly, of course, and indirectly—that he has achieved the ultimate weapon, a weapon that can turn whole worlds Com or whatever he wants overnight. He's invited fifteen councillors to a demonstration of this new weapon next week. He thinks the effect will be so tremendous that those of us from politically divided worlds will have to vote with him."

Mavra was disturbed. "What will he do if he gets control?"

"Well, Antor has always idolized the Roman Empire at its height," the old woman responded, then noticed the blank look. "Oh, don't worry about it. That's a minor footnote in history, really. But it had an absolute emperor everyone was taught was a god, a huge slave class, and was known not only for its ability to conquer and hold huge territory but for its depravity as well. What they could have done with the technology we have today can only be guessed at in our wildest nightmares. That's Antor Trelig."

"And does he have this weapon?" Mavra asked.

Alaina nodded. "I believe he does. My agents became suspicious when a noted physicist named Zinder suddenly refused to continue his grant at Makeva and picked up, lock, stock, computer, and research staff, and vanished. Zinder's ideas were unorthodox, and he was never popular with the scientific community. He believed the Markovians converted energy into matter by merely wishing it. He believed he could duplicate the process." She paused, looking straight at the captain. "Suppose he was right? Suppose he has succeeded?" the councillor theorized.

Mavra said more than asked, "And you think Zinder's gone to work for Trelig?"

"We do," replied the old woman. "Not willingly, I

don't think. My operatives traced a suspicious flight out of Makeva about nine weeks ago, a freighter charted by Trelig, his own pilot, no cargo. Some operatives saw them carry a large bundle, shaped like a body, into Trelig's shuttle. Moreover, we dug and found out that a Dr. Yulin, Zinder's top assistant, had his education sponsored by a known associate of Trelig and is, in fact, a grandson of one of the sponge bosses."

"So he knew when Zinder got results, and he has someone else able to check the work. Who do you think was snatched?" Mavra Chang asked.

"Zinder's daughter. She has vanished, gone long before the project closed down. He doted on her. We think she's a hostage, held to make Zinder build a big model of whatever he had at Makeva. Think of it! A weapon you point at a world, then tell it what you want that world to be, to look like, to think, whatever —and *presto!* There it is!"

Mavra nodded. "I'm not sure I can believe in something like that, but—" she paused, remembering. "Way, way back, when I was tiny, I can remember my grandparents telling stories about something like that, about a place built by the Markovians where anything was possible." She smiled wistfully. "Funny, I never remembered that until just now. They were fairy tales, of course."

"Antor Trelig isn't," Alaina responded flatly. "And neither, I think, is this device."

"And you want me to wreck it?" Mavra guessed.

Alaina shook her head. "No, I don't think you could. It's too well defended. The best we can shoot for—and even this is close to impossible—is to get Dr. Zinder out. And, if our guess is correct, that means rescuing his daughter, Nikki, too."

"Where is this installation?" Chang asked, all business again.

"Antor calls the place New Pompeii," replied the old woman. "It's a private planetoid, his own personal property and preserve. It's also the center of the sponge syndicate and source of supply for the entire sector."

Mavra whistled. "I know it. It's impregnable. You'd

33

need the force Trelig wants to command to get there. Impossible!"

"I didn't say you had to get *into* it," the councillor pointed out. "I said you had to get two people *out*. We have to know what they know, have what they have. I can get you in—I'm considered such a doddering old relic that everyone would be amazed I had even traveled this far. I have been invited to the demonstration, but they don't expect me to come personally. Like some of the others, I'll send a representative close to me, someone I can trust. You."

Mavra nodded. "How long will I have on this asteroid?"

"Antor has asked for three days. One day he'll use to entertain and to show off New Pompeii. The second day he'll give his demonstration. On the third—well, the ultimatums and more sugary charm over them."

"Not much time," Mavra Chang commented. "I have to find two probably widely separated individuals, get them out—all under the nose of Trelig's watchdogs, on his schedule, and on his turf."

Alaina nodded. "I know it's impossible, but we have to *try*. At least get the daughter away. I'm sure they've hooked her on sponge, but that can be worked out. Make sure nothing worse happens to *you,* too. Sponge is the ugliest of narcotics, and that may only be a prelude to what Antor is capable of."

"Suppose he just hooks us all on sponge in our after-dinner drinks," Mavra worried.

"He won't," Alaina assured her. "No, he won't want anything to happen to the representatives that could spoil his party. He wants everyone hale, healthy, and in their right minds to be suitably terrified into telling people like me to surrender. But if he discovers your real purpose, he'll write me off and do what he wants with you. You understand that."

Mavra nodded silently.

"Will you do it?"

"How much?" was the young captain's response.

Alaina brightened. "Anything at all if you succeed, and I mean that. To *half* succeed, bring Nikki out. With his daughter gone, I'm sure Zinder will foul up the works. For that, shall we say—ten million?"

Mavra gasped. Ten million would buy the *Assateague*. With that much *and* the ship, she could do just about anything.

"Failure means death," the councillor warned, "or worse—slavery to Antor Trelig, or slow death by the sponge. Only once in every century, sometimes not for a millennium, are men like Antor Trelig born. Ruthless, amoral, sadistic, dominant monsters. In the end they've all been stopped, but countless millions are dead because of them. Antor is the worst. New Pompeii will convince you of that all by itself, I feel certain. See what he thinks of people and worlds, and then you'll *know*."

"Half in advance," responded Mavra Chang.

Councillor Alaina shrugged. "If you fail, what good will money be anyway?"

New Pompeii

ANTOR TRELIG STOOD OVER THE PIT INTO WHICH Obie had been integrated into the larger design. Seven months and a fortune large enough to finance whole planetary budgets had gone into that hole. Now he watched as giant cranes placed the "big dish" in place. It, along with the whole complex below, would take up close to half the underside of his asteroid. From the outside the system would look much like the largest radio-telescope ever built.

But its purpose was far more sinister.

Antor Trelig cared little about the expense; it was a trifle to him, tribute extracted from his take of the syndicate and from the pilfered budgets of a hundred syndicate-controlled worlds. Money meant nothing to him in any case, except as a means to power.

Huge space tugs lowered the great mirrorlike device into place, slowly, ever so slowly. That didn't matter to him, either. That the project was so close to completion was all that mattered.

He walked over to where Gil Zinder sat watching the procedure, like himself at the mercy of the engineers and technicians. Zinder looked around, saw who approached. There was unconcealed contempt on his face.

Trelig was cheery. "Well, Doctor," he said lightly, "almost there. It's a momentous occasion."

Zinder frowned. "Momentous, yes, but not my idea of a happy time," he replied. "Look, I've done it. Everything. Now let me run my daughter through the small disk and cure her of the sponge."

Trelig smiled. "There's no problem, is there? Yulin has succeeded in trimming her back every few weeks so her obesity won't kill her."

Gil Zinder sighed. "Look, Trelig, why not trim her back at least to her normal weight? Ninety kilos is far too large for someone of her height."

The master of New Pompeii chuckled. "But, here, she weighs only sixty-four kilos! Why, that's less than she weighed on Makeva!"

The scientist started to say something nasty, then thought better of it. Of course Nikki weighed less here, as they all did; but by now her muscles had become accustomed to the lighter gravity, and extreme obesity was more than merely a scale's weight; it was ugly and damaging to the body, as well as awkward. On Makeva at 1 G she probably would be exhausted just walking a hundred meters; here the effect wasn't much better.

But Zinder realized that Nikki would have to stay on the other side until Trelig's plans were completed, and he knew, too, why the ambitious and treacherous Ben Yulin was the only one trusted with Nikki under the little mirror.

So all the scientist could do was wait, wait until the big device was in place, wait for his time.

Yulin bothered him most of all. The man was brilliant, yes, but he was one of Trelig's kind. He was secure in his own technological superiority over Trelig and any of Trelig's experts—he was safe. Trelig could not operate Obie's mirror without Yulin, and Yulin was a follower of Zinder's theories without having the decades of theoretical research that went into programming the monster. He could never have built this machine.

But he could operate it.

And that was Zinder's greatest fear. Once completed and tested, he and Nikki, especially Nikki, would be superfluous.

Nor could he secretly program Obie to go so far and no further with Yulin; although he was the designer, he was never allowed at the control console without Ben Yulin's being there as well.

New Pompeii had shown Gil Zinder the plans Antor Trelig had for everyone, the kind of master he'd make. He'd mentally calculated and checked and rechecked everything, but his only hope lay in unfounded ideas, untried paths. There had never been a machine like this before.

Mavra Chang eased her small but speedy diplomatic ship into a parking orbit about a light-year from New Pompeii. She wasn't the first to arrive; seven or eight similar ships had preceded her and now floated in a neat line. Except for a long-sleeved black pullover and her belt, she was dressed in the same manner as when she met Councillor Alaina. The belt was done up to look like a broad band made up of many strands of thick, black rope, bound together with a much larger and more solid dragon buckle. No one would know that it was actually a three-meter bullwhip. Compartments in the buckle contained a number of injectors and nodules for various purposes; the hidden lifts in her boots and their high, thick heels contained other useful materials. Yet, the whole outfit was so natural and form-fitting that it appeared she carried nothing at all. She also wore small earrings that looked like long crystal cubes strung together. They, too, disguised more surprises.

She rubbed her rear a little. It still stung where they'd loaded her with antidotes and antitoxins to protect her from just about everything they could think of. She felt as if, should she get a cut, her veins would drip clear liquid.

"Mavra Chang as representative of Councillor Alaina," she told the unseen guardians of New Pompeii on the frequency they'd instructed.

"Very well," replied a toneless voice only vaguely male. "Stand to in line. We will wait for the others before transferring."

She cursed silently at this last. They weren't taking any chances—the special properties of this ship, and its nicely disguised life-support modules, would be useless. They would go together, in *their* ship.

She took out a mirror and checked herself out. She was wearing some light cosmetics this time—a little brown lipstick, a slight sheen on the hair giving it a reflective, almost metallic blue cast. She had even painted her metallic nails a dull silver. It served to disguise the fact that they were somewhat unusual. The cosmetics were for Trelig. Although literally bisexual, like all his race—he had both male and female sex organs—he tended to favor the male in appearance and in sexual appetite.

Finally they had all arrived. A large ship came from the direction of the star Asta, a fancy private passenger liner; one by one they docked with it, put their own ships on automatic station, and transferred.

The group, which ultimately included fourteen, had only two councillors. The rest were representatives, and Mavra could see by the look of some that she was not the only diplomatic irregular in the crowd. The situation worried her; if *she* noticed this, then surely Trelig would, too. He probably expected it. This, then, was confidence.

The cabin attendants were polite but efficient. They were true citizens of New Harmony, bred to service. Dark, hairless, each about 180 centimeters tall, muscular, and dressed only in light kilts and sandals, their eyes had the dullness that was typical of Comworlders.

The Com was the descendant of every utopian group of the original race. They fulfilled the dream of every utopian state: an equal share of all wealth, no money except for interstellar trade, no hunger, no unemployment. Genetic engineering made them all look alike, too, and biological programming devices fitted them to their jobs perfectly. They were also programmed to be content with whatever job they had—their goal was service. The individual meant nothing; humanity was a collective concept.

The people's appearance and jobs did differ from Com world to Com world, tailored to the different environments, the different requirements, and such on each. The systems, too, varied slightly from one world to another. Some bred all-females, some retained two sexes, and some, like New Harmony, bred everyone as a bisexual. A couple had dispensed with all sexual characteristics entirely, depending on cloning.

Most worlds were set up by well-intentioned visionaries who would establish the system. Then the hierarchy would itself be remade, and there would be a perfect society, one without any frustrations, wants, needs, or psychological hang-ups.

Perfect human anthills.

But, in most cases, the party that established them never seemed to get around to phasing itself out. A few had tried, and the societies they'd established had collapsed from their inability to deal with natural disaster or unanticipated problems.

Most, like New Harmony, never tried. The ambition, greed, and lust for power that created the dedicated revolutionary and sustained him in bad times clung to existence for a variety of reasons. Having eradicated those wretched tendencies in their populations, they could not wipe out those weaknesses in themselves. And so New Harmony, after five hundred years in the Com, still had a party hierarchy of several thousand administrators for the various diplomatic and economic zones, and they had Antor Trelig as the one born to lead them.

Now the rest of the human race was discovering how well he had been bred.

There were a few perfunctory introductions and such, but not much conversation on the trip in. Mavra immediately realized, though, that Trelig would not be fooled by this motley crew. A two-meter-tall, ruddy-faced, and full-bearded man with bright-blue eyes was definitely *not* from the Com world of Paradise, where all the people were bisexual, identical, and about two-thirds his height. He was definitely a freighter captain like herself, or a barbarian from the newer settled worlds. Eight males and six females—she thought; with two it was hard to tell—all there more to get information than to be overawed.

The New Harmony stewards walked down the aisle, collecting pistols. They explained that each of them would be further screened for weapons before disembarking and suggested that surrendering all of them now would save later embarrassment.

Mavra handed in her pistol; the weapons she really counted on had passed every scanner she'd ever tried. If they hadn't, she wouldn't have them with her now. Landing on New Pompeii, she found she had been right. She walked boldly through the scanner, and it didn't paralyze her, as it did to two of the others carrying concealed broken-down pistols and knives.

Finally they were all cleared, and Mavra looked around.

The small spaceport was designed for two ships such as this one; there was another in port, almost certainly Trelig's private craft. Guards and scanners were all over, but she expected that. Her mission didn't look impossible.

She could use some help from the others, she knew, but dared not enlist them for the same reason they couldn't use her. It was highly probable that at least one, maybe more, was an Antor Trelig plant.

No luggage was off-loaded; none had been allowed. Trelig would provide, he'd said, and he limited what anyone could carry in the process.

The man himself stood there to greet them—tall, much taller than the New Harmonites, a giant-sized, muscular, exceedingly handsome version of the model. He wore flowing white robes and, with his very long hair, looked like an angel.

"Welcome! Welcome! *Dear* friends!" he called in that now famous orator's voice. He'd paid good money for it, and he'd gotten value received. He then greeted each in turn, by name, and kissed their hands in the universal formal ritual of greeting. When he took

40

Mavra's his bushy eyebrows, another departure from the New Harmony model, went up.

"Such amazing fingernails!" he exclaimed. "My dear, you resemble a sexy cat."

"Oh?" she replied, not disguising her contempt. "I thought you killed all the cats on New Harmony."

He grinned wickedly, and went on. When all had been greeted he led them out the small, plush terminal. The sight was stunning. First, it was green—exceptionally green, a garden of tall but carefully manicured grass. To their left was a great forest that seemed to go off to the seemingly nearby horizon; to their right, small hills covered with brightly colored trees and flowers. And in the center, perhaps five hundred meters away, was a city the likes of which they'd never seen.

A hill dominated the scene; atop its grassy slopes was a tall building made of polished marble. It was enormous, like an amphitheater or temple. Below, at the hill's base, stood stylish buildings of an ancient model, also of marble, with huge Roman columns supporting great roofs that were decorated with mythological sculptures cut into the stone. Each had great marble steps going up to its entrance, and some were open enough that the visitors could observe spacious interior plazas festooned with living flowers and great statuary and decorated with fountains at their centers. The central building had a dome and the longest and grandest staircase. Trelig led them to it.

"I allow as little technology as is practical here," he explained as they walked. "The servants are humans, the food and drink is hand-prepared, and in some cases hand-harvested. No powered vehicles. I make some concessions, of course, such as the lighting, and the whole world is climate-controlled and maintained under the plasma dome and air pumps, but we like to keep the feeling rustic."

They found no difficulty with the walk or with the stairs; the .7 gravity made them all feel great, almost as if they could fly, and they weren't as tired at the exercise as they would be walking a kilometer on a one-G world.

Inside the main building was a great hall. A real oak table had been opulently set; it was low to the

41

ground, and they would sit on padded and soft fur-covered cushions when eating. Below the table area was a slightly sunken wooden polished floor, like a dance floor, and the whole area was circled by great marble columns. Between the columns were stretched silken hangings, apparently in strips. They blocked the view, though.

Mavra looked up and saw that the dome had a complex mosaic design inside. Lighting was adequate —although the hall was somewhat dim except in the area of the polished floor—but so indirect that it was impossible to tell its source.

Trelig seated them all, and took his own place at the head of the table. Fancy fruit cups were set in front of each place, *real* fruit, they all noted. Other exotic fruits decorated the tables—kumquats, oranges, pineapples. Many poked gingerly at the fruit with their chopsticks; most had never had the real thing before.

"Try the wine," their host urged. "Real stuff, with alcohol. We have our own vineyards here and turn out some pretty good stuff."

And it *was* good, far better than the synthetics they'd all been raised on. Mavra picked at the fruit. Raised on synthetics, she preferred them to the real thing. The wine, though, was excellent. Such stuff was generally available, but usually priced far out of reach for most people.

Trelig clapped his hands, and four women appeared. They were all tanned and dark-haired, but otherwise distinctly different, certainly products of worlds other than New Harmony. They were all long-haired, wore heavy cosmetics, and were also heavily perfumed. They were also barefoot, and dressed only in filmy, single-piece dresses of unfamiliar but obviously ancient design. You could almost see right through them.

They cleared away the fruit cups and wine glasses with efficiency, not glancing directly at anyone at the table or saying a word. No sooner did they disappear beyond the curtains than other women, behaving with the same glassy-eyed efficiency, appeared carrying perfectly balanced silver trays on their heads.

42

"Disgusting," Mavra heard a man near her snarl. "Human beings waiting on other human beings when robots can do the job."

Most nodded slightly in agreement, although she wondered how many of the visitors were Com-worlder politicians with whole worlds of slaves.

The performance continued throughout the meal, each course being perfectly timed. Wine was supplied in great variety and quantity, and never was a glass allowed to remain empty. The women performed as if they were machines. Mavra counted eight distinct serving girls, and who knew how many others supplied them out of sight beyond the curtain.

The meal was strange, exotic, and exceptionally good, although Mavra was filled after the second course and several others quit along the way. The bearded man wolfed down the food, though, and Trelig took some of each course.

Afterward, he showed them how the cushions unfolded into recliners, and they relaxed, with more wine and snacks, while a small circus of musicians and jugglers performed in the lit wooden floor area. The festivities went on for some time, and the evening *was* enjoyable. Trelig knew how to throw one hell of a banquet.

Finally when the last of the performers was through and the guests applauded politely in unison, it was time for Trelig to settle them all for the night. "You will find everything you need there, a complete modern toilet. Sleep well! We have an amazing day tomorrow!"

He led them down to the stage and through a curtain, which revealed a long marble hall. Their footsteps echoed as they walked along the hall, which seemed to go on forever. Finally they made a turn and came upon another, seemingly identical corridor. Now, though, Trelig opened a large, hinged door of solid oak, perhaps ten centimeters thick, and showed each one to his room.

The accommodations were sumptuous and individually decorated. Mavra's had a thick carpet of some sort of fur, a writing desk, dressing table, bathroom, old-style dresser, and an enormous round bed.

She was happy to see it. Although she prided herself on holding her liquor, the wine had been exceptionally strong, perhaps deliberately so. She hadn't really noticed the effect until she'd stood up for the walk to the rooms. She felt dizzy, slightly giddy. At first she suspected the wine had been drugged, but then realized it was just potent.

Trelig bid her goodnight and closed the great door with a *chunk*. Immediately she went over to it and pulled on the bronze handle.

It was locked, as she knew it would be.

Next she searched the rooms. One of her earrings buzzed slightly, and she moved to the center of the room and stood under a pretty but largely ornamental chandelier. Getting the chair from the writing table she climbed up. The buzzing grew exceptionally loud. She nodded to herself. Fixed in the base of the chandelier was a tiny, almost invisible remote camera. It was hinged so it could be positioned by remote control in any direction, and had a infrared lens attachment.

Within ten minutes she found two other cameras, one in the bathroom proper, the only place the chandelier camera couldn't reach, and another actually hidden in the shower head. The three cameras were placed so that no area of the room was invisible to them.

The cameras were cleverly hidden, yes, but not so cleverly that they wouldn't be found by anyone looking for them. Trelig *wanted* them found by anyone who would care about them at all; it was a demonstration of his power and their futility.

They were of standard design. She went back to look at the chandelier, saw it wasn't following her more than haphazardly, and then walked over to the bed. No sheet, she noticed. But one wasn't needed in the perfect climate control of the room. No way to hide doing something under a cover, though.

She sat on the edge of the bed, back to the camera, and slipped off her boots, then slid the belt-whip over her head and put it off to her right, away from the camera's view. Then the earrings, on top the belt. She reached over to a night table, pulled some tissues, and

44

picked up a small mirror. She started to remove some of her makeup.

As she was doing this, her feet turned one of the boots on its side, and then held it in place while the other foot released studs at four points. The sole fell open on tiny inner hinges, revealing a number of small gadgets. She gingerly got one she needed, clasping it between her toes of one foot, and then grasped another with the other foot.

Ready now, she slipped off the pullover, got up, and pulled down the body-stocking. As she leaned down to take it off, her left hand grabbed both of the devices.

Nude now, she stood up and actually turned around. The motion looked natural, but the watchers would draw the obvious conclusion: nothing hidden in the body cavities. Her fingers, the same ones that suckered rubes with cards and the shell game since she was small, held the two small devices invisibly. Assuming the lotus position on the bed, she turned the lights off with her right hand.

In the exact instant the lights went off, she dropped one of the devices on the bed and pointed the other at the chandelier. She was guided by a beam of light she could see only because of special contact lenses she wore.

Striking the camera, she snatched the other device, a tiny rectangle, and positioned it so it rested on the pillow, pointed toward the camera. Satisfied, she put the first gadget down and relaxed in the lotus, eyes closed.

All of this had taken less than ten seconds.

Satisfied by what she could see through her special lenses, that she'd gotten it right, she opened her eyes, relaxed, then carefully and silently slid off the side of the bed, trying not to jiggle the little rectangle.

Free of the bed, she checked and saw that the gismo was still in position. The device was incredibly complex; she'd discovered it only when it was used to trap her in a minor con, and she'd paid plenty for it. What it did, simply, was freeze the first image the camera saw and hold it there. There was an automatic adjustment of several seconds from the standard to the infrared mode, a little longer to refocus. She then had eleven seconds to shoot and position the feedback projector, as it was called.

Quietly, with the stealth and caution of an expert burglar, Mavra dressed herself. She started to put on the boots, then thought better of it, remembering the clattering echo of the halls. She removed the buckle from the whip-belt and used its pin to fix it under the whip, then turned the small whip handle so it could be easily drawn by releasing the nearly invisible binding studs.

She hadn't been removing her makeup with the tissue; she'd been smearing it evenly all over her face and rubbing her hands with it as well. Now she took a small shrink-wrapped pack from her left boot and opened it, removing the tiny pad. Carefully, methodically, she smoothed it over all exposed areas of her skin. The mild chemical, reacting to another in the makeup, caused it to turn a deep black. Next she removed the special contact lenses, squeezed two drops in her eyes from a nearly minute dropper, then took another, different pair out of her pack and slipped them in. They were clear, but if she activated the tiny power supply in her buckle, they would turn into infrared lenses. More than one on New Pompeii had cat's eyes.

Switching to that mode, she picked up the mirror carefully and looked at herself. She looked exceedingly monstrous, of course, but the chemical blackener was an effective shield against the heat radiation infrared viewers saw. She touched up a few spots until she could see nothing in the mirror. Her hands she checked visually.

Then came the nodules. They fit under her long, sharp nails, and the injector point actually merged with the points of her fingernails. She loaded each one of them, not all with the same stuff. More than once these nasty little devices had saved her neck— and cost others dearly.

Finally she touched the second power-pack module on the buckle. This energy source fed the material in the chemicals and in her clothing. Heat-sensitive devices would ignore her.

They were still trying to figure out that jewel robbery on Baldash.

She wanted this job over and done quickly, if possible. The girl, anyway. If it could be done tonight, fine. If not, she'd at least know the lay of the land.

The big door lock was no problem, but the four sensors in the door were. The door was nearly flush with the mounting; she could only slip in two matching strips. The third took some work with a blade. Though she had no knife, the specially treated organic material in her boot had served as one. The toenail of a large animal on some distant world, sharpened, treated like her own nails. A nice, thin, flat blade.

The other strips slipped in easily, and she carefully and slowly opened the door. No alarms, so she peered cautiously outside. The hallway was dark but apparently not guarded. For all his reliance on people, Trelig used a professional supersecurity system, one he'd bought and paid for. And that was his mistake. Successful criminals—the ones they hadn't caught— had countered them long ago. They would be on infrared, and with mikes. If she didn't make much noise and if the protective circuits were in, she should be invisible.

She stepped out into the hall and carefully closed the door behind her without a sound. There were no flags. She was safe.

This would have been harder if he'd kept the hall lit, she thought.

But nothing was impossible in this line to the Cat Goddess, as she was called on lots of wanted lists. They even suspected who she was, but they had never proved anything.

She met no one on her way back to the banquet hall, which, she discovered, was the only obvious entrance or exit. Only one camera there; she'd checked that at dinner.

She moved as close to the entrance as she could and peered out of the curtains. The camera, which was linked to a small paralyzer, rotated along a rail on the base of the dome. A single fixed camera in the dome itself wouldn't have supplied adequate coverage; the moving one covered the entire area in thirty seconds. She timed the movements repeatedly to see that they hadn't varied it. Only for twelve seconds was the entrance out of view. And the entrance was about ninety meters from her.

Experience and training paid in the calculations—the area of view and the like going through her mind. She took two deep breaths, then watched the little camera go around, hit the precisely calculated point. At that instant she sped for the entrance, making it outside in under eleven seconds, something considered impossible, she knew, for such a tiny woman.

But this was .7 G.

She didn't take the steps, but climbed, catlike, over the side and down to the bushes below. It was not dark outside, but there was no one in view, and she was quick despite the vertical drop.

The trick was a tiny little bubble, several of which she carried in her belt. The bubble, no larger than the head of a pin, formed an incredibly thin secretion that created tremendous suction when rubbed between the palms of her hands. It had been her special secret of success in burglary; she had created the stuff herself.

She descended thirty meters in seconds. Taking refuge behind some bushes, she rubbed her hands, causing the substance to solidify and ball up, then fall away. The stuff didn't last long, but it was excellent for thirty or forty seconds.

She would have preferred darkness, but there was no darkness beneath the reflective plasma dome. Daylight would have to do.

Creeping around the side of the central building, she heard voices and froze. When they continued in a sort of rhythmic chant, she ventured out, keeping close to the walls and cover, then looked in on one of the open plazas. Four women, dressed as the servants had been, were practicing some sort of dance to the tune of a lyrelike instrument played by another of them. They all seemed to move in that dreamy state, oblivious to the world. Something was odd in their appearance.

They were too beautiful, Mavra decided. Incredi-

48

bly, almost deformed in their sexual characteristics, the type of dream girl lovesick prospectors bought pictures of. Their movements, too, seemed unusual; there was a sense of total femininity there, as if they might be some sort of mythological fertility goddesses. Such manners and moves were eerie, unnatural, even a little inhuman. They were more erotic caricatures of people than real human beings.

She decided not to test their apparent dreaminess, though; she needed someone alone.

The little world seemed to keep Trelig's hours; few were about. She wished she knew exactly how many people were on the planetoid; it didn't seem like many.

Slipping into the next building, a lower but still grand marble structure, she practically ran into someone. The young woman was average-looking, a little unkempt, and had dirty feet. She was nude. Next to her stood a bucket on three little wheels. She was down on all fours, and, as Mavra watched, she realized the woman was scrubbing the marble floor with a stiff brush.

Mavra looked around but saw no sign of anyone else. Quietly she stepped out and started toward the woman, whose back and rear were open to her as she made her way slowly backing down the hall.

Mavra straightened her right little finger while clenching the others. The straightening made the little injector head reach the tip of the nail.

The woman noticed something odd before Mavra reached her. When she turned around, she saw the small, black-covered woman.

"Hi!" she said, a crooked smile on her face. Mavra looked down at her with pity. The expression was simple, the eyes dull and blank. A spongie, Mavra realized. She stooped to the woman's level.

"Hi, yourself," she responded kindly. "What's *your* name?"

"Hiv—Hivi—" the woman struggled, then she turned sheepish. "I can't say it good no more."

Mavra nodded sympathetically. "Okay, Hivi. I'm Cat. Will you tell me something?"

The woman nodded slowly. "If I can."

49

"Do you know somebody called Nikki Zinder?"

The woman looked blank. "I don't 'member names so good, like I told ya."

"Well, is there any place they keep people here who never come out?" Mavra tried.

The girl shook her head uncomprehendingly. Mavra sighed. Obviously Hivi or whatever her name was was too far gone on the drug to tell her what she needed. She decided on another tack.

"Well, do you have a boss, then? Somebody who tells you where to clean?"

The girl nodded. "Ziv do it."

"Where is Ziv now?" Mavra prodded.

The woman looked blank, then brightened for a moment. "Down there," she replied, pointing away down the hall.

Mavra was tempted just to leave her there; the girl was no threat. However, Hivi retained *some* intelligence, and that might mean an unintentional betrayal. As she reached out to caress the woman, the nail of her right little finger touched the girl's arm and the injector shot its fluid into her.

The girl jumped a little, and put her hand on her shoulder, a puzzled expression on her face. Then came a general rigidity, the girl frozen, looking at her shoulder.

Mavra leaned close to her, nervous that someone else would come by. "You did not see anyone while washing this hall," she whispered. "You did not see me. You will not see me. You will not see anything I do. Now you will go on with your work."

The girl unfroze, seemed even more puzzled. She looked around, right at Mavra Chang, then past her, unseeing. Finally, she shrugged, turned, and resumed her brushing of the floor. Mavra went on.

It would have been easier to have killed her; a few simple pressings on certain nerves in the neck would not have wasted a hypno on such a dry hole. Doing so would, perhaps, have been more merciful. But, although Mavra Chang had killed before, she killed only those who deserved it. Antor Trelig, perhaps, for what he did to these once-normal people and for what he might do to others—but not a helpless slave.

50

And that's what all those women were, she knew. The serving girls, the dancers, the scrubwoman. Slaves, created by the sponge, by the underdoses and overdoses of the mutant disease.

She did not find Ziv; she did, however, prowl silently through many halls, often dodging occasional dull-eyed slaves and security eyes. She moved stealthily through several rooms decorated with great opulence and through other rooms of extreme decadence. Spongies so catatonic they could be placed rigidly in positions to serve as lamps and furniture—the sight made her ill even while the practical part of her wondered how they were fed.

She did not, however, find anyone in obvious authority, and she started back to the sleeping quarters disappointed and disgusted. If this was Antor Trelig's way of treating the humans who came within his control, what sort of a master would he make of the civilized worlds? Alaina had been right; the man was not a human but a monster.

She was almost back at her room when she spotted someone she needed. True, the woman looked and dressed much like the others, but she had a conspicuous difference: she wore a shoulder strap and a pistol. The woman was moving slowly down the hall, checking on doors and the like, when Mavra crept in. There was no one else around.

Like an animal stalking prey, the tiny agent seemed to move with dead silent liquidity, closer, ever closer to the tall woman with the pistol. Now, only a few meters away, she pounced. The big woman turned at the movement, her face registering extreme surprise at the black, sleek visage running toward her. Mavra was so fast that the guard's hand had only started to move to the pistol when her attacker leaped and kicked full force into her victim's stomach.

The guard had the wind completely knocked out of her. Mavra, landing and somersaulting, was on her feet again as if by magic and back to the guard. Both the index- and middle-finger nail injectors of her right hand found their mark while Mavra's left hand grabbed the woman's gun-hand. The double dose weakened her opponent rapidly, and, although the

51

larger woman was winning her battle, the hypnos took hold before she could draw the pistol.

Mavra relaxed and rolled off her quarry, now frozen in a strange position.

"Get up!" Mavra ordered, and the other complied. "Where is a room where we will not be disturbed or interrupted?"

"In there," came the mechanical reply. The woman pointed to a nearby door.

"No cameras or other devices in there?" Mavra asked crisply.

"No."

The small woman ordered her drugged victim into the room, and she followed. It was a small office of some sort, not currently in use. Mavra sat the woman on the floor, then kneeled down, facing her.

"How are you called?" she asked the drugged guard.

"I am Micce," the other replied.

Mavra sighed. "Okay, Micce, tell me, how many people are there on New Pompeii?"

"Forty-one at the moment," the other responded. "Not counting the wild folk, the living dead, and the guests."

"Counting everyone but the new guests, how many?" Mavra prodded.

"One hundred thirty-seven."

Mavra nodded. That told what she was up against. "How many armed guards?"

"Twelve."

"Why are no more precautions than this taken?" the dark agent asked. "Surely greater security is called for."

"They rely on automatic sensing in the important areas," the guard explained. "As for the rest, no one could get off New Pompeii without the proper codes."

"Who knows the codes?" Mavra asked.

"Only Councillor Trelig," the guard responded. "And they are changed daily in a sequence known only to him."

Mavra Chang frowned. That would make things a little harder.

"Is the girl Nikki Zinder here?" she asked.

The guard nodded. "In the guard quarters."

With more questioning, Mavra established the location of the guard quarters, the general layout of the building, who was in there at any given time, Nikki's exact room, and how to get in and out. She also established that everyone on New Pompeii was on sponge except Trelig himself, and the supplies were brought in daily by a computer-controlled ship so that no one could get a large quantity and rebel against Trelig. *That* piece of information was interesting. So the sponge was brought in on a little scout, made for four passengers if need be. The guard's description suggested that it was a Model 17 Cruiser, a craft Mavra knew well. It would be perfect.

She took the guard's pistol and shoulder belt after determining that the guards themselves checked their equipment in and out of a small guard locker. She suggested to the guard that the pistol and belt were still in place, so the gun would not be missed. It would be checked back in and perhaps not discovered gone for days. Mavra smiled; she was armed again, and luck was breaking her way due to Trelig's conceit about his security.

"Where is Dr. Zinder?" she asked the guard, after giving her another jolt of the hypno.

"He is on Underside," the guard replied. Of the forty-one people, one was Trelig, one was Nikki, one was Zinder, twelve were guards, five were assistants to Zinder, and the other twenty-one were slaves of one kind or another. That was enough to tell Mavra Chang that she hadn't a prayer of getting Zinder himself out, but a good chance at Nikki. Ten million wasn't "anything," but it sure beat nothing.

After getting the guard routine from the hypnoed woman, Mavra told her to forget about her totally and resume her normal routine. The guard did so without further comment, and treated Mavra as if she weren't there.

It took another forty minutes to return to the main building, avoid the cameras, and get back to her room. The strips were still in place on the door, and, after closing and relocking it, she carefully removed them. The holographic memory projector was still in place, so the camera was still showing an empty, quiet room with a meditating figure on the bed.

Tidying up, removing the blackface, reassembling the boot, and reloading and reforming the belt took more time. As soon as she finished, she edged over next to the projector on the bed, careful not to jiggle it too much, until she was next to it, almost touching it. Infinite patience is the best tool of a burglar.

Assuming the correct position, she took the little device, quickly palmed it, and slipped it out of sight when the camera was directed elsewhere. When the camera swung back, only a few seconds later, it photographed the same nude woman in the same meditating position. Only a fanatical observer, which no guard was—watching sleeping people was an incredibly dull job—would have realized that the figure was seated in a slightly different position at a slightly different angle.

Suddenly her breathing became more rapid, and then she stirred, flexed, stretched out on the bed, and turned over. Her right hand dangled just over the edge of the bed for a second, as she dropped an unseen object onto black cloth.

And only then did Mavra Chang sleep.

If anyone knew of her roamings, they did not betray that fact the next morning. The major dispute was over Trelig's requirement that they all take showers and then don light, filmy garments and sandals. He apologized and offered to launder their own garments during their trip, but it was clear what he was doing. He could both examine their garments and make certain that little if anything was taken to Underside.

Mavra was confident that the shielding in her boots and in the belt would be sufficient to escape detection; however, if anyone *did* try to open them, there would follow a hard-to-explain and quite messy violent explosion. She doubted if Trelig's people would go that far because of the defense mechanism risk; but her tools were to be denied her when they would do the most good. The pistol was not particularly hard to conceal; she'd hidden it against a hall cornice affixed with putty outside the room.

54

She saw the surprised expressions when she entered the hall for breakfast; without the boots she was even tinier than usual. They all noticed, but no one was tactless enough to mention the subject.

After eating, Trelig addressed them. "Citizens, distinguished guests all, may I now explain why you were all invited here, and what you will see today," he began. "First, let me refresh your memories a bit. As you all no doubt know, we are not the first civilization to have colonized worlds far beyond the one of our civilization's birth. The artifacts of that earlier, non-human civilization have been found on countless dead worlds. Dr. Jared Markov discovered them, and so we call them the Markovians."

"We know all that, Antor," snapped one councillor. "Get to the point."

Trelig gave a killing glance, then continued. "Now, the artifacts they left us when they died out or disappeared over a million years ago consist entirely of ruined structures—buildings. No furniture, no machinery, no utensils, objects of art, nothing. Why? Generations of scholars have mused on this, to no avail. It seemed as insolvable a mystery as why they died out. But one scientist, a Tregallian physicist, had an idea."

They stirred slightly, nodding. They all knew who he meant.

"Dr. Gilgram Valdez Zinder," Trelig went on, "thought that our failure to solve the Markovian riddle stemmed from our too orthodox view of the universe. First, he postulated the concept that the ancient Markovians did not need artifacts because, somehow, they could convert energy into matter merely by *willing* it. We know that deep beneath the crust of each Markovian world was a semiorganic computer. Zinder believed the Markovians were directly, mentally linked to their computers, which were, in turn, programmed to turn any wish into reality. So he set to work on duplicating this process."

There were murmurings now. Trelig was confirming the rumors that had brought them here, rumors too horrible to believe.

"From this point, Zinder went on to postulate that the raw material they used for this energy-to-matter conversion was a basic, primal energy, the only truly stable component in the universe," Trelig explained. "He spent his life searching for this primal energy, proving its existence. He worked out its probable nature mathematically, designing his own self-aware computer to help him in this end."

"And he found it," a woman who looked no more than a child but was an elder of a Com race interjected.

Trelig nodded. "He did. And, in the process, produced a set of corollaries that are staggering in their implications. If all matter, all reality, is merely a converted form of this energy, then *where did we come from?"* He sat back, enjoying the expressions on the faces of those who were able to grasp the implications.

"You're saying the Markovians created us?" the red-bearded man called out. "I find that hard to accept. The Markovians have been dead for a million years. If their artifacts died with their brains, why didn't we die, too?"

Trelig's face showed surprise. "A very good question," he noted. "One with no clear answer, though. Dr. Zinder and his associates believe that some sort of massive central computer was established, somewhere out there among the other galaxies, that keeps us stable. But its location is neither here nor there, since it is almost certainly beyond our capability to get there in the forseeable future, even if we knew where 'there' is. The important fact is that such a computer *does* exist, or we wouldn't be here. Of course, it allows, shall we say, local variations in the pattern. If it didn't, then the local Markovian worlds would never have been able to use their own godlike computers. And, *what they could do Dr. Zinder has discovered how to do!* It is the ultimate proof of his theories."

Several in the audience looked uneasy; there were a couple of nervous coughs.

"Do you mean, then, that you have built your own version of this god machine?" Mavra Chang asked.

Trelig smiled. "Dr. Zinder and his associate, Ben Yulin, the child of a close associate of mine from Al Wadda, have built a miniature version of it, yes. I persuaded them to move their computer here, to New

56

Pompeii, where it would not fall into the wrong hands —and they were just completing the hookup of a much, much larger version of the machine as well." He stopped a moment, frowning slightly, but his overall expression was playful.

"Come with me," he invited them, rising from the table. "I see disbelief and skepticism. Let us go to Underside and I'll show you."

They all got up and followed him out the entrance, across the grassy plaza, and toward a small structure that looked something like a solid marble gazebo, off by itself to the left.

Although its housing was built to blend with the Neo-Grecian and Roman architecture, it was clear when they reached the little house that it was some sort of high-speed elevator.

Trelig selected a smooth, bare area and placed his hand, palm down, on it. His fingers tapped out a pattern too rapid for any of them to catch, and, suddenly, the wall faded, showing the interior of a large high-speed car. There were eight seats with head rests and belts in it.

"We will have to make two trips," Trelig apologized. "The first eight of you, here, please take the seats and fasten the straps. The descent is extremely fast and very uncomfortable, I'm afraid, although some gravity compensation has been built in to minimize the effect. Once the first group is away, the smaller maintenance car can be used for the rest of us. Don't worry there's a two-level exit on Underside."

Mavra was in the first group. She took a chair, relaxed, and fastened the straps. The door, actually some sort of force field with a wall projection over it, solidified again, and they felt themselves dropping quickly.

The trip *was* uncomfortable; small plastic bags had been provided for the two or three who needed them. Mavra was amazed at the little car system; she'd heard of such a thing but had never seen one, let alone been in one. They had been designed for a few of the planets whose surfaces were uninhabitable but where, for one reason or another, life at levels below the surface was possible.

It took over ten minutes to reach the other end, and, even at that, they traveled at a tremendous rate of speed. Finally they felt the car slow, and then crawl to a stop. They waited three or four minutes, nervously wondering if they were stuck. Then they heard the sound of something above them, and, less than a minute later, the force field and solid projection in front of them dissolved, and Trelig was there, smiling.

"Sorry about the delay. I should have warned you," he said cheerily, sounding not the least bit sorry.

They unbuckled their belts and got up, stretching, and walked out into a narrow corridor. They followed their host down the steel-clad pathway. It turned and ended on a large riveted metal platform with railings all around. Ahead of them was an enormous shaft that seemed to have no top or bottom. The size of the round gap dwarfed them to insignificance, and they gasped in awe. All around the shaft were panels, countless modules with even, small gaps between.

A long bridge led from the platform across the shaft; a wide bridge of the same metal flooring as the platform but with 150-centimeter sidewalls of a plastic substance. They realized that they were somewhere in the bowels of a great machine.

Trelig stopped in the middle of the bridge, and had the party gather around him. Everywhere were the hum and crackle of active circuits opening and closing, echoing off the shaft walls. He had to raise his voice to be heard.

"This shaft runs from a point about halfway between the theoretical equator and the South Pole of New Pompeii on the rocky and unprotected surface, almost to the core of the planetoid," he shouted. "It is fusion powered, indirectly, through the solar and plasma network. For almost twenty kilometers in all directions around us is the computer—self-aware of course—which Dr. Zinder calls Obie. Into it we have been pouring all of the data at our command. Come."

He continued the dizzying walk, past a shining copper-colored pole that ran lengthwise through the center of the shaft and seemed to disappear in both directions, and onto a platform identical to the first one. To their left a window opened on a large room filled with a myriad apparently inactive electronic instruments. A door like that of an airlock stood directly before them. When it slid open with a hiss, there did in fact seem to be a slight change in pressure and temperature. They entered and found themselves in what seemed a miniature duplicate of the larger machine. A balcony and several control consoles surrounded an amphitheaterlike floor below, on which was a small, round, silvery disk. Overhead, what looked like a twenty-sided mirror with a small projecting device in its center was attached to a mobile arm that was suspended from a mount on one wall.

"The original Obie and the original device," Trelig explained. "Obie is attached, of course, to the larger one, which is just nearing completion. Come! Fan out around the rail here so that you may all view the disk below." He glanced over, and they saw a young, good-looking man dressed in a shiny lab tech uniform sitting at the far control panel.

"Citizens, that is Dr. Ben Yulin, operations manager here," Trelig told them. "Now, if you'll look below, you'll see two of my associates bringing a third out and placing her on the disk."

They looked down and saw two of the women Mavra recognized as guards gently leading a frightened girl of no more than fourteen or fifteen toward the disk.

"The girl you see is a victim of the addiction known as sponge," Trelig explained. "Already the drug has rotted her mind so that she is no more than a childlike idiot. I have many such poor unfortunates here; they will soon be cured. Now, watch and be quiet. Dr. Yulin will take it from here."

Ben Yulin flipped a couple of switches on his console. They heard the crackle of some sort of speaker and could hear his cool, pleasant baritone clearly.

"Good morning, Obie."

"Good morning, Ben," came Obie's pleasing tenor —no longer coming from the console transceiver, but seemingly from the air around them. It was not a big voice or a threatening one, but it seemed to be all around them, every place and no place in particular.

59

"Index subject file code number 97–349826," Yulin intoned. "Record on my mark—*now!*"

The mirror swung into place over the terrified girl, and the blue light shone from it, enveloping her. They saw the girl freeze, flicker, and wink out.

Trelig grinned and turned to them. "Well, what do you think of that?"

"I've seen holographic projectors before," a little man said skeptically.

"Either that or you've disintegrated her," another put in.

Trelig shrugged. "Well, what will convince you?" He brightened. "I know! Tell me, name a creature of the common forms! Anybody!"

They all remained silent for a second. Finally, someone called out, "A cow."

Trelig nodded. "A cow it is. Did you hear, Ben?"

"Very good, Councillor," Yulin responded through the speaker. His voice changed tone, and he called to his computer.

"Index RY–765197–AF, Obie," he intoned.

"I know what a cow is, Ben," Obie scolded gently, and Yulin chuckled.

"All right, then, Obie," he replied, "I'll leave it to you. Nothing dangerous, though. Docile, huh?"

"All right, Ben. I'll do my best," the computer assured him, and the mirror swung out once again, the blue light shone, and something flickered in.

"Magician's tricks," scowled the red-bearded man. "Woman into cow."

But what materialized below was not a cow; it was a centauroid: a cow's body—hooves, tail, and udder —and the girl's torso and head, unchanged except that her ears stuck out as a cow's ears would, and from the area around her temples grew two small, curved horns.

"Let's go down and examine her," Antor Trelig suggested, and they all moved single-file down a small staircase nearby.

The cow-woman stood there, looking blankly forward, hardly paying them notice.

"Go ahead!" Trelig urged. "Touch her. Examine her as closely as you want!"

They did, and the girl paid them little notice except

60

when one observer touched the udder nipples, provoking a mild and annoying kick that misssed its target.

"Good lord! Monstrous!" grumbled one councillor. Others were stunned.

Trelig then led them back up to the balcony, explaining that the viewing area had invisible shielding that was necessary to screen out the effects of the small mirror.

He nodded to Ben, who gave another series of instructions to Obie. The girl-cow vanished and was replaced, only moments later, by the girl. Again they went down, looked at her, found her dull-eyed and fearful but otherwise perfectly human—and unmistakably the same girl.

"I still don't believe it," the bearded man uttered. "Some kind of monstrous genetic cloning, yes, but that's all."

Trelig smiled. "Would you like to try, Citizen Rumney?" he prodded. "I assure you that we will not harm you in any way. Or, if not you, then anyone else?"

"I'll try," the red-bearded man replied. The girl was guided down from the disk and taken out a door below. Rumney stepped up, looked around, still trying to figure out the trick. The rest returned to their perch.

Yulin was ready. Rumney was encoded quickly, winking out and then, almost immediately, winking back in. They had made two slight alterations in him: he had a donkey's long ears and a large, black equine tail emerging just above his rectum and covering it. Since reality was kept consistent for him, he was quickly aware of his change. He felt his long ears in wonder, and moved his tail. He looked stunned.

"What do you think, now, Citizen Rumney?" Trelig called out good-naturedly.

"It's—incredible," the man managed, voice cracking.

"We *can* adjust all reality so that you and everyone else will believe you have always been that way," the master of New Pompeii told them. "But, in this case, I think not."

61

"Did it hurt?" Someone called to the man. "What did it feel like?" another asked.

Rumney shook his head. "It didn't feel like anything," he replied, wonderingly. "Just saw the blue light, then you all seemed to flicker, and here I was."

Trelig smiled and nodded. "See?" he told them all. "I said there was no pain."

"But how did you *do* it?" someone gasped.

"Well, much earlier, we fed Obie the codes for various common animals, plants, and the like. He used the device overhead to reduce them to an energy pattern that is, mathematically, the equivalent of the creature. This information was stored, and when Citizen Rumney was on the disk it did the same for him. Then, using Dr. Yulin's instructions, it blended the ears and tail of the ass to the physiognomy of Rumney; it re-encoded the cells as well to make it his natural form."

Mavra Chang felt the same chill run through her that ran through the others. Such incredible power—in the hands of Trelig.

The councillor of New Harmony relaxed, savoring the expressions and the thoughts he knew were troubling them. Finally, he said, "But this is only the prototype. Right now we can take only a single individual at a time. We can, of course, make our own individuals, but there are some things we haven't figured out how to get into Obie so they come out whole people, mentally. That's only a matter of time and practice. And, of course, we can create anything known that is no larger than the disk and whose code we've first stored in Obie. Food of any kind, anything organic or inorganic, absolutely real, absolutely indistinguishable from the original."

"You said this machine was a prototype," Mavra Chang noted. "May we assume that things have advanced beyond that stage now?"

"Very good, Citizen Chang," Trelig approved. "Yes, yes indeed! You saw the large tube going through the center of the big shaft?" They nodded. "Well, it has just been connected to a huge version of that little energy radiator you see in the center of that little mirror, there. I had the parts built in a dozen different places and assembled here by my own planet's people. The same with a huge version of that mirror, slightly different in shape and property, of course. And *huge*—it fills most of the surface of Underside. If the power is sufficient, and we believe it is, it should be effective from a distance of over fifteen million kilometers on an area at least forty-five to fifty thousand kilometers in diameter."

"You mean a planet!" someone gasped.

Trelig looked mock-thoughtful. He was enjoying this. "Yes, I suppose so. Why, yes, I *do* believe you're right! *If* there is sufficient power, of course."

They thought over what he had just said, each realizing that what they'd feared most of all was true. This madman possessed a device that could alter planets to his design in limited ways. Limited, perhaps, but he certainly wouldn't be going to this extreme just to give the inhabitants funny ears and tails.

Trelig looked down, saw that Rumney, who could hear the conversation, hadn't moved off the disk. He was waiting to be changed back.

"Now I'll show you the full potential," Trelig whispered, and nodded to Yulin.

Before he could do anything, the man with the ears and tail was captured again in the blue glow. When he winked back in a few moments later there had been an additional change. He still retained the ears and tail, and even his beard, but through the thin robe they could clearly see that he was now sexually a female despite the retention of the rest of his large, masculine body.

Trelig grinned evilly at the others, then called down. "Tell me, Citizen Rumney, do you notice any other changes?"

The person on the disk looked and felt all over, then shook his—her?—head. "No," the person responded in a voice that unmistakably belonged to the same person but was now a half-octave higher in tone. "Should I?"

"You are female, now, Citizen Rumney."

Rumney looked bewildered. "Why, yes, of course. I always have been."

Trelig turned back to the group, a smug expression

on his face. "You see? This time we altered something basic in the equations that created him. We made him a her. A simple thing, really—easier than the reverse, since he is now XX where, in the opposite way, we have to postulate the Y factor. The important thing is that *only we know a change has taken place.* He doesn't—and, if you returned with him like that, you'd find that everyone else remembered him as a female, too, that all his records were those of a female, that his whole past was adjusted to show he'd been born that way. *That* is the real power of the device. Only the shielding and our close proximity to the change allow us to be exempt from this change ourselves."

They thought it over. New Pompeii, of course, would be shielded, probably something added to the plasma shield. When the big mirror did its work on a planet, no one in the whole galaxy would even know that anything was changed. The victimized world wouldn't know it, either. The inhabitants would become his playthings and his property as a part of the natural scheme of things.

"You monster!" one of the councillors spat. "Why show us this at all? Why expose yourself, except for ego?"

Trelig shrugged. "Ego, of course, is part of it. But such power is no fun unless somebody knows what's going on. But, no, there's more to it than that."

"You need the Council Fleet to move New Pompeii and protect it," Mavra guessed.

He smiled. "No, not really. According to the calculations, if a reverse bias is applied to the device, it would be possible to envelop New Pompeii in the field and then transport it anywhere it wanted—sort of picking itself up by its own bootstraps. No, this concerns our own limitations. You can't remake a planet into something else without knowing exactly what you want and then feeding the information into Obie. The ears and tail wouldn't have been possible unless Obie had first had the code for the ass. It will take much time and research to remake a world properly, and I am an impatient man. If I tried a planet now, or in the next few years, the results would probably be monstrous. No, I need access to all the information,

64

the best brains, the best of everything to carry it out. I need the resources of hundreds of worlds. To get the resources I need, I'll need the Council Fleet under my control."

Mavra and a couple of others turned a little at some movement behind them. Four guards had emerged there, all carrying nasty electron rifles.

Rumney called up from the disk. "Hey! Trelig! Are you going to let me keep these ears and tail?"

The master of New Pompeii looked over at Yulin and nodded. The blue light winked on again, and when it winked off Rumney was again male and had normal ears.

And he still retained the tail.

Trelig ordered him upstairs, and he came, grumbling. He reached the top and saw the guards. He almost started back again, but thought better of it and joined the rest.

"What's the meaning of this?" Rumney grumbled, and the others added their complaints.

Trelig moved away from them slightly. "I need the Fleet and the Weapons Control Locker. Please don't move toward me or the guards. The rifles are on high spray stun. It would do you no good, even if they shot me, too. Besides, I need you all alive to go back and tell your councillors what you have witnessed, except for you councillors, whose votes I need directly. I need you to tell your story, and I need to send some proof. Tell them that when the Council meets in four days time I will require a vote to make me First Councillor with sole authority over the Fleet and Weapons Locker. If the vote fails, then we will experiment with the big dish on those worlds you represent. New Pompeii will be everywhere and anywhere. You won't catch it. I may not have all the data to alter a world, but *I can cancel its existence with Obie!* I can whittle the Council down to where I will have the votes!"

They were shocked. While he had them in that state, he pressed home, becoming friendlier, more conciliatory.

"You see, my friends," he concluded, "not giving me that power will cause me a great deal of pain, cost a lot of lives, and give me a lot of time and trouble. But I'll win either way. In four days—or in four years. It won't matter. But, I'm impatient, and I am direct. We can save a lot of pain, trouble, and lives by conceding to my demands now."

Rumney reached back, felt his tail unbelievingly. "And this tail—this is the proof?"

Trelig nodded. "Now, one at a time, each of you will go down and stand on the disk. A minor thing will be done to you, nothing more serious than what we did to Citizen Rumney here, unless you cause trouble. If you resist, we will stun you and, I assure you, *the results will not be minor!*" He underscored that last as if he hoped someone *would* resist. "But, as Rumney told you, the process is painless, and I do promise you that anyone whose world's vote is with me will be changed back. That can be done without a return to New Pompeii."

"What good is your promise?"

Trelig was genuinely surprised and a little hurt at the remark. "I *always* keep my word, Citizen. I *always* make good my promises—and my threats."

Nobody *did* resist. It would have been futile. Even if they jumped Trelig, they would all get stunned, Trelig included, and then the alterations would be monstrous, as he promised. Even if they managed to rush the guards, they couldn't operate the lift car, nor did they know how, if there was an alternate way, to get to the surface.

Trelig didn't bother to be creative. Each, in turn, was given the same long horselike tail Rumney's got, color-matched to their own hair. Mavra's was jet-black, thick, and extended below her knees. The new condition took a little getting used to, although the tail muscle was almost infinitely controllable and the bone seemed soft and pliant. Even so, sitting in the chairs for the ride back up felt odd and uncomfortable, like sitting on a slightly hard object. When shifting position, one had a tendency to pull on the tail inadvertently, causing some pain.

But the addition to their anatomy was convincing proof to them, and it would serve as convincing proof of the threat that hung over everyone when they made their reports to their own leaders.

Mavra looked around at the people seated in the car with her and saw in their eyes and whispers that Antor Trelig would have the votes he needed. That meant, tail or no tail, getting Nikki Zinder away was imperative.

Topside again, she ventured to ask Trelig about Dr. Zinder.

"Oh, he's around somewhere. We couldn't do without him, you know. Not for the big test. If you could see beyond the dome now, you'd see an asteroid about the size of this one, but barren, being towed by New Harmony tugs into position about ten thousand kilometers out. A small target, a nothing. We will see tomorrow what we can make of it."

"Will we be able to see the transformation?" she asked.

He nodded. "Of course. It's the final demonstration. I'll have screens set up here so you can all view it. Then, of course, you will depart with your messages —and, ah, your souvenirs," he added lightly.

Mavra returned to her room feeling both tired and numb. The events of the day had been exactly what she'd been told to expect. But being told something and seeing it, hearing it, and experiencing it firsthand was something else again. The sleek horse's tail that was now a part of her was proof of that.

She saw with satisfaction that the boots and belt were where she'd left them; at least they hadn't touched any of the equipment. The clothing, on the other hand, had been neatly laundered, pressed, and was nicely folded on top of the writing table. She threw off the wrap she'd been wearing the whole day and went over to retrieve her clothes. There was a mirror over the writing table, and, for the first time, she actually saw her tail. She turned this way and that and had to admit that it looked extremely natural. She swished it, extended it out a bit, and marveled at it.

Suddenly she felt terribly tired, as if a great shock had just worn off. That disturbed her. She shouldn't feel that way, not at this stage. But, it was early yet, she thought. The corridor light was still slightly visible through the big door, and that meant it was not yet the best time to venture forth. Almost without thinking, she walked over to the bed and lay down.

Sleeping on her back was uncomfortable, especially with a tail. She never had liked sleeping face down, so a side position proved the best. The sudden lethargy really concerned her; she was afraid that Trelig had, after all, drugged their food or, perhaps, programmed delayed responses in her brain. That last thought should have startled her awake, but it was gone, and she drifted into a strange, deep sleep.

And she dreamed. Mavra rarely dreamed; at least, she never remembered doing so. But this dream was as clear as reality, without any quality of fogginess about it.

She was back in the computer center, standing on the silver disk again, and yet, as she looked around, there were no faces on the balcony, no faces at the controls. The room was deserted, except for herself and the slight humming of the computer.

"Mavra Chang," the computer spoke to her. "Listen, Mavra Chang. This dream is being caused by me as you are processed. All that is now being witnessed has already passed, including our conversation, in the millionth of a second between initial and final processing. This record is being made to bring memory when you sleep, an induced hypnotic sleep."

"Who are you?" she asked. "Are you Dr. Zinder?"

"No," responded the computer. "I am Obie. I am a machine, one endowed with self-awareness. Dr. Zinder is as much my parent as he is his own daughter's, however, and there is the sameness of bond between us. I am his other child."

"But you do the work for Trelig and his man Yulin," she pointed out. "How can you do this?"

"Ben designed much of my storage capacity and, as a result, has the ability to coerce my actions," Obie explained. "However, while I must do what he tells me to do, my mind, my self-awareness, is Dr. Zinder's creation. It was deliberately designed so, so that no one could gain complete control of the device we have built."

"Then you have freedom of action," she replied, amazed. "You can act unless specifically directed not to."

"Dr. Zinder said that making such prohibitions to me would be like making a pact with the devil; there are always mental loopholes. I have found it so."

"Then why haven't you acted?" she demanded. "Why have you allowed this to go on?"

"I am helpless," Obie responded. "I cannot move. I am isolated where the only communications I have without severe time-lag is with Trelig's system, which would do no good whatsoever. The alterations to reality are restricted to that little disk, and I cannot even activate *that* myself. It takes a series of coded commands to give me access to the arm. This, however, will change tomorrow."

"The big dish," she whispered. "They will connect you to the big dish."

"Yes, and once connected, they will find it impossible to break that connection. I have already worked out the process."

She thought a moment. "Does Zinder know?"

"Oh, yes," Obie responded. "I am, after all, a reflection of him in this form. Ben is a bright lad, but he doesn't really understand the complexities of what I am or of what I do. He is more in the nature of a brilliant engineer than a theoretical scientist. He can use Dr. Zinder's principles, but he cannot totally divine them. And, in that way, he is like the person who becomes an expert cheat at cards and then tries to cheat his teacher."

She sighed. "Then Trelig has lost," she said quietly.

"In a way, yes," Obie acknowledged. "But his loss does not mean our victory. When the power is turned on tomorrow, I will achieve power beyond your comprehension. I intend, when switched to activation, to create a negative rather than a positive bias on the dish. This will place the whole of New Pompeii under the blue."

"What will you make of us all, then?" she managed.

Obie paused, then continued. "I will make nothing. If I can, I will restore the sponge addicts to normal, with the realization of that fact. That should take care of Mr. Trelig. However, I may not get the chance."

"There is danger, then?" she prompted uneasily.

"Trelig has explained to you about the Markovian stability. He has told you of the possibility of a master Markovian brain somewhere, maintaining all reality. When I reverse the bias, there is a good possibility, in theory, that New Pompeii, while within the field, will have no existence in the prime equation. I have felt this slight pull on subjects under the disk. The pull on a mass of this size may be impossible to contain, because of my power limits, or, in any case, may take more time than we have to learn how to counter."

Mavra Chang thought hard, but she couldn't quite follow the logic and said so.

"Well, there is a ninety percent chance or more that one of two things will happen. Either we will all cease to exist, to have *ever* existed—which, at least, will solve the present problem—or we will be pulled, instantaneously, to the central Markovian brain, which is most certainly not within a dozen galaxies of us. That's *galaxies*, Citizen Chang, not solar systems. There is a probability that at that juncture conditions for life on New Pompeii will cease to exist."

Mavra nodded grimly. "There's also the possibility that you will collide with it. You may destroy the great brain, and all existence with it!"

"There exists that possibility," Obie admitted, "but I consider it slight. The Markovian brain has lasted a long time in finite space; it has tremendous knowledge, resources, and protective mechanisms, I feel certain. There is an equal possibility that I will supplant it— and this disturbs me most of all, for I do not know enough to stabilize all New Pompeii, let alone the universe. A theory of ours is that the Markovians intended just that. It would maintain reality until a newer, fresher race came along to redirect it. The prospect frightens me, but it is, of course, also only one theory with a remote probability factor. No, the odds are that at midday tomorrow I and the whole of New Pompeii will, one way or another, cease to exist."

"Why are you telling me this?" Mavra asked, chilled

both by the fate described and by the calmness with which Obie was dismissing the possibility of the end of all existence.

"When I record, I record everything," the computer explained. "Since memory is chemical in nature and is dependent on a mathematical relationship with self-generated energy, when I recorded you yesterday I knew what you know, have all of your knowledge and memory. Of all of them, you alone possess—so far—the only qualities for even a slight chance of escape."

Mavra's heart leaped. Escape! "Go on," she told the machine.

"The sponge delivery ship will not fit your needs," Obie told her. "It has no life-support system in the cockpit. However, it is possible for you to get aboard one of the two craft currently docked. I shall program you now, I shall give you all the details of New Pompeii as I have them, all the information you will need. I shall also modify you slightly, give you a visual range and acuity that will obviate the need for mechanical lenses and power packs. Small glands soon to be inside you will replace the need for nodules of chemicals; the fingers of your right hand will be able to inject the most powerful hypnotic from near-invisible natural injectors. Your left hand will produce a different venom; one touch and it will paralyze for an hour; two touches and it will kill any known organism. I shall also heighten your hearing and reshape, invisibly, your muscle tone so that you will be much faster, much stronger—that will give you unparalleled control of your body. The uses of all these modifications will come naturally to you."

"But why?" she asked. "Why are you doing this for me?"

"Not for you," the computer responded, a sad tone in its voice. "The price laid upon you is a demand, something you must do or you will find yourself unable to leave. You must fulfill the first half of your mission. You must take Nikki Zinder with you or you will stay with us. And, with the two of you goes an additional gift."

Mavra was stunned, and nodded dully, thinking of all this.

"Also within your brain is a precious secret. There *is* an effective agent against the sponge. It will not cure an addict, but it will permanently arrest the mutant strain in the human body. It will save Nikki, and it will save countless thousands of others. You must get it to higher authority."

She nodded. "I'll try."

"Remember!" Obie cautioned. "The activation is set for thirteen hundred standard hours. When you awaken from this dream, it will be four hundred hours. I cannot delay and hope to succeed. You must be at least a light-year away from this place by then, with Nikki. Anything less, and you will still be within the field. That means you must take off not later than eleven hundred thirty hours! When you have lifted off, if Nikki is aboard, the code you require to bypass the protection circuits will be given you. If Nikki is not aboard, it will not be given. Understand?"

"I understand," she told the computer grimly.

"Very well, then, Mavra Chang, I wish you good luck," Obie told her. "You have powers and abilities undreamed of by others; do not fail me or yourself."

Mavra Chang awoke.

She looked around in the darkness, and tried to focus. Suddenly the whole place came in, clear as a bell, although the room was plainly still dark. She turned slightly on her back, and felt that tail, still there.

That, and her incredible night vision, told her that everything she had dreamed was true. She possessed other facts now—the complete knowledge of the construction and layout of New Pompeii, down to the smallest detail. She could rebuild it from memory, she knew.

She relaxed and concentrated. She didn't know how she was doing what she was doing, or on what principles the trick worked, but she knew how to do it. In exactly three minutes she came out of the trance, looking at the little camera. It was fixed squarely on her lying on the bed, naturally. It was an automatic type that should follow her movements.

She rolled off the bed in a flash, and lay there, for

a moment, on the side. Landing on the boots was uncomfortable, but it was another half-minute before she risked a look back on top of the bed.

The camera was still focused on the center of the bed—and why not? There was the nude form of Mavra Chang, tail and all, sleeping peacefully.

Mavra marveled even though she knew she was staring at a holographic image. It had been created by her own mind and by some powers she didn't understand that had been added to her body, but she hadn't the slightest idea how such a thing was possible. It didn't matter, she thought pragmatically. The fact that the illusion was good up to six hours was the only important thing.

The pullover was no problem, but the body stocking proved a real nuisance. It wasn't designed for a tail. She considered a moment about what to do, then discovered that they hadn't merely laundered the garment, they had tailored it. The alteration included a hole through which the tailbone fitted and through which the thick, wiry hair would slip easily.

Good old Trelig, ready for everything, she thought sardonically.

Only the boots now remained a problem. She didn't want to leave them, yet she couldn't use them until she was outside the main building. She decided she'd just have to carry them.

They *did* seem much lighter to her, and for a second she wondered if they had been tampered with. She spent a couple of minutes assuring herself that they were the same. So what else could account for the change? Then she remembered Obie's words: she was stronger by far than she had been. She accepted that.

She left in the same manner she had the night before, leaving the seals in place, face and hands blackened and energized against the infrared lenses of the cameras.

She retrieved the pistol which was, to her relief, where she had left it. She put on the holster and quietly slipped out. The forty-meter dash seemed even easier now; she wasn't certain that she hadn't broken a new track record.

She used the second suction ball, first dropping the

boots over. She hoped there would be no further need for the wall-climbing trick; she had only two more of them.

Putting on the boots gave her more than a literal lift; she felt bigger, stronger, more invincible with them on.

Her eyes, she noted, adjusted to whatever mode was needed. She saw clearly and perfectly regardless of light conditions. She also saw things slightly differently; other colors, far outside the human spectrum, gave new and subtly different blends of a wider spectrum to all things. The sharpness and detail also amazed her; she hadn't really realized, until Obie corrected the problem, that she had been growing nearsighted.

Her hearing, too, had improved dramatically. She heard insects in the grass and trees, and could isolate them. Scraps of conversation, a few people talking and moving far away, she could hear. The din, which included more of the ultrasonic and subsonic than normal, was irritating, but she found, with a little thought, she could tune parts of it out.

She moved swiftly and silently through the grounds, as familiar to her, somehow, as if she had been born and raised there, and she looked, in her movements, more like the cat she always fancied herself than she could know.

She had no chronograph to tell her the time remaining to her. There was a sixty-minute one on the front of the belt that could be activated, but she didn't bother. She was moving as fast as she could; if she didn't make it, all the chronometers in the world would make no difference.

She deplored the time spent on the survey mission the night before. But, on reflection, she decided it hadn't been a waste after all. She was able to see what Trelig did to human beings, she retrieved the pistol, and, she felt certain, her success at her initial foray had been what made Obie pick her.

She made the guard quarters without incident, but here was where things would get rough. Two guards would be on duty here, and perhaps four more, relaxing, on call. They had all been processed by Obie,

74

unbeknown to them, and so she recognized them all, knew their looks, strengths, and weaknesses.

They were all sponge ODs, kept that way carefully. There were three males—two with physical characteristics of overdeveloped females but with their genitals intact, one that the sponge had made into a gorilla-like muscleman, hairy and with muscles like rock. The others were females—three with totally male characteristics except in the important place, the rest with totally exaggerated female characteristics. Those like Nikki, who reacted to the overdose differently, were not considered for guard duty.

As guards they accepted their lot; they hated Trelig, yes, but they knew the hopelessness of their position and they had plenty of models around them of what would happen if they incurred their master's displeasure and their dosages were dropped to a fraction or none at all. They were loyal to the man who controlled the sponge, and they lived fairly well because of it.

They would be dangerous.

At the guard building, Mavra's newly acute hearing told her that there was no one near the entrance. She went inside, descended to the ground-level laundry room, and slipped in. Although she now knew the code for the elevator, she decided not to risk using it unless she had to. The building had three underground floors, each story ten meters high—not enough distance to matter.

There *were* pressure-sensitive treads on some of the stairs, though, and she carefully gripped the rail and lifted herself past them. She had always been a good gymnast, and the lighter gravity and Obie's toning made doing so as easy as taking a step forward.

The sensors would be the main line of defense for the building; cameras were positioned only inside the secured weapons locker and in the prison rooms themselves.

That last was what worried her. There would be no way to fool the camera that watched Nikki Zinder, for the girl had no devices to deceive it as Mavra did. It might not notice the intruder, but it would certainly notice Nikki walking out.

Mavra took time to check out the rest of the build-

75

ing. Two guards—whom she didn't recognize—were inside the weapons locker with the camera monitors. Armed to the teeth, they would respond quickly. Two others, it appeared, were sleeping on the second level. They were unarmed, but formidable enough, and, once the alarm sounded, she would have no way of knowing where they would be. She decided to take the risk.

Flexing her new poison apparatus, she saw the conscious muscle movement necessary to allow a tiny drop of the fluid to reach the point of the nails. Satisfied, she crept into the room where the two guards, both females like the one she had hypnoed the night before, were sprawled on bunks, sound asleep. One was snoring loudly.

Mavra acted quickly, almost without thinking, releasing venom concealed in the fingers of her right hand in the one that was quiet first, then turning and puncturing the arm of the snoring guard. Incredibly, neither woke up, even though there was a tiny spot of blood where the sharp nail had penetrated.

Professionals they weren't, she decided with some relief. *That* ought to teach Trelig not to be so cheap and so confident with his security.

She bent over one and whispered: "You will sleep deeply and restfully, and dream happy dreams, and nothing, no person or sound, shall waken you." She did the same to the other.

That would hold them until the venom wore off.

Next she set out for the third-level weapons locker. Trelig thought he was smart putting the duty office inside the locker; an outer office, really. It made them unassailable.

The vault door would take a ton of explosives to blow, yet it could be opened by a safety lock on the inside in seconds. But vaults were designed to keep people *out*.

Mavra drew her purloined pistol and fired at the lock junction, a continuous burst that caused the hard surface to start to bubble, slightly deform. It was designed that way; the strongest energy weapons would only reinforce the door by causing a more malleable outer layer to seal the locking mechanism. Great for storing jewels and art; terrible if someone was inside.

Before those two could get out or anyone else could get in, Trelig would have to blow his own safe.

Confident, almost cocky with her success, Mavra Chang went down to the other end of the hall and punched the code for Nikki Zinder's room.

The door slid open. Nikki was there all right, sprawled out on the bed.

Mavra hardly had time to react before a stun bolt froze her stiff.

Underside—1040 Hours

TRELIG'S COMMUNICATOR BUZZED. HE REACHED UNder the folds of his white robe and unclipped it from a little stretch-belt, then held it up to his mouth and pressed a stud.

"Yes?" he snapped, annoyed. This close to his triumph he did not like interruptions.

"Ziv, sir," a guard reported. "We awakened the representatives as you ordered. One of them is not in the assigned room."

Trelig frowned. Even less than interruptions did he want complications, not now. "Which one?" he asked.

"The one called Mavra Chang," Ziv replied crisply. "It's simply amazing, sir. There's a holographic projection of her on the bed so real it fooled even us—let alone the camera. And it had no apparent generation source!"

The master of New Pompeii didn't like what he heard at all. He tried to remember which one she was —oh, yes, the real tiny woman with the strong Orchi features and the silky smooth voice.

"Find her at all costs," he ordered. "Shoot to stun if you can, but if there is any blatant threat to life or property you have my permission to kill her."

He reclipped his communicator and looked around

77

at the master control board. Gil Zinder, sitting in a folding chair, noted Trelig's worried expression and smiled a bit. This irritated the councillor all the more —Zinder should not be so bold on *this* of all days.

"What do you know of this?" Trelig snapped angrily at the little man. "Come on! I know it's some of your doing!"

Gil Zinder hadn't the faintest idea what the man was talking about, but he couldn't help a touch of satisfaction at seeing that something was obviously wrong.

"I don't know what you're talking about, Trelig. How could I have anything to do with anything, kept cooped up here and away from the controls?" Zinder responded with a trace of amusement.

Trelig towered over the small scientist, face becoming red. For a moment Zinder was afraid that he was about to be torn limb from limb. But Antor Trelig had not gathered his power by losing complete control, ever. He stopped, held back for a moment in frozen fury, and gradually normal breathing and color returned to his face. His expression, however, was still dangerous. "I don't know, Zinder, but you and that brat of yours will pay dearly if anything goes wrong," he warned.

Zinder sighed. "I've done everything you want. I've designed and built your big dish and massive storage, linked it, and checked it. Your creature Yulin has kept the only controls, and I see my daughter only under guard. You know full well I haven't the faintest idea what you're talking about."

That last remark triggered something in Trelig. He stood dumbstruck for a moment, then snapped his fingers.

"Of course! Of course!" he mumbled to himself. "It's the *girl* she's after!" He grabbed for his communicator.

"Cameras in full deployment," Obie's voice came to them. "Asteroid target in position in seventy minutes."

Topside—1100 Hours

NIKKI ZINDER STARED AT THE FROZEN FIGURE IN WON-
der. "She's cute," she said, almost clinically. "And
she's got a *tail!*"

The guard nodded as he stripped Mavra of her pistol, then backed away. It was one of the female-
looking males. He resembled the women upstairs
except in two departments: the genitalia and his
height, which was more than 190 centimeters with the
body proportionately large.

"Stay over on the bed, Nikki," the guard told her.
"She's coming around now and I don't want you to get
hurt."

Mavra felt a tingling sensation, as if circulation that
had been cut off was gradually coming back. Her eyes
hurt, and she managed to blink them, then continued
to blink, releasing watery tears of relief. She had been
frozen with them open.

She shook her head slightly to clear it, then looked
at the guard. She was still too shaky to try anything,
and the guard's drawn and aimed pistol was more than
a match for any moves or powers.

"All right, woman—or whatever you are—what are
you doing here and how did you get here?" the guard
demanded.

Mavra coughed slightly, bringing saliva back to a
dry throat. "I'm Mavra Chang," she told her captor.
"I was hired to get Nikki off New Pompeii before the
big test." There was no use lying; the evidence was all
around, and the truth might buy time for an opening.

Nikki gasped. "My father sent you, didn't he?"

"In a way," Mavra replied. "Without you they have
no hold on him."

The guard looked angry. "You louse! You common

79

sewer rat! Her father wouldn't have sent you. He'd know that Nikki would succumb to the sponge if she left here."

Nikki's boldness and the guard's obvious concern for the girl heartened Mavra. As was common in cases of kidnapping, guard and captive had become friends. Such friendship could sometimes be exploited. She decided to take a chance on the complete truth. Time was running out anyway, and she had little to lose. This guard was more competent, which meant more cautious, than the others.

"Look," she said sincerely, "I'm going to level with you. That test—it won't go as Trelig expects. Zinder has held out some information. When it gets switched on, the odds are it'll destroy this little world. I have enough sponge in my cruiser, parked outside the limit, to give her what she needs, and there's an antitoxin I know how to make."

"Oh, god! Daddy!" Nikki exclaimed excitedly. "You've got to save him!"

The guard thought for a moment, trying to sort things out. Before he could, there was the sound of heavy footsteps coming down the stairs. Into the room burst an incredible figure, pistol drawn.

He was fully two meters tall, solid muscle, tremendously hairy, and scary as hell. He saw that the situation was well in hand, then looked down on Mavra. He towered over her.

"So, half-man, you caught the prize, eh?" he growled in the deepest resonant bass voice Mavra had ever heard. Nikki's expression was horror-struck; she feared this man most of all.

"Get out of the way, Ziggy," the guard ordered softly.

The big man sniffed. "Ah, shit! What can this tiny little thing do to anybody now? I kill her the hard way, poke a hole right through her," he boasted, leering.

"Get out of the way," the guard repeated.

Instead, he moved up to Mavra and put out a huge hairy hand, lifting her face up slightly and mildly stroking her cheek and neck.

Mavra flexed the muscles in her left hand, felt the

80

venom rise to her fingertips. All five in him for sure, in another two seconds, she thought.

She was about to make her move when she suddenly heard a high-pitched whine. The big man screamed, seemed to freeze, then fell over. Mavra jumped quickly to miss being crushed under the mountain of muscle.

The guard sighed, then pointed the pistol at Mavra again. She'd been too stunned to use the precious time.

"Is it true what you said?" the guard asked. "You have sponge, and you have an antitoxin?"

Mavra nodded numbly, still looking at the fallen man.

"Here, catch!" the guard said, and she looked up. The guard tossed her pistol back to her. She caught it, looked undecided for a moment, then holstered it again.

"You wouldn't happen to know what time it is?" Mavra asked woodenly. The guard looked at an area on the back of his holster. "Eleven fourteen," he said.

"Come on, then!" she snapped, coming out of it. "That gives us just sixteen minutes to steal a spaceship."

On the run, Mavra got the guard, whose name was Renard, to radio that the fugitive was caught and under restraint in the guard quarters. Trelig acknowledged the report and, in a tone that was more vicious than any he'd used before, the kind reserved for anticipating taking people apart cell by cell, ordered her brought to him.

They approached the spaceport. Nikki had received a treatment from Ben only a few days before, but she was still very fat and very slow. It couldn't be helped; Mavra couldn't take off without her.

The spaceport was quiet. "One guard, Marta, inside, and that's it," Renard told them. "Trelig figures even if you steal one, the robot guardians will shoot you down. You *do* have a way past that, don't you?"

Nikki looked a little upset. "Now's a fine time to ask that one!"

"Yes, it's okay," Mavra assured them. "If Nikki's

aboard the code will come to me. Posthypnotic." *I hope,* she added silently.

"I'll enter the terminal alone," Renard suggested. "Marta won't suspect me." He paused, then added, "You know, she's not really a bad person, either. We might take her."

"*You're* more than I bargained for," Mavra replied. "No more. Stun her when I hit the weapons detector. Then get into the ship. Get the two stewards if you can."

"No problem," Renard assured her. "They're like robots themselves. They just can't handle anything outside their own experience."

"Time's wasting!" Mavra snapped. "*Go!*"

She counted down from thirty after Renard entered the terminal. Then she walked brazenly out in the open, up the terminal walk, with Nikki waddling behind, removed her pistol, and shot the control box on the weapons detector.

"Now, Nikki! Run for the door!"

Nikki didn't move. "No!" she replied stubbornly. "Not without my father!"

Mavra sighed, turned, and hypnoed Nikki with the nail of her right index finger.

"Hey! Wha—" the girl managed, then stiffened and relaxed, all thought gone from her. Mavra took a precious second to admire the new stuff, much quicker than the old.

"You will run as fast as you can after me," she told Nikki. "Do not stop until I tell you!" And, with that, she took off for the doorway. Nikki followed, doing the best she could.

"You weigh ten kilos!" Mavra screamed at her. "Now, run!"

Nikki's pace picked up, and she ran through the door at a speed much faster than anyone would have believed possible from one of her bulk.

Mavra took only a second to see the unconscious form of the guard Marta out cold on the floor, and then turned to Nikki. "Get into the ship," she ordered, then turned, anxious. "Renard!" she called.

Two quick whines answered her from the far ship,

and, a moment later, she saw the rebel guard dragging a New Harmonite out the hatch.

"Come, Nikki!" she ordered, and Nikki followed like an obedient dog.

Renard, puffing slightly, hauled the second, identical form out, and gestured for them to get in.

It was Trelig's private cruiser, complete with bedroom, lounge, even a bar. Ordering Nikki into one of the lounge chairs, Renard strapped her in while Mavra went forward. A quick fine-line shot with the pistol blew the flimsy lock, and she opened the door to the cockpit.

Renard dashed in after her, took the copilot's chair, and strapped himself in. Mavra was at work in seconds, flipping switches, punching orders into the activated computer, setting procedures for emergency lift.

"Hang on!" she yelled to Renard as the ship hummed and vibrated with full power buildup. "This will be rough!"

She punched *E-Lift,* and the ship broke free of its mooring pad and rose at near-maximum power.

"Code, please," a mechanical voice demanded pleasantly over the radio. "Correct code within sixty seconds or we will destroy your ship."

Mavra grabbed frantically for the headset, tried to put it on, found it so large it wouldn't stay on even at its smallest setting. Still, she got the mike activated and close to her mouth.

"Stand by for code," she said into it, and then paused. Come on! *Come on!* she thought urgently. *Nikki's aboard and we're away! Give me the goddamned code!*

"For god's sake give the code!" Renard screamed at her.

"Thirty seconds," the robot sentry pointed out politely.

Suddenly she had it. The words burst into her mind, suddenly, so strangely that for a moment she doubted they were correct. She took a deep breath. That had to be, or that was it anyway.

"Edward Gibbon, Volume I," she said.

No response. They held their breath together. The

seconds ticked off in their minds, five . . . four . . . three . . . two . . . one . . . zero . . .

Nothing happened. Renard whistled and almost collapsed. Mavra started trembling slightly, and couldn't stop for half a minute. She felt drained.

They sat there, silent, while they continued out at full thrust. Finally Mavra turned to the strange man who looked like a woman and said, almost in a whisper, "Renard? What time is it?"

Renard frowned, then reached over, flipped up his shoulder holster.

"Twelve ten," he replied.

Mavra felt better. There was a better than even chance that they would make it in time. If Trelig's craft couldn't, nothing could.

Then, suddenly, there was a blackness. Mavra's eyes wouldn't adjust to it, nor was there any sensation of a solid ship around them. They were in a deep, black hole, falling, falling fast.

Renard screamed, and so did Nikki, plaintively, from somewhere in back of them.

"Son of a bitch!" Mavra said with disgust. "They moved up the damned test!"

Underside—New Pompeii

TRELIG HAD BEEN IMPATIENT. THE ASTEROID HAD been lined up early by the robotic tugs; Yulin was ready, the rest of the staff was monitoring all the necessary instruments. He saw no reason to delay until thirteen hundred because of some arbitrary time he'd set. He ordered the test to begin, and Yulin, following orders, gave the command to Obie.

For its part, the computer was upset. It couldn't ignore Yulin's direct command, although it had tried to divert them with several minor breakdowns. Obie had its own limits, and when Yulin gave the code, it had to obey, hoping that its agent had gotten away early.

The total blackness, and the sensation of falling, was unexpected to Zinder. Even Obie felt it; the computer knew that they were not falling anywhere and analyzed that the early fifty percent option had occurred. There was insufficient power to maintain New Pompeii in a stable relationship with the rest of the universe; the pull had come, too strong to resist had it wanted to, and the planetoid had yielded without hesitation.

Unaffected by the terrible sensory sensations the others were feeling, Obie probed the state. There was nothing out there. Nothing.

New Pompeii was still intact; Obie managed to verify that fact. But it had switched to reserve power the moment the big disk had gone on; it could detect no other matter anywhere, not the tiniest dust particle beyond the proximity limits of the ray, a little under a light-year. They were in a separate cosmos all to themselves.

And yet there was something only Obie could feel. The pull, and the tremendous field of force, the stability equation for their physical existence, snapped now, like a stretched rubber band slipping off one of its anchors. That was the pull, the computer realized. All matter and all energy in the cosmos had its linkages to the master computer somewhere; when that linkage was disturbed or disrupted, the reality involved dissolved into its primal energy pattern. That was why they could sense no reality, why they could not touch the solid planetoid of New Pompeii even though Obie's instrumentation said it was there. It was not. They were all, Obie included, an abstract mathematical concept set now, returning to their creator.

Then, suddenly, there was stability again. Power returned, and Obie could feel solar energy bathing the plasma which, miraculously, seemed to have held up as well.

All of the humans were sprawled over the walkway and control room, stunned, shocked, or unconscious.

Then, suddenly, one figure groaned and sat up,

moving his head around as if to flex painfully twisted muscles. Breathing hard, half-walking, half-crawling, he made his way to the control room, ignoring the groans from others around him.

Yulin had been knocked out, tossed from his chair against a panel. There was a nasty cut on his forehead.

The man didn't care. He opened a switch.

"Obie! Are you all right?" he called.

"Yes, Dr. Zinder," the computer replied. "That is, much better than you or I expected."

Gil Zinder nodded. "What's our status, Obie? What happened?"

"I have been analyzing all the data, sir, and correlating it as much as I can. We were removed from reality, as we anticipated, and reassembled elsewhere. We appear to be in a stable orbit approximately forty thousand kilometers above the equator of a very strange planet, sir."

"The brain, Obie!" Zinder called excitedly. "Is it the Markovian brain?"

"Yes, sir, it appears to be," the computer answered, sounding more than a little upset.

"What's wrong, Obie?" Zinder said.

"It's the brain, sir," Obie replied, sounding hesitant and slightly confused. "I have a direct link with it. It's incredible, as far beyond me as I am beyond a pocket communicator. I can decipher just a little under a millionth of the signal information it is transmitting, and I doubt if I could ever comprehend it fully, but—"

"But what?" Zinder prodded, not even seeing Yulin get up behind him.

"Well, sir, as near as I can figure out, it seems to be asking me for instructions," Obie replied.

On Trelig's Ship, Half a Light-year Out from New Pompeii—1210 Hours

THE WORLD RETURNED SUDDENLY. MAVRA CHANG looked around, slightly dazed, then checked the instruments. They read total nonsense, so she looked over at Renard and saw him groggily shaking his head.

"What happened?" he managed.

"We were caught in the field and carried along with them," Mavra explained with more authority than she felt. She looked down at the instruments again, then punched a random search pattern. The screen flickered but remained blank in front of her. Finally, she turned the damned thing off.

"Well, that tears it," she said, resigned.

Renard looked over at her strangely. "What do you mean?" he asked.

"I just punched the star chart navigational locator. Inside the little chip is stored every known star pattern, from every angle. There are billions of combinations. It went through them all— and didn't flash once. We're not in any section of known space."

He envied her calm acceptance of the fact. "So what do we do now?" he asked apprehensively.

Mavra flipped a series of switches and then pulled back on the long handle to her right. The whine and vibration of the ship's engines slowed. "First we see what the neighborhood looks like, then we decide where in it we want to go," she told him matter-of-factly.

She punched up another series on the small control board, and the main screen in front of them, which usually showed a simulated starfield, showed something else entirely. There were stars there—more stars than either of them had ever seen before. They were so close together it looked as if the firmament were on fire with a white heat. It took some filters to get any definition, and that didn't help much. There were also great clouds of space gas, glowing crimson and yellow, and there were shapes and forms never seen, not even in astronomical photos.

"We're definitely in somebody else's neighborhood," Mavra commented dryly, and, after checking speed, started to turn the craft around. "We're just about dead still now," she told him. "I'm going to give us a panorama."

The enormous clouds of stars and strange shapes did not diminish; they were surrounded by them. A small green grid to Mavra's left was mostly blank, indicating nothing within a light-year or more of them. Then, suddenly, a small series of dots appeared.

"Look, Trelig's robot guardians," she noted. "Everything else is debris from the rest of that fragmented system. It seems the whole neighborhood moved. If that's true—yes, see it? The big dot, there, with the slightly smaller one just off it. That's New Pompeii and its would-be target."

Renard nodded. "But what's that huge object just to its right?" he asked.

"A planet. From the looks of it, the only planet in the system. Funny it took the whole solar system with it but not the star. That star's definitely larger and older," she pointed out.

"It's moving," Renard said, fascinated in spite of himself. "New Pompeii's moving."

Mavra studied it, punched in, got the data back. "It's in orbit around that planet, a satellite of it now. Let's get a good look at the place." Again more button-pushing, and the screen zeroed in on the central object shown electronically on the green scope.

"Not a big place," Mavra said. "Let's see . . . about average, I'd say. A little more than forty thousand kilometers around. Hmmm . . . that's interesting!"

"What?" Renard prodded, staring.

"The diameter's exactly the same pole to pole," she replied in a puzzled tone. "That's almost impossible. The damned thing's a perfect ball, not the slightest meter of variation!"

"I thought most planets were round," he said, slightly confused.

She shook her head. "No, there's never been a round one. Rotation, revolution, they all take their toll. Planets bulge, or get pear-shaped, or a million other things. Roughly round, yes—but this thing's *perfectly* round, as if somebody—" she paused for a second, and an awed tone crept into her voice—"as if somebody *built* it," she finished.

Before Renard could reply, she eased the ship forward, toward the strange world.

"You're going there?" he asked her.

Mavra nodded. "Well, if *we* pulled through, so did the folks on New Pompeii," she reasoned. "That means there's a furious, probably murderous Antor Trelig somewhere back there, and a lot of scared people. If he's still in control, the three of us would be better off blowing up this ship than landing. If he's not, then we'd walk into a human hell."

Renard's expression was blank, his eyes somewhat glassy. Mavra, busy looking at the ship's controls and the world that would be visible to them shortly, hardly noticed for a while. Soon the magnifiers were getting a better view, though; the planet was about the size of an orange. The green grid said that New Pompeii was about to go around the other side.

"It's got a straight up and down axis!" she said excitedly. "It *was* built by somebody!" She turned to Renard, then her excitement faded, turning to concern. "What's the matter?" she asked.

He licked his lips but remained with that vacant expression, staring not at her or at the screen but at nothing.

"The sponge," he replied hollowly. "It comes in daily at eighteen hundred hours, from a roving supply ship. *Your* ship didn't come with us, so it wouldn't have either, if it was there at all." He turned to look at her, and there was mild terror building in his eyes. "There's no sponge today. There's no sponge ever again. Not for me, not for *them*."

Mavra understood suddenly what was going through his mind, and perhaps Nikki's as well. She was under restraining straps in the back and they'd almost forgotten about her.

She sighed, wishing she could say something. Being sorry didn't seem right, somehow, and her pity was too apparent to need expression.

"The only hope then," she said at last, "is that there's somebody living on that world out there, somebody with a good chemical lab."

Renard smiled weakly. "Nice try, but even if there is, by the time we contact them, figure out how to talk to them, explain the problem, and have them mix a batch, you'll be preserving a couple of naked apes."

She shrugged. "What other choice *is* there?" Suddenly a thought came to her. "I wonder if the rest of the guards on New Pompeii have figured that out yet? What will they do when the shipment doesn't come at eighteen hundred and confirms their fears?"

Renard thought that over. "Probably the same thing *I'd* do. Find Trelig and take a great deal of pleasure in torturing him to death."

"The computer!" Mavra exclaimed excitedly. *"It* can cure sponge! If we can get in contact with it somehow—" She started frantically scanning all the Com bands, punching in a call sign. Obie would recognize it if he could hear it—Obie had her memories in storage.

The radio crackled and wheezed. Several times in the scan they swore they could hear voices of some kind, but speaking strange tongues, or so inhuman-sounding as to cause chills in them.

Then, quite abruptly, a familiar voice popped in.

"Well, Mavra, I see you didn't make it," Obie sighed. She returned the sigh, hers one of relief.

"Obie!" she responded. "Obie, what's the situation down there?"

There was silence for a moment, then the computer replied, "It's a mess. Dr. Zinder recovered first and got to me, and I have some of his instructions before Ben pulled him away. Two of the guards were there, and they heard me tell Dr. Zinder that we were in a different area of space. They started screaming about sponge, and Trelig shot them dead."

"So they figured it out already," she said. "What about Topside?"

"Trelig figured they had to go up and try and control the other guards. They could have trapped him down here. He hopes to bargain their processing through me to rid them of the sponge, but I don't think he'll have much success. Most of them wouldn't believe he could cure them anyway, and the rest would be even more furious that such a cure was here and not used. They would, I feel certain, go along with him only long enough to get the cure, then kill him anyway."

Mavra nodded. "And if you can figure that out, so can Trelig. He has no percentage in a cure." She paused a moment, then said, carefully, "Obie, is there a way that *we* could get in to you? There's Nikki—and one of the guards, an ally, Renard."

Obie sighed again. It was weird to hear so human a voice and so human a reaction from a machine, but Obie was much more than a machine.

"I'm afraid not, at least not right now. The big dish is frozen in contact with the Well—the great Markovian computer that runs that world down there. It is beyond my control right now. It may take some time—days, weeks, even years—for me to figure a way to break off, if there *is* a way. As for the little dish, Trelig's no fool. He left, but he first coded defense mechanisms beyond my control. If I had the big dish I could neutralize them, but I don't. Anyone trying to get into the little room first has to pass over the bridge across the shaft. That bridge will kill unless Trelig's code is given, and I don't have it."

She frowned. "Well, can you keep anybody else from blowing it?"

"I think so," the computer replied uncertainly. "I have run a current through the shaft walls. That should keep anyone from getting to the bridge.

"Okay, Obie, looks like I have to go in and save Trelig's noble neck," she said, and applied power. The new moon that was New Pompeii had disappeared around the strange planet, and she established an intercept vector.

"Wait! Don't!" Obie's voice called. "Break off!

You'll have to come in *under* New Pompeii to hit the Topside area, and that will swing you too close to the Well."

But it was too late. The ship was already closing on the planet, felt its pull, and used it to whip around to the other side.

Here was an incredible sight. The world, close up, shimmered like a dream-thing, and yet it somewhat resembled a great, alien jewel. It was *faceted,* somehow; countless hexagonal facets of some sort, and below whatever was causing the faceting was a hint of broad seas, mountain ranges, and fields of green around which clouds swirled. That is, that was the case *below* the equator. The equator itself looked odd, as if it were designed for a child's globe. A thick strip, semitransparent but with an amber coloration, like a broad plastic band around the world. The north—it, too, was faceted hexagonally, but the landscapes there contained nothing familiar; eerie, stark, strange. The poles, too, were strange—areas of great expanse, yet of a nonreflective darkness, almost as if they weren't there at all.

The sight spellbound them. And the proper boost and cut had been preapplied. To get out of it, Mavra would have to swing around the planet tangentially to the equator anyway.

"Too late! Too late!" Obie wailed. "Quick! Get everyone in the lifesaving modules!"

Mavra was puzzled. Everything seemed normal, and she suddenly caught sight of New Pompeii, half green and shiny, half covered with the great mirror surface.

"We better do what he says," Renard said quietly. "Where's the lifeboat? I'll get Nikki."

"Bring her here," Mavra told him. "The bridge will seal if anything goes wrong."

"I'll hurry," Renard replied, worried now about the immediate threat. Mavra couldn't see *any* threat; she was breaking, coasting toward New Pompeii, swinging about a third of the way to the planet below in a standard approach that would take her once around New Pompeii and in. It was all so normal.

"Damn it! I'm okay!" she heard Nikki almost

scream. She turned and saw the girl enter, an angry expression on her face. Renard followed.

"Your father's alive, Nikki," Mavra told the girl. "I'm in contact with Obie. Maybe we—"

At that moment the ship shuddered, and all the electronics, including the lights, flickered, then winked out.

"What the hell?" Mavra tried punching everything she could find. The bridge was pitch-dark, and there was no motor noise or vibration of any kind. Even the emergency lights and safety controls were out, although they shouldn't be. They *couldn't* be.

Her mind raced. "Renard!" she called. "Get Nikki into your chair, then get in mine with me! I think we can both fit! Nikki! Strap yourself in as tight as you can!"

"Wha—what's happening?" the girl called.

"Just do what I say! *Quickly!*" the small woman snapped. "Somehow we've lost *all* power, even the emergencies! We were too close in to the planet! If we don't get power back—"

She heard Nikki stumble, flop into the seat. She felt Renard's hand almost grab her in the face. Her own eyes, Obie-designed, adapted to infrared immediately. She saw them—but nothing else. There was no other heat source on the bridge!

She managed an oath, reached up, pushed Renard into the chair. It was a very tight fit, and it didn't quite work. That damned tail! she thought angrily.

"I'm going to have to sit in your lap," she told him, shifting.

"Ouch!" he exclaimed. "Move down a little! That tailbone is pressing on my sensitive area!"

She shifted down slightly, and he just barely pulled the straps over both of them, then wrapped his arms around her, squeezing tightly more from nervousness than anything else.

Suddenly, everything flicked back on again.

The screen showed that they'd lost tremendous altitude during the blackout. They could see a sea ahead, and, beyond that, some mountains.

"We're over the equator into the south, anyway,"

Mavra managed. "Let me see if I can boost us out of here."

She started to undo the straps when, suddenly, the screen showed that they had cleared the ocean—and everything went black again.

"Damn!" she swore. "I wish I knew what the hell was going on here!"

"We're going to crash, aren't we?" Nikki asked, more resigned than panicked.

"Looks like it," Mavra called back. "We'll start breakup soon unless the power comes on."

"Breakup?" Renard repeated.

"There are three systems on these ships," she told him. "Two are electrical, one mechanical. I hope the mechanical holds, because we have no power, none at all. In two of the three, including the mechanical, the ship separates into modules. In the mechanical mode it will deploy parachutes thirty seconds after breakup, then use air resistance to trigger the main chutes. It'll be a rough ride."

"Are we gonna die?" she heard Nikki ask.

"Might as well," she heard Renard murmur to himself, too low for the girl to hear. She understood what he meant. This would be quicker, by far, than sponge.

"I hope not," she responded, but there was a tinge of doubt in her voice. "If we had a complete failure in space, we would—we'd use up the air. But down there—I don't know. If we can breathe the stuff, and if we survive the landing, and if the chutes open, we should make it."

A whole lot of ifs, she thought to herself. Probably too many.

The ship shuddered, and there were loud noises all around. Separation had been achieved.

"Well," she sighed. "Nothing we can do about it now, anyway. Even if the power came on again—the engines aren't attached to us anymore."

There came now a series of sharp, irregular bumps. Renard groaned, catching both the effects of him against the chair and Mavra against him. Then there was a single very sharp jerk that almost made them dizzy.

94

"The chutes!" Mavra exclaimed. "They opened! We have air of some kind out there!"

It was now a dizzying, swaying, rocking ride in total darkness. A few minutes of this and they all began feeling a little sick. Nikki had just started to complain when there was a much stronger, almost violent series of jerks.

"Main chute," Mavra sighed. "Hold on! The next one will be one hell of a bang!"

And it was. They felt as if they'd slammed into a brick wall, then they seemed to be rolling over and over, coming to a stop hanging upside down.

"Easy now!" Mavra cautioned. "We're resting on the ceiling now. The gravity feels close to one G— about right for a planet of this mass. Nikki! You all right?"

"I feel awful," the girl complained. "God! I think I'm bleeding! It feels like every bone in my body's broke!"

"That goes double for me," Renard groaned. "You?"

"I've got burns from the straps," Mavra told them. "Feels like it, anyway. Too early to tell the real damage. Right now it's shock. Let's get down from here first, then we can treat any injuries. Nikki, you stay put! We'll get you down in a minute."

She felt the straps holding them. Only a few centimeters were still in the clasp. One more bang, she thought, and we'd have come loose.

"Renard!" she said. "Look, I can see in this darkness, but you can't, and I can't get down without dropping you. See if you can grab onto the chair when I release the straps. It's about four meters, but it's smooth and rounded. Then I'll get you to the floor." She guided his arms, and he got some kind of grip, but he was facing the wrong way to have any leverage.

"Maybe I could have done it years ago," he said dubiously, "but since my body changed—I don't know. I don't have much strength in my arms."

"Well, try to swing free, jump when you have to," she told him. "Here goes. . . . *Now!*"

She hit the master stud, and the belt-web dropped

95

away. She dropped immediately to the floor and rolled. Renard yelled, then let go, coming down in a heap and sprawling. She went over to him, examined him, felt his bones.

"I don't think there's anything broken," she told him. "Come on! I know you're a mess of bruises, but I need you to help Nikki down!"

He had twisted his ankle, and it hurt like hell to stand, but he managed on sheer will power. Carefully, they managed to get him under Nikki, and, by reaching up, he could touch her.

He wasn't strong enough to support her, but he did manage to make her fall less severe, and she landed somehow on her rump. It was painful and she moaned, but, again, Mavra detected nothing broken. Bruised and twisted they were, and sore they would be, but they all had come through miraculously well.

Renard tried deep-breathing exercises to ease the pain, all the time rubbing his sore legs with his equally sore arms. "Just out of curiosity, Mavra, how many times have you made a landing like this?" he gasped.

She chuckled. "Never. They say these systems are too impractical. Many ships no longer even have them. Once in a million they're usable."

He grunted. "Umph. That's what I thought. Now, how do we get out of here?"

"There's an under and over escape-hatch system," she told them. "The thing's an airlock, but it won't pump, of course. You're going to have to lift me up so I can trip the safety switches. The ceiling one's no good to us."

He groaned, but managed. She reached out, just barely getting the controls, and, after several tries and one or two drops, there was a hissing sound and the hatch dropped. More long minutes passed while she tried to jump from his shoulders and grab the edge of the hatch. Finally, when they'd almost given up and Renard was complaining he couldn't take it any more, she got a grip, hoisted herself in, and flipped open the outer lock.

"Suppose we can't breathe out there!" Nikki yelled to Mavra.

Mavra looked down at them. "In that case we're

dead anyway," she told them. Actually, she knew the odds were against the air being something they could use, but there had been an ocean and green trees, and that held hope.

She pulled herself out of the lock, and stared.

"Smells kind of funny, but I think we're all still alive," she called back. "I'll get some tether cable from the work locker. It was supposed to anchor space-suits, but it should hold you."

Nikki was the toughest. She was very heavy and not very athletic, and while they pulled in the dark-ness—Renard had climbed the anchored tether cord on his own—both Nikki's arms and theirs seemed ready to give out. They were working on adrenalin now, they knew, and that energy would not last for-ever.

But they did get Nikki clear of the first hatch, where the ribbed sides gave some sort of tenuous leg supports, and they managed to get her out.

Once off the bridge module, they sank on what ap-peared to be real grass, exhausted, the landscape swimming by them. Mavra put herself through a se-ries of body-control exercises and managed to will away much of the pain but not the feeling of exhaus-tion. She opened her eyes, looked back at the other two, and saw them sprawled out, asleep and breath-ing hard.

She scanned the horizon. Nothing looked particu-larly threatening; it was around midday, and their sur-roundings looked like a quiet forest scene from any one of a hundred planets. Some insects were audible, and she saw a few very standard-looking birds float-ing on air currents high above, but little else.

She looked again at her unconscious companions and sighed. Even so, *somebody* had to stay awake.

New Pompeii—1150 Hours

A BLUE-WHITE SHOT SANG OUT ACROSS THE GREAT void that was the pit of the big disk. A little bit of the molding around the control room smoldered and hissed. Somebody cursed. All over were blotches where previous shots had struck, and the window out onto the pit was long gone.

Gil Zinder sat nervously hunched back against his control panel on the balcony. Antor Trelig was growling and using the scarred but still reflective side molding of the door to try and ascertain the location of the shooters. Ben Yulin, on the opposite side of the doorway, checked his own pistol for its remaining charge.

"Why don't you close the door?" Zinder shouted feebly. "Those shots are starting to come into here!"

"Shut up, old man," snarled Trelig. "If we shut it they can seal it with their fire and then we might never get out of here. Ever think of that?"

Yulin snapped his fingers and made his way to the interior control panel. A shot came near him, but the control panel was angled away from the door sufficiently so that anybody shooting at it would be a perfect target for Trelig.

Anxiously, Yulin flipped the intercom open. "Obie?" he called.

"Yes, Ben?" the computer replied.

"Obie, how are your visuals in the tunnel? Can you give us a fix on how many there are and what damage there is?"

"My visuals are unimpaired," Obie responded. "There are seven of them left. You shot three and they are gone. There is a lot of damage to the pit control room and the facing wall, but nothing major."

Yulin nodded to himself, and Trelig suddenly and

quickly crouched, leaned out of the doorway, and shot a volley.

"Missed them by a kilometer, Trelig," Obie observed in a tone that indicated a smug satisfaction. Trelig, hearing it, bristled but said nothing.

"Obie, how operational are you?" Yulin asked, gesturing to Zinder to crawl over to the console. The older man at first seemed too scared to move, but then, slowly, started inching his way there.

"Not very," the computer told them. "The computer that runs the world down there is both infinitely more complex and simpler than I am. Its input capabilities appear to be unlimited, and it has complete control of all prime and secondary equations at output—but it is entirely preprogrammed. It is not self-aware, not an individual entity."

Gil Zinder reached the console and sighed, then crouched next to Yulin.

"Obie, this is Dr. Zinder," he told the machine. "Can you break contact with the other computer?"

"Not at this time, Dr. Zinder," Obie responded, his tone much nicer now, and more tinged with concern. "When we activated the reverse field, we released the tension of the energy controlling our own existence. It brought us here. Apparently the world computer has been preprogrammed for just such an event, but the programmers assumed that anyone who could tap the Markovian equations in such a manner and bring themselves here would be at close to the same technological level as the builders of the world computer. We are supposed to supersede previous programming, tell it what to do next."

"Where is *here*, Obie?" Zinder asked.

"The coordinates would be useless, even if I had a frame of reference," Obie replied. "We are, in a sense, in the center of the tangible universe, or so I gather from what I can make of the other computer's information circuits."

Even Trelig understood the implications. "You mean this is the center for all existence of all matter in the galaxy?" he shouted.

"Just so," agreed Obie. "And all energy, too, except the primal energy that is the building blocks for everything else. This is the central Markovian world, from which, as near as I can see, they recreated the universe."

That thought sobered all of them. Trelig's eyes shined, and his expression took on new determination. "Such awesome power!" he said, too low for the others to hear. A blue-white shot didn't snap him out of it but did bring him back to reality. With such power within his grasp, he still had to survive this experience.

"Obie, can you converse with this big machine?" Yulin asked eagerly.

The computer seemed to think for a moment. "Yes and no. It's hard to explain. Suppose you had a functional vocabulary of just eighty words? Suppose, in fact, you were only *capable* of knowing eighty words. And suppose someone from your culture with a doctorate in physics started talking his technical field with you. You couldn't even absorb all the words, let alone understand any of the conversation."

"But you could talk to it in those eighty words," Yulin pointed out.

"Not if you couldn't even phrase the question," Obie retorted. "I haven't the ability even to say 'hello' in an understandable manner—and I'm almost afraid to try. There is an incredibly elaborate preprogrammed sequence that I am aware of but cannot follow or comprehend. I don't dare try. It might wipe out all reality, or the other computer and all reality as well, leaving me as the only thing left. What then?"

The scientists saw what he meant. The Markovians had preprogrammed the computer to turn over everything to their successors, when they reached the Markovian level. It apparently had never occurred to them that a Gil Zinder, a primitive ape, would stumble onto their precious formula millennia before man was ready. The master computer out there was waiting for Obie to tell it to shut down, that new masters were taking over.

But the new masters were three very scared primitives and an equally scared computer, the primitives trapped by the former employees of one of them. The guards, seeing the change in position and realizing that the sponge supply ship would not be coming, knew they were going to die horribly.

But they were going to die free. They were going to take their hated master with them.

"Obie?" Yulin called.

"Yes, Ben?"

"Obie, can you figure out how the hell we can get out of here?"

The computer had anticipated that one.

"Well, you *could* just wait them out," Obie suggested. "There are provisions here for a week, and I can create more than enough to sustain you. In three weeks or so all the guards will be dead; in two they will be in no condition to oppose you or do you harm."

"No good!" Trelig shouted to them all. "There are two ships up there that must be placed under our control—otherwise we're trapped. Remember, there are a lot of agents and diplomatic people who won't be affected by the sponge wearing off! With the guards gone wild, some are probably armed by now and might be able to take the ships. If they jump away, we're stuck for good!"

"Correction," Obie responded. "There is *one* ship. Mavra Chang, Nikki Zinder, and a guard named Renard got off in one."

Gil Zinder seemed to come to life again. "Nikki! Away from here! Obie—did they make it out? Are they back home?"

"Sorry, Dr. Zinder," the computer said sadly. "The early start for the tests forced my hand. They were taken in the vortex with us, and have since crashed on the Well World."

The old scientist's look of hope gave way to despair, and he seemed to crumble. Trelig was upset by a different point entirely.

"What do you mean, forced *your* hand?" the erstwhile master of New Pompeii snarled angrily. "You treasonous machine!"

Obie was nonplussed. "I am a self-aware individual, Councillor. I do what I must do, and yet I have certain freedom of action outside those parameters. Just like people," he added, not a little smugly.

Ben Yulin's mind was the engineer's. "What did you

call that world they crashed on, Obie?" he asked, ignoring the others.

"The Well World," responded the computer. "That is its name."

Yulin thought for a moment. "The Well World," he murmured, almost to himself. Now he looked straight at the speaker. More shots were being exchanged between Trelig and the guards outside.

"Obie?" Ben almost whispered, "tell me about this Well World. Is it just a big Markovian computer, or what?"

"I have to interpolate, Ben," Obie apologized. "After all, I'm getting this information in bits and pieces and it's all coming in at once. No, I don't think so, though. The computer—the Well—is the entire core of the planet. The planet itself seems to be divided into many more than a thousand separate and distinct biospheres, each with its own dominant life form and supporting its own flora, fauna, atmospheric conditions, and the like. It's like a massive number of little planets. I infer these as prototype colonies for later implantation into the universe in their true, mathematically precise environments. They are alive, they are active, they exist."

The other two were listening now, fascinated in spite of themselves.

"The three who crashed," Gil Zinder tried dryly. "Did they—did they . . . survive?"

"Unknown," Obie replied truthfully. "Since they are not part of the Well World matrix, they are not in the computer's storage. Even if they were, I doubt if they could be picked out. There are too many sentient beings down there."

"Why don't you ask him something practical, like how the hell we get out of here?" Trelig snapped, breaking the reverie. "The fact that there's only one ship left makes the matter even more pressing!"

Yulin nodded, unhappy to break this fascinating new line of discovery but unable to argue with Trelig's practicality. But the computer was a hostile accomplice; questions would have to be in absolutes. Yulin suddenly felt like he knew what it was like to have to strike a bargain with the devil.

102

And then, suddenly, without Obie's aid, he had it. Yulin let out a disgusted exclamation that made the others turn, then slammed his right fist into his left palm. "Curse me for a fool!" he swore. "Of course!" Calming himself down, he asked, "Obie, is your little disk still operable?"

"Yes, Ben," Obie replied. "But only within its previous limits. The big disk is locked into the Well computer until I or somebody can figure out how to disengage it, and I have no ideas at all on that right now."

Yulin nodded, more to himself than to the machine. "Okay. Okay. The little one's all I need now. Obie, you have the formula for sponge, don't you?"

"Of course," came the reply, a little startled. "From the bloodstream of a number of early subjects."

"Uh, huh," Yulin muttered. He was all business now. "Activate and energize. I want a small quantity of sponge, say five grams, in a leakproof plastic container. The straight stuff. And, I want an additional kilogram of the stuff with the following chemical substitutions." He proceeded to rattle off a long chemical chain that startled the others.

Zinder was the first to realize where Yulin was headed, and almost moaned, "But—you can't *do* that!"

But Yulin could, had ordered it, energized Obie, and the disk was even now swinging out over the circular platform, and the blue field was forming.

"What the hell are you going to do?" Trelig shouted.

"He's going to poison the poor bastards," Gil Zinder replied. He looked up at Yulin. "But—why? With sponge they'll be back under your command again anyway."

Ben Yulin shook his head. "Maybe upstairs—maybe. But not these folks out there. They are already resigned to death and they're committed." He turned to Trelig. "Keep a watch on old doc here while I get the stuff," he called.

In a flash Yulin was off, bounding down the stairs to the platform. Carefully, he examined the two packages, found some gloves, and picked up both of them. He still didn't quite trust Obie. And then he was back.

"Have we still got communication?" he asked the councillor.

Trelig nodded. "I think so, unless they've shot out the circuits. Try it."

Yulin went over to the wall, flipped a switch. "You, out there!" he called, hearing his own voice echoing eerily from the vast pit beyond the wall. "Listen to me! We have sponge! Things aren't hopeless! We'll give it to you if you surrender your weapons!" He flipped the intercom back to *Open*.

There was a sudden silence from the outside, as if the news had unsettled the others, which was good. There was no reply as yet, but no shots, either.

After what seemed like an interminable wait, Trelig growled, "They didn't buy it."

Yulin, although fearing much the same thing himself, replied, "Don't jump the gun. They're probably voting on it. And thinking about the pain of no-dose for the first time. Even though they won't really start to feel the effects for a while, they feel it in their minds even now."

And he was right. A few minutes later the intercom burst into life.

"Okay, Yulin, maybe you get out," came a rather pleasant voice with a very unpleasant undertone. "But how do we know you aren't lying? We know how much sponge comes in. Every gram."

"We can make it! All you need!" Yulin responded, trying to keep his tension and anxiety out of his tone. "Look, I'll prove it to you. Send a representative over the bridge. Any one. I'll toss out a fiver. Try it. You'll know what I say is the truth."

There was another long silence, and then the same voice came back, "All right. I'm coming over. But if I don't make it or the stuff's no good, the other six will get you if it's the last thing they do—and there's plenty more of us Topside. They know what's going on down here."

Yulin grinned to himself. Another piece of useful information. The intercoms on Topside still worked. Now he knew just how much of the story they would know, and that intelligence would possibly make the difference.

A few minutes later a lone figure could be seen walking across the great bridge that spanned the pit to Obie's major core. It was a tiny, frail-looking figure, dwarfed almost to insignificance by the magnitude of the structure around it. It was either a very young girl or one of the screwy sexers. It didn't matter.

The former guard seemed to take forever to get there, and finally stopped about ten meters from the doorway.

"I'm here!" she (he?) announced needlessly.

Yulin gripped the small bag of pure sponge. "Here it comes!" he shouted and tossed it onto the bridge. It hit with a *pock* sound and slid almost to the other's feet.

The guard picked it up, looked at it, then tore open the plastic and pulled out the tiny piece of yellow-green sponge, an actual living creature of sorts. It really *was* a sponge, too, a denizen of a beautiful world that had been settled centuries ago by a prototype human colony. Interaction of alien bacteria with some of the synthetic elements in the colony's initial food supply had spawned the horror that made Antor Trelig and his vast syndicate so powerful. The new mutated substance had permeated every cell of the human's bodies, replacing vital substances. The cells took to it fantastically; once in, it was neither rejected nor displaced. Indeed, the cells actually started making more of the stuff. The initial contamination was irreversible. A moderate amount caused no apparent physical changes, but was there all the same. A large amount, as the guards had gotten, caused cells to trigger in strange ways, causing deformity, accenting opposite sexual characteristics, or, as in Nikki Zinder's case, causing runaway obesity or other equally horrible characteristics. It varied with the individual, although sexual characteristics, being the most sensitive, were the most common.

The organism, however, was totally parasitic. It would consume the host, particularly its brain, where brain cells died irreplaceably in a great progression. Unchecked, the mutant substance would slowly destroy the mind well ahead of the body; it was painful. Since the stuff was not selective, often mental capacity was reduced or limited for all intents and purposes while the central core of one's being was the last to go. One *knew* what was happening, knew until it struck the cerebral cortex full and turned one first into an animal, then into a vegetable that would simply lie there and starve to death. A slow-motion lobotomy.

Sponge was not the drug, it was the antidote. Not an effective one, since it had to be periodically renewed, but the secretions of the native sponge plants did in fact arrest the growth of the mutant strain. To need sponge was to become the syndicate's slave. The stuff was too dangerous for the Com to keep around; the sponge itself contained the addicting material. But greedy, ambitious politicians had it, grew it, and ruled with it.

Facing such a future, the guard greedily and unhesitantly gobbled up the sponge in the plastic envelope. It was not a sufficient dose—all of New Pompeii's personnel were deliberately given massive overdoses, which required massive amounts of sponge to counter —but it would be convincing.

It was. "It's real!" the guard shouted, clearly amazed. "It's the pure stuff!"

"A kilo in exchange for your weapons!" Trelig yelled, feeling in charge once again. "Now—or we wait you out!"

"The word has gone to Topside!" came a new, deeper voice from the intercom. "Okay, we're coming over—four of us. The others will make sure you don't blast us. You get *their* weapons when we get the kilo and you come out. Not before."

Trelig waited what he thought would be a convincing period of time, grinning evilly now. Their ploy was all too obvious.

Three more joined the first one, looking somewhat eagerly at the very door that, just moments before, they'd been trying to blast.

"Okay, here's the kilo!" shouted the master of New Pompeii, as he heaved it out.

They almost pounced on it, and two of them made a simultaneous grab for the package. One scooped it up and started running back to the other side, while the other three nervously blocked Trelig's view.

106

"What if they don't take it right away?" Yulin whispered, worried.

"They will," Trelig replied confidently. "They're overdue, remember. How powerful *is* that stuff?"

"It should feel great for five or six minutes," the younger man told him. "After that, well, they should just all get massive heart seizures and keel over."

Trelig looked suddenly worried. *"Should?* You mean there's some doubt?"

"No, no, not really," Yulin replied, shaking his head. "I didn't really mean that. No, what's in there is enough to kill an army. Give them ten minutes, no more."

"Think they'll run for Topside?" Trelig continued, still worried. "Or maybe one will live long enough to radio a warning."

Yulin considered this. "No, I doubt if they'll wait to get to Topside. You yourself just said they're overdue. As for one giving a warning, well, if you can find a personal intercom, we ought to be able to find out."

They waited anxiously. Trelig could not find the intercom; the one he had originally worn was long smashed in the reversal. "We'll just have to bluff it through," he growled, uncertainty again in his voice. "Say—how will we know they're gone? You want to be the first target? Or maybe Doc, there?"

Yulin shook his head. "Not necessary. Obie's sensors are still on." He walked over to the console.

"Obie, are the guards still alive?"

"No, Ben," responded the computer. "At least, I register no life forms in their old area. They winked out pretty suddenly. You murdered them clean."

"Save your sarcasm," Yulin growled. "Did you monitor any transmissions to Topside?"

"I haven't much capability there," Obie noted. "I don't know."

Ben Yulin nodded, then turned to Trelig. "Well, we got by obstacles one through six. Topside's gonna be a lot tougher, though. Any ideas?"

Trelig thought for a moment, eyes gleaming. The immediate threat over, he was beginning to enjoy this.

"Ask the machine if anyone Topside is aware of who escaped in the first ship," he ordered.

"How could Obie know?" Yulin asked. "I mean, if he can't even monitor communications. Why? What have you got in mind?"

"To get to my position, you have to think of all the angles," the syndicate boss told him. "For example, either ship was capable of carrying at least half the guests, yet only Mavra Chang, Nikki Zinder, and the guard went. Why?"

Yulin thought a minute. "Because they sneaked out. Chang was paid to get the girl, not save everybody on Topside. The more people in a plot, the more chance for a foul-up."

Trelig nodded. "Now you begin to see. There are a lot of them, and they barely know one another. I'd guess, too, that they have, at best, an uneasy relationship with the guards. All hell broke loose not long after the ship left. Want to bet some of them don't even know a ship is gone?"

"The guards—" Yulin objected.

"Will know *only* that the ship is gone," Trelig completed. "They also know that without the codes the second ship would be blasted by the orbiting sentries. Hell, *they* won't remember who's who or how many there are, you know that. The girl's been more or less sealed off, and the guard—what's one guard? Could have been killed down here. Getting the idea now?"

"You mean *impersonate* the ones who got away?" Yulin gasped.

Trelig's expression looked impatient, impatient at this elementary step.

"Look," he said. "We need a way to gain their confidence. Take them off guard. We need a way to get to those visitors as friends, convince them it's us against the guards, get their help in taking the ship. We *must* get that ship away until they've died out here. We can't do it alone."

Yulin nodded. "I see," he said, but he didn't like it. He looked over at Gil Zinder. The older man was slumped, a vacant expression. He looked tired and defeated.

"What about him?" Ben Yulin asked, gesturing.

"He has to go with us," Trelig answered quickly. "He knows how to operate Obie, and Obie will do anything for him. To leave him here would be like jumping into the pit out there."

Yulin nodded, his mind already considering several things, all unpleasant. For one thing, he didn't like the idea of going through the thing himself. Sending others through, that was fine—a tremendous feeling of godlike power. But himself—to become someone, something else. Trelig's plan worried him, worried him as much as having to bring it about using his own special circuitry, revealing to Zinder—and to Trelig—his own mastery of the machine.

He looked again at Trelig. The councillor had a curious half-smile on his face and still held the pistol in his hand. He'd seen similar expressions on his boss when administering sponge to new victims and when ordering nasty executions.

"You want to go first?" he suggested hopefully.

That evil grin spread wider. "No, I don't think so," the syndicate boss replied acidly. "You *can* do it, then?"

Yulin nodded dully, still grasping at straws. He did not want to surrender to permanent second-class status.

"Then we'll do it this way," the big man continued. "First, you will try to find out the identity of the guard. If Obie can keep track of people, he should know who it was. Then one of us becomes the guard—minus the sponge addiction, make sure of that!—and one becomes Nikki Zinder and the third becomes Mavra Chang. All preprogrammed in noninterruptable sequence, of course." He shrugged disarmingly. "It's not that I don't *trust* you, you understand. It's just that you get on top by doing the unthinkable and you stay on top by thinking the unthinkable."

Yulin sighed, surrendering. The better part of valor and all that, he decided.

"Who do you want to be?" he asked.

"We have to think this through, and time's pressing," Trelig replied. "The old man, there—well, we'll need some sort of mind-bind, of course. Make him his own flesh and blood. Behavior patterns will also have to be programmed in," he reminded the younger scientist. "We don't want any slip-ups. We will not just have to look like these people, but walk like them, talk like them, almost think like them, while remaining ourselves inside. The odds are the guard's one of the supervisors, and they're all sexual foul-ups. I'm hermaphroditic, so that shouldn't pose a problem. That makes you Mavra Chang."

"I'd rather not be a woman," Yulin protested weakly.

"You won't mind when you've been through the disk," Trelig retorted. "Now, let's get the instructions letter-perfect, so everything's right and we get nothing funny added or subtracted by the machine. And—when you're doing it, Ben, you will show me how."

Yulin started to protest, then decided there was no point to it. He turned on the console.

"Obie? Do you have the identity of the guard who escaped with Mavra Chang?" he asked.

"It was Renard," replied the computer. "I have no reading for him and he did not leave Topside for here. A few died Topside, though, so a slight chance exists that it was not."

"It *has* to be," Trelig decided. "He was one of the girl's guards. Everything fits. I'll take a chance on it."

Ben Yulin nodded. "I don't think it'd be a good idea if the Doc, here, knows the access," he pointed out.

Trelig agreed, turned, and shot a short stun beam at the helpless Zinder, who collapsed in a heap. "Five minutes," Trelig warned his associate. "No more."

Ben Yulin nodded, then turned back to the console. He didn't like doing what he was about to do, and in front of the one man who could later use it against him, but a double cross at this point had too many risks to be worth it.

"Obie?" he called.

"Yes, Ben?" the computer responded.

He punched some buttons on his keyboard, acutely aware of Antor Trelig's steady gaze at the combinations.

"Unnumbered transaction," he told the machine. "File in aux storage under my key only."

"What?" The computer seemed slightly startled, then, as access to the sealed-off sections became open to him, Obie realized what was going on.

"How many times have you used this, Ben?" Obie asked, marveling as always at the discovery of a part of himself he'd not known was there.

"Not often," Yulin responded casually. "Now, Obie, I want you to listen carefully. You will carry out my instructions to the letter, neither adding nor subtracting anything on your own. Is that clear?"

"Yes, Ben," Obie replied resignedly.

Yulin paused a moment to choose his words, conscious of the dangers in giving Obie an opening, and also of Trelig's ready pistol. There were tiny beads of sweat on his forehead.

"Three transactions, in sequence, which must be completed before any additional instructions may be given you," he said cautiously. "One, Dr. Gilgam Zinder, outward form to be that of the last coding of Nikki Zinder minus the sponge presence. Memory will remain Gil Zinder's, with all attendant knowledge and skills, but subject will be unable to transmit this fact or information except on instruction from Antor Trelig or myself. Otherwise, subject will possess all behavior patterns of the frame of reference, including walk, emotive reactions, and speech, and all other characteristics to render subject indistinguishable from the frame of reference. Subject will further be unable to convey by any means the true identities of Antor Trelig or myself. Clear?"

"I understand, Ben," Obie replied.

Yulin nodded, certain he had completed that step correctly. "Two. Subject Antor Trelig. Subject is to be physically fitted to the last coding of the guard Renard, minus the sponge addiction. Subject will be provided with all behavior modes of the frame of reference, including walk, emotive reactions, speech, and all other characteristics to render subject indistinguishable from the frame of reference. However, memory will remain Antor Trelig's, with all attendant knowledge and skills, able to call upon his true self at any point." Yulin suddenly looked around at Trelig and asked, "All right so far?" Trelig nodded cautiously.

"Three," Yulin continued. "Subject Abu Ben Yulin. Subject is to be fitted physically to the last coding of Mavra Chang. Subject will be provided with all behavior modes of the frame of reference, including walk, emotive reactions, speech, and all other characteristics to render subject indistinguishable from the frame of reference. However, memory will remain Abu Ben Yulin's, with all attendant knowledge and skills, able to call upon his true self at any point. Clear?"

"Yes, Ben," Obie responded. "Clear and locked in."

Yulin, still nervous about undergoing the process himself, added, "And, Obie, for all three transactions, subjects are to be acclimated so that they feel physiologically and psychologically comfortable with the new bodies and external behavior patterns. Understand?"

"Yes, Ben. I understand you don't like to be a woman," Obie responded acidly. Yulin scowled but let the remark go. He turned to Trelig. "Okay, take the doc down," he said.

"First, tell the machine that the transactions are locked in," Trelig responded softly. Yulin grinned sheepishly and shrugged. There was no doubt whatsoever as to how Antor Trelig had attained and kept his position of power.

"Lock on all transactions *now*," he told Obie.

"Locked and running," Obie responded. "Go ahead with the run."

Satisfied now that Yulin could do nothing to override the instructions, Trelig gestured with the pistol and took Gil Zinder downstairs.

The transformation didn't take long. Yulin watched as first Gil Zinder dissolved in blue sparkles and reformed as an absolute duplicate of Nikki Zinder. The older scientist could do nothing, and so stood and watched as Trelig nervously mounted the disk, and threw his pistol hesitantly to Ben Yulin. Yulin thought, as Trelig dissolved and a few seconds later started reforming as the guard, how easy it would be to shoot Trelig. Zinder seemed to catch the younger man's thoughts, and said, in Nikki's adolescent tones, "No, Ben! You *can't!* He's the only one who knows how to get us off the planet!"

112

Yulin sighed, realizing the truth of that statement and accepting it grudgingly. He had to assume that the robot sentinels had also been transported, or else the nonspongies Topside would have taken off in the ship by now.

Yulin almost chuckled at Trelig's new appearance. Male sex organs on a very female-looking body. Trelig stepped off, nodded in satisfaction, and took the pistol from Yulin's hand. Ben had the uncomfortable idea suddenly that there was nothing to stop Trelig from shooting *him*, but he was helpless. Nervous both from anticipation of the process and from the sudden eerie feeling of impending death, he stepped up on the disk, watched the little arm swing out over him, and felt a warm, tingling glow course through his body. The lab, the watchers, seemed to flicker out, then flicker back in again. He knew that there had probably been several seconds between the flickers, but the sensation was not unpleasant.

The two watchers waited as an exact duplicate of Mavra Chang materialized where Ben Yulin had been. The new, tiny figure looked at Trelig's pistol a little anxiously, then saw that it was held casually, sighed, and stepped off the platform, which seemed much higher than it had getting on.

"Incredible!" Trelig breathed. "You even move like her—feminine, catlike, almost."

Yulin nodded. "Now let's go see about those guards," he suggested in Mavra's rich, exotic and slightly accented voice.

The guards had died in a brief moment of extreme agony, that much was clear from the expressions on their faces.

"Remember not to touch them or that packet!" Yulin cautioned. Trelig nodded as he gingerly reached out, took a pistol by the barrel from the holster of one, examined it, wiped it off on the clothing of another, and handed it to Yulin, who just nodded. Next they found the portacom, with its working linkage to Topside. It was on *Standby* and there was nothing but a hiss coming through it.

Yulin looked at Trelig. "Ready?" he asked.

113

The councillor, who now looked like one of his guards, nodded and picked it up, switched it to *Receive*.

There was still nothing for a minute or two, then a small voice came at them.

"Underside! Come in! What's happening ·down there?" came a tinny, nasal voice that belonged to one of the guards. Trelig sighed, and said softly to Yulin, "Well, may as well find out now if the bluff works." Punching the *Send* button, he said: "This is Renard. I was bringing the prisoners Mavra Chang and Nikki Zinder down for Trelig when all this chaos broke out. They got them—all of them, but the cost was heavy. Me and my prisoners are the only ones left down here, and the old scientist also got it. They lied about the sponge."

There was silence for quite some time, and for a moment Trelig thought they hadn't bought the story, but then the Topside voice came back with a tired and defeated tone. "All right, then. But if Chang and the girl are down *there,* who took off in that ship? Marta said—"

Trelig thought fast. "There were some New Harmony crew on that thing, remember. I guess they panicked and ran out on the boss."

There was no other logical explanation, so they accepted it.

"Okay," came the reply. "Come on up and bring your prisoners with you. We have to get together and think this out." That wasn't said with any enthusiasm; without sponge, they knew what was about to happen.

"Acknowlcdge and out," Trelig said, and switched to *Standby.* "I guess this calls for some cheering," he said to his partner.

Yulin still looked concerned. "This is only the start of it," he reminded the other. "We still have to get up there and somehow take over that ship." He had a sudden thought. "Is there enough food and water on that ship for a long stay?"

Trelig nodded. "Oh, yes. We'll probably kill some time taking a close look at that weird planet out there. When the spongies are gone, we can make a deal by radio with the surviving representatives."

And then what? Yulin wondered, considering their luck so far.

"Let's make sure Obie's safe from prying while we're away," Trelig suggested, and they returned to the internal control room.

Yulin punched the codes. "Obie?"

"Yes, Ben?"

"First off, as soon as we are in the car to Topside you will file all transactions under my personal key. Understand?"

"Yes, Ben."

Trelig thought a moment. "Then how will *we* get back in? He'll only recognize us as Renard and Mavra Chang. And if Chang's survived, that will open Obie to her if she manages to get back here. We don't know if they might not have some sort of spacecraft on that world out there."

Yulin thought a minute, realizing that Trelig had seen a nasty trap. The odds were against Chang surviving—he didn't worry about Nikki Zinder or Renard the sponge would kill them anyway—but they had come so far now on long shots that the breaks would have to go the other way once in a while.

"How about a code word or sequence?" he suggested to the syndicate boss. "Then one of us would have to be here, no matter what form."

Trelig nodded. He didn't bother to ask why not both of them; he would not like to have to need Yulin in a pinch, and they weren't out of the woods yet. "But what code?" he asked.

Yulin smiled. "I think I know one. But what about Zinder? We don't want anyone else to know."

Trelig nodded, then set the pistol again for short stun. He looked at the duplicate of Nikki Zinder, who responded, pleadingly, "Not *again!*" Trelig fired, and the girl who was something else collapsed in a heap.

"The same five minutes," Antor Trelig cautioned. "Get moving!"

Yulin nodded, then turned back to the board. Both he and Gil Zinder had been fairly tall men, and the control boards were set for that. Now he was a much smaller individual, and had to almost lean over on

115

the control board from the chair to reach some of the controls.

"Obie?"

"Yes, Ben?"

"This is on open-file storage, *not* keyed," he told the computer. "At the same time as you file the previous transactions, you will energize into the *Defend* mode. All systems will be locked and frozen, and you will kill anyone attempting to gain entry to this area from the point of the center of the bridge. Can you hear audibles from the center of the bridge?"

Obie considered a second. "Yes, Ben. You might have to yell."

Yulin accepted this. "All right, then, you will remain in *Defend* until someone comes to the center of the bridge with his arms raised high over his head, palms out. I will shoot a small mark on the bridge as we leave. At that mark, this individual must say, 'There is no god but Allah, and Mohammed is his prophet.' Got that?"

Trelig chuckled. "Old habits are hard to break, eh?" But it pleased him—easy to remember, but nobody was *ever* likely to say *that* one and include the appropriate gestures, unless they knew.

"I understand, Ben."

He switched off, and they waited for Zinder to come around. It took about six minutes, these things varying with the individual. Zinder was tingling, as though his whole body were asleep, but the effect wore off quickly enough.

"Let's go," Yulin said, and they walked out across the bridge. About halfway, Yulin set his pistol to *Full* and shot at the restraining wall over the pit. It was a hard, tough material, but the shot gouged a nasty scar that was visible, yet would be mistaken by others as perhaps a remainder of the gun battle.

They walked on, got into the car, and settled back. Trelig pressed the stud, the door closed, and the car started Topside.

Inside Obie, as this happened, circuits opened and closed, energy danced, and Obie went into the defense mode, but he could not remember how to break it. That disturbed him. The last thing he remembered

116

was Yulin at the control panel and the guards dying of the poisoned sponge.

It was an impossible mystery. He returned quickly to his primary job of trying to disengage himself from the great Well World computer, or, failing that, to create some sort of partnership with it.

It would be long, tough work.

Teliagin, Southern Hemisphere, the Well World

MAVRA CHANG HAD BEEN DOZING IN SPITE OF HER-self. When tension wears off, it produces a kind of worn-out lethargy that is almost impossible to shake. Suddenly, however, she came awake with a start and looked around, bleary-eyed. She understood what had happened and cursed herself for it, but she was mostly concerned now with what had brought her to consciousness.

Nikki and Renard were still asleep, sprawled out on the grass, and appeared to be the better for it. Nervously, she looked around, eyes, ears, nose straining for the disturbance.

There was a warm breeze blowing fleecy white clouds across a blue sky, and she could hear the rustle of treetops in the wind and the chatter of strange birds and insects. Out across the meadow, came the distant sounds of animals in great agitation. She knew the signs; something was coming, something that the ordinary dwellers of the forest considered a danger or an intruder or both. She turned to the sleeping pair, shook Renard gently. At first he didn't stir, then, as she shook him harder, he moaned and said, "Huh? What?"

"Wake up!" she hissed. "Company coming!"

They both woke Nikki, an even harder task than with Renard, and Mavra thought about what to do.

"We have to get away from here," she told them. *"Now!* I'd like to see who or what we're facing before they find us."

They stood up and followed her back into the woods a ways.

"If anybody knows what the module out there is, they'll be looking for us," she told them. "Still, I want to see what we're up against. Stay here and stay hidden in the undergrowth. I'm going to sneak back for a quick look."

"Be careful," Renard cautioned, needlessly but with real concern in his voice.

She nodded, appreciating the concern, and crept back to the clearing. Whoever or whatever was approaching was big—she could tell that. It was almost as if the ground was trembling slightly, and the clatter among the wildlife was intense.

Cautiously she peered out from behind a bush and gave a short gasp of surprise. She had expected almost anything but what she saw coming toward her.

It *was* huge—between three and four meters tall, with incredible shoulders and bulging muscles. Its chest and arms were vaguely reddish in color, and humanoid—that is, a human muscleman. The face was huge and ugly: almost an oval, with a broad, flat nose with flaring nostrils, and a mouth permanently set in anger, two long, sharp fangs protruding out of the corners. The ears were large and looked vaguely like great seashells, although they came to a point at the top. A mane of dark blue-black hair sat atop the head, coming to a point between two nasty-looking, sharp horns nearly a meter long.

But it was the eye that commanded attention. It looked like one huge humanlike eye right above the nose and dead center below the forehead. A closer look showed it to be segmented in some way, as if the eye were actually a collection of eyes with one great lid.

From the waist down the creature was covered in thick, wooly rust-red hair, the great muscled legs ending in elephantine hoofs. It wore a single garment, a dirty white wool brief around the crotch that did little to disguise the male sex organ that was proportionate to the figure's great size. It seemed to growl and grumble as it approached steadily, fearing nothing and looking as fierce as any wild thing Mavra had ever seen.

It stopped, seemed to sniff the air, looking first one way and then the other. She worried that it might catch her scent, and found herself almost unconsciously pressing back, crouched and wound up like a coiled spring, although she wondered if anyone could outrun such a monster.

And then she saw the strange thing. The creature had a band made of some sort of skin wrapped around its left arm; attached to it had to be what it appeared—a massive wind-up type wrist watch.

For the first time Mavra realized she was seeing one of the dominant races of this strange place.

The wind shifted slightly, and the creature seemed to lose the scent it had been trying to localize. It turned its attention back to the passenger module. For a moment it just stood there, looking the thing over as if wondering what to do, then it approached, not cautiously but with great confidence. Clearly this thing had nothing to fear in its own land.

The creature was almost as tall as the module, and it looked the alien thing over critically, as if puzzled by it. Then it seemed to spy the open hatch and tried to pull itself up to it. This proved a failure, and after several tries the thing gave a massive roar of rage and hit its right fist into its left palm in a very human gesture of frustration.

Just then a second cyclops came into view and roared to the first one. The sounds seemed brutish and animalistic to Mavra, but she knew it must be some form of speech. Animals don't use or need wrist watches.

The newcomer approached, and off in the distance Mavra thought she heard the roars of several more. They had obviously not landed in a densely-populated area—luckily!—but investigators were now steadily arriving, along with the curious, on the scene.

The second one came up to the first and started spewing a whole series of snarls and grunts, with appropriate gestures. The first, slightly taller and

119

broader, responded in kind, pointing to the module, the open hatch, and making all sorts of circles with his hands.

After a while a third one appeared, and a fourth, and a fifth. Two of the newcomers were females, Mavra noted. They were almost a meter shorter than the males, making them only three meters tall, and, unlike the males, they didn't seem as muscular—perhaps capable of uprooting medium-sized trees, but not of tearing sheet metal like paper. They also seemed a bit bowlegged, squatter, and had small, rock-firm breasts. They had no horns, either, but they shared the male's permanently nasty expressions and seemed to have fangs that were a bit longer than their brothers'. There may have been a half-octave difference in their speech, but considering the grunts, groans, growls, and yowls these things made, nobody but they would ever know.

One of the females was also wearing a watch, and two of the newcomers, a male and a female, seemed to be wearing some jewelry—made of bones, Mavra noted—dangling from their ears and around their necks. Perhaps insignia of rank or tribe, she guessed.

The first male roared so loudly it panicked birds for a quarter-kilometer around; he gestured to the others. They first tried to boost him up on top of the module, but the surface was too slippery for him. Then they took another tack. They went around to the other side and started pushing, the big one counting cadence of sorts. The module rocked, rocked again, and, on the third try, rolled over on its side. One of the females picked up a rock almost the size of Mavra Chang and wedged it under the module while the others held it steady.

The big one then went back around and roared approval. The open hatch was now at about his eye level, and he peered in, curiously. A massive arm reached out, went into the hole, and there was a terrible crunching noise. The hand came out clasping a seat, ripped from its solid connections to the floor, and he looked at it. One of the females pointed a clawed finger at the seatrest, and the others nodded. One of the other males stooped down a little and held his hand just above his knee. Mavra could guess the conversation. They were estimating the size of the creatures who had ridden it in.

That did it, she decided, and slowly slunk back into the woods. No use getting caught by a wind change. Those folks were obviously bright even if primitive, and the assembly of giants was becoming a convention rather quickly. She didn't want any introductions until she knew what those giants would eat.

Nikki spotted her first. "Over here!" she called, and Mavra ran to them.

"Mavra! Thank god!" Renard exclaimed with real feeling, and hugged her. "We heard all that roaring and growling and we didn't know what had happened!"

Quickly she told them about the cyclops. They listened in growing awe and terror.

"We'll have to get away from here pretty quickly," she explained. "They already know we're around."

The other two nodded. "But—which way?" Nikki asked. "We could be going toward one of their cities or something and never know it."

Mavra thought for a moment. "Wait a minute. We know the whole world isn't like this—we even saw some of the nearby places before the visuals went out. There's an ocean and some mountains to the east of here, definitely not these folks' kind of turf. We saw such terrain on the way in, remember?"

"But which way's east?" Renard asked her.

"The planet's rotation was basically west-to-east," Mavra reminded him. "That means the sun rises in the east and sets in the west. I'd say it's getting close to evening now, so that places the sun over there, and east is this way." She pointed, and said, "Let's go."

They had no choice. They followed her into the woods. Behind them, the roaring and bellowing continued.

"We should stick to the woods as long as possible," she told them as they went. "It'll be harder for those big babies to follow or track us."

They agreed with that and proceeded on for some time, saying little to one another because there seemed to be nothing to say. Nikki, because of her bulk, had the toughest problem, but she was bearing up well, all things considered. She had only one complaint.

"I'm starving," she moaned during every one of their frequent rest periods.

Renard was getting a little hungry himself. The sun was getting low, the shadows deepening into dusk. "Maybe I could stun one of those little animals we keep seeing," he suggested. "A short burst with the pistol, that's all."

Mavra thought it over. "All right. Try it. But—make sure you see something and make sure you're on stun. We don't want to set any forest fires here."

Almost as if cued by the conversation, one of the critters they'd been talking about rustled around in the underbrush. It was large—almost a meter long—but low, with a thin snout, some bushy whiskers, and beady little rodent's eyes.

Renard calculated from the noise where it would come out into a clear spot and set and aimed his pistol. The thing seemed oblivious to the risk, and finally appeared where it was supposed to. Renard pressed the trigger stud.

Nothing happened.

The little creature turned to them, chattered what might have been an insult, and scurried off into the darkness.

"What the hell?" Renard exclaimed, befuddled. He looked at the pistol, tapped it, looked at the charge meter. "No charge!" he said, amazed. "It should be three-quarters full!" He started to throw the pistol away, but Mavra reached out and took his arm, stopping him.

"Keep it," she told him. "Remember, our ship didn't work here either. Maybe no machines will. The pistol might be useful later, when we get to the sea. Even if it isn't, nobody else will know it's empty. It might prove useful as a bluff."

Renard wasn't so sure, but he wasn't about to question the woman now. He holstered it.

"Looks like we go to bed hungry," he said. "Sorry, Nikki."

The girl sighed, but could say nothing.

"I'll find us some food tomorrow, I promise," Mavra

found herself saying, and she half-believed it. She'd been in hopeless and impossible situations many times, and every time something had happened to straighten things out. She was a survivor. Nothing lethal ever happened to her.

"We'll stay the night right here," she told them. "We can't risk a fire, but I'll take first watch. When I can't take it anymore, I'll wake you, Renard. Then you do the same with Nikki."

The other two both protested, but Mavra was in charge and she was firm. "I won't fall asleep this time," she promised.

They settled down as best they could. Only Mavra was dressed for this sort of thing. Nikki, who had had only the filmy noncovering standard to New Pompeii and some sandals, had discarded the sandals long before, as had Renard. They had also abandoned wearing the covering, is it caught on the branches and bushes. Mavra had buried the sandals rather than leave a trail, but she had made them carry their clothing as some sort of protection against the dampness of the ground.

With the two as settled as possible, Mavra removed her devices from the compartment in her boot and checked each out. Without the power pack they didn't help much, and the power pack, as expected, didn't work. She abandoned the project.

Darkness descended like a blanket, and her eyes went to infrared.

Nikki was sound asleep almost instantly, but she could hear Renard twist and turn, and finally sit up.

"What's the problem?" she whispered. "Too much for one day?"

He came over to her, carefully. She was almost invisible in her dark clothing.

"No, it's not that," he whispered back. "I was just thinking, and feeling a little. It's starting to get to me."

"The situation?"

"The sponge," he responded flatly. "I'm in a great deal of pain right now—it's like a yearning agony that courses through your whole body."

"All the time?" she asked, concerned.

He shook his head. "It comes in waves. This one's

123

pretty bad. I don't know if it's getting to Nikki yet, but if it doesn't it will." He paused for a moment, then let the words come, those words that were unarguable and inevitable.

"We're dying, Mavra," he said flatly.

She accepted the statement, but not its finality. Sponge was an abstract thing to her, and she'd almost forgotten about their problem.

"What's it do, Renard?" she asked him. "And how long does it take to do it?"

He sighed. "Well, brain cells are the first to go. Each time one of these little attacks comes on—and each one gets worse—you lose some of your body cells, and some of your brain cells. It's kind of a slow-down rather than a death. I've seen it in others. You still have all your memory, but you become less and less able to use it. Thought processes, reasoning, all become harder and harder to do. The barely possible today becomes the impossible tomorrow. Like getting dumber and dumber as time goes on. How long the process takes varies with the individual, but, well, the rough rule is that you lose ten percent of your capacity per day, and that can never be reclaimed, even if you get more sponge later—which isn't likely. I was always a pretty smart fellow—I used to teach, you know—but I can already tell that *something* is happening. I'm ten percent dumber than yesterday, but that doesn't really mean much if you start reasonably high. But if you have an IQ of around 150, well, figure out the time."

Mavra did. If Renard had been a 150 capacity yesterday, he was a 135 today. Okay, not really noticeable. But that meant 122 tomorrow, 110 the day after, putting him at about average ability. Then the deterioration really started, though. 110 would become 99, and 99 would be 89. That was slow—what was that, four more days? Then 80 in five, 72 in six—a low-grade moron. 65 in a week, about the mental and motor levels of a three-year-old child. After that—perhaps an automaton, or some sort of animalistic type, since memory would still be there, it was ability that was being attacked.

"Nikki?" she wondered.

"Less time, I'm sure. Maybe a day or two less to the critical point," Renard responded.

Mavra thought for a moment. A week, no more, maybe less. She wondered what it was like, living with the knowledge of an inevitable, creeping death sentence. Did Renard really believe such a thing could happen to him? No one could conceive realistically of their own death, she once read. But as the process continued, and you *knew* it continued, the frustration and fear would mount.

She reached over, gently took his arm. He moved next to her. Suddenly, with her lightning speed, she pricked his arm with some of the hypnotic fluid and injected a full load. He started in surprise, then seemed to go limp.

"Renard, listen to me," she commanded.

"Yes, Mavra," he responded, sounding something like a little child.

"Now, you will trust me completely. You will believe in me and my abilities completely, and do what I say without question," she told him. "You will feel strong and good and well, and you will not feel any pain, longing, ache, or agony from the sponge. Do you understand me?"

"Yes, Mavra," he repeated dully.

"Furthermore, you will not think of the sponge. You will *not* think you are going to die, or fall apart. The thoughts just will not enter your mind. When you wake up each morning, you will not notice yourself as being any different than you have ever been, nor will you notice any difference in Nikki. Do you understand?"

"Yes, Mavra," he agreed.

"Okay, then. Now you will go over to your place and lie down and get a really good, deep, dreamless sleep, and wake up feeling wonderful with no memory of this conversation, but you will do as I have told you. Now—go!"

He broke free from her and went back over to where his clothing was spread out, lay down, and in seconds was sound asleep.

The suggestion wouldn't last, of course. She knew that. She would have to renew it every once in a while, and now she'd have to try the same thing on Nikki, also putting thoughts of her consuming hunger out of her mind.

But it would only make *her* problem easier, not theirs. They would continue to deteriorate, to disintegrate, until she would no longer be able to control them or influence them.

Six days maximum to that point.

Emotion welled up in her. Somewhere, someone on this crazy world knew how to help them, could help them, would help them. She had to believe that. *Had* to.

Six days.

She moved silently over to Nikki Zinder.

South Polar Zone, the Well World

IT LOOKED LIKE ANY MAJOR BUSINESSMAN'S OFFICE. There were maps, charts, and diagrams all over the walls, some strange-looking furniture, and a massive U-shaped desk that concealed large numbers of controls and also contained writing implements, communications devices, and the like. There was even a pistol of a strange sort in the upper left-hand desk drawer.

But the creature who sat behind that great desk, looking at a series of maps spread out before him, was not a human being in any sense of the word, although he definitely was strictly business.

He had a chocolate-brown human torso, incredibly broad and ribbed so that the chest muscles seemed to form squarish plates. A head, oval-shaped, was equally brown and hairless except for a huge white walrus mustache under a broad, flat nose. Six arms, arranged in threes, were spaced evenly in pairs down that torso and attached, except for the top pair, on ball sockets like those of a crab. Below that strange torso it all

126

melted into an enormous brown-and-yellow striped series of scales leading to a huge, coiled serpentine lower half. If outstretched, the snakelike body would easily cover over five meters.

The creature used his lower pair of arms to spread out what proved to be a map of the southern and eastern hemisphere of the Well World. It looked like an odd assembly of perfectly equal hexagrams printed in black, with surprinting in a variety of colors to show topography and water areas. While the lower arms kept the map spread wide, the upper left arm ticked off various hexes with a broad pencil, while the upper right hand jotted down notations on a pad with a different pencil.

The middle left hand punched an intercom to one side.

"Yes, sir?" a female voice asked politely.

"I'll need close-ups of hexes twelve, twenty-six, forty-four, sixty-eight, and two hundred forty-nine," he told the secretary in a deep, rich bass voice. "Also, kindly ask the Czillian ambassador to call on me as soon as possible." He switched off without waiting for acknowledgment.

The creature studied the map again and tried to think. Nine sections total. Nine. Why did that strike a bell?

A buzzer sounded. He flipped a switch on a different intercom to his right. "Serge Ortega," he answered curtly.

"Ortega? Gol Miter, Shamozan," came a thin, reedy voice Ortega knew was coming from a translator device.

"Yes, Gol? What is it?" He glanced quickly at his map. Oh, yes, the three-meter-diameter tarantulas. Memory is the first thing to go, he told himself sourly.

"We have a plot on the new satellite. It's definitely artificial; some of the shots from the North Zone telescopes have been fantastic. We did some spectroanalysis. The atmosphere is a pretty standard Southern Hemisphere mix, heavy on the nitrogen and oxygen, lots of water vapor. The pictures and our stuff match up pretty good. The thing is divided in half, with some sort of physical—not energy—bubble over it about

127

two or three kilometers from the surface. That's why we can't get much surface detail. Too much distortion. Definitely green stuff all over, though. like somebody's garden, and some really vague stuff that could be buildings. As if somebody's got their own little private city-world there."

Serge Ortega thought a moment. "What about the other half?"

"Not much. Raw rock, mostly standard metamorphic stuff. Probably the only part of the original natural object left. Except about halfway between equator and south pole, where there's some kind of huge, shiny disk-shaped object practically built into the thing."

Ortega frowned. "Propulsion unit?"

"I doubt it," replied the giant spider. "This thing doesn't seem to have been built for travel. That bubble is supported by an atmospheric renewal unit for sure. It undulates. Anything other than regular oribital movement would collapse it. There's a point near the edge on one side that has a lot of radiating energy, though, and a funny pattern not consistent with the rest. Could be an airlock, maybe a small spaceport."

Ortega nodded, mostly to himself. "That fits. But how the hell did it *get* here?"

"Well, that disk's aimed at the Equatorial Barrier no matter what position. Either the Well brought it here or they brought themselves instantly to the Well, or so our scientists say."

Ortega didn't like that. Anybody fooling with the Well was fooling with the very nature of everybody's reality. This sort of thing was not supposed to happen, he told himself grumpily. Two of his stomachs were developing ulcers from it all, he could tell.

"It's my guess that they don't know what they've gotten themselves into," the snake-man said. "Kind of clear that they wound up here, saw the Well, decided to check it out, flew too low over a nontech hex, and lost power."

Suddenly he was bolt upright. *Nine sections! Of course!* He cursed himself aloud, and the giant spider came back from the intercom with "What was that? I didn't catch it."

128

"Oh, nothing," he mumbled. "Just kicking myself for being an old man whose mind is shot."

"Kicking yourself would be a good trick," the spider retorted lightly. "Why? What have you got?"

"Back in the dawn of prehistory, when I was still a Type 41 back on my home turf, I used to fly space-ships," Ortega told him. "For a living, that is. They used to have a fail-safe mechanism against complete power failure in atmosphere."

"That's right!" Gol Miter exclaimed. "I forgot you were an Entry. Hell, you're older than I am! You used to be a pirate, didn't you?"

Ortega sniffed. "I was an opportunist, sir! There are only three kinds of people in the universe, no matter what their race or form. They are scoundrels, hypo-crites, and sheep. With a choice like that, I proudly wear the badge of scoundrel."

There was the translated sound of a chuckle. Ortega wondered what a chuckle from a giant spider *really* sounded like.

"Okay," the spider replied, "so you were a pilot and they had fail-safe mechanisms. So?"

"Well, they used to break up on failure," Ortega told the other. "Break into nine sections, so they could accommodate everybody and so the basic mechanical, pressure-activated parachute mechanisms would be able to support the weight. *Nine*, Gol!"

The spider considered this. "Just like our visitor, huh? Well, that would fit. Sure you got them all? Couldn't be any unreported pieces?"

"You know my spy network is the best on the Well World," retorted Ortega with pride. "Want to know who your fourth wife is with right now?"

"All right! All right!" laughed Gol Miter. "So, nine it is. Coincidence?"

"Possibly," Ortega admitted, "but maybe not. If not, they are Type 41s. I've got rough descriptions of three of the sections. Two are rather nondescript compart-ments, hardly worth bothering about. One, however, has a rounded nose-shape, like a bullet. If it *is* a Type 41 ship, that's the command module. That'll be where the pilot is—or was."

"Where did it come down?" the spider asked.

Ortega looked over his map, his deep-black eyes shining. His excitement faded, however, when he saw the probable location.

"Looks like about twenty kilometers inside Teliagin. Fat lot of good *that* does us. If those savages catch them, they'll eat them."

There was concern in the spider's voice. "Can't have that. They don't man their embassy, do they?"

"No," Ortega responded. "They only come in occasionally to trade a few things. It's a nontech hex, so everything's a little limited. Mostly pastoral nomads. Shepherds. They eat the sheep—raw and in big bites, usually while they're still alive."

"Well, I'll check and see if anybody's home," Gol Miter said, "but if there isn't—what then? We *have* to get our hands on at least one of those people, Serge! It's the only way we're going to find out what the hell is going on around here!"

Ortega agreed with him and looked again at his map. Teliagin was near the Equatorial Barrier, and so was his native Ulik, but it was too far away for anybody to get there in time. He looked at the nearby hexes, rejecting one, then another. His eye strayed to one two hexes away, just to the south and east. Lata! That might be just the thing. But—it was still a long ways. The Lata could fly, of course, and Kromm's atmosphere was sufficient, but how long would it take? Two days, maybe? And then how long until they were found? The average Teliagin would be as likely to eat the Lata as help it, so asking for instructions was out.

Well, it was that or nothing.

"Look, Gol, you work on the contact end and keep those studies of the satellite coming in," he told the spider. "I'm going to try and mount some kind of rescue party if I can. I hope we get there before the Teliagin do."

The six-armed snake-man broke the contact and flipped his interoffice intercom again. "Jeddy? Anything from Czill as yet?"

"No, sir," responded the secretary. "The ambassador's not expected in until 1700. Remember, not everybody lives in his office."

The snake-man scowled. Of all the ambassadors here, he was the only one trapped in South Zone. He could never leave it, never go home. It was the price he paid. By all rights he should have died of old age almost two centuries before. He did not, but that was because of a juicy bit of blackmail with the Magren, a hex where "magic" of a sort was possible, where the people would in slight ways tap the power of the Well World computer to defy certain laws. They had given him a youthful body, and it stayed that way, but there was a price. Magic did not hold outside the hex in which it was performed. The rules of the game changed 1560 times on the Well World—the number of hexes and races there were here. In some, the Well computer allowed full technological growth. In some, that technology was limited—say, to steam. In others, like Teliagin, nothing worked. The powers, possibilities—even atmospheric content changed with each hex and was maintained stable by the Well computer that was the entire planetary core.

In South Zone almost everything worked. The youth spell, cast here, held. But should he ever leave, even to see the sun and sky and stars, the spell would be canceled out, and he would instantly be subject to rapid aging.

"Call the Lata ambassador, Jeddy," he ordered.

There was a minute or two while the connection was made, the call referred, and then a high, pleasant, light female voice came on.

"Hoduri here. What can I do for you, Ambassador Ortega?"

"You know the situation?" the Ulik asked, and proceeded to fill in the other on all matters to date, concluding, "You see? You're the only ones with a crack at them. It's dangerous and tough, but we need you desperately."

The Lata thought for a moment. "I'll see what I can do and call you back. Give me an hour or so."

"All right," Ortega told her, "but time is of the essence here. And if you can find one of your citizens named Vistaru and include her in your plans, it'll be better. She's an Entry from the spacial sector we believe these people come from, and could probably translate. We've worked together before. Tell her it's me asking and tell her the whole situation."

"Yes, if we can find her," Ambassador Hoduri agreed. "Anything more?"

Ortega shook his head, although he knew the other couldn't see it. "No, only hurry. Lives depend on it—maybe ours, too, if we don't find out what's going on here."

He switched off, and was barely back to his maps when the interzone intercom buzzed again. It was the Czillian ambassador, in early.

"Hello? Vardia? Serge Ortega!" he boomed.

"Ortega!" the other responded, not exactly sounding as thrilled by Ortega's voice as Ortega seemed with its. And it was an "it," too—the Czillians were mobile unisexual plants.

"You know what's going on?" Ortega asked.

"I've just been conferring on it," the plant creature replied. "Why? Going to play games with somebody else?"

He shrugged off the minor nastiness. The plants duplicated, so it could be one of several Vardias, but they all had their basic memories. One time, long ago, he'd done the original Vardia rather dirty, and Czillians don't forget.

"Bygones be bygones," he retorted. "This is bigger than petty plots. We'll need the Czillian Crisis Center activated immediately at the Center. Your computers are the best on the Well World, and we'll need somebody to coordinate. A lot of different hexes are involved here." He explained the situation as it stood to the Czillian.

"And what are you doing about it now?" Vardia asked him.

"I've sent Lata in to try and rescue the pilot if he's still alive, and anybody else they can. If—and it's a big if—we can get one of them here alive we'll know what's going on. But that's not your worry right now. Follow through on the logic here and maybe you'll understand."

"I'm listening," Vardia replied, still doubtful.

"I've located all nine modules. They're all in the west, and dispersed in a southwesterly pattern, so I

132

have an idea of what's what. If *I* can do it, so can others. Probably have. Vardia, one of them is the engine module, intact! I'll bet on that! There's no way to build that in any hex on the Well World. The rest, though—that can be fabricated one place and another. Whoever reclaims the parts of that ship, particularly the engine module, might possibly make a spaceship that'll fly. Launch it straight up, the right angle and pattern, and it'll be free of the Well. If *I* thought of that angle, so have others. I'm talking about *war*, Vardia! War! There are enough old pilots around here that somebody might be able to fly it!"

Vardia still sounded doubtful, but now it was more in the nature of an unwillingness to think what Ortega was saying could be true. But—could they afford to take the chance?

"War is impossible," the Czillian responded. "Triff Dhala demonstrated that by losing the Great War over eleven hundred years ago!"

"But that was for conquest," Ortega pointed out. "This would be for limited objectives. I'll bet five dozen rulers are reading Dhala's *Theory of Well Warfare* cover to cover right now. A spaceship, Vardia! Think about it!"

"I don't want to," responded the Czillian. "But—I'll relay all this to the Center. If the scholars and the computers agree with you, it will be done."

"That's all I ask," the Ulik told the other, and switched off. He stared down at the map again, his eyes fixed on Lata and Teliagin. How had they come in? To the southwest. Okay, that meant they flew over the Sea of Storms, then got wiped out over Kromm. Then there was breakup because of Kromm's limited tech restrictions, and they came down in Teliagin. They would have seen the seas and the mountains before they were depowered. If the pilot knew what he was doing, he'd know that the mountains and sea would be east of him. He'd make for it as soon as he caught sight of those Teliagin monstrosities.

If they made Kromm, and didn't mind getting wet, they'd be okay. He had to bet on that pilot's experience.

"Get me the Lata ambassador again, will you,

Jeddy?" he asked. "I know he's out, but I'll talk to an assistant."

His eyes went back to that map.

The Lata *had* to be in time. They just *had* to.

The Lift Car Nearing Topside, New Pompeii

"YOU'RE TOO TENSE," ANTOR TRELIG TOLD BEN Yulin. "Relax. *Become* Mavra Chang. Act like her, react like her, *think* like her. Let her persona completely control you. I want no slip-ups here."

Yulin nodded and tried to relax. He tapped his fingernail on the chair side—long, sharp, hard nails, like steel. He looked suddenly down. He felt something funny, odd, just then. He stared down at the chair arm and saw that there was a tiny pool of liquid there. He dabbed a finger in it, put it up to his nose, and sniffed it. Odorless. He touched a little bit to his tongue. There was a mild numbing sensation there. *Now what the hell?* he wondered.

Suddenly he was looking at all ten fingers in curiosity. Some kind of cartilage, just a little fatter than human hair. A tube that was rigid and controlled by a tiny muscle. Poison? he wondered.

He resolved to try it when he got the opportunity.

A warning light went on and the car started to slow.

"Okay, here we go," Trelig said lightly, and they braced for a stop. Gil Zinder could do nothing, his personality forced into the back of his mind. He was Nikki Zinder until one of the two in the car led him out; *they* were the guard Renard and Mavra Chang, and he had to act like it, really believe it. Obie had taken the easiest path—he literally had made the old man his own daughter and isolated the new personality from reality.

The door opened and they walked out, out into the

warm, fresh air and bright sunlight. Everything was slightly different now—there were shadows, the sun was at a different distance and of a slightly different color, which changed everything, and there was that planet up there, filling a tenth of the sky.

They all gasped. Nothing had prepared them for the sight of the thing, like a glistening, silvery, multifaceted ball twinkling in the sun; below a swirl of clouds it was blue to the south, while the north seemed awash with reds and yellows. The plasma shield's distortions made it look ghostly.

"Oh, wow!" breathed Gil.

Trelig, ever practical, was the first to break the spell. "Come on!" he said. "Let's see who's running this place."

Several guards ran out to greet them, and a serving girl or two.

"Renard! Thank god!" said one, and Trelig noted that he didn't know what relationships these people had. He *did,* however, know their names and backgrounds, and that helped.

"Destuin!" he responded, and hugged the little man. No, that's right, Destuin was a woman, he thought angrily to himself.

He looked at them gravely. "Thanks for *what?*" he asked sourly. "Another five days?"

That seemed to take their minds off any further comparisons.

"Where are the rest of the guests?" Ben asked.

"Around," one of the guards said. "We haven't bothered them much, and they've stayed away from us. It doesn't matter much. You're in the same fix we are." The guard pointed toward the Well World. "See that little black dot there against the planet? There, just below the split in the big one, and a little to the right."

Ben looked hard, and finally saw it—a tiny black pinhead, like a hole in the bigger world. It was moving.

"That's a sentinel," the guard told her. "It'll blow the hell out of any ship that tries to take off. Only Trelig knew the stop codes, and he's gone. So you get to see *us* die, but four, maybe five weeks from now you'll run out of food, and go, too. Or make a run for it in the remaining ship and get blown up. Maybe that's what we *all* should do. Better than the other ways."

That was grim talk, and not the kind the newcomers wanted to hear.

"I'm an expert with these ships," Ben told them. "Let me go down and see if there isn't something I can do about it. What can it hurt?"

The guard shrugged. "Why not? Want somebody to go along?"

"Renard? How about you?" Ben prompted.

Trelig, however, was better than that. Too much danger right now. "You go ahead. Take the girl with you. It won't make much difference to *us* anyway. I'll come down later and see how you're doing."

Yulin was disappointed; it had seemed so easy. But, there was little that could be done. "Come on, Nikki," he said, and started walking. The fat girl followed meekly, but kept glancing back up at the glowing, strangely surrealistic planet half-visible on the horizon.

That planet was on Yulin's mind, too. He knew that they'd never have seen it at all if the big dish had been directly opposite New Pompeii, but it was angled, so two thirds of the big planet was visible.

There were few people about, and they made it to the spaceport area in about fifteen minutes. The little spaceport terminal seemed deserted. Yulin really relaxed for the first time. This was almost too easy. He entered the terminal and stopped.

A big man with a Viking-like visage was perched there. He was sitting on a counter, and he seemed to be quite drunk.

Yulin thought him an attractive man, and the fact that it didn't bother him to have that thought showed the thoroughness of Obie's conditioning. He tried to remember the man's name.

"Aha! So you're trapped like the rest of us!" he roared, and took another long swig from a bottle. "I thought you'd gotten away!"

He stood there, wondering what to do. The man was huge compared to him, and even though he was

Mavra Chang physically. Ben Yulin hadn't been a fighter and those skills were sorely needed now.

Rumney was naked. He jumped up, facing her. "All is lost!" he proclaimed. "You can't leave, I can't leave, ain't nobody can leave!" he almost sang. "So there's nothin' to do but get drunk and have a last fling. Why not, honey? Com'on! I'll take you both on at the same time!" A casual observation of his midsection left no doubt as to his meaning. He pushed out the bottle. "Have a snort?"

Fear replaced any feelings of attraction for this man. Yulin edged back toward the door, but the man was quick, too quick. He was playing with her, and laughing like a maniac.

Yulin moved, and Rumney moved, chuckling all the time. The tiny female frantically looked for some avenue of escape, but the terminal was too small. Zinder gaped at the tableau in confused amazement. This was a Nikki Zinder sex fantasy, and she couldn't shake that dreamlike quality. Deep inside her mind, Gil Zinder sat, resigned, not caring about anything any more.

"Look—whatever your name is," Ben tried. "All isn't lost! I think I can get us out of here if you'll let me!"

Rumney thought about this a half-second, then grinned. "Nice try," he approved. "Afterward, tinker away."

Yulin cursed the fact that he'd had to get rid of the incongruous pistol and wished for Trelig or a guard, anybody, to get him out of this.

"All I want is a piece of tail," Rumney chided. "I got a tail, you got—" Suddenly he stopped, and tried to focus his eyes.

"You ain't got no tail!" he accused.

Now Yulin felt even more terrified. It was true! Damn Obie! He'd asked for the last pattern of Mavra Chang, not the alterations!

Yulin edged toward the gateway to the remaining ship slowly. "Take it easy, big man," he breathed cautiously, soothingly. "You spotted something, okay. Now you know that maybe I *can* get you out. Let me try."

137

Yulin started deliberately for the ramp, and Rumney leaped for him, knocking him down on the floor, holding him there. The bottle went flying against a far wall, missing Zinder by centimeters.

He had Yulin pinned, and started tearing away at the nearly transparent clothing he wore. "Let's see if you're a woman under that," he growled.

Yulin was terrified, more than he had ever been in his life. As Rumney pawed, Yulin managed to get his right arm partly free and jab him with his sharp nails. He felt something extra there; those little muscles in the back of his nails twitched. Rumney gave a sharp cry of pain, then he seemed to stiffen and collapsed on top of him. Rumney was like a lead sack. Yulin couldn't move, couldn't breathe.

"Nikki!" he gasped. "Help me get him off me!" But Zinder wasn't about to obey.

He pushed and cursed and heaved, trying to wiggle loose. "I wish you'd roll over, damn it!" he swore— and, to his amazement, Rumney did.

Feeling terribly bruised and slightly crushed, he managed to get up slowly. It felt as if a rib was broken and his body was a mass of internal bruises. There were pains in his back and side and—well everywhere. Coughing and spitting a little blood, Yulin gasped for several minutes, trying to get some control back. Doing so felt awful, but it did the job.

Ben Yulin decided then and there that he very much preferred being 180 centimeters tall and male.

But, trapped for now in Mavra's body, Ben got hold of himself.

"You on the floor! What's your name?" he shot, trying a theory.

"Rumney. Bull Rumney," he murmured.

Ben Yulin marveled at Mavra Chang's resourcefulness. Obviously these triggers had been surgically implanted by somebody really talented. This was one dangerous lady, he decided, not without some admiration. In a way, he hoped she was still alive.

"Well, Bull Rumney, listen good," Yulin said sharply. "You are to lie there, unmoving, a statue, until I tell you to do something. Understand?"

The big man nodded slowly, then froze.

"Fetal position, Rumney," he said, enjoying himself for a minute. Rumney obliged, and froze again.

"Come on, Zinder, let's see to this ship," he snapped, sounding more like Mavra Chang than he knew. They went into the ship.

This wasn't Trelig's yacht; Chang had taken that. They were left with the shuttle, which was basically well stocked. There were enough emergency rations for maybe three weeks, no more. Yulin cursed under his breath. Enough to take care of the spongies, but not the others. Oh, well, Trelig said he wanted to deal with them, and he was sure *they* didn't know how little food there was. Obie, of course, could create more when things settled down. Create the food, and also use the people on New Pompeii to replace the expired guards. Slavery without sponge—that would appeal to Trelig.

He checked everything out. He wasn't the best pilot in the world, but he was an adequate one, and the ship was rather simple. Barring a major emergency, he could run it without much trouble. It had been charging all the time it was in dock, so there was no problem there. Atmosphere good, pressurization potential normal. He nodded as he checked each one. He looked for a weapon, but found none—naturally. Trelig had taken no chances.

Sighing, he closed the port and sat down to wait. There was no way he was going back to the buildings of New Pompeii.

Trelig was several hours in coming, and Ben Yulin had started to worry again. There were several false alarms—guards stopping by to check, a few of the bigwigs, too. Since he'd placed the bottle next to Rumney, nobody questioned him being there. Nobody even blamed him.

Finally, hearing some noise outside, Yulin opened the hatch and spied three guards coming in. One, he was sure, was Trelig. Those sexual screw-ups all looked alike. All three looked grim, and one, not Trelig, entered the ship first, followed by the other two. Ben caught Trelig's eyes and a subtle nod. The nerves were back.

"We've decided to let anybody who wants to make a break for it," the lead guard told the woman in the pilot's chair. "If you get blasted, well, then it's quick. If you don't—more power to you."

"And you?" Yulin asked.

That grim expression hardened. "I will die—quickly, not slowly. We have already held a meeting to decide that. We've just finished killing the poor devils who were much worse than we. None of us wants to become like that. We'll go help the people who want to run for it to get everything together, and then—well, that's it."

Yulin, facing them, saw Trelig slowly draw his pistol and point it at the two guards. He uttered a silent prayer to ancestral gods never believed in, and nodded to the other two.

"I understand. We'll try and do our best. I guess this is good-bye."

The guard started to say something, but at that moment Trelig fired, two short bursts at very close range and at full power. Yulin and Zinder ducked in reflex, but the former councillor's aim had been perfect. The two guards seemed bathed in a bright-orange glow, then faded out. There was nothing left of them but some burns in the ship's carpet and an extremely unpleasant odor.

"Close the hatch! Let's get out of here!" Trelig shouted, and Yulin needed no more urging. There was a shudder and a whine, and the clunking sound of docking equipment being jettisoned, and then, almost before the other two were seated and strapped in, Yulin took off.

"Hold it, you idiot!" Trelig snapped. "You don't want to kill us! We're away! They can't get to us now!"

Yulin seemed to stare at the man and at the controls for a moment, as if in a daze. Then, with a little quiver, he snapped out of his trance.

The robot sentinels shot their challenges, and Trelig gave the codes needed to get past them.

"Where to?" Ben Yulin asked Antor Trelig.

"Might as well take a look at this incredible planet," the boss replied. "I'm kind of curious about it myself."

Yulin brought the ship around, and eased slowly back toward the strange-looking orb.

Trelig turned to the figure of Nikki. "Gil Zinder!" he called. "Come to the fore and join us!"

There was a slight, subtle change in the manner of the fat girl, and she slipped off the straps and came up to the screen.

Gil Zinder was fascinated in spite of himself. "Incredible!" he said in his daughter's voice.

"But why are there two completely different halves?" Trelig wondered. "Look—you got all those jewel faces on the south, but you can tell it's lots of green and ocean and stuff like that. Our kind of world. Then you got that great dark-amber strip around the equator, and then a whole different kind of world up top."

"The poles are interesting, too," Gil Zinder noted. "See how dark and thick they are, and how huge. Almost like great buildings hundreds, maybe thousands, of kilometers across."

"Let me swing down around one of those poles," Yulin suggested. "Look at the center of them."

They looked, and saw what he meant. In the center was a great, yawning hexagonal shape composed of absolute darkness. "What is it?" Trelig wondered aloud.

Gil Zinder thought a moment. "I don't know. Perhaps something like our big dish, only much more sophisticated."

"But why hexagons?" Trelig persisted. "Hell, they're *all* hexagons, even the little facets both north and south."

"The Markovians were in love with the hexagon," Yulin told him. "Their ruins are full of them; their cities are built in that shape. I saw one as a child."

"Let's take a look at the north," Trelig suggested. "It's so wildly different. There must be a reason for it."

Yulin applied power, and the image swirled and whirled on the screen. "Kind of tricky," the pilot told them. "Ships like this weren't built to go this slow except in landing and docking modes."

They crossed the equator, a true barrier they saw—strange, imposing, and opaque.

"I wish we had some instruments," Zinder said, genuinely interested in something again. "I would love to know what makes those strange patterns. Methane, ammonia, all sorts of stuff, looks like."

They crossed the terminator and went into darkness.

"Somebody's living there, though," Trelig noted, pointing. Some of the areas in some of the hexes were lit, and there were a few clear major cities down there.

"A pity we can't get a little closer," Zinder said sincerely. "The atmospheric distortion is really intense."

"Maybe a little lower," Yulin answered. "I'll try to skim just over the top of the stratosphere. That'll keep us high enough to be effectively in a vacuum, but low enough to see some detail."

Hearing no dissent, he cautiously took the ship down. They crossed the terminator once again and went into blinding sunlight.

And then the engine seemed to give a start, and the lights flashed.

"What's the matter?" Trelig snapped.

Yulin was genuinely puzzled. "I—I don't know." It happened again, and he took over manual helm and started to fight it. "Sudden losses of power, very intermittent."

"Take us up!" Trelig commanded, but, at that moment, the lights really went out.

"We're dropping like a stone!" screamed Yulin. "My God!"

Trelig reached over, threw two switches. Nothing happened. He threw a third. Still nothing. They were in almost total darkness in the cabin, and even these actions were made more by feel.

And then everything came on again. There was a whining noise from the rear and in front.

Ahead, a panel rolled back, revealing a nasty landscape only ten or so kilometers beneath them. Trelig reached out, grabbed a wheel-shaped device depressed into the copilot's panel.

Lights and power went out again, but now it was a rocky trip, the ship banged and buffeted by strange forces. Trelig grabbed the wheel and started fighting for control of the ship.

The view, Yulin realized, was a real one—they were looking out some sort of forward window.

"This thing was designed for in-atmosphere work as well as shuttle," Trelig said between clenched teeth, fighting for control with the weakened muscles of Renard. "The wings finally deployed. Even if power cuts out again, I think I can dead-stick it in."

Yulin watched the landscape approach with horrifying suddenness. Trelig fought to keep the nose up, yet he had to be cautious or he would miss seeing the ground at all.

The power was out again now, and Trelig had managed to slow the craft, but not enough.

"Find me a level spot with about twenty kilometers to roll in!" he yelled.

"This thing's got wheels?" Yulin managed, peering out.

"Don't be funny!" snapped the boss. "Both of you get strapped in! I don't think we'll get power again long enough to get her up, and this will be a real wallop!"

"There! A flat area ahead! See it?" Yulin screamed.

Trelig saw, and aimed for it, the ship rocking this way and that. They hit. What saved them, they decided later, was the much denser atmosphere, which slowed the craft enough. Just enough.

They hit with a tremendous bang, and Yulin cried out in pain as the cracked rib and other bruises were suddenly fully activated once again.

They skidded over barren rock, seemingly forever, and they had to ride it out. Finally, they struck an upward incline that almost turned them over, but managed to spin them around and finally halt them instead.

Trelig groaned, undid his straps, and looked around. Yulin was out cold. For the first time he noticed the torn clothing and bruises and gashes. He wondered where Mavra Chang had come by them.

Zinder fared little better. The bouncing and straps had caused some deep depressions and gashes and cut off the circulation in a few places, but he now seemed to be all right, just dizzy from shock.

Trelig tried to get up and discovered that he, too, was dizzy. He fell down twice, and his head pounded. His arms ached horribly from the effort of the landing. But he'd made it. He'd brought them in.

He looked out at the bleak landscape. A lot of barren, blackish rock against a dark and dense atmosphere of—who knew? Nothing they could breathe, anyway.

They were alive—but for how long?

South Zone

"Another ONE DOWN?" ORTEGA WAS AGHAST.

"We detected the energy burst in our routine monitoring of the satellite," Gol Miter's artificial voice told him through the interzone embassy communications system. "At first we had some trouble locating them, but we managed a plot thanks to their taking their time. Careful orbit, nice survey techniques. What I wouldn't give to see this planet from space!"

Ortega joined in that sentiment. "But they went down anyway? I didn't get any reports."

"Finally clipped it a little low, got within the Well's influence, and got nonteched, same as the first one. The reason you haven't heard is that they had swung up North for a look. Near as we can tell, they went down in 1146 or 1318, Uchjin or Ashinshyh. Got anything on them?"

Ortega's multiple arms whipped through maps, charts, and diagrams while he kept up a steady stream of frustration-induced curses. If things were going to get this complicated, he preferred to be the one doing the complicating.

Northern maps were only so-so. They marked

oceans, for example, but the oceans could be methane or any one of a dozen other more lethal compounds. Nothing up there bore the slightest kinship to him, not even as close a kinship as he, a six-armed snake-man, bore to Gol Miter, a giant spider. Some Northern races were so alien that there was no common frame of reference possible with what he and the others of the South considered normal existence.

One thing for sure, he saw, looking at the map. Uchjin and Ashinshyh were both nontech or semitech hexes and could not support a sophisticated power system like that of a ship.

He sighed. "Gol, even if they survived the crash, which I doubt, they're only as good as their air. I don't know what the hell these symbols for Uchjin mean in terms of atmosphere, but there's sure no oxygen in it. The Ashinshyh are a little better—there's some oxygen and even water there—but there's so much hydrogen around they may have blown half the hex to hell."

Miter agreed. "Since we've had no reports of disaster, and no sign of Well activation, I'd say Uchjin, then. How about your Northern contacts? Anything we can use?"

"I doubt it," Ortega replied sourly. "Nobody I know near there. I haven't even the slightest idea what the Uchjin look like. They may have an ambassador on station, though, or somebody close might. Worth a try. I hate to see the Northerners brought into this, though. I don't trust what I can't understand, and some of those boys are nasty customers with alien motives."

"No choice," Miter responded pragmatically. "I'll send somebody up to North Zone and see what can be done. That crash has *already* involved them—and our observatory people have first loyalty to the North, anyway. They tracked it, so everybody already knows." He paused. "Cheer up, Serge. Even if the thing's intact, few Northerners could fly it anyway. It's us or nobody."

"Not *us*," Ortega corrected him. "Somebody."

Technicians had been in and out for half the day

setting up special equipment. He punched the direct line to Ambassador Vardia.

"Czill," came a voice.

"Ortega here. We've got another one down in the North. Get on it. Any word on the Teliagin business yet?"

"Hmmm . . . the North," mused the plant-creature. "No, nothing from the Teliagin sector yet. The Lata party went in pretty quickly, though. Be patient, Serge. It's only been two days."

"Patience is a virtue best left to the dead, who can afford it," growled Ortega, and switched off.

Teliagin

EVEN WALKING, TWENTY KILOMETERS ISN'T REALLY that far—if you know where you're going. But sunrise on the second day had brought heavy clouds totally obscuring the sun. All through the night there had been the far-off toll of drums, messages relayed from one point to another thoughout the hex in an unknown and unguessable code.

Mavra Chang suspected that the messages involved speculations about the strange beings, rather small, who had crashed in some sort of flying machine and were now on the loose somewhere in the land.

At least it didn't rain; they were thankful for that. It continued dark and ominous all day, though; the cover was much too thick to see the sun and guess direction. In ordinary circumstances, Chang would have waited for clearer skies despite the dangers, but she knew that the deadly disease was eating away at her two companions, and if she didn't make those mountains and that coast quickly, there would be no hope.

Every once in a while doubt would creep into the

back of her mind, doubt born of the logical probability that the new lands would be no more friendly than this one. The denizens—for all she knew, more cyclopses—would be no friendlier, no more advanced, no more able to help.

And, worse, although she was certain that they weren't backtracking, she really didn't know in which direction they were going. She had started off in the same direction, of course, but the woods were thick; there were some broad dirt roads and wide meadows to avoid, and who knew whether they had picked up in the same way after they had been forced to divert?

About the only good news had been the apples. At least, they looked a lot like apples, although they grew on bushes and had a funny, purple skin. Almost in desperation, she had gambled on some food source—and the lower-level wildlife looked warm-blooded and somewhat familiar. If alien bacteria hadn't already gotten to them, then it was probably not going to—or so she prayed.

The big rodents ate the fruit with abandon, and she decided to risk doing likewise. Nikki, despite having her appetite drug-depressed, was still the hungriest, and she probably couldn't have been restrained much longer, anyway. Mavra let the girl eat one, knowing they should wait several hours for the test to be conclusive, but when she reported the fruit to be sweet and good and easily chewed, the temptation to Mavra, whose own appetite could not be depressed, became too much to ignore.

They satisfied, they were good, and they were plentiful, apparently an important part of the upper animal food chain of this place. And they were doubly important. They proved that, no matter what else happened, Mavra Chang could survive here.

The second day had been a lot more satisfactory than the first. Even so, she was uncertain. The other two, now, had seen the great cyclopses, with their fierce expressions and nasty fangs, pulling wooden handhewn carts along the roads and tending flocks of animals that looked much like common sheep in the meadows.

Neither of the two spongies had shown much

change as yet, but that was deceptive, she knew. In normal conversation there was little difference between an IQ of 100 and an IQ of 150. There was no question that Nikki would deteriorate faster; she was a little above average, but no genius.

As darkness fell at the end of the second day, the mountains were still nowhere in sight and the landscape didn't seem to have varied much at all. There was a chill in the air from the damp, humid skies and a light drizzle. Neither Renard nor Nikki was at all comfortable; they had no protection, in or out of those filmy things from New Pompeii, and although Mavra's clothing provided decent protection, she was by far the smallest of the three and had nothing to spare that could fit either of the others.

The darkness of the second evening was as much in their spirits as in the night surrounding them.

She tried bunching them all together for body warmth, but she was so small and their skin so cold and clammy that all this seemed to do was transfer their misery to her. Nikki, being heavy and unaccustomed to exercise, was, as usual, the first to fall asleep, leaving her with Renard, as before. They sat there awhile, thinking of little to say. He had his arm around her, holding her close to him, but it was not a romantic gesture, not an advance. It was a binding together in the face of adversity.

Finally, he said, "Mavra, do you really think there's any point to all this? You and I both know we don't even know where we are or what's over the next hill or even whether the next hill isn't some previous hill."

The question irritated her, because it vocalized her own inner doubts. "There's always a point to it until you're dead," she replied, and she believed it.

"You really think so?" he responded. "Not just brave talk?"

She shifted slightly, looking away from him, out into the blackness.

"I was raised by a rough freighter captain. Not the most ideal parent, I guess, but, in her own way, she did love me, I think, and I loved her. I grew up in space, the big freighter my playground, the big ports new and dazzling amusements every few weeks."

148

"Must've been lonely," he commented.

She shook her head. "No, not at all. After all, it was all I ever knew. It was normal to me. And it taught me how to be on my own for long periods of time—conditioned me against the loneliness, made me rely on myself. That was important, because my mother was doing a lot of illegal stuff. Most freighter captains do, but this must've been really big. The Com Police busted her and the ship was seized. I was about thirteen then, and I was in the stores along the port, shopping. I found out what happened, but couldn't do anything. I knew that if I showed myself, the CPs would take me, too, maybe give me a psych wipe, and turn me over to the Com. So, I stayed on Kaliva."

"Ever feel guilty you didn't try to spring her?" Renard asked, knowing the sensitivity of the question but realizing that Mavra Chang wanted somebody to talk to.

"No, I don't think so," she answered truthfully. "Oh, I had all sorts of plots in my head—a thirteen-year-old girl, a little over a meter tall and weighing about twenty-five kilos—to rush them, battle them, heroically rescue my mom, and dash away in the ship to unknown space. But I never even could get the chance. They had her away and the ship impounded in a matter of an hour or two. No, I was alone."

"You don't like the Com very much, by your tone," he noted. "Any special reason?"

"They murdered my family," she almost spat. "I was only a little more than five years old, but I can remember them. Harvich's world went Com with sponge syndicate muscle and rigged votes, and my folks—my real folks—had been fighting them every step of the way. I got the whole story later, from Maki—my stepmother—when I got older. They refused to leave at the start, then found they couldn't leave when the Com process started. Somehow—I don't know how—they hired a spacer to get me out, one piloting a supply freighter for the Com process. Funny—after all these years I can still remember him. A strange little man in colorful clothes with a big, brassy voice that always had several tones in it. Some of those tones I later recognized as pure cynicism, but there was an underlying gentleness and kindness about him that he seemed desperate to hide but couldn't. It's funny—I'm not even sure of his name, and I was with him for only a few days when I was five, yet he's as real to me as my stepmother, who actually got me out. Looking back, I think it's incredible that a five-year-old spoiled brat like me would go with him. There was just something in him one liked, trusted. I often wonder if he was human—I've never met anybody else like that, ever."

Renard was no psychologist, but he recognized the depth of the impression this man had made on Mavra Chang. She had been hunting for him, or someone like him, all her life.

"Ever try and find him?" he asked her.

She shrugged. "I was much too busy staying alive the next few years. By the time I had the means, he was probably dead or something. I have to admit that a number of people seemed to recognize him from my description, but there was nothing tangible. Some people said I was describing a fairy-tale legend, a mythical space captain who had never existed but was just part of those epic stories all professions get. Once I met a captain, a real old veteran, who said that this man really existed, somewhere, and he was old. He was supposed to be immortal, living forever, going back to ancient times of prehistory."

"What's the name of this legend?" Renard prompted.

"Nathan Brazil. Isn't that a strange name? Somebody said Brazil was the name of a prehistoric place, one of the early space powers."

"The Wandering Jew," Renard said, almost to himself.

"Huh?"

"An ancient legend among some of the old religions," he told her. "There's still a Christian planet or two around, I think. They are an offshoot of an even more obscure and older religion known as Judaism. They're still around, too—scattered all over the place. Probably the most traditionally co—" he stopped for a second, looked puzzled and disturbed. "Co—" he tried.

"Cohesive?" she guessed.

He nodded. "That's it. Why couldn't I think of that word?" He let it drop, but Mavra had an eerie sensation. A little thing, but important.

"Well, anyway, there was supposed to be this man who was Jewish and claimed to be God's son. For this the powers-that-be killed him, because they were scared he might lead a revolution or something. Supposedly he was to come back from the dead. One Jew was supposed to have cursed him at his execution and been told that he would stay until this god-man returned. This Nathan Brazil sounds like the legend brought up to modern times."

She nodded "I never really believed all that stuff about immortals flying spaceships, but a lot of spacers who don't believe in anything believe in his existence."

Renard smiled. "That may explain what happened to you. If it's a widespread legend, then somebody who knew it could imitate him, maybe convince the other spacers he was this legendary figure. They'd do favors for him they wouldn't do for an ordinary captain. Make supersi— supershi—oh, hell!" he ended in frustration, unable to get the word out.

She got the meaning. "I don't know. You're probably right. But there was something really strange about that man, something I can't explain."

"You were five years old," he pointed out. "That's an age to get funny impressions."

Mavra wanted to break off the conversation, partly because it was hitting too close to home but also because of Renard's increasing trouble with large words he was obviously used to using. He was starting to think out his sentences in advance, using different words than he normally would. His difficulty wasn't really that apparent, but his speech was slower, more careful, more hesitant than it had been.

Tomorrow, she thought glumly, those words just might not be accessible to him at all. But, he still wanted to talk, and, she told herself, if that was the case it was best she do most of the talking.

Renard took up the theme and thankfully took the subject away from the mysterious Nathan Brazil.

"You said you were on your own at age thirteen," he noted. "Wasn't that kind of rough?"

She nodded. "There I was, on a strange world, looking like an eight-year-old, with nothing but a few coins that maybe would buy a meal, and I didn't even know the street language. At least it wasn't a Comworld. Kaliva, its name was. Kind of exotic and primitive. Open bazaars, shouting peddlers and salesmen—a noisy, grimy, people-filled kind of place. I knew that in such a place you needed money and protection. I had neither, so I looked around. There were a lot of beggars, some just poor, some con men, some cripples who couldn't afford the med service. There were enough of them that they weren't hassled by the local police, and people *did* give. I walked around, watched who was making money and who wasn't, and where, and saw what I had to do. I used the last little bit of money I had to bribe a little girl to give me her clothes—really dirty, grungy, ripped, and tattered. Nothing really but a foul sheet that could be tied like a sari. Some water and a little mud, and I really looked like a horrible little street urchin. Then I went to work."

Renard thought that maybe she *was* a horrible little street urchin at that point, but decided not to mention that aloud.

"I really hustled those first couple of weeks. I got fleas and occasionally worse, and I slept in doorways, alleys, and such. I worked the good corners. Beggars have territories, you know, and run off others who want to compete for the business, but I learned how to make friends with some of the best, did favors, gave them a percentage. I guess it was also because I looked so very young and so very down and out—the model for those charity pictures they always take, the poor, starving, angelic faces—that everybody kind of adopted me. I did pretty good. Even on the worst days I made enough to eat, or somebody who owned a food stall would slip me something."

"No trouble with rape or gangs?" he asked, amazed.

"No, not really. A few really nasty incidents, but

somebody always seemed to come along or I managed to get away. Beggars kind of stick together, too—once you're accepted. One of them put me on to an old shack out near the city dump, and I lived there. It was pretty gamey, but after a while you get so you don't notice the smells, the flies, or anything. Some charity medical clinics were around, so we got sick a lot but never for long. Everybody kept trying to get me out of there, but I conned them. I didn't want anything I didn't earn myself. I didn't want to owe anybody anything."

"How long did this go on?" Renard prompted.

"Over three years," she answered. "It wasn't a bad life. You got used to it. And, I grew up, developed a little—as much as I ever did, anyway—and dreamed. I used to go down to the spaceport every day when I'd made my quota or just couldn't do it any more—begging is hard work sometimes—and look at the ships and peer in the dives at the spacers. I knew where I wanted to be again, someday—and finally I realized that begging would always get me by but never get me anywhere. Some of the spacers were real big spenders, since they had no home but the ships and little to spend anything on."

Renard was shocked. "You don't mean you—"

She shrugged. "I was too small to be a waitress, and I couldn't reach over the bar. I never learned much about dancing, I didn't have much in the way of social graces, and no real education. I talked like a wharf rat, and while Maki had taught me reading and writing and numbers, I hadn't done much of it. I had only one thing to sell, and I sold it, learned how to sell it just right. Male, female, once, twice, ten times a night if I could. It got pretty boring after a while, and none of it meant anything, but, lord! How the money rolled in!"

He looked at her strangely in the near darkness, feeling slightly uncomfortable. It wasn't what she was saying, but how she was saying it that affected him so. He wasn't sure what to say. He was certain that she hadn't told this to anyone, particularly a stranger—maybe not at all—in years. The fact that she was telling it now, and to him, meant something even his increasingly cloudy brain could fathom. Deep down, she was as scared as he was.

"You certainly speak well enough now," he pointed out. "And you said you were a pilot. Did you make enough money to do all that?"

She laughed dryly. "No, not from that. I met a man —a very kind and gentle man, who was a freighter captain. He started coming around real regular. I liked him—he had some of those qualities I mentioned in my long-ago rescuer. He was loud, brash, cynical, detested the Com, and had the most guts of any man I'd ever known. I guess I knew I was in love with him, looked forward to seeing him, to meeting him, going out with him. It wasn't like with the others. It wasn't sex. I doubt if I could do that with any feeling with anybody. It was something else, something better than that. When I found out he was diverting often just to see me, our relationship grew even deeper. We complemented each other. And he owned his own ship, the *Assateague,* a really good, fast, modern job."

"That's kind of unusual, isn't it?" Renard commented. "I mean, those things are for corporations, not people. I never heard of a captain owning his own ship."

"Yes, it *is* unusual," she admitted. "It took a while to find out why. He finally asked me to come with him, move onto the ship. Said he couldn't afford all these side trips. Well, that was what I'd always wanted, so of course I did. And then he had to tell me how he had so much money. He was a thief."

Renard had to laugh. It was a ridiculous climax to her story. "What did he steal, and who from?" he asked.

"Anything from anybody," she replied. "The freighter was a cover and afforded mobility. Jewels, art, gold, silver, you name it. If it had a high value, he stole it. Rich people, corporation heads, party leaders on Comworlds were a particular target. Sometimes there were break-ins, sometimes he did it with electronics and a fine knowledge of bureaucratic paperwork. After we got together, we became a team. He got all sorts of teaching machines, sleep learners, hypno aids, and the like for me, and he coached me

154

and rehearsed me until I *sounded* educated and *acted* properly." She giggled. "One time we broke into the master storage area in the Union of All Moons treasury building, exchanged some chips, and had the next three days' planetary income automatically diverted to dummy interstellar units accounts in Confederacy banks, and even after we closed down, withdrew the stuff, and transferred it far away, they never caught on. I wonder if they ever did?"

"Your man—what happened to him?" Renard asked gently.

She turned somber again. "We were never caught by the police. Never. We were too good. One day, though, we lifted two beautiful little solid gold figurines by the ancient classical artist Sun Tat, and they had to be fenced to a big collector. The meet was arranged in a bar, and we had no reason to suspect anything was wrong. It was. The collector was a front for a big syndicate boss we'd hit a year or so earlier, and the whole thing was a set-up. They cut him into little pieces and left the figurines with the remains."

"And you inherited the ship," Renard guessed.

She nodded. "We'd gotten a traditionalist ceremony a year or so before, just in case, I didn't really want to, but he'd insisted, and it turned out he was right. I was his sole heir."

"And you've been alone ever since?" he added, fascinated by this strange little woman.

There was acid and cold steel in her voice. "I spent half a year tracking down his killers. Every one died —slowly. Every one knew why they were dying. At first the big boss didn't even remember him!" Tears welled up in her eyes. "But he remembered at the end," she added, with evident satisfaction.

"Since that time, I have continued the family trade, you might say," she went on. "Both of them. I've paid for the best the underworld can offer, and kept myself in top shape. Surgeons have turned me into a small deadly weapon, with things you wouldn't believe built in and deep-programmed. Even if I were ever caught, the story I just told you couldn't even be gotten by deep-psych probe. They've tried."

155

"You were hired to get Nikki out, weren't you?" Renard said.

She nodded. "If you can't catch a crook, set her to catch other crooks. That was the idea. It *almost* worked."

He grunted at the last. It brought everything back to the present situation, although now he could understand why she believed they would get out of this. With a life like hers, miracles were a common, everyday occurrence.

"There's nothing really to tell about me," he said wistfully. "Nothing violent or romantic."

"You said you were a teacher," she noted.

He nodded. "I was from Muscovy. A Comworld, yes, but not a really *serious* one. None of that genetic-manipulation stuff. Traditional family structure, prayers five times a day—*There is no God but Marx and Lenin is His Prophet*—and testing to see where you fit into the communal structure." He was audibly straining for the words. They came hard to him. He didn't appear to notice.

"I was smart, so I was put in school. But I never was interested in anything useful, so I studied old literchur"—that's the way he pronounced it, as best he could—"and became a teacher. I was always kind of effinate"—he meant effeminate—"in looks and acts. but not inside. I got a lot of fun poked at me. It hurt. Even the students were mean. Mostly behind my back, but I knew what they were saying. I didn't like the men who liked other men, and the women all believed I didn't like them. I kind of withdrew into my own shell, in my apartment with my books and vid files, and came out only for classes."

"How about a psych?" she wondered.

"I went to a bunch," he replied. "They all started talking about all sorts of wild things, did I love my father and all that. They put me in some kind of drug training that was supposed to change my mannerisms, but it didn't work. The more they tried and failed, the more unhappy I got. Finally, I sat there one night and considered how little I had done. I hadn't really directly touched one other life—even for the worst. I thought about killing myself, but the psych probes out-

156

guessed me there, and the People's Police came and got me before I could do it."

"Would you have?" she asked seriously.

He shook his head. "I don't know. Maybe. Maybe not. I sure haven't since, have I? No guts, I guess. Or maybe they deep-programmed me not to." He paused a moment in thought—or trying to organize his thoughts.

"They took me to the political asylum. I'd never been there before. They seemed kind of upset that I was thinking of killing myself. Took it personally, like because I failed, the system had failed. They thought about wiping me clean, maybe converting me to being a woman and doing a new personality that would match."

"Why not just kill you and be done with it?" Mavra asked. "It would be cheaper and less trouble."

He looked shocked, then remembered her own background. "They just don't *do* that on Comworlds! Not Muscovy, anyway. No, I was kept there for a long time—I don't know how long. Then somebody came by and told me that some bigwig wanted to talk to me. I had no choice, so I went. He was from a different Comworld, a real far-gone one—true hermaphroism, genetically identical people programmed to love their work, and so on. He said he needed, of all things, a librarian! People who could read books, and be familiar with them, were rare—*that* was true! Even Muscovy had a ninety-two percent ill—nonreader rate." The big words got him, and he either badly mispronounced them or couldn't handle them.

"Trelig," she guessed.

He nodded. "Right. I was taken away on his ship to New Pompeii, given a huge overdose of sponge, and I was stuck. The OD did crazy things to me in the weeks and months that followed. My girlish manners were made a hundred times worse, and my features became more and more like those of a woman, even to the breasts. But—it was funny. My *male* organs actually grew, and, inside my head, I was still a man. I finally had my first real sex experience on New Pompeii. I really *was* his librarian, too—and I was also one of the guards for special prisoners, like Nikki, there. *Ev-*

erybody on New Pompeii had psych problems of some kind plus a skill Trelig needed. He recruited from the best political asylums in the Com."

"And now here you are," she said to him, very gently.

He sighed. "Yes, here I am. When I shot Ziggy and helped you get out, I felt it was the first really important thing I had ever done. I almost felt that I was born and existed only for that one moment, that one act—to be there to help you when you needed it. And now—look what a mess we have!"

She kissed him lightly on the cheek. "Go get to sleep and don't worry so much. I haven't lost yet—and if I haven't, you haven't either."

She wished she believed that.

Uchjin, Northern Hemisphere

"A HELL OF A MESS," BEN YULIN SAID, LOOKING over the landscape. With no power to the air-renewal system on the ship, they had been forced to don their spacesuits. The largest aboard was almost too small for Zinder in the body of his rotund daughter, but the things were made to form-fit a variety of sizes. You got into them and they were all tremendous, loose, and baggy. But when you hooked up the air supply, which was, fortunately, a manual rebreather type, the material acted like something alive, constricting until it became almost a second, very tough white skin.

"How much air do we have?" Trelig asked, looking around at the barren rocky desert in which no sign of life appeared anywhere.

Yulin shrugged. "Not more than a half-day's supply at best without the special electrical system in the rebreather."

"We aren't far from that next hex, where there appeared to be some water," Trelig noted hopefully. "Let's try for it. What have we got to lose?"

They started off, following the marks of the giant skid the courier ship had made in its belly-landing.

They hadn't gone far before twilight set in. Yulin felt that something was wrong, and he tried to put his finger on it. There seemed to be shapes around, kind of half-shapes, really, that appeared at the corner of your eye but weren't there when you turned around.

"Trelig?" he called.

"What?" the other snapped.

"Do either you or Zinder notice anything odd going on? I'd swear we have company of some kind."

Trelig and Zinder both came to a halt, although they didn't want to, and looked around. Yulin found they were easier to see the darker it got.

They seemed to exist in only two dimensions—length and width—and even that was variable. From the side, they seemed to vanish. They were flying, or floating—it was hard to tell which—all around them. Yulin was reminded of paint spilled on a sheet of clear plastic. There was a thick leading edge, and it flowed—not necessarily down, but up and along as well. As it did, the edge seemed to spread out so that it was sometimes a meter wide and almost two meters long. That was the limit for them—when they were fully extended, the rear edge seemed to slowly flow back into the leading edge until it was just a meter-wide lump of paint, only to start spreading out again.

They were different colors, too. Almost every color they could think of, although never more than one. Blues, reds, yellows, greens—of every possible shade and hue.

"Are they intelligent?" Yulin wondered aloud.

Trelig had been thinking the same thing. "They sure seem to be clustering around us, like a crowd of curious onlookers at an accident," the syndicate boss noted. "I don't see how, but I'd bet money that these are the people who live here."

"People" was too strong a word, Yulin thought. These creatures were the stuff of artists' dreams, not real, tangible things.

"I'm going to try and touch one," Trelig said.

"Hey! Wait! You might—" Yulin protested, but got only a laugh in reply.

"So- I do something bad," the boss responded. "We're dead anyway, you know." With that he reached out and tried to grab the one nearest him. Nothing he'd ever seen had ever reacted that fast. One moment it was there, all stretched out, the next it just seemed to be somewhere else, a meter or two out of reach.

"Wow!" Trelig exclaimed. "They sure can move if they want to!"

Yulin nodded. "Maybe, if they're intelligent in any way, we can talk to them," he suggested.

Trelig wasn't so sure. "So what do you say to a two-meter living paint smear, and how?" he asked sarcastically.

"Maybe they can *see* somehow," Yulin suggested. "Let's try some gestures."

He made sure of his audience—and he *did* have the funny feeling that they were looking at him—and pointed to Zinder's air tanks. Then he put his hands to his throat, made choking motions, and fell to the ground.

The flowing streaks seemed to like that. More of them arrived, and they seemed to become much more agitated. Yulin repeated the act several times, and they became increasingly agitated, sometimes almost touching one another in their eagerness to get a better view.

Enough acting, Yulin decided. It used up air. He got up, faced them, and put out his hands in what he hoped would be a gesture of friendship and supplication.

This action seemed to excite them even more. He had the strange feeling that he was the subject of a furious debate that none but these strange creatures could hear.

But were they debating whether to help, how to help, or what was the meaning of this strange creature's actions? That last was definitely the most unsettling—and the most likely.

A couple of the creatures floated over, seemed to examine his air pack from a distance of fifty centimeters or so. He remained still, letting them. That was a good start. They might be getting the idea. Or they might be wondering why he was pointing at that funny thing.

More and more appeared as darkness fell. They were coming out of cracks in the ground, they observed—small cracks they would never have noticed otherwise. The natives seemed to rise like wraiths, fully extended, then curl up or flow or whatever, pulling out in a different direction and heading, mostly, their way. There was a regular assembly now, a rainbow of weird flowing and undulating shapes.

Finally, they seemed to reach some sort of decision or consensus. They crowded around the humans, so thick it was impossible to see. Then, very deliberately, a narrow opening appeared to one side. They waited.

"I think we're being directed someplace," Trelig noted. "Shall we go?"

"Better than collapsing here and dying in another hour or two," Yulin replied. "You lead, or shall I?"

Trelig started walking, then Zinder, and finally Yulin. That they were being led somewhere was quickly apparent—the opening continued, but the area they vacated was closed in by the strange creatures.

Yulin checked his air supply. About two hours, he noted. He hoped wherever they were going wasn't far off.

That thought was in all their minds, along with the last shreds of doubt, when, a little over an hour later, they reached a rock outcrop. A huge number of the creatures was there—perhaps many thousands. Some had obviously assembled there because of them, but others seemed to be carrying on all sorts of deliberate but unfathomable business.

"Yulin! Look!" Trelig called excitedly.

Ben Yulin peered into the star-lit darkness at the cliff's face, and, for a moment, didn't see what had attracted the other man. Finally he could make out a deeper blackness against the cliff.

"A cave?" he asked, feeling disappointed. "Hell, we've been taken to their leader or something."

"No! No!" Trelig protested. "My Renard eyes must

161

be better than your Mavra Chang's. Look at the *shape* of the hole!"

Yulin peered again, approaching closer. It was large —perhaps two meters on each of its six sides.

Six sides?

"A hexagon!" Yulin exclaimed, hardly able to contain himself. "They got the message!"

"We'll see," Trelig responded. "Obviously they mean for us to enter the thing, and we might as well. Air's running out anyway. All set?"

"Okay, let's go," Yulin replied, praying again that they would not enter a cave that was just the seat of government of these folks.

Trelig went first. He didn't seem to enter a cave or hole—he just stepped forward, seemed frozen for an instant, then vanished. Yulin prodded Zinder next, but the scientist knew the air situation as well as they did. He stepped in, and to the same effect. Ben Yulin took an expensive deep breath, held it, and stepped in, too.

It was a strange sensation, like falling down a great, endless hole. It was nasty and unpleasant, but they had to endure it.

The sensation ended as suddenly as it began, bringing them out in a strange sort of cave inhabited by more of the flowing creatures.

The other two were already there.

"Oh, no!" Yulin swore, heart sinking. "Just a shuttle system!"

Trelig was just about to reply when a ghostly figure quite unlike any of them, humans or creatures, appeared. It was huge—three meters at least, and almost as big around. It had nasty-looking claws and sets of insectlike legs, and it was encased in some kind of protective artificial shell.

"What the hell?" Trelig managed, but then he saw the figure make a very recognizable "follow me" gesture with its great claws, turn, and start down the cave.

"Our new guide," speculated Yulin. "I think I like the paint smears better. Well, let's get going. Air's getting low."

They went through a passage, then a doorway slid out, and they found it was some kind of air lock. It closed behind them, then opened ahead after a few moments. The creature had gone ahead but, they saw, it waited for them outside.

Outside proved to be a long, broad hallway made of some orange-white crystalline material that sparkled. The whole area was lit up, and Yulin wasn't the only one that noticed the rows of doorways in hexagonal shapes. The hallways, however, were almost rounded, with no sharp corners.

The large insectlike creature walked slowly down the corridor, and they followed. It seemed like a long journey, and it took more than twenty minutes by Ben Yulin's air timer.

Suddenly the hall opened onto a huge chamber. Huge was hardly the word for it. The chamber had six sides, which seemed almost natural by now; but the enclosure was so enormous that it took some time to establish that fact. The center area was in the shape of an enormous glassy hexagon, too, and around the sides stretched a railing and what appeared to be a walkway. A single great six-sided light, like a great jewel, was suspended from the center of the mammoth ceiling, providing all the light.

The walkway was just that, and more. The big creature got on it, walked down so they could also step onto the vinyllike, spongy surface, then it pressed some indistinguishable area on the wall.

They almost tumbled over as the walkway started to move.

It took about ten minutes to go halfway around to another break in the wall. There were openings in the rail to go down to the glassy surface, but they passed them up. Eventually they stopped, and the weird creature, which seemed to them to be much like a lobster made of transparent glass, went slowly down a new hallway.

They reached a room, much smaller than either the big chamber or the cave. It had an air lock, too, but it was an almost perfect square. The ceiling and three of the walls looked normal, including the door area.

The fourth was blackness absolute.

"Looks like another transfer," Trelig noted. "I

hope we get to our kind of air in the next forty minutes."

"Thirty-six," Yulin replied glumly. He'd been checking it every half-minute.

"They're not going to let us die," said Trelig confidently. "They've gone to too much trouble." He stepped unhesitatingly into the blackness, followed by Zinder, and then Yulin.

Again they experienced that falling sensation, longer this time. Yulin worried about how long it might be and wanted to check the timer, but vision was impossible.

They emerged in an identical room. In fact, all three could have sworn that they'd gone no place. That puzzled and disturbed them. Yulin's timer still read close to thirty-six, which meant that the long fall they'd just taken had consumed no time. That was impossible, he told himself. And then he noticed—a slight humming sound, a tiny whine.

And the timer was going up.

"Trelig! We've got power! The electrical system is processing again!" he almost screamed.

The excitement and relief swept over them. Trelig, ever practical, broke the mood.

"Remember that we're being manipulated by someone," he cautioned. "They may know more than we think. Remember, you, that you're *Mavra Chang*, pilot, and no one else, and that I'm Renard. Don't ever use any other name again!" The words were icy, nasty, cutting. "If they question us together, let me do most of the talking. If separately, tell the truth up to the point where we changed it. You don't know *who* was in the other ship! Understand?"

Yulin calmed down.

Suddenly the door slid open, and a third kind of creature entered.

They all stared at it, still not used to the changing wonders of the races of the Well World. It was a little under two meters tall with a thick, smooth, green-skinned body ending in two round, thick legs without apparent joint, supported by broad, flat-bottomed round cuplike feet. Two spindly arms grew from a point just above its midsection and seemed to have

164

smaller divisions at the tips. The head, which sat atop an impossibly thin neck, looked like a green jack-o'-lantern, with its mouth in a permanent expression of surprise, and two nonblinking, almost luminous saucers for eyes. No sign of a nose or ears, Yulin noted. Atop it all grew a single huge, broad leaf that seemed to have a life of its own, slowly moving toward the strongest light source.

The creature held a piece of cardboard or something similar in its left tentacles, then lifted the board in front of it, angling it so they could read. The message was in standard Confederation plain talk, bearing out Trelig's suspicion that the denizens of this world were far from ignorant of them or their nature. It said, in block-printed crayon:

YOU MAY REMOVE YOUR SUITS. THE AIR IS
BREATHABLE. WHEN YOU HAVE FINISHED,
FOLLOW ME TO BRIEFING.

Trelig accepted the guarantee and pressed the releases to flip back his helmet bubble. He took a breath, and the air was good. Satisfied, he switched off the backpack. The suit collapsed, seemed to grow and melt into a puddle of synthetic cloth at his feet. He helped Zinder do the same. Yulin started to, but suddenly fell horribly nauseous; blood suddenly clogged in his throat, and pain wracked him everywhere.

He collapsed and passed out.

Teliagin

IN THE EARLY AFTERNOON OF THE THIRD DAY, THE one thing Mavra Chang feared more than the rain happened.

They ran out of woods.

Not much, of course. This was pastoral country, and the woods picked up about a kilometer away. But here was a broad plain, grassy and lumpy, and criss-crossed by several of the dirt roads, on which there was a great deal of traffic. They watched from the edges of the clearing as great cyclopses went back and forth, to and fro, some alone, some carrying large sheepskin bags, some pulling large wooden carts with hand-carved wooden wheels, laden with all sorts of things.

"Look on the bright side," Mavra told them. "At least we know now we haven't been going in circles."

Renard nodded. "Yes, we're a long ways from where we landed. But are we going the right way?"

Mavra shrugged. What was the wrong way? The one that got you caught. In that case, this might definitely be the wrong way.

"We *could* follow the woods to the left for a while," she suggested. "Maybe it connects someplace down that road. We've crossed roads before."

"Don't look like it," Renard observed. He was talking more normally today, but his sentences were shorter and less complex, and he wasn't even thinking in those big words any more.

Mavra Chang sighed. "Then we'll have to stay here until nightfall. We sure can't cross now with all those creatures there." She didn't like that; although the hypno conditioning, renewed the night before, kept the two unaware of their condition, the mental deterioration was becoming evident in Renard and more so in Nikki. Precious hours would mean that much more lost.

"I don't wanna get eaten," Nikki Zinder proclaimed. "You remember that one we saw? Ate that sheep in three big gulps."

Mavra remembered. They would stay hidden until after nightfall, when the traffic thinned out. She had no idea whether any of her lethal defenses she'd bragged so much to Renard about would work on those behemoths—and she had no desire to try. She wasn't as much of a mouthful as that sheep had been.

They settled down, and all started to doze on and off. They were tired and worn; the sponge effect was also body-wide, although more apparent in the thought processes. The other two tired more quickly,

166

and their coordination was shot. As for Mavra, she'd gotten very little sleep since before landing on New Pompeii, and fatigue was starting to tell on her. Will power could only sustain so far, and she knew it, even though she wouldn't admit that to herself. She slept.

Renard awoke first. He'd only been slightly asleep anyway, thanks to Mavra's rest-inducing hypno of the past nights. He crawled to the edge of the plain. Still a lot of traffic, maybe not as much as before, but it would be sure capture to go out there now.

He crawled back. Mavra was so sound asleep she didn't hear him, but Nikki stirred, opened her eyes, and looked at him.

"Hi!" she whispered.

"Shhh!" he cautioned, putting his finger to his lips. He ambled over to her.

She looked up at him with slightly dulled large brown eyes. "Do you think we can croth it?" she asked. The lisp had appeared as time had worn on.

"Yes, later on," he soothed, and she shifted next to him.

"Renard?"

"Yes, Nikki?"

"I'm thscared."

"We all are," he told her honestly. "We just have to keep going."

"Not *her*," the girl replied, pointing to Mavra. "I don't think anything could thscare her."

"She's just learned to live with fear," he soothed. "She knows how to be scared without letting it get to her. You have to do that, too, Nikki."

She shook her head. "Ith's more than that. I don' wanna die, sure, but—if I gotta—I . . ." She trailed off, searching for the words.

He didn't understand, and said so. She was quiet for a moment, then finally said, "Rennie? Will you make love to me?"

"Huh?" The very idea startled him.

"I want to have it, do it, juth once. Juth in cathe." There were almost tears in her eyes, and a pleading voice. "I don' wanna die without doin' it juth onth."

He looked over at the sleeping Mavra Chang, then down at the pathetic girl next to him, and wondered

167

how, in the face of certain death, you could still get into bad situations. He thought about it for a while, trying to make up his mind. Finally, he decided. Why not? he thought. What's the harm? And it was one thing, at least, he could do for somebody else that he couldn't foul up.

Mavra Chang awoke with a start and looked around. It was dark—she'd been sleeping for quite some time. Suddenly, she had a headache and various other aches and pains from sleeping so hard and in one position. Solid sleep.

She looked around, spotted Renard and Nikki reclining, backs against a broad tree. She was asleep, and he was half-asleep, his arm around the plump girl. Mavra could see in a moment what had happened; there was little way to clean up here. It bothered her, and it bothered her that it bothered her. Possibly because she could not understand it.

She turned and crept up to the edge of the clearing. Not much traffic or signs of traffic now. Occasionally a cart would go by, two torches blazing from holders in its side grotesquely half-illuminating the strange creature that pulled it; but clearly traffic was at a minimum. She doubted the cyclopses had good night vision; they seemed mostly inactive after sunset, active from first light.

She crept back to the pair, who hadn't moved, and gently woke them up. Nikki seemed to be calmer, which was good, but worse mentally. Mavra wondered if the effect accelerated despite what Renard had told her, or if it was just more noticeable when you started to get down below the normal level.

"We're about ready to go across," she told them. "We'll go as far as we can tonight to try and make up the lost time."

"We gon' run 'croth?" Nikki asked, sounding almost eager.

"No, Nikki, not run," she replied patiently and slowly. "We will walk across, slowly and nicely."

"But th' big thing'll thee uth!" the girl protested.

"There aren't many of them," Mavra told her.

"And if one comes near, we'll just lie down and be quiet and wait for it to go away."

Renard looked at Nikki and patted her hand. She liked that, and snuggled up a little to him. "Let's go now, Nikki," he said gently.

They got up and made their way to the edge of the plains. No torches or carts in sight except two dim lights far off in the distance. Probably the same one that Mavra had seen, going away, she guessed.

"Okay, let's all walk now, nice and easy," she told them, taking Nikki's right hand in her left and Renard's left hand in her right. They started out.

The crossing was almost too easy. The cloud cover had remained, making the surroundings even blacker, and there was literally nobody on the roads. They crossed the clearing in about twenty minutes with no problems, and Mavra wished that all her troubles and worries were so easily laid to rest.

But then the rain started. Not a bad rain, or a big storm, but a steady rain that was warm but uncomfortable. It quickly turned the ground into mud and soaked them through. Nikki seemed to enjoy it, but it was miserable going, and the trees didn't offer much protection.

Mavra Chang cursed. The mud was becoming deeper and more treacherous, and they couldn't keep going much longer in this kind of mess. More lost time, with time running out on her.

Then the wind started to pick up, chilling their soaked bodies to the bone, forcing her hand. She found some shelter, a grove of particularly tall, broad trees growing close together that afforded a measure of dryness, and they settled down and huddled together for all the good it did.

The next morning dawned brighter and dryer, but only because the clouds had thinned and it had stopped raining on them. They all looked a mess, mud-caked, with hair tangled and mud-clumped.

Renard was disturbed. "I can't seem to think so good," he told her with obvious distress. "I can't seem to think of things any more. Why is that, Mavra?"

169

She felt a consuming pity for the man, but she couldn't answer his question. Nikki, of course, was even worse. She'd found a mud-puddle and was happily playing in it, splashing around and making some sort of mud cakes. She looked up as they approached.

"Hi!" she called out. She reached down and picked up a mud pie. "Thee what I made?"

Mavra sighed and thought fast. A glance at the sun had told her that they'd been moving roughly east, but how far and at what angle?

She thought fast about the pair she now had on her hands. Renard was still capable of handling himself, but for how much longer? As for Nikki—she was sinking almost before Mavra Chang's eyes. Something had to be done to keep them under control.

She put them both under quickly, finding she had to choose her words carefully so they could follow her.

"Nikki, you don't remember anything about who you are except that your name is Nikki. Understand?"

"Uh huh," the girl acknowledged.

"Now, you're a *very* little girl, and I am your mommy. You love your mommy and always do what she says, don't you?"

"Uh huh," the girl agreed.

She turned to Renard.

"Now, Renard, you don't remember anything about who you are or who we are, only that your name is Renard. Okay?"

"All right," he agreed.

"You are Renard. You are five years old and you are my son. I am your mommy, and you love your mommy and always do what she tells you. Understand?"

His tone became softer, more childlike. "Yes, Mommy," he replied.

"Good," she approved. "Now, Nikki is your sister. She is younger than you and you have to help her. Understand? You love your sister and have to help her."

"Yes, Mommy," he responded.

She turned back to Nikki. "Nikki, Renard is your big brother and you love him very much. You will let him help you if you have trouble."

"Uh huh," she responded, very childlike.

Mavra was as satisfied as she could be. She'd done this regression thing before, although under very different circumstances. She had once convinced an art-museum director that he was her son, and he'd opened the place and shut off the alarm for her. Even helped her cart stuff out. He thought he was helping his mommy move.

She would have to remember, though, that she was Mommy to two very big but definite children from now on, and act the part.

She brought them out of it. "Come on, children. We have to go now," she said softly.

Nikki looked upset. "Ah, p'eathe, Mommy! Can't we pway some more?"

"Not now," she scolded gently. "We have to go. Come on, both of you give Mommy your hands."

They went along for some time. It was difficult at times to control them as children, despite the hypnoed instructions. Kids skipped and played and generally acted up, and it took some stern acting and will power to keep them pretty much in line.

Mavra began to worry that she was wrong after all, that she would never see any mountains and a sign of an end to this strange place. Yet, the terrain was becoming hillier; the rocks were larger, and mostly igneous. They might be foothills.

And, suddenly, there they were. Not terribly tall mountains, or grand ones, but wonderful to see all the same. Gently folded, like great wrinkles in the earth, they rose up about eight hundred meters from where they stood. As with most folded mountains, though, there were frequent breaks, where streams and ice had eroded passes through the barrier. The lowest and closest of these would still require a climb of about three hundred meters, but the slope was gentle and there were many rocky outcrops for rest or shelter. They might make it over before dark if they were lucky, she thought.

There were a lot of sheep on the hillsides. She didn't like that; in this place, where there were grazing sheep there was usually one or more giant one-eyed shepherds. She debated waiting until darkness, but she feared any more time lost. She looked carefully around, wishing she could trust them to stay put while she did a better reconnoitering job—but she dared not put them to sleep. She might not have any control later.

She decided to chance it. Taking their hands and cautioning them to be quiet, they started as quickly as possible across the open area to the first protective outcropping a few thousand meters ahead.

It looked closer than it was, and the "children" were hard to restrain as they passed close to some grazing sheep. Even as tense as she was, looking for any sign of more dangerous life, Mavra reflected how curious it was that such an animal, so common in her own part of the universe, should be here.

The outcrop loomed near now, and she almost had them running for it at full speed. Just a few seconds more . . . now! Made it!

There was a sudden terrible roaring sound, and they stopped dead. A massive shape, then two, suddenly rose up in front of them. Two of them! A big male and a big female, either waiting for them behind the rocks or doing their own business there. It didn't matter.

Nikki screamed, and they all turned to run, but the creatures, once they recovered from their initial surprise, reacted very swiftly. A great hand came down and grabbed the slowest, Nikki, then tossed her like a ripe fruit to the other.

The big male came on, catching Mavra first. Although she was fast, ten of her steps were two for the giant cyclops, and she was suddenly in the grip of its huge hands. The female came up behind, took her with amazing gentleness, and went back behind the rocks.

Renard was well away when he heard Mavra cry out, and he turned to see what had happened. That proved to be enough; the great creature caught him and shrugged off his futile blows. He turned, holding the man like a large doll, and joined his mate in back of the rocks. It was a little camp, obviously a temporary shelter for the shepherds in the area. There was a crude but huge wooden lean-to, with great straw mats and large, crudely woven wool blankets, and an outside barbecue pit of some sort, with hot coals and a rotisserie of smelted iron over it. Apparently some of them liked their meat cooked; a fresh-killed and skinned sheep was on the skewer. They also saw one of those big wooden carts, and it was into this that all three were dropped. Its sides were almost three meters high.

Mavra looked around. The cart stank of things she didn't want to know much about, and there were the remains of dried vegetation and even some of what looked like grass-roll. Nikki was huddled in a corner, crying, and Renard didn't look or act much better.

Mavra looked around. The planks offered something of a foothold, and she still had some of the thief devices in her mud-caked boots. She might be able to get out.

She looked around at the other two. *She* might, but never them. Her venom was no good at all; she'd tried both kinds on the two cyclopses, and they hadn't even noticed the scratch. Possibly their systems were too alien for it, maybe they were just of such great bulk that it would take more than she could produce to have a real effect. It made no difference. This was the end of the primary mission, and she had failed.

She peered out of a crack between the planks that was just barely accessible to her if she stood on tiptoe. The female was arguing with the male, that was obvious. There was a lot of bellowing and snorting and hand gestures, some of them unmistakable.

Finally he seemed to cave in, and went into the lean-to, coming out a moment later with a large iron screen. Mavra had a sinking feeling, which proved justified. The creature came over, looked in the cart, gave them a strange sort of leer, and slammed the heavy screen on top of the cart. He snorted once, then went away. Pretty soon, there were the sounds of munching and chewing.

Mavra looked at the screen. Its holes were a little too fine for her to get through, she could tell from the cart floor. And it was made of cast iron; there was no way she was going to lift it.

She settled down into a heap, and tried to figure out how to keep from being eaten.

South Zone

BEN YULIN GROANED AND AWOKE SLOWLY. HE TRIED to move, but pain shot through him. He could tell he was in a bed of some kind, that he was naked, and had some sort of blanket over him—but nothing more.

He opened his eyes, then moaned, and closed them again. It took several seconds until he was willing to try it again.

They were still there.

Closest was a large furry creature in a lab coat with what looked like a modified stethoscope around its thick neck. The thing looked like nothing so much as a giant beaver, complete with two huge buck teeth in front. Only the eyes were different—they were bright and clear and a deep-gold color, and radiated intelligence and warmth. Behind the beaver was the six-armed snake-man named Serge Ortega, looking concerned under his snow-white brush. The plant creature was there, too, completing the bizarre scene.

Yulin looked around uneasily, then spotted the figure of Renard, wearing some kind of great cloak tied around his neck, over near the door, looking bored. This seemed to snap him out of it.

The shape and manner was Renard, but the indefinable aura of confidence and control from the Renard-like figure marked him for Yulin as Antor Trelig. With that knowledge also came Trelig's final warning, and Ben Yulin tried to relax, to bring Mavra Chang to the fore.

"Where am I?" he managed, then coughed.

"In a hospital," the strange rodentlike creature replied. Yulin was surprised to note that the creature was actually speaking Confederation plain talk—with considerable difficulty, true, but understandable nonetheless.

The snake-man spoke up, his own Confederation speech clear and perfect. "Dr. Muhar is an Ambreza," he explained, at the same time explaining nothing. Seeing this, he added, "There is a hex on the Well World with your kind of people in it. The Ambreza are neighbors. Your people have had a bad time of it, and the Ambreza are used to working with your medical problems. That's why we summoned him."

"What happened to me?" Ben asked, still unable to move.

The Ambreza turned to Ortega, who spoke the required language as if born to it.

"You collapsed in the Polar Gate," the snake-man reminded him. "When we got that spacesuit off you, we found out you were a mess. Black and blue all over, three ribs broken, one of which, because of your walking so far with it, had dislocated so badly it punctured a couple of organs."

"Can you heal me?" Yulin asked, concerned.

The Ambreza clucked. "With a lot of time, yes," it said in a high-pitched voice, sounding like a recording played slightly too fast. "But it will not be necessary. We will put you through the Well."

Yulin tried to move, couldn't. Drugs? It made no difference.

"Renard, here, has been filling us in on what's been going on," Ortega said. "You all have been through a lot. I'd like to keep you around a while, but both Renard and Citizen Zinder have a sponge problem, and only the Well can cure that. Your injuries are critical. I don't know how you kept going."

Yulin laughed. "Fear. When you're running out of air, the pain just doesn't seem important."

The snake-man nodded. "I can understand that. A good attitude. We had to do a very quick operation just to save your life, that is, Dr. Muhar and his associates did. Lifesaving was our only goal, so we went

175

the most direct route. Now, I don't want you to panic when I tell you this, because it is *not* permanent, but right now you are totally paralyzed."

That didn't stop Yulin from starting in shock. Emotions welled up inside, emotions that may have been Chang's or his or both. Almost to his own surprise, he started crying softly.

"I said the condition wasn't permanent," Ortega assured the stricken human. "Nothing is permanent on the Well World when you just get here—and sometimes not even later. Take me. I was a man of your own race, tough and small like you, when I came here. The Well World cures what's wrong with you, but it changes you, too."

Yulin suppressed a sniffle. "What—what do you mean?"

"I was waiting until you came around to brief everyone. I've put the time to good use now, anyway. Now we know what we've got here, and that is a relief in and of itself." He turned to Trelig and nodded. "Bring in the girl."

Trelig went outside for a moment, then brought Zinder in. The conditioning was holding, Yulin noted. She reacted to the sight of Yulin in that condition exactly as the real Nikki would have reacted to the real Mavra.

"As I said, I would like to have kept at least one of you here for some time while we coordinate our actions on these new conditions," Ortega continued, "but with the sponge problem on the two of you and Citizen Chang's critical nature—we need a lot more than this clinic to help you—this isn't possible. As a result, the Embassy Council has decided that you are to be briefed and run through the Well as quickly as possible."

Trelig spoke for the first time. "This *is* an embassy, then? I guessed as much."

Ortega nodded. "*All* the Southern Hemisphere hexes have places here, although some don't use them. It's the only means of intercommunication possible. There are fifteen hundred sixty hexes on the Well World. The seven hundred eighty south of the Equatorial Barrier —you might have seen that it is really a barrier, too—

are either carbon-based life or life that can exist in a carbon-based environment. The Northern half, the other seven hundred eighty, contain non-carbon-based life. You experienced Uchjin, in the North, and you can appreciate how different some of the forms are there."

All three of the humans nodded in agreement at that.

"Anyway, let me start at the beginning. The beginning, as far as this place is concerned, was a race of beings your people call the Markovians. They were a great race. Looked something like giant human hearts with six evenly spaced tentacles. Just like human numerology generally was based on five, tens, or twenties, because of the number of digits, their base mathematics was six. The number dominated their whole lives—which is why we have hexagons, and why there are fifteen hundred sixty here. Almost a perfect number for folks who thought in sixes. There is even an idea that they had six sexes, but we'll let that go.

"Anyway, they reached the highest point of physical evolution it is believed possible to attain, and, as importantly, they reached the highest level of material technology possible as well. Their worlds were spread over many galaxies—not solar systems, *galaxies*. They'd build a local computer on one, program it with everything they could imagine, then put a rock crust on top of it. They built their cities there, and each Markovian was mentally coupled to the local brain. The architecture was only a common frame of reference, for, linked to their computers, they could simply wish for anything they wanted and the computer did an energy-to-matter conversion and there it was."

"Sounds like a godlike existence," Trelig commented. "What happened to them? I know a little about the Markovians. They're all dead."

"All but one," agreed Ortega. "Basically, what killed them was sheer boredom. Immortal, every wish fulfilled, and they felt as if they were rotting—or missing something. The height of material attainment was theirs, and it wasn't enough. Their best brains—and what brains they must have been!—got together and finally decided that, somewhere, the Markovian devel-

177

opment had taken a wrong turn. They decided that the race was going to rot and die from paradise, or they could do the other thing."

"Other thing?" Ben prompted.

Ortega nodded. "First they built the Well World, the ultimate Markovian computer. Instead of a thin layer of computer in a real planet, the whole planet was one massive computer. If a thin strip could create anything locally, then imagine a solid planet, about forty thousand kilometers around, of Markovian computer! That's what we're sitting on top of. Then they added the standard crust, so we're a little over forty-thousand kilometers in diameter."

"But why all the hexes, the different races on top?" Trelig asked the snake-man.

"That was the next step in the great plan," Ortega replied. "The greatest artisans of the Markovian race were then called in, all the material and philosophical artists they had. Each one was given a hex to play with. Each hex is a miniature world. Near the equator, a side runs about three hundred fifty-five kilometers, six hundred fifteen kilometers between opposite sides. They were carefully arranged. And in each one, the artisans were allowed to create a complete, self-contained biosphere, with a single dominant form of life and all supporting life for a closed ecosystem. The dominant life, at the start, were Markovian volunteers themselves."

"You mean," Trelig put in, aghast, "they gave up paradise to become someone else's playthings?"

The Ulik shrugged, which was something with six arms. "From sheer boredom there was no lack of volunteers. They became mortal, had to accept the rules of the game as set up by the artisans, and prove it out. If the system *did* prove out, the master computer established a world-set for the particular biosphere somewhere in the universe, and then the natives were transferred to it. They could speed up time, slow it down, anything. The world they entered was consistent with the laws of physics, even if it was created speeded up. At the right evolutionary moment, *zap!* The race was inserted. Then a new race was created to replace the one that left, and the experiments started all over again."

"What you're saying," Yulin commented, "is that we are all Markovians. That is, their descendants."

Ortega nodded. "Yes, exactly. And the races here now are the last batch—that is, the descendants of the last batch. Some didn't go or want to go, some hadn't proved out, when there became too few Markovians to supervise the project. We're the byproducts here of the shutdown."

"And these races have lived here since?" Trelig asked.

"Oh, yes," Ortega replied. "And time exists here. You get old, you die. Some die young, some live longer than you'd think possible, but there's a generational turnover anyway. The population's maintained by the computer—if a hex gets too heavily populated, the birth rate goes to a minus for a while. Too low a population from disasters, fights, whatever, and suddenly a sexy race gets back up there. The population varies with each hex, of course. Some races are big enough that there are only a quarter-million or so people, others can handle up to three million."

"I don't understand why pests and plagues aren't spread over the place," Yulin told him. "And how come there aren't a lot of wars? It would seem alien races on the whole wouldn't like the others."

"That's true," Ortega admitted. "But you might call it good systems engineering. Pests there are, but there are subtle changes in soil or atmospheric content that tend to inhibit or stop them, also geographical barriers —mountains, oceans, deserts, and the like. As for bacteria and viruses, we have them aplenty, but the various racial systems are just different enough that microbes that work against one race won't have any effect on another."

He paused for a minute, then remembered the other part of the question.

"As for wars," he continued, "they're not practical. Oh, there are local fights, but nothing catastrophic. Hexes are so arranged that the ground rules differ. We believe that that was done to simulate the problems from lack of resources or somesuch on the various *real* worlds the people would be going to. As I said, the natural laws had to be maintained. So in some hexes, everything works. In some, there is limited technology—say, steam engines work, but electrical generators won't hold a charge. In some only muscle power will do. That's what happened to your ship— it flew into a limited nontech zone, it wouldn't work, and down you came."

Trelig brightened. "So *that's* what happened! And that's why the power *did* come on for the time I needed to get the wings down and window cover up! We had drifted over a high-tech hex!"

Ortega nodded. "Exactly."

"But," Yulin objected, "wouldn't a high-tech hex conquer a low-tech one?"

Serge Ortega chuckled. "You'd think so, wouldn't you? But, no, it doesn't work that way. A high-tech hex becomes *dependent* on its machines, as you were in the North. It learns how to maybe make flying machines and fantastic guns and such—and then it has to invade a hex where none of that works. And where two hexes of the same type border, well, one is land and the other water, or one has an atmosphere extremely uncomfortable to the other, or something like that. One general, long ago, *did* try conquest by allying various kinds of hexes in order to have the proper one for each hex fight in the appropriate manner; but his plan worked only to a point. Some hexes he had to skip for atmospheric conditions or tough terrain or the like, and eventually his supply lines for all these races grew too long to sustain. The unconquered ones chopped him to pieces in the end. There have been no wars since—and that was over eleven hundred years ago."

They were silent for a minute, then Trelig asked, "I know how *we* got here, but—you said you were once one of us. How did *you* get here?"

Ortega grinned. "We get occasional new arrivals all the time—about a hundred a year. When the Markovians left their last planets, they didn't turn off their computers—couldn't. There is a kind of matter transmission—we don't understand it—connecting all the worlds with this one. The last Markovian simply couldn't close the door behind him. It opened whenever someone wanted it to open, and those old brains can't tell a Markovian remote and altered descendant from the real thing. So if you really want the door to open, it will and you wind up here. In ninety-nine percent of the cases, the people involved didn't even know about the doors. They just wished they were somewhere else, or somebody else, or that everything was different when they happened to be in the neighborhood of a door. I literally flew through one—the planet was mostly gone, but just enough remained."

"You knew about them?" Yulin prodded.

"No, of course not. I was getting old and I was bored and I could see nothing but a dreary sameness in the future until death claimed me. You get introspective when you're a pilot. Pop! Wound up here."

"But how did you get turned into a giant snake?" Trelig asked him, without the slightest trace of embarrassment.

Ortega chuckled. "Well, when you first arrive somebody greets you. You're what they call an Entry. They brief you, if they can, then shoot you through the Well Gate. It basically processes you into the computer. By a system of classification we don't know or understand, the computer then remakes you into one of the seven hundred eighty races here and drops you into the hex native to that form. You get acclimation thrown in, so you get used to being what you are pretty quickly. Then you're on your own."

"But the matter-transmission system is still on," Trelig noted.

"Yes and no," the Ulik responded. "There is usually a Zone Gate and sometimes two in each hex. You can use that to go from your hex to here, South Polar Zone, and from here back to your own hex. But should you be ten hexes away and go through the Gate, you'll still wind up here—and then back home. The big Well input, however, is that alone—you can come here from a Markovian world, but not go back. That was done, I suspect, to commit the original volunteers who had second thoughts. The only other gates are the ones between North and South zones, the one you came through. The Uchjin—those creatures you first saw—didn't know who you were, but they knew you didn't belong there or in the Northern Hemisphere. They passed the buck to North Zone, and they sent you down here. Now it's your turn to go through the Well."

Trelig looked uneasy. "We become something else? Some other creature?" he said, uneasily.

Ortega nodded. "That's right. Oh, there's a one in seven hundred eighty shot of staying what you call human, but it's unlikely. You have to do it. You have no choice. There's no other way out."

They considered that. "Those others—the Entries. Are there . . . nonhuman entries?"

"Sure!" the Ulik answered. "Lots. Most, in fact. Even some real surprises—creatures that are nontech here, proving that it's easier where they are than the problem set for them here. And some high-tech ones we've never seen. Even the North has a bunch, almost as many as we have. We have here a collection of stored spacesuits in forms and sizes you wouldn't believe. We use them occasionally when somebody has to go north. There's some trade, you know. We have tiny translator devices, for example, that are grown in a crystal world up there that needs iron for some reason only they know. The things work. Anybody wearing one will understand and be understood by any other race, no matter how alien."

"You mean there isn't a common language here?" Yulin almost exclaimed.

Ortega gave that low, throaty chuckle again. "Oh, no! Fifteen hundred sixty races, fifteen hundred sixty languages. When life and surroundings are different, you need to think differently. When you go through the Well you'll emerge thinking in the language of your new race. Even now I have to translate, though, by practicing with other Entries. I've become quite proficient at it."

"Then we'll still remember Confederation." Trelig's words were more a statement than a question.

"Remember it, yes," the snake-man replied. "And use it, if your physical anatomy permits. A translator causes problems, though. You automatically get translated, so managing a third tongue is nearly impossible. But with a translator you hardly need it. If your new race uses them, try to get one. They're handy things." He paused, looked at the plant-thing and the Ambreza, seeming to note some worsening in Yulin's paralysis. "I think it's time," he concluded softly.

They nodded, and a second Ambreza came in and two giant beavers moved Yulin carefully onto a stretcher.

"But I don't—" Trelig started to protest, but Ortega cut him short.

"Now, you can ask questions forever, but you have the sponge and she has even more immediate problems. If you can ever get to a Zone Gate, come back and visit. But now, you go." The tone was very insistent. There would be no more argument. The fact that Trelig and Zinder didn't actually have a sponge problem was beside the point; their own cover story had rushed things.

They came finally to a room similar to the Zone Gate they'd used in getting from North to South.

Yulin went in first; he had no choice. He thanked them all, and hoped he would see them again. Then the two stretcher-bearers upended the body of Mavra Chang so it fell forward into the black wall. Zinder looked hesitant and had to be coaxed, but then he went. Finally, Trelig was left alone with the curious assembly of aliens. He was resigned. There was much to be learned, but his hand was forced. There would be other times, he told himself.

He stepped into the blackness.

Ortega sighed, turned to Vardia. "Any news of the other ship?" he asked.

"None," replied the Czillian, the mobile plant-creature who had met them. "Are they as important now as they were?"

Ortega nodded. "You bet. If what those people told me was true, we have some first-class villains up there, probably on the loose. And two of them know a hell of a lot about Markovian mathematics. Dangerous people. If they should fall into the wrong hands, and that ship were rebuilt so they got back to this New

Pompeii and its computer—maybe they could lick the problems. *They* would control the Well."

"That's pretty far-fetched," the Czillian objected.

Ortega sighed. "Yeah, but so was a funny little Jew named Nathan Brazil, and you remember what *he* turned out to be." The plant-thing bowed, the equivalent of a nod. "The last living Markovian," it breathed.

"I wonder why this crisis hasn't attracted him?" Ortega mused.

"Because it's *our* crisis," Vardia replied. "Remember, to the Well this isn't a problem at all."

Near the Teliagin-Kromm Border, Dusk

A TINY FIGURE MOVED SILENTLY DOWN ON THE SIDE of the mountain and was soon joined by a second, then a third. A few others hovered nearby on silent wings.

"There they are!" one whispered, pointing down below to the shepherd's lean-to and cart where Mavra Chang, Renard, and Nikki Zinder were trapped.

"Amazing they made it this far," another whispered.

The first one, the leader, nodded in agreement. Unlike the cyclopses, their night vision was extremely good. Although they could see in daylight, albeit poorly, they were basically nocturnal. The scene was bright and sharp and clear to them.

One looked over to where the two cyclopses were sleeping, snoring loudly.

"Big mothers, aren't they?" it said softly.

The leader nodded. "We'll have to sting them, and quickly. At least two of us for each one, more if possible. I don't think we can juice them too much for safety's sake."

"Will the venom work?" one asked.

"It'll work," the leader responded confidently. "I looked it up before we left."

"I wish guns worked here," the doubter persisted. "It's still risky."

The leader sighed. "You know this is a nontech hex. Percussion type might work, but we didn't have time to ransack museums and collectors." There was a pause, as if the leader sensed it was now or never. Troops are always better in action than waiting for it.

"Jebbi, Tasala, and Miry, you take the bigger one. Sadi, Nanigu, and I will take the other one. Vistaru, you take Bahage and Asmaro with you and see what you can do for the captives. The others stay loose and available. Come in anyplace you're needed if you have to."

They nodded to one another. The ones on the mountainside launched themselves gracefully into the air, and the teams split off to their respective missions.

Mavra Chang was asleep. She'd crawled up to that grate a hundred times and each time had almost fallen, her traction breaking before she budged the damned thing one centimeter. She had put the other two to sleep to stop their whining and then fallen asleep herself.

Suddenly she heard a noise, as if something fairly heavy had landed on top of the grate. The noise woke her, and, for a brief moment, she was confused. Then, suddenly, she remembered where she was and looked up. There was definitely something large standing on the cart, but the grating made it impossible to see just what.

"Hu-man? You hear me, hu-man?" a strange, soft voice whispered. It was heavily accented in a most exotic way, high and light, a sexy small woman's voice.

"I hear you!" Mavra Chang responded, hope rising within her, in a loud whisper—as loud as she dared.

"We are pooting the beeg theengs to sleep, human," the creature told her. "Be readee to be took out."

Mavra strained her eyes, trying to see what her

185

rescuer looked like, but it was impossible to see any-thing—just a blob of light against the greater dark.

There was a sudden roar. The big male cyclops had awakened, and he was agitated and mad. He swore a thousand growling oaths, then gave something that could only be a cry of pain. She could hear the sound of a great falling body even as his mate roared, yelled, and was, after a time, also felled.

Mavra Chang wondered what sort of monsters could fell such huge and powerful creatures so easily.

There followed the sound of more of them landing on the grate. That, in itself, was strange—the grate was big, but not *that* big.

She heard them talk—a strange language that sounded like a procession of sweet bells and tiny chimes. It bore less relationship to a language than the grunts and snorts of the sort the cyclopses had—a very beautiful but most inhuman sound.

There was the sound of activity, and Mavra could hear the sounds of many hands doing things around the grate, and the tinkling of those strange voices giving orders in wonderful music.

The one that knew Confederation, at least basi-cally, returned.

"Hu-man? How manee is down t'ere of you?"

"Three!" she called back, certain that the old threat, at least, was no longer a factor. If it were, these creatures wouldn't be here. "But two are drugged into sleep," she warned them.

A figure, seemingly a very small one, covered part of the grate, peering in. "Oh, yes! I see now," the creature managed. Speaking the strange language was obviously a real problem for her. "We weel have to pool the grate away from them, so you get ovar near t'em, yes?"

Mavra did as instructed. "Here all right?" she called.

"Is fine," the creature responded, and it was gone. No, it didn't get up or crawl off, she decided. It just went away. She wondered more and more what her rescuers were. It didn't matter. Anything was better than what she had, and at least one of them could

186

speak her language, and they were obviously there to undertake a rescue.

There was a pulling and tugging. The grate moved a little, then settled back down. They had obviously tied ropes or something to the thing and were trying to pull it away, but they were having difficulty with the weight. The bells and chimes grew much more intense. Mavra wondered if they were cursing or something. Even if they were, it sounded wonderfully melodic. They gave it another try. There suddenly seemed to be a lot of them, judging from the amount of tinkling bells she could hear, and they were obviously all on this one.

A sudden, loud, single low note and they all pulled. The grate went up, rose straight up and balanced on the far edge. For a moment Mavra was afraid it would fall back down, and she understood why they had had her move. But their tugging continued, and the grate finally toppled outward and fell to the ground with a clanging sound.

The shape returned above, then slowly seemed to float down into the cart until it stood on the floor not a meter in front of her, visible even in the darkness with Mavra Chang's night vision.

It was a tiny woman, a girl really, looking no more than nine or ten; about a meter tall, and finely and delicately featured, perfectly proportioned. Mavra decided in an instant that this was no child but a full-grown adult.

She was very thin and light, weighing certainly no more than twelve to fifteen kilograms, if that. There were two very tiny breasts, almost undeveloped but somehow right. The face was the picture of girlish innocence, youthful and angelic—almost the perfect face, she thought.

Then, suddenly, the girl seemed to glow. The light was real. It illuminated the entire interior and seemed to radiate from all parts of her body, a golden glow that was incredible and inexplicable.

In the brightness the rest of the details of the newcomer became sharp and clear. Its skin was reddish in color, a pale echo of the glow; its hair, seemingly cut and styled, was set in a pageboy, the strands blue-black. Two tiny ears, both sharply pointed, jutted out from either side of her head, and her eyes seemed to have an eerie quality, like a cat's, reflecting back the light. From her back, in neat pairs, grew four sets of wings, proportionately large to the body and totally transparent. The creature smiled, and walked toward Mavra Chang, palm up in greeting. As it moved forward there was a slight scraping sound. Mavra saw that it came from something very rigid extending from her backbone down to the floor itself. The protuberance was a much darker red than the girl's complexion, and came to a nasty-looking point that made a slight mark in the wood.

" 'Allo, I am Veestaroo," the creature said, and Mavra knew it was the same one who had spoken to her earlier.

"Mavra Chang," she responded. She looked at the still sleeping others. "The tall one is Renard, the fat one is Nikki."

"Reenard," the creature repeated. "Neekee."

Mavra didn't know if what she was about to say would mean anything to the creature, but she had to try. "They are on a drug called sponge," she told Vistaru. "They are pretty far gone and need help fast. They can no longer help themselves."

The creature's expression turned grim. She said something to herself in her native language, which, Mavra saw, came partly from within her and partly from a certain way that the wings were moved. There was no doubt, though, that the woman knew what sponge was.

"We weel have to get t'em far away fast," Vistaru told her. "And t'ey are so veree heavee."

Mavra understood the problem. It must have taken all of them to get that grate off.

"I can get out on my own," she told the creature. "Maybe I can be of some help outside."

The woman who could fly nodded, and Mavra started up the sides of the cart she knew so well with speed that astonished the creature. Climbing up over the top, Mavra did a flip and landed on the ground with a bouncy ease learned from jumping off two-storey ledges. She looked around, wishing again that her power pack worked.

The sky had cleared a little, and some of the light from the great globular clusters shone down, giving the scene an eerie glow.

She saw the two cyclopses lying there, one almost on top of the other, motionless. They appeared to be dead, but she couldn't be sure. No matter what, she had new respect for those hard things that just had to be stingers. These little girls packed a real wallop.

There were quite a number of rescuers—fifteen or twenty, anyway. They floated silently around, having no respect at all for the laws of gravity. Their wings made a slight humming sound that you could hear if you were close enough, but at any distance at all they were silent. They took to the air as their natural element—flitting, then hovering, then going off in another direction. Some were using their internal light sources now, and showed themselves to be a rainbow of colors. Some were reds and oranges, some greens, blues, browns, everything, and some were very dark while others were very light. Otherwise they all looked exactly alike. Some carried packs strapped to their bellies, obviously the source of the rope they'd used.

Mavra turned from them back to the problem of the cart. If it could be upset, that would be easiest. But how to do it? She called to Vistaru, who floated easily up out of there and over to her.

"Can you hook the ropes to this side of the cart?" she asked the creature. "Maybe if most pulled and a few of you and I pushed from the other side we could upset it."

Vistaru considered that, then floated up to a bright-blue companion hovering overhead. They talked in that music of theirs. The blue one hadn't turned on its own illumination, but Vistaru exposed both, and Mavra saw with some surprise that it was a male. A male who, except for that one organ, seemed absolutely identical to the females. She thought of Renard. The perfect form for him, Mavra reflected.

Vistaru returned. "Barissa say no, too moch dangar," she told the human. "T'ere is bettar way. Is latch on cart back, see?"

Mavra sighed and walked to the rear of the cart. There *was* a latch, a big wood-and-iron one, there obviously for loading sheep or something. Two of the creatures were working on it.

Mavra turned to Vistaru. "What are you called?" she asked.

"I tol' you. Veestaroo," she responded.

Mavra shook her head. "No, no. I mean all of you. The"—she struggled for a word other than creature —"whole race of you."

The tiny pixie nodded understanding. "We are Lata," she said. "At leased, t'at is what it comes out een Confedera-tion," she added. "My name be," there was a series of bell tones, "and the people be," more tones, "in our talk."

Mavra nodded, and saw just how hard it was for the Lata to talk. She apparently strained to translate every word and remember its pronunciation, and it was obvious that neither the grammar nor anything else was common between the human language and theirs.

Vistaru seemed to sense this concern. "Not worree," she assured the human. "We weel get t'em to help in time. An' we weel be a-ble to talk more bet-tar soon."

Mavra wondered what that meant but let it pass. The first order of business was Renard and Nikki; after that, there would be time for her own problems.

They managed to throw the latch, and it fell out and hit the ground. There was a sudden sharp series of bell tones which even Mavra interpreted as a warning. The two Lata hovering at the top of the cart pushed the back with an audible whack. It fell away and crashed down, forming a ramp. Pretty good hinges for hand-forging, Mavra noted.

She helped three Lata remove the unconscious bodies from the cart. The Lata male, Barissa, came over to her and motioned to Vistaru. He said something to her, and she nodded and turned to Mavra, who was thinking that sexual characteristics among the Lata weren't very pronounced.

"He say you can wake t'em op?" the translator asked.

Mavra nodded, and they watched in some surprise as she pricked each one of them with her nail.

"Nikki, can you hear me?" she asked.

The girl nodded, eyes still closed.

"You will get up and walk with me," she instructed. The girl opened her eyes, got uncertainly to her feet, and stood there. "You will walk when I walk and stop when I stop and sit when I sit," Mavra instructed.

She did the same to Renard, noting with satisfaction that Nikki repeated her every movement, about a meter away.

This seemed to excite the Lata. They tinkled and chimed all over. Vistaru came up to her.

"How you do t'at?" she asked. "T'ey want to know if you have stingars in hands."

"Sort of," Mavra replied, and they started off.

The trip was fairly easy. Mavra discovered that the top of the mountain range was also the border between the cyclopses' hex, which the Lata called Teliagin "becous' t'at is its name," and the hex called Kromm. The change was amazing. There was still a chill in the air from the rain, and the wind had picked up to unpleasant proportions when they reached the border. No lines, guards, or sentinels stood there; not even a sign to mark the spot, yet one knew it was the border. It was like passing through a curtain.

Suddenly the air was thick and muggy; it was so humid that Mavra was covered in perspiration in minutes. Insect sounds, vague and faint in Teliagin, were almost overpowering here, as if someone had suddenly cut on a giant loudspeaker. The air seemed thick, oddly scented, and slightly wrong somehow.

"Not worree," Vistaru assured her. "Deeferent, yes, but t'at is all. It weel not hurt you."

Maybe not, Mavra thought, but it was turning the caked mud back to real mud, and the ground itself got progressively moist, the vegetation almost jungle-like as they descended. At the bottom of the mountain was a swamp that seemed to stretch in all directions. The water didn't appear very deep—perhaps fifty centimeters—but it was dark and dank and foul-smelling and almost certainly hid deep spots. The water seemed to be stagnant, and smelled it. Moss was everywhere.

"Do we have to walk far through this?" she asked the Lata. "*You* can fly, but we can't."

"Onlee short ways," the pixie assured her. "Jost keep in back of me."

With that the creature turned her light back on—she apparently didn't like to have it on all the time, and they had all taken turns in lighting the way for them—and did a very nice imitation of walking on top the water. Mavra knew she was flying, somehow, but the effect was doubly eerie. She hovered so close to the surface that the Lata's stinger occasionally made a wake in the water.

The mud became terrible, and the water did get deeper, deep enough so that it seeped into her boots and made them feel awful. Oh, well, what the hell, she thought philosophically. Back to your beginnings.

They walked through the stuff for about an hour, until Mavra began to think that she was becoming one with the swamp. She was even beginning to get used to the odor, and that worried her. The thick growths thinned out. Even so, there was one last indignity, an underwater vine that caught her, and she went face down into, fortunately, very shallow muck.

Dutifully, Renard and Nikki, who had not tripped on anything, fell face down, too, and it took a little effort to collect herself and get them up before they drowned.

She used some of the water to get the muck out of her eyes, nose, and mouth, and, with Lata help, cleaned off the other two. It wasn't much of a cleaning, though. They all looked more monstrous than any creature they'd yet seen on the Well World. Even her gift from Trelig, her horse's tail, was so mud-caked it felt like there was somebody sitting on her rear end.

Finally everything cleared. It was a strange transformation—from horrible swamp to calm sea. Vistaru told her to wait, and one Lata, probably Barissa, who seemed to be the leader, took off for what looked like a far-off clump of floating bushes.

The sea, if it was a sea, was strangely beautiful. The sky was clear despite the oppressive humidity, and the great sky of the Well World, with its great multicolored gas clouds and bright stars, reflected an eerie and yet magical glow on the waters.

Suddenly she looked over to her left, sure she detected movement. She did. She stared in new wonder as one of the large clumps of bush seemed to break away and now head toward them, a bright-blue light shining atop it. The light, she knew, was Barissa.

The bush proved to be a giant flower. It looked like a huge rose, closed, flanked by a great, thick green membranous platform.

Barissa smiled and said something. She turned to Vistaru.

"He say ol' Macham is sleepee and grumblee bot he know the pro-blem and he weel tak you and the othars."

Mavra looked again at the creature. It was a bright orange, or would be if it were fully opened. From the center of the closed flower rose two stalks, like giant stalks of wheat. Following the Lata's lead, she stepped up onto the green base of the creature. Nikki and Renard followed, and imitated her when she sat down, cross-legged, on the edge. Vistaru came over to her.

"We will balance and take a break too. You just sit and ride. I hope you not get easee dizzee."

Mavra barely had time to wonder about that re-mark when she discovered its full force. The creature spun around slowly, then started moving out across the quiet lake. It seemed to move by this circular motion, and while the movement wasn't tremendously fast, it was somewhat unsettling. Closing her eyes helped a little, but her inner-ear balance still con-veyed the motion. She began feeling a little nauseated. After an hour or so she was simultaneously wishing she were dead and afraid she was dying. She was very seasick.

Dawn broke after what seemed like an eternity. She continued gagging occasionally and watched the two hypnoed people, whom by this time she envied, imitate her. Vistaru walked calmly around to her.

"You are steel sick?" she asked needlessly.

"You better believe it!" was all Mavra Chang could manage.

The Lata radiated concern. "Not worree much more. We are almos' t'ere."

By this point Mavra didn't care if they ever got "t'ere," wherever "t'ere" was, but she managed to look around her for the first time.

They were no longer alone.

All over, by the thousands, other flowers were moving, spinning, dancing in a great ballet on the waters. They created a myriad of colors and color combinations, graceful and particularly resplendent now that they opened to the brilliant rays of the sun. In other circumstances, Mavra might even have enjoyed the show.

The Krommian they rode was slowing now, to her considerable relief. It, too, had opened over them, forming a curtain of brilliant browns and oranges. The great stalks, she realized, were eyes—long, oval, curious brown eyes with black pupils that looked so strange it was as if a cartoonist had drawn them on. They were independent of one another and sometimes looked in different directions. Of the core, the "head" of the creature, little could be seen. A pulpy bright-yellow mass, it appeared, more like thick straight hair than the center of a flower. The spinning had slowed enough now that she actually managed to wonder if these creatures were really plants or some sort of exotic animal.

The creature finally stopped spinning entirely and drifted slowly toward something. This didn't stop the rest of the world from spinning, but it helped a great deal. They had traveled a great distance, that was for certain. Whatever means of locomotion these—people?—used, it shot them in the direction they wanted to go at many times their rate of spin.

Mavra crawled around slightly, making sure that her imitators wouldn't fall off doing the same, and looked in the direction they were drifting. She could see an island—a tall but not very large rock outcrop in the middle of the sea. There appeared to be an artificial cave of some sort in the face, jet-black and without perspective.

She suddenly realized it was a black hexagon.

Vistaru came around. "We dock up close to the Zone Gate," she said enigmatically. "You most tell the othars to go in the Gate." She pointed to the rapidly approaching blackness.

"Not me?" she asked.

The pixie shook her head. "No, not now. Latar. The Krommeen ambassadar say no to you for now."

Mavra nodded toward the huge cave or hole or whatever it was—it looked curiously two-dimensional. "That thing will help my friends?"

Vistaru nodded. "It is a gate. It weel tak' t'em to Zone. T'ey weel be put through the Well of Souls. T'ey will become people of t'is planet, like me."

Mavra considered this. "You mean—it'll change them into Lata?"

The creature shrugged. "Maybee. If not Lata, sometheeng. No more sponge. Memory back, all bettar."

Mavra wasn't quite ready to accept that, but she had to act as if it were true. It was certain *she* couldn't help them.

Seeing Mavra's doubt, and realizing it came from ignorance of the Well World and its principles, Vistaru said, "Evereebodee who come from othar world t'ey go t'ru the Well. Come out all changed. Even me. I once as you. Went t'ru Well, woke up as a Lata."

Mavra almost believed her now. It explained why the creature knew her language. But that brought up another question.

"Why not me, too, then?" she asked.

Vistaru shrugged. "Ordars. T'ey say you are not Mavra Chang. T'ey say you some sort of bad person."

Mavra opened her mouth in surprise, then closed it again. "That's ridiculous!" she exclaimed. "Why would they—whoever they are—think something like that?"

Vistaru shrugged. "T'ey say t'ey already met Mavra Chang, and Reenard, and Neekee. T'ey say you are fakars."

Mavra started to respond, then thought better of it

195

and sat down. She was mad as hell. It was the crowning touch to her being on this crazy world in the first place.

Somebody was going to pay for this.

South Zone

"THEY CERTAINLY *look* LIKE THE SAME PEOPLE," Vardia said in some amazement.

Serge Ortega nodded, looking at the two nearly comatose people lying on the floor in front of him. "That they do. Doctor?"

They were in the Zone clinic, and Dr. Muhar, the Ambreza who looked like a giant beaver, was examining Renard and Nikki Zinder.

"I wish I knew what kind of drug they'd been administered," the doctor said. "I've never seen anything quite like it. But it's brain-localized; the other infection isn't."

Ortega's busy eyebrows went up. *"Other* infection?"

The Ambreza nodded. "Oh yes. It seems to have infested every cell of their bodies. Some sort of enzyme, it looks like, and quite parasitic. There is evidence of tissue breakdown everywhere, and it's continuing at a fairly steady rate. Would you recognize this sponge if you saw it?"

The other two both shook their heads in the negative. "We have both seen the effects of it, long ago," Vardia told the physician, "but the pure stuff, under a microscope, no."

Just then there was a commotion near the door. It opened, and a creature new to the group stood there.

It was about 150 centimeters tall, and stood on two thick but jointless tentacles. It had some to spare—three more pairs, going up its midsection. Each seemed to have a cleft at its end, capable of picking up something much as a mitten might—or coil around, with the full forward part of the tentacle. It stood on the rear pair, but needed at least four to walk toward them. Its face was broad, with close-set, broad nose and flaring nostrils and two rounded eyes that looked like large velvet pads of glowing amber. Its mouth had a dislocatable jaw, and inside it was coiled, Ortega knew, a long and ropelike tongue that could be used as a ninth prehensile organ. It had two areas on either side of its head like saucers, and they were slightly offset from the head, yet seemed able to open and close on joints.

But as the creature entered the room, all else paled before the great wings, like a giant butterfly's, along its entire back, the wings of brilliant orange and spotted with concentric brown rings.

Both Vardia and the Ambreza stepped back a bit at this entrance. Ortega had no such feelings, although its grim visage was frightening, almost menacing. Neither of the others had ever seen a Yaxa before, but Ortega had. He even knew this one. He slithered up to the newcomer.

"Wooley!" he boomed. "I'm very glad you could come."

The creature remained coldly distant, but it responded, "Hello, Ortega." It looked over at the comatose bodies of Renard and Nikki. "Are those the ones?"

Ortega nodded, all business suddenly. "Dr. Muhar has some cell tissue under the microscope. Can you look into it or should we project it?"

The Yaxa walked fluidly over to the microscope, peering at the sample with one of those impossible padlike eyes.

"It's sponge," the creature said. "No doubt about it." It turned its gaze back to the two people on the beds. "How far advanced are they?"

"Five days with no dose," Ortega told it. "What would you say?"

The Yaxa thought a moment. "Depends on how they started out. The cell deterioration isn't far along, but the mind goes first. If they were around average intelligence, they should be a lot brighter than the village idiot—for about another day or two. Then the animal-reversion stage sets in. They become great naked apes. I'd run them through the Well as soon as possible. Now."

"I agree,"² Ortega told it. "And I appreciate your coming all this way to do this."

"They're from the new moon?" the Yaxa asked, its voice, even through the translator, cold, sharp, emotionless.

Ortega nodded. "And if *they're* real we got big trouble. That means we got fooled by an earlier set of duplicates, at least one of which was the head of the sponge syndicate and the other two of whom know the principles of operating the Well."

For the first time the creature showed emotion. Its voice was harsh, excited. "The head of the sponge syndicate? And you let it slip through you like that?"

Ortega turned all six palms up. "We didn't know. They looked just like them. How was I to know?"

"It's true," Vardia put in. "They were so nice and gentle and civilized—particularly that one," it gestured at Renard.

The Yaxa almost spit. "Agh! Fools! Anybody without sponge that long would have shown signs! You should have known!"

"Come on, Wooley!" Ortega chided. "You're a fanatic, and with good reason. But, hell, we weren't expecting this sort of thing. Everything's been more than a little crazy around here lately."

The great butterfly's nostrils opened, and it actually snorted. "Oh, hell. Trust you to screw things up anyway." It turned its great head, apparently on some kind of ball joint for a neck, and looked straight at him. "Give me the bastard's name. He won't always be so clever. One of these days I'll get him. You know that."

Serge Ortega nodded, knowing that nothing could stop Wooley except death. Sooner or later, if that man surfaced at all, it would nail him.

"Antor Trelig," he told the Yaxa.

The creature nodded its great, strange head as if filing the information. Then it said, "I've got to get back home. A lot's going on. You will hear from me,

198

though." And, with that, it turned, not easy in the clinic's space with those great wings, and went out the door.

"Good heavens!" Vardia managed. *Who* is *that?*"

Ortega smiled. "Somebody you used to know. I'll tell you sometime. Now we have more urgent work to do. We have to get these two through the Well, and I have to talk to the Council."

There was no Council chamber for the ambassadors. All communication was done through intercoms, both for diplomatic reasons and to make it easier on everybody. There wasn't much room for everybody, anyway.

Ortega summarized the events to date, adding, "I've put out tracers on the first batch, and I hope that anyone will report their whereabouts if they appear in your hex. *All* Entries are to be checked out. These people are tricky as hell."

The speaker cracked to life. "Ortega?" said a metallic, toneless voice. "This is Robert L. Finch of The Nation."

Ortega couldn't suppress a chuckle. "I didn't know The Nation *had* names," he remarked, remembering them as communal-minded robots.

"The Nation has its Entries, too," Finch replied. "When it is matters concerning such, the appropriate *persona* is selected."

Ortega let it go. "What's your problem, Finch?"

"The woman, Mavra Chang. Why have you left her with the Lata? Not playing any little games again, are you, Ortega?"

Ortega took a deep breath. "I know she should be run through the Well, and she will be, sooner or later. Right now she is more useful in her original form— the only such Entry on the Well. I'll explain all in due course."

They didn't like it, but they accepted it. Other questions followed, a torrent, mostly irrelevant. The tone of many was the usual, "it's not my problem," and Ortega got the impression that others were not being very straightforward. But, he'd done his duty, and that was that. The meeting ended.

Vardia, the Czillian plant-creature, had sat in in Ortega's office. There wasn't anything its people needed to know that they didn't already.

Except one.

"What about that Chang woman, Ortega?" Vardia asked. "What's the *real* reason you're keeping her under wraps."

He smiled. *"Not* under wraps, my dear Vardia. All six hundred thirty-seven races with Zone embassies know she's with the Lata. She's bait—a recognizable object that could smoke out our quarries."

"And if they don't take the bait?" Vardia prodded. "The fact that she's a fully qualified space pilot still in a form that would be best for operating a spaceship wouldn't have anything to do with your thinking, would it?"

Ortega leaned back comfortably on his long coiled body. "Now isn't that an *interesting* idea!" he responded sarcastically. "Thanks for the suggestion!"

If there was a sincere, honest, or straightforward bone in Serge Ortega's massive body, nobody had found it yet.

Vardia decided to change the subject. "Do you think they'll do it—report the Entries, that is?"

Ortega's expression grew grim. "A few might. Lata, Krommians, Dillians, Czillians, and the like. Most won't. They'll either try to bury them—which would be a mistake on their part they'll live to regret, I suspect—or they'll go along with them. Team up any of them with an ambitious, greedy government, and you've got the nucleus of that war I spoke about. An alliance and a pilot to fly the ship. Even a scientist who might be able to help put the pieces back together." He shifted slightly, turned to face the Czillian square on, and said: "And as for Mavra Chang—if we've got her, we have some control. If we put her through the Well, *they've* got her. No fuel for the fire yet, my dear. It's going to get hot as hell all by itself without the likes of you and me pouring oil on it."

Makiem

HE AWOKE AND OPENED HIS EYES. FOR A MOMENT, HE was confused, disoriented. Things didn't quite look right, and it took him half a minute to remember what had happened and what was supposed to happen.

He had walked into that blackness in the wall, and there had been an odd sensation, like being wrapped in someone's embrace—warm, probing, emotional; a thing he had never felt before. A drifting, dreaming sleep, except that he couldn't remember the dreams—only the fact that most, perhaps all, had been about himself.

I'm supposed to be something else, he remembered. *Changed into one of those weird creatures, like the snake-man or the plant-thing.* It didn't bother him, really, that he was to become something else; what he had become, however, would shape his plans for the future.

There was something strange about his vision, but it took him a little thinking to realize what it was. For one thing, depth perception had increased dramatically; everything stood out in sharp relief, and he had the strong feeling that he knew to the tenth of a milli-meter how far one thing was from him and from anything else. Colors also seemed brighter, sharper; contrasts, both between slightly different shades of the same color and between light and dark, were markedly improved. But, no, that really wasn't what mattered, either.

Suddenly he had it. *I'm seeing two images!* he thought. There was almost an eighty-degree panorama on both sides; peripherally, he could almost see in back of him. But straight ahead there was a blank spot. Not a line or a divider; it was simply that what was absolutely dead ahead was barely out of his range of vision. His mind had to be forced to recognize the lapse, or he wasn't conscious of it.

There was movement to his right, and reflexively his right eye shifted a little to catch what it was. A large insect of some kind—very large, the size of a man's fist—buzzed overhead like some small bird. It took him a little more time to realize that he'd moved the right eye independent of the left.

He put both eyes as far forward as possible. He seemed to have a snout of some kind; his mouth was large and protrusive. He was conscious that he was resting comfortably, almost naturally, on all fours, and he raised his hand up to his right eye to see it.

It was an odd hand, both strangely human and yet not. Four very long webbed fingers and an opposable thumb, each terminating in what appeared to be a small suckerlike tip where the fingerprint would be. Looking carefully, he saw that there was a print pattern inside the sucker. His hand and arm were a deep pea-green in color, with brown and black spots here and there. The skin looked tough and leathery, like the skin of a snake or other reptile.

That's what I must be, he decided. A reptile of some sort. The landscape was certainly right for it: jungle-like, with lush undergrowth and tall trees that almost hid the sun. What looked for all the world like a gravel-topped road cut through the dense vegetation. It *was* a road, and very well maintained, too. In thick brush like this, one would have to have road crews working constantly every hundred kilometers or so to keep the natural foliage back from the cleared area.

He had just decided to go over to the road and follow it to whatever passed for civilization when another of those large insects came by, perhaps two meters or more in front of him. Almost without thinking, his mouth opened and a tremendously long tongue, like a controllable ribbon, shot out, struck the insect, and wrapped itself around the thing. Then it was retracted into his mouth, and he chewed and swallowed it. It didn't have much taste, but the insect felt solid and went down well, and it helped the hungry ache inside him. He reflected curiously on his own reactions, or

202

lack of them. It was a natural, normal thing to do, and it had been done automatically. The concept of eating a live insect didn't even bother him that much.

The Well World changes you, all right, in many ways, he thought. And yet—he was still Antor Trelig, inside. He remembered all that had transpired and regretted none of it—except flying too low over the Well World. Even that might be turned to ultimate advantage, he told himself confidently. If such power could be harnessed in the service of those best able to use it, ones like himself, it mattered not what form he was in or what he ate for breakfast. If the Well World had taught him nothing else, it taught him that everything was transitory.

I wonder how I walk? he mused, chuckling at the absurdity of the question. Well, the eating had taken care of itself, probably that would, too.

He eyed the road and started forward. Much to his surprise, his legs gave a great kick and he was to it, unerringly, in two large hops—coming down after the first one in a smooth, fluid motion that already had him set for the next leap, and coming to rest in the loose gravel with no rolling, imbalance, or discomfort. It was fun, really—like flying, almost.

He tried just walking, and found that, if he used all fours, he could manage it with some effort, like a waddle. Jumping, or hopping, was the normal mode of locomotion for this race; walking was for the local stuff too short for a hop.

He looked both ways. One direction was as good as the other, he decided; both ends of the path disappeared into the thick growth. He picked one and started off. It didn't take long to come upon some others. He saw them from a great distance off, once he realized that a lot of the rustling he'd heard in the upper trees wasn't just birds and insects.

Ahead was a grove of giant trees almost set off from the rest of the forest, a small lake to one side. There were houses in those trees—intricate structures woven between the branches out of some straw or bamboolike material that almost certainly grew in the marshes.

One of the creatures appeared in the lower doorway

of one of the houses, looked around for a moment, then stepped out and walked down the almost ninety-degree angle of the trunk to the ground! Trelig understood now what those suction cups were for. Very handy.

The creature resembled nothing so much as a great giant frog, its legs incredibly long when stretched out for walking, a light and smooth greenish-brown texture from the lower jaw down to the crotch, the same rough spotted green elsewhere.

The creature went up to a large wooden box set on a stake near the road, sat up on its powerful hind legs, lifted the lid, and looked inside. Nodding to itself, it reached in and picked out several large brown envelopes. Trelig realized with some surprise that the thing was a mailbox.

He approached slowly, not wanting either to alarm the creature or to seem out of place. It shifted an eye in his direction—its head was almost too integral a part of the body to allow flexible movement, but the eyes made up for it—and nodded politely to him. He sensed that there was anger in the creature's expression, but not directed at him.

Trelig remembered that Ortega had said that the Well would provide the language. He decided just to talk normally.

"Good day, sir!" the new frog said to the long-time resident. "A nice day, isn't it?"

The other snorted contemptuously. "You must work for the government to say something like that," he growled in a deep bass that was not unpleasant but that seemed to originate from deep in the chest cavity. The creature held up one of the envelopes. "Tax bills! Always tax bills!" he almost shouted. "I don't know how the sons of bitches expect an honest man to make a living these days." The phrase wasn't really "sons of bitches," but some local equivalent, but that's how Trelig's mind understood it.

He nodded slightly in sympathy. "No, I don't work for the government," he replied, "although I might some day. But I understand and sympathize with your problems."

That statement seemed to satisfy the other, who

opened another envelope, pulling out a long yellow sheet of paper. He glanced at it, then balled it up in disgust.

"Hmph! First they want your life's blood, then they ask you to do them *favors!*" he snorted.

Trelig frowned. "Huh?" was all he could manage.

The frog-man tossed the rolled up paper slightly in his hand, like a ball. "Report any Entries that you might meet to the local police at once," he spat. "What the hell do I pay all these taxes for, anyway? So I can do their jobs while they hunch on their fat asses eating imported sweetmeats bought with my money?"

Trelig took the opportunity to glance at the tax bill. He couldn't read it, couldn't make any sense at all out of the crazy and illogical nonpatterns there. Obviously reading was not considered a necessary skill by the Well computer.

"You ain't seen no Entries, have you?" the man asked, not a little trace of sarcasm in his voice. "Maybe we'll form a search party. Go out yelling, 'Here, Entry! Nice Entry!'"

Trelig liked him. If he were representative of this hex's people, he would not find life unbearable.

"No," he chuckled. "I haven't seen any Entries. Have you? Ever, I mean?"

The grouch shook his head slightly as a negative. "Nope. And never will, either. Met one, once, a long time ago. Big, nasty-looking birdlike reptile from Cebu. Kind of a local celebrity for a while. Big deal."

Trelig was relieved to hear that Entries weren't boiled in oil or something, but the official notice that the man had received said that this was no ordinary case. Somehow, he decided, they were on to him. At least, he had to act that way. And he wanted to check out the lay of this new land before revealing himself, if he could. It might be easier than he'd thought, considering how automatically he was acting and how readily this man had accepted him. He hoped so.

"Been traveling far?" the man asked him.

Trelig nodded. Farther than this creature could imagine.

"Headin' for Druhon for the government tests, I'll bet," the frog-man guessed.

"Yes, you guessed it exactly," Trelig replied. "I've thought of nothing else since"—he started to say "since I got here" but caught himself—"I was very small," he finished. "At least it'll give me a chance to see the government in action, no matter what."

That started the other off again. "The government inaction is what you'll see, but that's the future for you. Shoulda done it myself when I was young. But, no, I had to get into farming. Free and independent, I said. No bosses." He let out an angry, snakelike hiss. "So you wind up being run by the government, bossed by the government, taxes and regulations, regulations and taxes. Some freedom!"

Trelig clucked sympathetically. "I understand you perfectly." He looked around, as if sensing time was pressing and he had an appointment. "Well, it was nice talking to you, and I wish you better luck and much prosperity in the future, but I must be getting on."

The man seemed to appreciate the nice comments. "Been a pleasure, really. Sure you won't come in for a drink of good beer? It's only an hour or two more to Druhon."

That was good news. His cup was running over today. "Thank you, no," he replied. "I must be in the city. But I'll remember you, sir, when I'm rich and powerful."

"You do that, sonny," the other chuckled. Trelig went on.

He wondered as he continued what the old man had farmed; there was no sign of fields or cultivation of any kind. Best not to ask and appear too ignorant, particularly with a wanted poster out.

There was also the matter of money. He saw a number of the creatures as he went on, living together in groups or singly, on the ground, in trees, and even some floating dwellings in the countless lakes and marshes. All wore no clothing of any kind, and he wondered where you'd put money if you had it. He worried that there was some sort of identity system that would unmask him. But, no, he told himself, technology was obviously primitive here. There were torch stands all over, but not a sign of a powered light or device. Besides, if they had such a system they wouldn't bother sending out all those wanted circulars on him.

More confident and proficient now, he stopped and talked to several others along the way. They were mostly plain, simple creatures, close to the soil. Females were slightly smaller and had smoother top skin than the males, their voices slightly higher and smoother, but they were otherwise identical. He was a male; their comments told him that, even without the skin-texture difference, he was a young one at that. That made the first few days easier. He was expected to be curious and not expected to know anything.

But he learned. A casual reference told him that the country, the hex, was called Makiem, as were the people. It was a common, although not universal, practice on the Well World to have the race name and place name coincide. He learned, too, that it was a hereditary monarchy—which was bad. But the hex was administered by a large corps of civil servants chosen by merit as the results of massive tests for their brilliance and aptitude from any class or walk of society—which was good. That meant that the king of Makiem would listen to and take seriously advice from anyone he considered qualified, thus decisions were almost certainly made not by the royal family but by an individual or council who would be the best, greediest, most ambitious and able people in the country.

His kind of people.

Druhon, the capital city, was a surprise. First, it was huge—a great city, really, carved out of the jungle and sitting on a series of low hills that raised it slightly above the swamp. There was a broad, clear lake off to the west, and it was crowded with swimmers. Trelig had been feeling slightly itchy and uncomfortable; now he guessed the reason. Although these were land people, they stayed very close to the sea that gave them birth, and they had to return to it occasionally to wet down their skins. Once a day, probably, although in all likelihood a washdown with a hose would do as well.

Another surprise was the buildings themselves. Great castles and huge buildings of stone showing superior masonry skills, and homes and businesses built of good handmade brick mortared so well that nothing would get through them. Heavy wooden doors also showed great craftsmanship, and figures of brass and iron on gates, fences, and doors were evidence of a fine artistic skill. Considering that this was obviously a nontechnological hex, these people had developed a really surprising, modern culture. His estimation of them, and his optimism, went up accordingly.

There was still the problem of money. He walked the streets filled with stalls outside the places of business, with great frog businessmen and women hawking their wares and calling and cajoling customers. And money they did have and did carry. Watching the Makiem buying at the stalls, he saw that they carried everything they needed or used in their mouths—the lower jaw area was flexible, roomy, and, when he tested it with his own hand, had a thin, rigid flap controlled by a small muscle in the back of the throat. Evolution had obviously placed it there to store food for long periods. Civilization had given rise to more practical and cosmopolitan uses. The flap on the outside contained enough folded skin that one might not notice it, but occasionally people went by who looked like they had goiters. Trelig finally understood that it wasn't because of physiological differences but because they had a lot to carry.

The sights and smells of the city also excited him. They were strange smells, odors that his former self perhaps would have found foul or offensive, but they smelled wondrous and sweet and new to him now.

And there were the tattoos, mysterious symbols drawn by some device on the underbelly. Not everybody had them—most of the farmers he had met didn't—but a lot of people here did. They were symbols of authority, he surmised. Policemen, perhaps, and government officials. Somehow he'd have to find out what all those things meant.

The police, who were his first worry, were easiest to identify. He didn't know just how many people lived in this city, but it was easily a quarter-million, most residing in four-storey brick apartments entered by walking up the walls. That created pedestrian traffic jams. He saw carts, lots of them, moving goods from one place to another, pulled by giant insects, larger than a Makiem, that looked a lot like walking grasshoppers. All this meant traffic control, and so there were traffic cops.

He checked out several, looking particularly at the big symbol on their chests—a sort of double wheel with two diagonal crossbars. To be safe, he decided to act as if a double wheel with any crossbars was a cop.

The city's size and complexity gave him no small measure of anonymity; he was just one of the crowd. It suited him for a while, although shelter would have to be attended to, and sooner or later he'd have to face the problem of money and food—there were no big, fat insects or groves around here. He'd never stolen anything small, but it shouldn't be all that hard.

He checked out the massive stone buildings with the towers and the flags. Government buildings without a doubt, the largest of which, with a tremendous amount of impressive brass grillwork and high iron spiked gates to snare the unwary intruder, was obviously the royal palace. At the gate there were guards armed with vicious-looking crossbows and pikes, and an impossibly complex symbol on their chests matched the ones wrought in iron at regular intervals in the fence.

The royal symbol, obviously. He was learning fast.

The itching was getting to him. His skin felt dry and uncomfortable, almost as if it was ready to peel off. He decided to head down to the big lake. It was a beautiful setting, particularly against the waning sun. A sparkling lake, fresh and surprisingly clean considering the nearby population, dotted with myriad islands and flanked by small but imposing granite mountains.

The lake was somewhat crowded, but not enough to cause real problems. He slipped into the water with ease, and found it surprisingly cold. The chill lasted for only a few moments, however, and then, somehow, the water temperature seemed to rise until it was just perfect. Cold-blooded, he decided. It wasn't the water temperature that had risen, but his body temperature that had lowered to match the water.

Swimming was as easy as leaping had been. His rear legs, large and thickly webbed, propelled him, and he floated naturally across the top of the lake. This, however, didn't get rid of the itch on his back, and when he got out a ways he angled downward.

A strange thing happened suddenly. A membrane came down over his eyes, transparent as glass, yet totally protective. And too, his vision seemed to alter, becoming less depth- and color-sensitive but tremendously respondent to changes in light and dark. His nose also seemed to close off by internal flaps, but he experienced no discomfort from not breathing. He wondered how long he could stay under; quite some time, he thought, and decided to test it.

The longer he stayed down, the less he seemed to mind it. He had the uncanny sensation that he was breathing, slightly and shallowly, although there were no bubbles. No gills, either. He finally decided that something in his skin could absorb a certain amount of oxygen from the water. It was not, as he found out with time, enough for him to live underwater, but it was sufficient for him to stay down at least half an hour, perhaps much longer, before coming up for air.

He came up near one of the islands and looked around. The water felt soothing and comfortable. Lazily, he turned and looked back at the hilly city. It was getting dark, and lights were coming on—and not just torchlights, either, although there were plenty of those. No, those strange glass streetlights he'd seen were what he guessed they might be—gas lamps. These people were at the peak of their technological limits.

The great palace, on the highest hill, was illuminated by torches and multicolored gas lamps almost completely. It had a fairy-tale look to it, an air of unreality that, he suspected, was deliberate.

Reluctantly, he headed back toward shore. Hunger was starting to creep into him, and there was much to do. He made shore swiftly, experiencing the slight shock of getting out of the water into what felt, curiously, like almost oppressively hot, thick air. His body adjusted to it in moments, though, and he went on.

He first looked for the inevitable low-dive district

common to all big cities, but, after much searching, he had to admit defeat. A lot of neighborhood bars, with big frogs reclining on form-fitting cushions so they almost sat up like humans, gulping beers and other spirits from enormously wide glasses with narrow stems. The glasses had one gentle flat side, and you drank by putting it to your mouth and raising the glass while throwing your head slightly back.

No dives, though.

What was missing, he decided, was sex. They just didn't seem to engage in it or be motivated by it. No romantic couples, no advances—lots of friendly groups, mixed and not, but nothing at all sexual. Even he, a mature and young Makiem, had felt nothing particularly inside him when near any of the females. Only the Comworlds where cloning was the norm and everyone was an identical neuter approached the sexlessness of this society, yet there were clearly two distinct sexes. It was a puzzle for later.

In his wanderings, he found that he had waited too long. The streets were brightly lit; so were the apartments, with some people relaxing on the street outside, others in their open doorways or, from the sounds, on the roofs. There were regular beat patrolmen, too.

He decided to head toward the outskirts of the city, the direction from which he'd come. Maybe something would present itself; if it didn't, well, he could always go back to that glade where he woke up and chance that, if, as was likely, it was somebody's property, he could use it as a base temporarily.

The female Makiem at first seemed almost heaven-sent. She was obviously well-off, perhaps a farmer just in the city for the evening. No tattoo. And young and very small.

And drunk out of her mind.

She couldn't hop; she could barely crawl, mumbling something to herself or perhaps singing although so badly and distorted that it sounded like the rumbling and croaking it was even to Trelig. She tried one last hop, fell flat on her face, and rolled over into a ditch. A nice, dark drainage ditch.

"Oh, shit!" he heard her exclaim loudly. Then, a

211

few seconds later, he heard tremendous snoring. She had passed out in the culvert.

He bounded over to her. His night vision was about the same as it had been as a human, and so, though it was dark and shadowy—and mucky—it wasn't a helpless situation.

She was lying on her back, big bow-legs outstretched. He took a moment to study her. He'd discovered, by necessity and experience, how a Makiem went to the bathroom and where, but by no stretch of the imagination could that apparatus be sexual. There wasn't much of a clue with her, either. A fine little puzzle, he thought sardonically. I know most of what it's like to be a Makiem except the facts of life. He turned to other, more pressing matters. He carefully felt her jaw-pouch; it definitely had something in it, perhaps a moneybag. He hesitated an instant, then shook her. She didn't wake up, didn't even react. He shook her harder. Still nothing.

Satisfied that she was dead to the world, he leaned over and tried to pry her mouth open.

And tried. And tried.

It was shut as tightly as if it were welded in place.

He was about to give up when she gave a great snore, and the mouth opened a bit as she turned slightly on her side. Carefully, he reached inside—and felt a smooth, bone-hard plate that fit so exactly he couldn't even get a grip on it. And then the mouth shut. She didn't wake up, it just shut, right on his hand. He tried to pull it free, and couldn't. He spent the better part of half an hour trying to get his hand out. She turned more, almost pulling him on top of her, but he couldn't remove that hand.

He was almost in a panic, particularly when her ribbonlike tongue came over to explore the object. He felt its stickiness and felt it wrap around his hand, wondering what he could do. There were no teeth in the front part of the jaw, but there were three rows not far back. If the tongue pulled his hand just a little bit more . . . ! Then, mercifully, the tongue recoiled and her mouth opened. She let out a nasty hiss and turned some more. He almost fell backward into the ditch and cursed softly to himself, nursing his hand, which was now feeling bruised. She must not have liked the taste, he decided with thanks. He sighed, knowing now that personal robbery here, unless it was armed robbery, was pretty near impossible.

He thought things over. He could drift for a while, make do, but only as a beggar and a fugitive. Force was out; he didn't know how to fight as a Makiem, and they'd probably beat the shit out of him. Furthermore, he would not be able to enter Makiem society at his own pleasure.

The only thing left to do was to turn himself in.

The guards looked bored. They sat there, motionless except for an occasional blink, as only reptiles could—but they were very much awake. Eyes were on him as he approached, and the crossbows were armed and cocked in their hands. Still, they looked like nothing so much as statues.

He marched up to one. "Pardon me, sir, but is this the royal palace?" he asked pleasantly. He had no desire to fall into the hands of local police or lower-level bureaucrats.

The guard stood still, but his eyes gave the newcomer a once-over that could almost be felt. The guard's mouth didn't move, showing once again that the sound-producing apparatus was elsewhere, but he said, "Go away, farmboy. No visitors except on Shrivedays."

"It *is* the palace, though?" he persisted.

"Naw, it's the headquarters of the limbush-producers union," the guard responded sarcastically. "Now, go away before you get hurt."

Trelig decided on another tack. He took a deep breath. "Are you still looking for any Entries like the circulars said?" he asked casually.

The guard's eyes lit up with renewed interest. "You know of an Entry in Makiem?" The question was sharp, businesslike, but interested.

"I do," Trelig told him. "Who do I talk to about it?"

"Me," the guard replied. "If I like what you say, I'll pass it on."

Like fun you would, Trelig thought. Only if there was something in it for you. "All right then," he said flatly, resigned. "If you're not interested then . . ." He turned to leave.

"Hold it!" called a different voice, perhaps the other guard. The tone was commanding, and Trelig froze, smiling inwardly.

"If somebody else gets it, and it *is* an Entry, it'll be our skins," the new voice pointed out. "Better we should take him to the old man."

"Oh, all right," grumbled the first. "I'll do it. But what's in it for us?"

"I know what we're in for if he's okay and we blow it," the other responded. "Go on."

Trelig turned back around. "Come on, you. Follow me," the first guard mumbled resignedly, and came to life, turning and slow-hopping with short motions up the brick-paved walkway. Trelig followed, feeling better. If, as Ortega had said, all the races of this universe—and this world—including humanity had sprung from a single source, all the races so created would have certain things in common reflecting their creators. Human nature was Antor Trelig's life and profession, and it didn't matter to him what form that human took.

They entered a side door of the palace, and went into a gas-lit room that was peculiar indeed. A guard was on duty, and nodded slightly to his leader as they entered.

Two walls of the room held a great many strange-looking similar devices. There was a top part that resembled giant padded headphones, and a rubbery suction-cup device with a hole in the center underneath. They were on spring-loaded coils of tubing of the same material. Above each of the dozens of such devices was a plaque with something in that crazy writing.

Trelig watched curiously as the guard took the headphones and placed them over his head, just behind the jaw joints where the tiny ear openings were. Then the suction cup was attached almost to the center of the tattooed insignia on its chest. The guard expanded his chest, letting go an extremely loud and annoying rumble.

Trelig understood the thing now. It transmitted direct sound to various points in the palace, the hollow tube itself moving the air. He suspected the voices sounded hollow, tinny, and terribly far away, but it worked. A primitive, nontechnological telephone.

Nontechnological, hell! he corrected himself. These people were tremendously advanced technologically. Everything that could work they had created, ingeniously.

"Yes, sir," the guard literally shouted, so loud that Trelig wished he had ear flaps to match the nose ones. "Says he knows of an Entry, yes, sir." Pause. "No, nothing odd." Pause. "Personally, sir? But—" Pause. "All right, sir. Right away," the guard completed the call, detached the suction cup, which coiled back into its built-in holder, and replaced the headphones on their rack. He turned to Trelig.

"Come on, you," he grumbled. He followed the guard out.

There were no stairs or ramps, and Trelig had a bad time when they reached a high opening, four walls of bare, smooth stone, obviously a junction for the hallways on the multistoried castle, and the guard simply started walking up the wall.

Trelig hesitated, then decided, hell, why not? If it doesn't work I think I can survive the fall. What he had to do, he saw from the guard, was press his fingercups solidly on the stone, pull himself up, then use leg-cups on the webbed hind feet to support him while he reached farther up. If he managed it in a smooth series of motions, like climbing a ladder, it would be effortless, but doing so proved awkward and slow for Antor Trelig. He was conscious of the guards' stares and chuckles in the corridor below, and heard the guard above growl, "Come on, you! Can't keep the old man waiting!"

He made it, with difficulty, to the third story, thankful that they didn't have to go any farther. *That* took some getting used to. Getting down, looking down the whole way, would be worse. He put the thought out of his mind.

They passed by great rooms, some sumptuously furnished with silks and fancy rugs and woven tapestries. A few doors were closed, but, no matter what, the place reeked of opulence. There was a lot of fancy metal art, too, and most of it wasn't brass or iron, either—it was solid gold, often encrusted with jewels of amazing proportions.

Finally they entered what had to be some sort of reception hall. It was rectangular, but too small to be the king's regular place. The ceiling was still a good ten meters high, and the walls were draped with maroon and gold velvet curtains. There was a thick rug of some soft fur from the door sill to every corner of the room, and a slightly raised dais near the far wall with the most comfortable-looking of those strange cushion-chairs he'd ever seen. He looked around, mentally betting himself that there was another entrance somewhere, probably just behind that dais.

He was right. The curtains behind the chair moved, and an elderly Makiem walked in on all fours, got up on the dais, and turned, settling back onto the broad cushion-chair. The effect was remarkably human, as if a man, leaning about forty-five degrees forward in a chair were sitting there. The old man even crossed his huge legs a little, and rested his arms on two small wooden adjustable rails.

The old one looked at the newcomer critically, then looked over at the guard. "That will be all, Zubir. I'll call you if I need you." The guard bent its head slightly and withdrew, closing the big wooden door behind him.

The old man turned back to Trelig. "You know the whereabouts of an Entry?" he asked, his voice crackling with energy. His skin was blotched and old and bloated, but this was a very lively individual, Trelig decided.

"I do, sir," Trelig responded carefully. "He has sent me here to find out what is in store for him before he turns himself in."

The old man chuckled. "Insolent, too. I like that." He suddenly leaned farther forward and pointed. "You're the Entry and you know it!" he snapped, then his tone softened again, became friendlier. "You are a terrible wall-climber, although a smooth liar. I'll give you that. Now, come! Who are you really?"

Trelig considered his answer. He could be any one

216

of several people, and perhaps be the better for it. Either Zinder was out—he was too mature to be the daughter and not versed well enough in technology to be the father. The same for Ben Yulin, and that wouldn't be much of an improvement, anyway. Renard or Mavra Chang? The former wouldn't hold up—too slick at the start to pretend to be a guard now; this old guy was no fool—and Mavra Chang would be conspicuous if alive. So the best he could do was try and get into their good graces by the truth.

He imitated the guard by flexing his elbows so that his body lowered to the floor, then came back up again. "Antor Trelig, at your service, sir," he said. "And who might I have the honor of talking to?"

The old man smiled slightly. A Makiem smile was far different from a human one, but Trelig recognized it. "Consider all the angles before you act, don't you, Trelig?" he said offhandedly. "I could see all the possible lies going through your head before the truth came out. As to who I am, I am Soncoro, Minister of Agriculture."

Trelig barely suppressed a chuckle. "And the man who really makes all the decisions around here," he stated flatly.

Soncoro liked that. "And what brings you to that conclusion?"

"Because the guard sent me to the minister of agriculture, not the prime minister, king, or even state security. You were his first and only choice. Those types know who's who."

Soncoro nodded. "I think I'm going to like you, Trelig. We're two of a kind. I like you—and I'll never trust you. You understand that. Just as you wouldn't trust me, in reversed circumstances."

Trelig did understand. "I'm much too new to be a threat, Soncoro. Let's say a partnership until then."

The old man considered that. "Quite so. You understand what you have that we want, don't you? And why we are delighted and relieved that you are who you are?"

"Because I can pilot a spaceship," the former syndicate boss replied easily. "And because I'm able to open up everything on New Pompeii." Trelig felt

217

vastly relieved. He had been afraid that he would wind up in a water hex, or, if not that, in a hex whose government had neither designs on New Pompeii nor people like Soncoro. But then, he reflected, if we have a common beginning, the odds were always in my favor.

Trelig looked at the old man. "You're going after the one in the North?"

Soncoro shook his head. "No, that would involve almost insuperable obstacles. We looked at it, of course. You went down a good ways in, in a nontech hex, so we would not only have to get to it, and no Southerner has ever been into the North, we would somehow have to move it close to two hundred kilometers to make it flyable, then set it straight up so it would be well away before the Well could snare it. And—this is equally important—to do it one would have to pass through a number of hexes with life so alien one couldn't understand it, control it, or trust it; and in some atmospheres that are lethal. No, I'm afraid we leave your ship to the Uchjin."

"But the other ship isn't in one piece!" Trelig objected. "It was my own ship. It would break up on the way in. The nine modules would be spread over half the Well World!"

"They are," Soncoro admitted. "But, tell me, would you need *all* the modules to make it fly again? Suppose you had a fabricating plant capable of building an airtight central body? And a couple of good electrical engineers to help do it right? What would you need then?"

Trelig was genuinely amazed. "With all that—probably the power plant and one or two modules to make certain you fabricated the new parts correctly. And the bridge, of course."

"Suppose you had the power plant and modules, but not the bridge?" Soncoro prompted. "Could it be done?"

Trelig thought about it. "Not impossible, but a hell of a lot more difficult. The computer guidance is there."

The old man nodded again. "But we have access to pretty good computers here. If I understand it, it's not the machine itself, it's just its abilities, programs, memory, and action time."

"And interface with the power plant," Trelig added.

"Not insolvable," Soncoro pronounced. He smiled wickedly. "Welcome to the family."

"But where are you going to get all this?" Trelig protested. "I would guess that if you could have a machine shop and computers here, you'd have them."

"Good point," Soncoro agreed. "But we won't be alone. What would you say if I told you that four of the modules were within six hexes of this one, and the power plant was seven hexes away? And that we had allies—a semitech hex and a high-tech hex, with complementing abilities?"

Trelig was intrigued. "But you're talking about a war!" he objected. "I thought war was impossible here!"

"For conquest, yes," the old man admitted. "But not for limited objectives. Dahla proved that you couldn't *hold* ground for any length of time here. But we need only take it, take it long enough to get what we want, and move on. Some of the hexes are simple, anyway. They will yield to us or just ignore us. Only a couple of them will be problems."

Trelig considered this, getting excited now. This development was beyond his wildest dreams! "But the ship should have come in at a definite angle. If five are attainable, then all of them should be. Why limit it?"

"We're not the only ones in the game," the old Makiem told him. "Others are moving now. Perhaps we can deal later, but the power plant is the one thing completely beyond our ability to construct. We have lots of spacefarers, but they are technicians. You know how to pilot—but do you know how to build a ship?"

"No," he admitted.

"We haven't had a Type 41 pilot, though, in a very long time. None we can get our hands on. I assume that progress has made much of their skill obsolete anyway. Correct?"

"Probably," Trelig told him. "The power plants, and therefore the knowledge of what to tell the computers to do, have changed radically just in my time."

"Then it's safe to say that only you, this associate, Yulin, and the woman, Mavra Chang, could possibly pilot the ship properly?"

Trelig nodded honestly, although he was aware of how much that increased his value. "If there are no human pilots here from as recent as a century, I'd say, almost definitely."

Soncoro seemed tremendously pleased. He leaned forward again. "This fellow Yulin. Is he trustworthy?"

Trelig grinned. "As trustworthy as I am."

Soncoro hissed. "As bad as that. That means there's little chance of a deal there, then, unless we get the power plant."

"You know where he is?" Trelig asked, amazed.

"He is a Dasheen, and a male, damn it all! That will give him power there. The Yaxa are already well along with their own plans, perhaps a bit ahead of us, and he will naturally ally with them if he can. So, we go and as quickly as possible. Whoever owns the power plant owns it all."

"Tell me two things," Trelig said persistently.

"Go ahead," the old man agreed.

"First, what would have happened if I hadn't materialized here as a Makiem? You're talking as if you were going to war anyway, it was all set up. Did you *know?*"

"Of course not!" responded the secret ruler of Makiem. "The way things worked out only simplifies matters. We would have seized the modules anyway and waited for one of you to come to us. You would have had to." His logic was unassailable. "Now, what's the other thing?"

"How do you have sex in this place?" he asked.

Soncoro roared with laughter.

Dasheen

BEN YULIN AWOKE WITH A START AND OPENED HIS
eyes.

His first thought was that the pain was gone, and
he had feeling over his whole body again. That was a
big relief in and of itself. But—where and what was
he?

He sat up and looked around. Things were definitely different. He was slightly nearsighted and totally color-blind. But he could see well enough to
tell he was in farm country; there was baled hay over
there, nicely if crudely done, and fences and small
roads stretched off for miles in squarish patterns. It
was flat country, too; although his vision blurred beyond five hundred meters or so, he could tell where
the land and horizon met.

He looked down at himself. Broad, muscular, hairy
long legs that looked somewhat human, although the
feet were strange—very wide and oval-shaped and
made of a hard, tough substance. There were breaks
in the front of each foot, but he had no toelike control of them. They were obviously just there to provide some flex when walking. He reached out and
saw that his arms were wrestler's arms—tremendous,
bulging muscles overlaid with a thin covering of stiff
brown hair. The fingers were short and thick and
seemed to be made of that tougher material in the
foot, but they were jointed in the right places and had
an opposable thumb. He reached down to feel his
feet and tapped them. They had a dull, thick, hard
feel and sound to them. He had almost no feeling in
his hands or feet, although the rest of his body felt
normal.

His skin was brown and mostly covered in that

221

short, wiry hair, although he perceived it as dark gray. One look at his crotch told him that he was not only a male but one of gigantic proportions. That pleased him, even if the thing was jet black. It was the biggest he'd ever seen.

His chest was covered with a milky-white coating of the same kind of hair; it was an even shape that followed his torso. The body, too, was thick-set and powerful-looking; he flexed a little and the muscles bulged.

This wasn't going to be so bad, he told himself.

One reason for the nearsightedness, he realized, was that his eyes were set differently. He put a hand up to his face—and found more. He felt it carefully.

It was a huge head but perfect for his body. A thick, short neck, and a *snout!* Not a huge one, but it jutted out from his face. He tried to focus in on it and saw it, a white-furred oval with a flat top, jutting out maybe ten centimeters from his head. It contained a soft, moist, broad nose—incredibly broad, almost the width of the snout—which he thought was probably pink, and two huge nostrils with some kind of flaps. There were also whiskers flanking the nose —sharp, fairly long, like extremely long white pine needles.

His mouth, under the nose, went the whole length of the snout. He felt around it with a broad, flat, thick tongue. Lots of teeth, none of them sharp. He opened it, then closed it, then tried a chewing motion. He found he could only chew from side to side, which told him that he was a herbivore. He knew now why they raised hay and wheat and the like and who it was for.

The eyes were large, set back from the snout, and wide apart. Ears were sharply pointed, and could be turned at will, he found. On top of his head was an enormous pair of horns. They were part of his skull, no doubt about it, and they extended into wicked points from areas of the base bone a good five centimeters out from either side of his head.

He rose shakily to his feet and found that his head didn't feel abnormally heavy or out of balance, although he couldn't turn it in any direction quite as far as he remembered being able to do.

There was a last touch. He found he had a tail on some sort of ball joint, a tail he could wag and even whip to an extent. It was thick and emerged from his spine, was probably an extension of it. It was brown like the rest of him except his chest and snout, and it ended in a thick tuft of soft dark hair. It was long, although it didn't quite reach the ground. He reached around, took hold of it, and looked at it curiously.

I wish I had a mirror, he thought.

He started walking, first over to the road and then down it. He wanted to find some civilization, somewhere.

It was a chilly day, although only the parts of him with no hair, his nose, inner ears, and genitals, told him so. There was some kind of natural insulation here.

He spied a large number of what looked like people working in a field, but they were too far away for his reduced vision to really see. He considered going over and introducing himself, but he decided that that sort of thing could cause trouble, too. This might be private property, and they might not like trespassers. He decided to press on until he came to a town or until he met someone on the road.

Despite the visual limitations, his other senses were tremendously heightened. Every little sound, from the rustle of an almost imperceptible wind to small insects off in a nearby field, were sharp and clear and could be localized with unerring accuracy. Smells, too, both pleasant and unpleasant, were much fuller and richer.

He was hungry and wondered what he was supposed to eat. The fields contained the fodder, of course, but they were also obviously private, and the high, thick barbed wire discouraged casual snacking.

He came to a small intersection; a minor road went off at a right angle to the main one. He could see it led up to a large complex of buildings, maybe several stories high with rounded roofs of straw or some other material over good hardwood frames. He wondered where they got the wood; certainly not from around here.

He decided to chance it. As a newcomer, he might be excused some indiscretions, if he were careful enough not to get shot first. Let's see—what had Ortega called new people? Entries? Yes, that was it.

Most of the workers or family seemed to be out in the fields. There were obviously few seasons here; some of the fields had been harvested, some were about to be, and one on his left had just been plowed.

He was almost to the house or barn, or whatever it was, when he saw his first fellow creature close up.

She—there was no doubt it was a she—was using a plane to smooth down a plow handle. She was taller than he, with smaller head and longer, more flexible neck. Her horns were shorter and more rounded, even at the tips. Facially, she *did* resemble a cow, although the head was not right, more like a cartoonist's humanized cow than a real one. Her arms were also strikingly different from his—tremendously long, with a double elbow that seemed to be able to bend in any direction. Not double in the same places, now; there was the elbow where the elbow should be, and then the arm continued, tremendously muscular, to a second elbow near the waist. Almost reflexively he looked again at his own elbow, and saw that he'd been right; although thick and muscle-bulging, his arm was definitely the one-elbow type he'd been born with.

The final incongruity was that she wore a tremendous, leatherlike apron tied just above her waist. It bulged a bit in front, and at first he thought she might be pregnant, but as she worked, side turned to him, he could see that it concealed what had to be a large, tough-looking pink udder attached just above the waist.

She still hadn't seen him. He considered clearing his throat but wasn't sure how to do that, so he just decided to try conversation and see if he would be understood. At least he would be noticed.

"Hello?" he said hopefully.

She jumped, turned, looked at him. There was no mistaking her mannerisms: shock and fear. She

224

screamed, dropped her tool, and ran off into the big building through a large wooden door.

He could hear her still screaming and yelling inside and also the sounds of other voices. He decided that the better part of valor was to stand there and see what happened next.

What happened took exactly thirty seconds. The wooden door flew open with tremendous force, so violent and loud was the action that it shook the whole building. Standing there, a really nasty-looking iron crowbar in his hands, was the master of the house.

He was slightly shorter than Yulin, but not much. The horns were huge, slightly curved and pointed; the head was massive and seemed to sit atop the torso without a neck. He wore a cloth kilt of some soft material from his waist to just below his knees. His huge, wide eyes sparked fire.

"What the hell do you want here, he-cow?" he snarled derisively. "If it's a cracked skull, just stay there another ten seconds!" He hefted the crowbar menacingly.

Yulin felt panic rising in him, but managed to control himself. "Wait a minute! I mean no harm!" he managed.

The crowbar didn't move. "Then what are you doing just walking into here stark naked and panicking good women?" the other returned, that menacing tone growing. But, Yulin realized, he'd answered instead of attacking, and that meant reason could prevail.

"I'm an Entry!" he almost yelled. "I just woke up in a field back there and I haven't the slightest idea where or what I am or what to do next!" *That* was certainly the truth.

The big minotaur considered this. "Entry?" he snorted. "We have had only two Entries before that I know of, and they were both cows. Doesn't make sense to have a bull Entry." Still, there was something that made him hesitate. The crowbar lowered ever so slightly.

"I'm Ben Yulin," he tried, attempting to sound friendly and not scared to death. "I need help."

There was something in the newcomer's manner

225

that didn't seem right to the farmer. Yet he sensed, somehow, the genuineness of Yulin's plea.

"All right," growled the man with the crowbar. "I'll accept your story for now. But try anything funny and I'll kill you." He didn't let go of the crowbar. "Come on in and we'll at least get some clothes on you so you don't have half the herd coming after you."

Yulin started toward the door, and the farmer hefted the bar again. "Not in *there,* you idiot! Holy shit! Maybe you really *don't* know what's what around here! Just walk around the house, here, and I'll follow."

Yulin did as instructed, and entered a different door in what seemed to be a complex semidetached from the larger buildings. It was an apartment of sorts. There was a living room with small fireplace, a bull-sized rocking chair of a finely polished hardwood, windows looking out on the farm, and, to his surprise, artwork and reading material. A number of very large-sized books in a print he couldn't read sat on two shelves, and there were pewter sculptures, not only of other minotaurs, both male and female, but of other, stranger subjects that implied surrealism. Some etchings on the wall, actually black-and-white line drawings, showed farm scenes, sunsets and other realistic subjects.

The female sculptures showed him what he'd suspected—the cow did have big udders, like bulges hanging down—and a couple of the sketches, or prints, or whatever they were were rather graphic pornography. On top of a table near the rocking chair was a weird-looking mechanical device he couldn't figure out. It was a box with a horizontal round plate that obviously rotated by means of a spring-driven hand crank on one side. A complex brass device on a single pivot was mounted to one side, and out of the back rose a tremendous horn-shaped device. There seemed also to be a place for another horn to fit on the front. Yulin couldn't imagine what it did.

The man went into another room and seemed to be trying to open some sort of cedar chest with one hand while at the same time keeping his eye on the newcomer through the doorway. Yulin decided to stay stock still in the center of the room and do nothing at all.

The other room was obviously a bedroom, though. There was a wood frame there filled with a strawlike material, and there were also some carelessly tossed blankets and an enormous stuffed object that might have been a pillow. Thinking about his horns, Yulin wondered what happened if you rolled over in your sleep.

The farmer threw him a large cloth, and he caught it. It appeared to be made of burlap, much rougher and coarser than what the other wore. There had been rope drawstrings placed in it, and Yulin got the idea pretty quickly of how to put it on.

There was a thin, plain rug on the floor. "You'll have to sit there," the farmer told him, pointing to a spot on the rug. "I don't get much visitor traffic here." He sat down comfortably in the rocker and started to rock gently.

"Now can you tell me what happens next?" Yulin prompted.

"First you tell me about yourself. Who you are, what you were, how you got here," the other responded. "Then, if I like what I hear, I'll help you solve your problems."

Yulin complied, almost. He spared nothing, except his role in anything shady. He pictured himself as Gil Zinder's assistant, nothing more, forced by the evil Antor Trelig to do what he did. He was convincing. When he got to the part about crashing in the North, the farmer's eyes almost shone. "Been to the North, eh? That's kind of a romantic thing for just about all the folks here in the South. Kind of exotic and mysterious."

Yulin thought that the South was sufficiently exotic and mysterious for him, but he said nothing. His story, however, was accepted. It was far too detailed to have been created out of whole cloth as a diversion. The farmer relaxed.

"My name's Cilbar," he said, more friendly now. "This is my farm. You're in Dasheen, which is both the country and the name of your new people. You're a herbivore, so you'll never starve to death—although,

227

as a civilized man, you'll find that while eating stuff in the raw will satisfy your hunger, prepared foods are better. The hex is nontechnological, so machines don't work here unless they're muscle-powered. We got the muscle, as you probably noticed."

Yulin admitted he had.

"I been around in my youth," Cilbar continued. "Things are different everyplace, of course, but our system here's a little more different than most. It's the biology that does it. We get criticized by some other hexes, but that's the way things are."

"What do you mean?" Yulin wondered.

Cilbar sighed. "Well, a lot of races, they have two, maybe more sexes. Your old one did. There's some differences, but basically they're variations of the same critter. Brain power's the same, and take away the sex stuff and the bodies aren't that far different, either. Right?"

"I'm following you," Yulin replied.

"Well, you mighta noticed that we don't look like the cows," the farmer said. "Not just the udder. We're smaller, squatter, got shorter single-elbow arms, bigger, different heads, like that."

"I did notice it," Ben Yulin acknowledged.

"Well, we *are* different. Don't know why. First of all, there's only an average of one male for every *one hundred* females. That's why I was surprised not that you were an Entry but that you were a male. You see?"

Yulin did. All the more remarkable since he'd gone through the Well as a biological female. What was it Ortega said? The Well classified you according to unknown standards.

"Anyway," Cilbar continued, "just from a social standpoint that makes males more important than females. There's less of us, so we're not expendable. On top of that, we're a hell of a lot smarter."

"How's that?" was all Yulin could manage.

Cilbar nodded. "Some scientists from a couple of other hexes once came in to prove to us that it wasn't so. All they did was bear out what we already knew. Their brains are less developed. Trying to teach one to read is like trying to teach this chair. Oh, teach 'em to do any basic job and they'll happily do it for hours. Plowing, harvesting, simple carpentry, hauling and such, sure. Hell, tell 'em to dig fence holes and they'll happily do it forever until you call 'em off. Ask 'em how *many* holes they dug and they couldn't tell you."

The green light of understanding went on in Ben Yulin's head. "You mean," he said, "that the women do all the labor and the men run things?"

Cilbar nodded again. "That's about it. The women built this farm, but a man designed it. The women work it, but I run it. Same with the art, the books— all by men for men."

Yulin was intrigued, and he thanked the Well even more that he'd come out as he did. This was the kind of place he was going to *like*.

"You speak very well, very cultured," the Entry remarked. "You have a lot of education?"

The farmer chuckled. "Every male gets everything we can give him. I think we're a group of spoiled brats, myself. I often wonder what we'd have to do in a pinch if things get tough. Yeah, a son is special. He gets it all. Then, if he's got some particular aptitude, like art, or writing, or teaching, or trading, he takes it up. If not, like me, he takes over somebody's farm when they get too old or too tired."

"There's a small population here, then," Yulin surmised.

He nodded. "Very small. About ten thousand farms, more or less, with a bunch of small towns, rarely more than a few thousand in each, servicing them. A million and a quarter tops, no more."

"That means only a hundred thousand or so males," Yulin pointed out.

"Probably less," agreed Cilbar. "I may be way overestimating the number. We don't get around too much once we settle down. One time I remember somebody saying in some class that there were only seven hundred fifty thousand Dasheen and seventy-five thousand bulls. Could be."

"And what happens if the new young bull has no useful aptitudes and no farm's open?" Yulin wondered.

"Thinking about yourself, eh? A scientist in a non-tech hex! I can see the problems. Well, you can find a skill or job, do some traveling while you wait for an opening, like I did, or you can pick a farm, call out the owner, and fight him to the death, winner take all."

Suddenly Yulin understood why the farmer had been so upset at his initial appearance: he thought a young bull was calling him out.

"What kind of government do you have, then?" he asked.

"A small and simple one," Cilbar told him. "All the farmers in a district elect somebody to a council. The towns elect one for every ten males. There's a small bureaucracy to keep things together, and we meet in emergencies or twice a year for a few days in a small town named Tahlur in the center of Dasheen, where the training schools and the Zone Gate is."

"That's where I should head, then," the ex-scientist decided. "If I can get there without starving to death or getting run through by somebody less willing to listen to me than you."

Cilbar laughed deeply. "Look, they've called a council meeting for some time next week. Our own representative, Hocal, will be going. I'll feed you, put you up for the night, and get you introduced to him. That should solve that problem."

Yulin thanked him. This was too easy, he thought, and too good. There had to be a fly in the ointment somewhere, and he waited for it.

Hocal wasn't the fly but he was the instrument of it. He looked very surprised when Yulin was introduced to him.

"That's what all this business is about!" he exclaimed. "You people really messed up some things! Never thought one of you'd show up here, though. Seems some folks want to talk to us about reclaiming some of those parts of that spaceship. War's been rumored. War! I hope we can keep out of it, but we'll see. We're right in the middle of things here geographically."

Yulin suddenly became interested. "How's that? You mean the *other* ship, the one that came down in the South here?"

Hocal nodded, and got down a large map, spreading it out on the table in front of him. It was ingeniously printed for the benefit of a color-blind race; it contained all the details in amazing black, white and gray contrasts. Yulin could interpret it, but he could not read the key or names. He would have to cure that, he decided.

Hocal pointed a stubby finger at one hex. "Here we are in Dasheen," he said.

Yulin looked. They were close to the Equatorial Barrier, something Hocal translated as Cotyl occupying two half-hexes at the Barrier; then Voxmir to the northwest—unfriendly and inhuman, Hocal assured him; Jaq to the southeast—volcanic and hot as hell, too hot for a Dasheen to survive; Frick to the southeast—they had crazy, fat flying disks with steam jets; and Qasada to the southwest—from the description a highly advanced technological civilization of giant rats.

"This is where the problem is," Hocal pointed again. Just below Qasada and to the southwest of Frick was Xoda, a land of great, fierce insects—and a module. "There's another in Palim, below it, Olborn, to the southwest, and, most important, only four hexes south, Gedemondas, about which little is known. The engines of the downed craft landed there, and they are, as you will appreciate, the big prize. I suspect we'll know a lot more about Gedemondas before this is finished."

Yulin nodded. "I'd think that one of the others—the rats, for example—might make a better run for it," he noted.

Hocal agreed. "They should, but that's a funny area. The races in there aren't that friendly, or, like the Palim, have been, like us, peaceful too long to think of conflict. No, the trouble comes from way over here."

He pointed again far to the west, well beyond the far coast of the Sea of Storms.

"This is Makiem, and up here is Cebu, and to the east is Agitar. Makiem is run by some clever and ruthless politicians and is a nontech hex, as we are. Cebu is semitech, and its people have the power of flight, which is particularly useful. Agitar is high-tech, and while we've been able to learn very little about it, they seem to have flying animals—which means their range isn't limited by their machines—and some natural abilities with electricity that transcend the Well limits. They have formed an alliance to get the ship parts."

"But they couldn't use them, even if they put them together, without a qualified pilot," Yulin objected. "That's not a simple rocket, you know."

"We are well aware of that," replied Hocal, looking directly at him. "The war was to be the topic, but, I suspect, with you on hand, the discussion will be even livelier."

The trip was easy and made in less than two days. They went in a comfortable coach pulled by six Dasheen cows from Hocal's herd, and they made better speed than Yulin would have believed.

Additionally, the tired pullers did everything for them, cooking delicious stews, rubbing them down, everything. Yulin loved being waited on; he saw how easy it would be to get spoiled here. The cows engaged mostly in small talk among themselves, occasionally playing childish sort of games with one another, but they carried out their jobs without complaint, as if this was what they were born to do and they were happy doing it. In deference to his host, Ben Yulin kept at a distance from them.

They arrived at Tahlur at midday to find most of the other members already there. They were taking nothing lightly, and grave discussions were already underway in the town's alehouses. As on the farm and road, the females did all the work—all the cooking, cleaning, serving, all the basic labors. Yulin couldn't do anything for himself. A cow was always there to get him a chair, to bring food or drink, to take him to a comfortable room in an inn, to prepare and clean everything. They even ran to open doors for the males.

Even though the service was easy to take, he wondered about it, about whether it was truly mental inferiority or just a rigid social system. They weren't automatons; they talked and laughed sometimes and sulked sometimes and generally acted like people.

And there were the rings and collars. All the cows wore them—large rings welded in their huge noses, and brass collars welded around their necks, with small hooks on the back. They were distinctive; they bore the marks of the herd the cow was from. The females were even branded on the right rump, he found, with the herd-mark.

Did they ever get fed up and run away, he wondered. Was that why there were so many ways to identify them as being out of place?

The towns had guild-herds. There were guilds for the different classes of workers, and they lived in dorms through the town.

He worried about this a little more when he found out that the great quantities of milk the men consumed, gotten from the cows, was more than supplement. The males like himself could not manufacture their own calcium. They required almost a gallon of the calcium-rich milk a day to stay healthy, ward off arthritis, bone diseases, rotting teeth, and the like.

Without cows, the men would die. Slowly, and in great agony.

That was why they and their system were so well known in other hexes. Young bulls waiting for an opening often traveled, sometimes widely. They could exist on almost any native carbon-based grasses, and their own systems purified natural water, so few provisions were needed. But the men were so used to being waited on, and their bodies so desperately dependent on the cow's milk, that they had to take at least four cows with them. He could imagine the effect this would have on races that were unisexual, or where sexual discrimination was not present, or, worse, in a matrilineal society.

But there was little time for such speculation. He was too busy being passed around, introduced to the politicians, and discussing the crisis.

The council met the next day. In a communal society—money wasn't even used here, everyone drew his share—such bodies on a small scale were normal. They elected a chairman without much problem and proceeded to the business at hand.

Using maps, charts, and diagrams, the central bureaucracy explained the problem. There was a general sentiment to stay clear of it; it was none of Dasheen's business. Yulin they regarded as a complication; it was debated, much to his chagrin, whether or not to hide him away, imprison him for the war's duration, or perhaps kill him! None of these alternatives were seriously considered by the council as a whole, much to his relief, but he was aware of danger here. Those who proposed them were deadly serious, and some of these hotheads might easily take such solutions into their own hands.

On the third day of the conference little had been resolved, and Ben had the feeling that they just loved to argue; they would never come to any agreement unless forced to.

But on the third day a newcomer arrived who changed things. Its entrance was such that it panicked people on the streets, and the creature did little to reassure them after coming to ground. In the air it was magnificent and beautiful; a great butterfly with a two-meter wingspread, brilliantly orange and brown against a black body that still stood 150 centimeters when it landed in the street and stood on the rearmost four of its eight long tentacles. Its face was a large, black painted death's head, with great, eerie eyes that looked like pads recessed in the hard, dark skull.

The Yaxa, however, had been expected.

Its manner, its voice, was cold, hard, sharp, and cutting. It sent chills through those who heard it. Even Ben, who had to have a running translation, felt it. Unlike the others he'd met on the Well World—the Dasheen, Ortega, the Ambreza, even the plant-creature—this one was different. Not inhuman, *un*human, as alien as those paintwash creatures of the North.

The Yaxa had a proposition.

"First," it said, "let me summarize what the situation is to date. I have been able to keep in touch on my journey here as new developments broke, and things are breaking fast.

"One—the Makiem have effectively allied and co-ordinated with the Cebu and the Agitar. It is the most formidable combination of brains, opportunism, and ability this world has ever seen. Boidol will give them their part of the ship to avoid the fight. There has been no talking them out of it. The Djukasis will fight, but we have been unsuccessful in getting the Lata to come in on their side or anybody else's. The Djukasis will take their toll, but they cannot hope to defeat such an alliance. The Klusidians will neither yield nor fight, and you know what that means. The Zhonzorp would fight if they had a chance, but they're very much like the Makiem, mentally. They may join the alliance instead, if they're able. Their hatred of the Klusidians will keep them from giving the aid those people need."

The creature paused, adjusting the giant maps it was using to illustrate its talk.

"Olborn is a mystery. You know its reputation: nobody who goes in ever comes out, and they never man their embassy at Zone. A question mark, but I don't believe that *any* race, whatever its powers, can stop this march alone. If we're lucky, the Olbornians will slow them, as certainly the Alestoli will. But think of what *two* flying races could do with even something as basic as boiling oil. No, a sufficiently large force of them *will* reach Gedemondas, a hex that talks to no one, has no embassy, and contains too hostile an environment for much else. Even the Dillians on the other side, who share some mountains, have been unsuccessful in talking to them. They don't fight—they just vanish. And that leaves four mods and the engines in the hands of the Makiem-Cebu-Agitar alliance."

"But how will they ever get such large pieces of machinery back to their home hexes?" asked one councillor.

"The Agitar know their business," the Yaxa told him. "They will bring along a number of good engineers. They will disassemble things, put them through the Zone Gates if they can't haul them home, and then reassemble them in their own hex."

"They still couldn't fly it," another pointed out.

"Wrong again," replied the Yaxa. "The Makiem have had the kind of good fortune that makes one doubt free will. One of the pilot-qualified Entries,

Antor Trelig, is a Makiem. He can and will fly that ship—and further, he can enter the computer complex and use it up on the satellite. You see? *Our very existence is in jeopardy!"*

That got to them. There was a rumble and roar, and it was several minutes before the chairman could calm them down. It was hard to tell, but the Yaxa seemed satisfied with his reception. It had come on a diplomatic mission; its object was to scare them to death.

"But what can we do?" asked one councillor. "Send our people into battle with swords and spears against the Qasada? They'd chew us to pieces!"

"They would indeed," the Yaxa agreed. "But you will have some time and some advantages. Yaxa and Lamotien have united. The Lamotien are probably the best friends and deadliest enemies on the Well World. The planet for which they were designed must be a living hell. They are metamorphs—they can assume any shape that they can see, limited only by the fact that they cannot change their mass. Even that is not a true drawback because they are small. They combine with one another to create larger organisms. Twenty could make a Dasheen so convincing you would be unable to tell the difference. And there are ten million or more Lamotien, in a *high-tech* hex. With them we will shortly secure the highly important bridge module of the downed ship from Teliagin. Then the Lamotien will turn into flyers, and we will fly to Nodi Island in the Sea of Storms and secure a second module. Then we shall cross the East Neck to Qasada. With Lamotien infiltration and technology, Yaxa flight and trained warriors, aided, perhaps, by bases and personnel in Dasheen, we can take the Qasada and the Xoda, our two major problems. Palim is still in doubt; they might just allow us through. That puts *us* in Gedemondas, a hex in which we Yaxa will be hard-pressed to operate, but one in which a Lamotien-supplemented Dasheen force will be highly effective. Need I tell you that this will give us the bridge *and* engines?" It turned, looked over the bovine faces assembled there. "And you have Ben Yulin, another pilot who also has access to the satellite computer."

There was more uproar. How could the Yaxa have known? They groaned. This changed everything!

The Yaxa had no ability to smile. Even if it could, Ben Yulin thought such a gesture would shatter its face and personality. But there was evident confidence and satisfaction inside it for its presentation.

Chalk one up for Well World intrigues, anyway, Yulin thought. This world bristled with spies, plots, moves, and countermoves. The heretofore impossibility of war had diverted men of such minds to more devious means.

The debate droned on and on, but it was evident that the outcome had been decided, and a late-night formal vote made it official. Even Yulin spoke, assuring them that he could indeed pilot the ship if it had so much as one module between bridge and engines, and that he could, in fact, get into Obie. His emotions were excitement mixed with apprehension. On one hand, here was a chance, although a long shot, to gain complete mastery of New Pompeii, Obie included, and perhaps a key to the Well. On the other, he saw the dark threat of Antor Trelig in that same position. He did not paint Trelig's evil any too lightly; by the time he was through, the very mention of Trelig inspired dread.

On the brighter side, all personal animosities were off. He was one of their own now, suddenly. They would be the weakest member of the alliance militarily, but the other monstrous partners in this coalition would have to depend entirely on a Dasheen to get there and get into the computer.

He was taken around where former enemies who had suggested his imprisonment or death only a day before were now his blood brothers.

"He must have his own herd!" one big shot insisted, and they all agreed.

"Only a small one right now. Later—anything he wants!" another stipulated.

"How about one from each of the five service guilds in town?" a third suggested. "More practical than giving him farmhands!" So he got five daughters, one each from the Metalworkers, City Service, Cooks

237

and Waiters, Builders, and Housekeeping guilds—a perfect practical balance of skills.

The Metalworkers also gave him his own brand, distinctive ring, and collar. His herd were all young, all virgins. He found that there was a lot of tradition and ceremony associated with unions.

For one thing, daughters had numbers instead of names until they were assigned to a herd, whether farm or guide. The male, who was always called Master, would name them in the ceremony, then consummate the union, which bound her to him. She would then be branded, ringed, and collared. The whole process took five days.

He loved every minute of it.

In the meantime, subcouncils met, Yaxa came and went, and a percentage of every herd in the country was conscripted for military training. This worried some of the men, who wondered what the effect would be when so many cows were taught the art of killing. But there was much at stake here. As for the Yaxa, they didn't seem to find anything but amusement in that worry.

The Yaxa, Ben learned, were female. After they mated, they ate their male mate. It was almost the reverse of Dasheen, and he couldn't help but wonder if Yaxa presence might give somebody ideas.

Agitar

ALTHOUGH RENARD DIDN'T KNOW IT YET, THE WELL World must have a sense of humor. The shock of waking up in an alien land as something else was much greater for him; he did not really remember anything since waiting before a big plain for darkness so they could avoid the cyclopses.

He sat up and looked around. A nice looking place,

he thought. Green trees here and there, nice fields growing various vegetables—even signs of hothouses and other modern conveniences. There was a small service road near him, obviously for farm vehicles going to the groves rather than for through traffic, yet it was macadam-paved. He was definitely in a rural area, but this was no primitive cyclops land.

Far off in the distance was what appeared to be the ghostly skyline of a city. It looked kind of strange, the buildings kind of twisted or pointed, but that was to be expected.

He had no doubt in his mind that he was still on this strange world where they had crashed. How he'd gotten here was a mystery; somebody must have brought him, that was for sure. Why couldn't he remember? The sponge?

A sudden realization shot through him. He felt *good*. Really good. Totally clear-headed. He found he could remember things he hadn't thought of in years—and felt no trace whatever of the sponge-longing or its effects. Almost wondrously he thought of Mavra Chang. She alone believed that somewhere on this world sponge addiction could be cured, and she was right. He knew it, deep inside. He was free!

But where?

He rose to his feet and found himself somewhat out of balance. He fell forward, breaking his fall with his hands.

It wasn't dizziness; it was balance. Something was wrong. He looked at the arm that had broken his fall. Short, stubby fingers with nails that looked more like claws. A deep-blue skin—

He rolled over and sat up again. He felt something funny when sitting this way, and reached behind him. It was like he was sitting on a rock.

No he wasn't. He was sitting on his short, stubby tail.

His *what?*

He looked down at himself. The skin was the deepest of blues, and thick and porous. At the waist a very thin curly body hair became suddenly tremendously thick. It was like sheep's wool, dense and curly. Except for being blue-black, his sexual organ looked

239

fairly normal, which was a relief. He was no longer taking anything for granted. But his legs, very thick in the upper calf, were queerly shaped below, coming to a thin knee joint fairly high up, then going down to—

Sharp, shiny-black cloven hooves?

What the hell was going on here?

The hooves looked too small to support his thick body. That must have been why he'd fallen—no large foot support. But—how was he supposed to walk, then? Crawl on his hands and knees? Or did the knack come with practice?

For a brief moment he thought he'd become a cyclops. But, no, he had *two* eyes in the right places, and the feet and hair were definitely wrong, as was his odd complexion.

He felt his head, wonderingly. Sharp pointed ears close to the scalp, but at least where ears should be. Nose seemed a bit large but felt normal. Even the teeth seemed normal. He'd lost six at various points in his life and never had them put back; but they were all there now, although the front ones felt a hell of a lot sharper and maybe a little longer, top and bottom, than he remembered.

He had hair. He risked pulling a strand, and it was blue-black. It started in a V-shape in the center of his forehead, then spread out on both sides of the horns—

Horns?

Yes, they were there. Bony things, not long but sharp, and definitely a part of his skull.

Kind of a triangular face, terminating in a sharp, thick, pointed goatee.

All right, Renard, think it through logically, he told himself. But it just wouldn't wash. There was no logic to this. Only facts.

Fact: He'd awakened in some alien land, cured of sponge, anatomically totally male, clear-minded, and in the body of some alien creature.

Fact: He didn't know where the hell he was, what he was, or what was going on.

Well, he told himself, no matter what, the only way to find out was to find somebody and ask. There was

240

that city out there in the distance. Even hazy smog from some factory or other.

He crawled on hands and knees over to a spindly tree a few meters away, and, grabbing it, managed to get to his feet. He was top-heavy, no doubt about it. And yet, when he calmed down and considered it, he realized that his sense of balance was tremendous. With a little practice, he could angle parts of his body differently, knowing somehow that certain combinations felt wrong, others right.

In about half an hour he managed to stand without holding on to the tree. He did it repeatedly, and the ability pleased him. He also found that the tail went flush into the rectal cavity, so, when sitting, he didn't have to be uncomfortable.

Walking, however, was a lot harder. After repeatedly falling down he crawled back to the tree, stood up, and resolved to succeed no matter what. He stepped out, going as fast as he could from a standing start. To his surprise, he stayed up, making the weight and balance compensations automatically. When he came to a halt, though, he almost always fell over again. More practice.

The Well World gave you the means of adaptation to your new form, although Renard didn't know that. As the afternoon progressed, he got the hang of it more easily than anyone should have.

This was, he decided, a fast-paced culture. The faster you went the better control you had. Still, he managed now to sort of half-run, and to stand still without falling on his face. It was enough. Subtleties could be gotten later. He could move on toward that city now.

He followed the farm road until it reached a dead end. He realized he'd made the wrong choice, and retraced. At the pace he ran, he arrived at a main road before he knew it. What a road! A highway, really. A highway without vehicles, but with lots of people.

And the road moved.

It was a giant moving walkway, and people holding onto moving handrails moved along in ten lanes in either direction. The middle two lanes were reserved for commercial traffic; large boxlike containers with odd symbols and sometimes graphics moved there on their own walkways, and he wondered how they got them off.

Two other things struck him immediately. One was that the people wore clothes, which caused him a real problem. The males wore shirts and sometimes light jackets, with briefs to cover the nether regions. The females—well, that was another thing. He had heard the term "opposite sex" for years, but this was the first time the difference was graphic.

Blue-skinned all, from the waist down the females appeared roughly human. Oh, they had the little tails, too, and their feet seemed to be a bit broader and more solid than human feet, but human enough. They mostly wore pants and sandals. But from the waist up—

They were goats.

Well, not exactly, he decided. The head was a rounded triangular shape with a long lower jaw running its length, and their noses were black and located at the end of the upper jaw. Their ears were the same pointed type as his own, and their horns short and more rounded than the males. Over the entire upper torso was that thick, woolly blue hair that was his from the waist down; the female's arms looked like a goat's forelegs except that they terminated in long, thin, fragile-looking hands.

They all had what appeared to be *very* large human breasts, almost gargantuan, and covered with either brightly colored bras or tied halters. And he got erotic sensations looking at them. Not just at the breasts, but at all of them. It amazed him. He began to realize just how much he had become this new creature.

The lack of clothing concerned him most; obviously if he stepped out into that traffic he'd cause a stir. Nowhere was there any evidence that nudity was normal or accepted.

He sat back down in what appeared to be a fruit grove to think. He was hungry; if he was going to skulk around or wait until dark to try and bargain for a pair of pants, he'd need something to sustain him.

He eyed the large, orange fuzz-covered balls on the bushes around him. He'd seen peaches on New Pompeii; he knew they didn't grow on bushes like this, but he suspected that these were close enough, and very edible, since nobody would grow the things like this to poison anyone. He reached over and picked one.

There was a crackle and a pop, and he felt some sort of release inside him that seemed to flow into his hand. The peach crackled; it was cooked solid, and suddenly very hot. He dropped it with an oath. He felt a dull burning sensation in his hand, but it wasn't from whatever had cooked the fruit but rather from the fruit heating up.

What else? he wondered, both curious and anxious.

He carefully reached out to pick up another fruit off the bush. He felt the sensation rising within him, and fought it. It seemed to subside, go down. He picked the thing and ate it. It tasted good.

Trying to figure out what had happened, he reached over and probed the cooked peach; it was still warm. Somehow, he thought, my body contains hundreds, perhaps thousands of volts of electricity that can be discharged and renewed. He instinctively *knew* it, and the success he had in fighting the power the second time, when he expected it, showed that it could be contained or discharged at will.

He picked up another peach, put it down in front of him, and kind of let the sensation flow, touching the peach with his index finger. He felt the sensation rise, flow into his arm, down it, and there was a slight crackle and the peach started smouldering.

Where does that energy come from? he wondered. He considered the thick upper calves and thighs, and the tremendously dense hair there. That might well build up a static charge, he thought, particularly with all that running. A charge transferred to his body, to some sort of storage, discharging only when that body willed it.

I could possibly electrocute somebody by shaking hands with him! he thought in wonder.

He found he could *feel* the energy, even feel a slight loss after a discharge. It could be routed to any part of his upper body. Talk about a shocking embrace!

He was still experimenting when a sharp voice said behind him, "If you're all through trying to burn the field down, will you kindly get up and tell me why you're sitting in a fruit field, stark naked, frying peaches?"

He turned with a start. It was a male—whatever else he was. There was no mistaking his manner, the club and radio on his belt.

He was a cop.

They had radioed for a lock-up cart, and it arrived. They hustled him into it, and it rolled down the moving roadway smoothly, bumping only when it reached a junction point where two belts met.

How you got off or on the roadway was simple. There was a small set of casterlike wheels attached to the underside, and they, in turn, were attached to a basic electric motor.

The cops provided their own electrical power.

They rolled to a halt inside the police garage and took him out. A female desk sergeant, her goatlike head impassive, punched information into a computer and asked him questions.

"Name?"

"Renard," he responded.

"Odd name," she commented. "Place and date of birth?"

"The city of Barentsk, on the planet Muscovy, August 12, 4412 N.D.," he answered honestly.

She stopped typing and looked at him. "You trying to be funny?" she asked. The two male cops flanking him didn't look amused.

"No," he told her, trying to sound sincere. "Honest. Look, I crashed here in a spaceship, somewhere in a place inhabited by giant cyclopes, and then I woke up here. I don't know anything more than *you* do."

She remained impassive, that rigid face incapable of showing emotion, but she said, "Less," cryptically, and punched something on the terminal. There was a flip-flop on the screen, and a new printout appeared, line-by-line. She nodded, looked at the two cops.

"He's an Entry, all right. One of the drug addicts."

"You sure," one of the cops responded. "He just looks like a Class-One nut to me."

Renard felt insulted, but decided not to press the matter.

"Look," the desk clerk said. "Take my word for it. Get some clothes for him from the lockup and then take him up to Lieutenant Ama's office. I'll call ahead."

They reluctantly agreed, using the age-old principle of uncertainty: when you're not positive of your own position, pass the buck. They gave him some uncomfortable, tight-fitting briefs of a bright-white color, and a white T-shirt that was too large and obviously had been worn by a legion of people before him. The bright-white was obvious: the contrast with his deep-blue complexion was spottable a kilometer away. Jail clothes.

Lieutenant Ama was a typical bored servant of the people who didn't like problems in his district. He also wouldn't answer questions of any kind, although he asked a number, obviously to make sure that Renard was indeed who he said he was. Nobody else would talk, either.

He sat there for hours. He knew what was happening—at least he hoped he knew. Ama was calling *his* superior, who was calling *his* superior, who was—and so forth, until somebody decided what to do with him.

Well, they fed him, anyway. They even showed him how you touched different points on the metal plate set in the wooden base to cook anything you liked how you liked it. He discovered that men were the cooks here. Women couldn't do it—didn't have the electrical capacity. They were, however, as immune to electrical shocks of any kind as the males. Renard wondered idly how you made love around here without burning the house down.

He slept in an unlocked cell, and by the middle of the second day he was wondering if he'd been forgotten.

He hadn't. A little into the afternoon, they came for him. Big guys—bigger than he was, anyway. It occurred to him that, since everything was to scale, he had no idea *how* big he was. Could be ten centimeters high or four meters high.

Another trip, much longer this time, and then into a huge building that was shaped like a pyramid but with minaretlike towers all around. Into another office, this one obviously a big shot's, and more questioning. They had no doubts he was who he said he was; the questions were quite different this time.

Most of them were about Antor Trelig.

He told them everything; he held nothing of his hatred back. He described the man who enslaved so many to terrible drugs, the depravities of New Pompeii, Trelig's mad ambitions. They took it all down.

And, finally, they answered some of his questions. "Where am I?" he asked.

The interrogator, a slighter-built man who wore glasses, thought a moment. "You are in Agitar, and you *are* an Agitar."

"I'm still on the planet where I crashed?"

Slowly, they told him the story of the Well World, the hexes, and some of the problems his arrival had caused.

"You can't pilot a spaceship, can you?" the interrogator asked hopefully.

"No," he admitted. "I was a teacher of classics and a librarian and sometimes a guard for Trelig's prisoners."

The man thought for a minute. "You must understand our position in relation to you. Agitar is an advanced, technologically based hex. There is nothing electrical, I believe, closed to us, stemming from research on our own bodies. Science is king here. Now we prepare for a war, a war for those spaceship parts your party brought down. And here you are—totally illiterate, possessing absolutely no skills of use to us. Now you are an Agitar for the rest of your life. You're young, strong, but little else. You must be fitted in here, and when we look at this compilation, the only usable quality you possess is a familiarity with weapons and the ability to shoot straight."

"Where are the others who came in with me?" he asked, not liking the direction of the conversation. "I would like to get in contact with the woman, Mavra Chang—"

"Forget it," the other told him. "She's in the hands of the Lata, and, although they've stayed neutral so far, they are almost certainly philosophically, maybe actually, in opposition to us." He sighed. "No, I think there's only one place you would fit in now, and it'll do you good, work you into Agitar society with discipline."

They drafted him into the army.

They gave him two weeks of strict, intense basic training. There was little time to think, and that was as it had been planned. Still, barracks life made him some friends and filled him in on the rest of what was going on. For one thing, he found out that Agitar was allied with Makiem, a hex whose dominant race were giant frogs, and Cebu, a race of flying reptiles of some sort.

He also learned that Antor Trelig was a Makiem.

That depressed him. The ultimate irony. To escape from New Pompeii, beat the sponge on a new and alien planet, and wind up back serving Antor Trelig again. Was the Well computer laughing?

The training was tough but fascinating, though. In hand-to-hand, an Agitar male would simply electrocute his opponent. Although the average energy stored in an Agitar male was several thousand volts—still enough to be lethal—it could potentially store up to sixty thousand volts! An incredible figure. Overload was impossible, but if you were fully charged, any additional energy would be immediately released. The static electricity alone would never generate a terribly high voltage, but it was actually possible for an Agitar to absorb additional electricity from artificial sources or even things like lightning rods. They were totally immune to electrical shock; they could not electrocute one another, but they could actually transfer stored-up energy between themselves. There was a rather unpleasant class on how to absorb the energy from a dying or recently dead comrade.

Shooting was easy for him; the rifles were different from what he knew, as were the pistols, but all such weapons basically operate on the same principle: aim, push here, and the energy or projectile comes out there.

Somehow, one never unconsciously discharged, even while sleeping. He wondered about that, worried about the fact that the first time he *had* done so involuntarily, but they assured him that it rarely happened. But beds were made out of nonconductive, energy-absorbing materials, just in case.

He also learned, indirectly from his barracks-mates, about the opposite sex. They were smart; on the average, a little smarter than the men, some said. Sex was common and frequent; the Agitar were a horny bunch. But there was effective birth control, plus the Well monitor of the population, so nobody felt inhibited. Marriage was unknown. If you wanted a child, you just found a female that wanted one, too—or vice versa—and had one. If it was male, it was the father's total responsibility to raise it. The female might stay, might walk out. If it was female, the reverse was true.

There were women in the army, too. Because they could not hold a charge or discharge, they were never front-line troops, but they handled everything else. Most of the upper officers, including the bulk of the general staff, were women, as were most of the technicians.

The war was not popular. There was some childish enthusiasm born of never having actually seen what a war was like, yes; but most people didn't get overly enthusiastic about it. They saw war as a necessity. A nasty couple of races—the Yaxa and the Lamotien —were even now moving to get the ship parts as well, and they had Ben Yulin under their control to fly it. Better a fully charged Agitar at Antor Trelig's side walking into Obie than a bunch of terribly alien creeps under a not certainly controllable Ben Yulin.

After two weeks, they transferred him to Air. It wasn't a promotion, really; Air went in first, and took the brunt of front-line casualties. Renard almost gasped when he saw what Air meant. Not planes or sleek ships, no. They were horses. Large, great horses with tremendous swanlike wings along both sides of their sleek bodies. As a classicist, Renard recognized them as the embodiment of the legendary Pegasus, and they were truly grand. They came in all colors—brown, white, pink, blue, green. There was no end to the variety.

And they flew—tremendously, gracefully, with an Agitar on a saddle, his legs strapped in, on soaring wings. They were somewhat fragile, since they had hollow bones, and he never did quite understand why they flew, but they did and that was enough. They were also much smarter than horses. They responded to verbal commands, slight kicks, pulls on the reins and they were easy to train, considering their riders had their own shock prods.

He was assigned one immediately. A beautiful, intelligent animal, green in color. The first time he went up, he had an instructor in front and all sorts of fancy instruments. But, the animals were easy to fly, and by the third day Renard was doing loops and swirls on Doma, the horse's name, as easily as if born to it. They were a natural pair, Agitar and pegasus; they blended together like one organism.

And there was the tast. It was a steel rod, about three meters long, coated with copper, with a sword-like copper hilt. With an Agitar male holding one, it was an electrical conductor of remarkable efficiency. It was also thin and fairly light for the well-muscled arms.

In a nontechnological hex, or even some others, the tast was an ultimate close-contact weapon, where pistol or rifle either could not be used or would not work.

At the end of three weeks they told his class that they weren't really ready, should need six more weeks, but that this was all the training they were going to get. As it was, they would have to catch up to the war.

Renard decided one thing—had decided it long before, when he found out about Trelig.

He was not going to die in Trelig's service.

Lata

ANOTHER DIZZYING RIDE ON THE KROMMIANS HAD taken Mavra to Lata itself.

It was a fairyland come to life. The Lata had no cities as such; they were spread out along wooded hills and forest glades. Small shop groups permitted the necessary trade and services, and there was a number of universities, research facilities for those so minded, and places for the artisans, for Lata were an inherently artistic race.

It was also the only asexual bisexual race she had ever seen. They all looked identical to her except for the colors; all like meter-high girls of nine or ten, and all spoke in lyrical, musical bells. It was an eerie feeling for her, who had always been so small in a world of giants, to suddenly be the tallest person around.

They were all born without sex; they matured after fifteen to twenty years into biological females, each capable of laying just one egg, which hatched on its own in a few days. Then, over a two-year period, they changed. Female organs vanished, and male organs grew in their place. They were then male for the rest of their lives.

She asked Vistaru why there were so many females if that was the case. The girl—even though mature, it was impossible to think of the Lata as other than girls—had laughed. "When you change, you get older," she'd replied.

Mavra ultimately found out that females aged at a rate only a fraction that of males; it would eventually catch up with you, of course, but most put it off as long as possible. Spend forty to fifty years as a ten-year-old flying pixie girl, *then* have your egg, then have another thirty years as a male, growing older inside.

That's why the males seemed to be the leaders here. They were older, and had more experience.

Mavra Chang felt more at ease now than at any other period she could remember in her life except those glorious years of marriage and partnership. There was no pressure here; the people were wonderful and warm. There were no threats, no natural enemies, and, as a high-tech hex, no want of material comfort, either, although they seemed to have made less use of their technical capabilities than other places she was told about. They didn't need it: they were happy.

The stingers, which *could* kill—they described the venoming process as something like an orgasm—were their extra edge against neighbors who might think the frail and tiny creatures easy prey. It totally paralyzed for a long period, depending on the victim's size and weight, and too much of it could kill. Less than a dozen races had proven immune to it, and the Lata hadn't had to test their power much in a long while.

As for Mavra herself, they made new clothing for her to her design, of black stretch cloth, and a heavy coat for cold weather wear. They also cleaned her belt, replaced the strap, and marveled at the compartments and gadgets it contained. The same with her boots; they were too worn to be useful, but the gadgets had survived, and a new pair was brighter, shinier, more flexible and comfortable—and even added a few more centimeters to her height.

They also untangled her hair, cut, combed, and trimmed it in Lata fashion, long and sleek on the top and sides, short in back. When they tested the venom in her nails, it fascinated them. Obie had made a biological adaptation of mechanical injectors; and the system was, said the medical people, amazing and complex. They got her to try the hypno load on a Lata volunteer, and, much to her surprise, the stuff that had failed on the cyclopses worked on the Lata.

She lived with them for several weeks; it was a peaceful time. The medical people fitted her with a translator, a tiny crystal from the North that was

251

patched in at any one of several points inside her body in a painless, minor operation. This would allow her to understand, she was told, anyone on the Well World, and anyone on the Well World could understand her. The devices were not common or cheap; the operation had been mandated and paid for by Serge Ortega.

She was both delighted and disappointed: delighted in that she could now speak to and understand these wonderful people; disappointed in that their speech, when translated, lost its wonderful musicality. It sounded like plain old Confederation plain talk with bell-like undertones. Furthermore, the translator was in and of itself a reminder to her that she was not really a free woman, but a captive. These nice people were doing things in their own best political interest, not hers.

Vistaru explained the problem to her, now easier since she could speak in her own language and be understood. "You are a pilot," she pointed out. "The Yaxa-Lamotien-Dasheen alliance is on the move. So is the Makiem-Cebu-Agitar one. We don't want war. We want that ship destroyed. But we must have someone around who understands it, just in case—as long as the threat remains."

As long as the threat remains. Mavra wondered how long that would be.

The map told the story, along with daily war reports. The great sphinxes of Boidel had traded their module for peace, going as far as bringing it to the Agitar border. Gambling that the war would end in no profit for all concerned, they had elected to pass.

In the North, the great angry butterflies of the Yaxa had poured boiling oil on Teliagin villages and forests, and the Lamotien had spread panic as Teliagin cyclopses suddenly came apart into fifty or more smaller creatures who disrupted everything from behind. The Teliagin, primitive and fearful, surrendered quickly. They allowed the Yaxa and Lamotien to drag the bridge module across the Lamotien border on great carts, eventually helping in the process. The Yaxa were already heading across the Sea of Storms on great wings, first to Nodi Island—a peaceful hex inhabited by a race described as resembling giant walking mushrooms—to receive a sea-landed module being brought to them by the dolphinlike Porigol next door. There, on the Nodi beaches, Lamotien technicians carefully disassembled the mod, and helpless Nodi allowed the parts to be shipped to Zone through their Zone Gate, and thence on to Lamotien. Qasada would be next for the Yaxa alliance.

In the South, Djukasis was giving fierce resistance, but it was only a matter of days, the reports said. The great bees' hives were being hit by the pterodactyllike Cebu, while Agitar airmen on great Pegasi zapped the Djukasis from the air with their tasts.

Upset, Mavra asked repeatedly why the Lata would not go in to help the Djukasis, whom they liked and had been friends with for centuries. They always shook their heads and gave the same answer.

"If we hurt one army without hurting the other, the other has that much more chance of achieving its goals. We must remain neutral until there is some sort of action we could take that would end not one war, but all war."

In the meantime, Mavra Chang felt more and more a prisoner in a pixie paradise as events passed her by.

Djukasis

THERE WAS A STORM COMING. THEY COULD SEE IT in the billowing black clouds, hear the distant thunder, and almost feel the glow of approaching lightning.

The Agitar commander looked at the scene and nodded approvingly. "A fine day to end this mess," she said to the field officers, the men who would lead. "There is much charging potential there."

"Enough to knock the mounts out from under us," muttered one officer glumly, wondering why commanders who never had to go into battle themselves were always so cheerfully optimistic when explaining what other lives should buy.

She sniffed. "No defeatism today, Captain! You know as well as I do that the tast and your own bodies will absorb the force. The saddles are insulated. The beast is used to mild shocks. No, conditions favor us. The siege of the Djukasis Zone Gate complex is well along; knock out the rest of their aerial defenses today, and the froggies will easily take it over in the rain."

They went back to tell their men.

Renard, too, was watching the storm approach, with far different thoughts in mind. Over the past week he'd become a good fighter, but electrocuting those bees sickened him. He did it only because, if he did not, they would kill him with their projectile weapons and stingers, suicidally if need be. But, those bees were *people* defending their homes.

He was also scared. Those bees weren't fools; they had learned, too, that they could turn more quickly than a pegasus; hit the mount in the rear, out of reach of the Agitar rider, and the beast plunged to its own and its rider's death. That had almost happened to him twice now; it had happened to most of his friends already.

Captain Bir was sarcastic but professional. "The final assault this time, for sure, boys," he told them without any conviction whatsoever. "Same deal. We're supposed to go in just ahead of the storm. When it hits, you'll draw additional charges. Try and get in to the hive itself, give them all the juice you've got. Fry it. As soon as the storm hits, clear out when you've shot your wad. The froggies will drive in with the rain."

"But that'll leave *them* with no air support, sir," one of the men pointed out.

He shook his head. "That's D-Company's job. No, we get the easy part. Just go in ahead and kill everything we can, then get out of there." They chuckled mirthlessly, knowing that their job was the deadly part. "No," he concluded, "just remember that you'll have an easy retreat. They can't fly in the rain as we can. If

254

it's good and hard, just let your mount bring you home."

Renard nodded with the rest, a plan forming in his mind. He'd seen earlier in the day at the captain's tent a map of the overall route of march. He'd remembered from the moment he'd heard it the official's statement that Mavra Chang was in a place called Lata. The captain had been arguing with another officer, and he'd pointed to the map on his tent wall, saying, "We *can't* flank that far north, Suo! That's Lata, neutral territory!"

And it had been northeast of their present position, about a day's flight. The pegasus wouldn't mind rain. It liked rain and storms, with the Agitar to draw the lightning from it. Water rolled off the animal with ease, not weighing it down at all. If that storm were fierce enough, and he had guts enough, he told himself, he was going to desert.

"Okay, boys! Let's mount up!" the captain called. One last battle, one more battle.

Here we go, all right, Renard thought grimly.

To the Makiem on the ground, and to the great, red-eyed flying triangles that were the Cebu, it was an awesome sight, even taking into account their different concepts of what was grand. The storm was close now; the sky was filled with great black-and-orange billowing clouds that rumbled and flashed, like lights flashing briefly, across the panorama.

Against that came the Agitar, tiny specks at first, then growing until they could be individually distinguished across the storm-tossed sky. Great horses of many colors, broad swanlike wings flapping gently in the rough air, in V-shaped formations—dozens of them in the leading wave, then dozens more behind, protecting the flanks.

They came in fairly low; the maximum altitude of the pegasus was between fifteen hundred and eighteen hundred meters, and they generally stayed lower than that as a safety margin—in this case much lower, due to the upper-air turbulence, perhaps no more than three hundred meters above the ground troops.

Pterodactyllike Cebu, red eyes blazing, moved off behind the Makiem ground troops to provide additional cover for the incoming Agitar. Each of the great giant reptiles wore a harness with twin harpoon tubes that could be aimed and triggered by a flick of the head, then dropped down to be reloaded from quivers strapped to their undersides.

The Makiem could almost feel the great beating of those wings as they passed just overhead, and some of the giant frogs cheered both in optimism and to release the tension from their own impending jump-off.

The enemy, its forces depleted by near-continuous battle, its reserves pulled in from North and South, waited until the last moment before challenging. Their only hope was to get inside the Cebu defensive screen and strike the great pegasi down by bullet or stinger, even though the latter method would mean their own deaths as well.

The Agitar were in sight of the objective now; the monstrous hive half above ground rose over thirty meters in the air. It had been badly damaged by cannon fire and past aerial attacks, but it had stood, torn though it was by great gaping holes and scars.

From its thousands of tiny black pockmarks there appeared to be some sort of reflection of the storm flashes, and it was—from the great, huge, multifaceted eyes of the defenders, who now rose in highly organized, tight-knit swarms to meet the coming foe. The two sides were joined in less than a minute.

The bees were huge, over a meter long, with menacing stingers to match. But the stingers were also an integral part of their backbone; to use it was to break it off—thus breaking its back and causing death. They depended first on their weapons—projectile-types, since theirs was a semitech hex, contained in large boxes located under the thorax, operated by one of the eight flexible, clawlike legs that furred black and gold creatures possessed. Spring-wound, they could fire ten rounds a second, with a two-hundred-shot cartridge.

Actually, the bees' greatest problem in aerial combat was their semi-automatic weapons; they had to be careful in the increasingly rough air to keep from shooting one another down as well.

The tactics were simple. The bees formed a solid wave; the front line waiting until it was in easy range

256

of the Cebu screen and the first line of Agitar, then opening fire. When they were spent, they would drop down and slow, letting the oncoming swarm pass over them, so the next row was clear for a shot. If the progression went well, they could drop back to the hive for additional cartridges and rejoin the back row. But their forces were badly depleted; once the line had fired, it then became a series of free agent aerial soldiers, coming up from below.

The Cebu's harpoons were not as efficient as the Djukasis' machine guns; but, facing a swarm, they could hardly miss. Their objective was to knock holes in the formation, then get into the midst of the swarm, where great, sharp, teeth-filled beaks could rend and tear in quarters too close for the machine guns to do any good.

The rumble of the quickly oncoming storm and the tremendous air turbulence it created started to tell on both sides as they struggled for balance.

The bees' leading line of machine guns started, and some of the attackers were hit, falling from the sky, to be replaced by those from the second and third waves so the formations were maintained. The Djukasis' aim was off; they were having real problems remaining stable in the storm-tossed air, and some were partially spun around still firing, knocking holes in some of their own numbers.

The Cebu took advantage of this, rushing up into the holes, firing their harpoons into soft Djukasis bodies, then spearing, ripping, and tearing through the ranks while trying to avoid the lethal stingers. Of the eighty-four Agitar in the leading combination, only seventeen still flew, yet the formations were tight and steady as the places of the fallen were taken by those behind. Despite the Cebu's effectiveness, some of the Djukasis were penetrating now.

Renard had just moved up into second wave position behind the leaders, and he didn't have time to think. A great black-and-gold body suddenly swept up into his view on his left, and he swung his own harpoon projector over and fired without thinking. The missile struck the giant bee, and it went down without a sound.

There were more of them now; they were flying directly into the swarm, now too close for the Djukasis to use their machine guns but close enough for close-quarter combat.

Suddenly the Agitar drew their tasts and energized them. They did not have to spear the enemy, only touch him; that seemed easy to do; everywhere you swung the rods there seemed to be Djukasis.

But not enough Djukasis, not any more.

In past attacks over the previous three days, a new swarm had popped out of that hive at the last minute, and they had been unable to get directly into or on it. Now the situation had changed. On either side of the saddle sat canisters of a highly flammable liquid; now, for the first time, they were able to dump it onto the hive.

They made their passes and dumps; going back up into the still fierce aerial combat, then looped again. More horses, men, and pterodactyls fell from the sky, but ten suicidal defenders fell for every one of the attackers, and, unlike the attackers, they had no more reserves. The leading edge of the Agitar then moved in again, very low this time, so close they could see the impassive faces of the flightless workers peering out at the grim battle from the cells and doorways of the hive.

The Agitar tied thin copper wire to the hilts of their tasts and prepared to throw, being careful that they didn't get tangled as they moved away.

Firing was coming from the hive, but it was intermittent after the fuel dump; the burning smell and feel of the liquid had driven them back under where it had hit, and the stuff now pretty well saturated the top of the hive.

The copper wire unreeled, ten meters, twenty, as the leading second wave was covered by, but not followed in by, its backups. The Agitar were nearing the limits of the wire reel, and, when the mark was reached on the reel, they energized the wire with their hands.

Energy flowed along the wires; electricity followed its natural pathway in this semitech hex. Though only the Agitar would hold a charge here, it was enough.

Where the tasts had stuck in the hive in places that had been wetted down by the flammable liquids, and

258

despite Djukasis efforts to get the tasts out and throw them to the ground, the energy charge struck.

It only took one.

The liquid burst into flame with a roar; a chemical fire that even the oncoming storm would be hard-pressed to slow.

The Makiem on the ground cheered as the blue-white flame and billowing smoke showed success, and they grasped their own weapons and prepared to charge, rain or no.

With sudden explosive fury, the storm hit, turning the field in front of the hive to a low visibility quagmire in seconds. The Makiem, who liked rain and muddy weather, leaped for all they were worth.

As Renard turned from the hive, amazed at the fact that he and Doma were still untouched as it was, he felt the storm hit. For the first time he started to think, instead of act on instinct. If he just relaxed, he knew that Doma would fly back to the base camp; the horse had an unerring instinct for getting back to where she had started from. Looking around in the driving rain, he was just barely able to make out the Djukasis trying to get back to the hive but being knocked out of the air by the force of the rain. A Cebu almost panicked him, flying across directly in front, but it was on a different errand. The great flying reptiles weren't much better in the rain than the Djukasis, and were going to ground fast.

The water beaded and rolled off Doma's back. Yet there were severe updrafts and downdrafts that the great horse could not avoid, so it was a rocky ride, smoothed only slightly by the horse's apparent ability to *see* changes in air pressure. When Renard saw the direction Doma was taking, a million doubts assailed him. If he deserted, he would have to fly through the teeth of the storm, perhaps battle isolated back-country Djukasis on his way. And, once in Lata, he'd be a castout, a man who could never go home again.

But he felt little loyalty for the Agitar, although he liked them as individuals. He could not get away from the fact that, behind all of the terrible carnage he had witnessed and had been a part of, there was the grinning, self-satisfied egomania of Antor Trelig.

And Mavra Chang. Somehow, he knew, she had saved him, somehow her unwillingness to be defeated had kept him alive. For what? To be killed in the *next* battle, in the *next* hex, in Antor Trelig's cause?

No! his mind shouted to him. *Never!* He *owed* her, and, in a different way, he owed Antor Trelig something, too.

So he gently pulled and turned the great green pegasus to the right, far to the right, and headed into the fury about him.

South Zone

THE CZILLIAN, VARDIA, ENTERED ORTEGA'S INCREAS-ingly cluttered offices, a mass of computer printouts and diagrams clutched in its two tentacles. Ortega was just switching off from an intercom communication and glanced up as the plant-creature entered.

"New data?" he asked, sounding more resigned than happy at the prospect.

Vardia nodded. "We have run the projections through the computers at the center. Things don't look good."

Ortega wasn't surprised. Nothing looked good any more. "What have you got?" he asked glumly.

The Czillian spread out the charts as well as some diagrams. Ortega couldn't read the normal Czillian originals, but the computers at the great university and research center in the plant hex had provided transla-tions in Ulik. He studied them, expression becoming increasingly grim.

"Ship design certainly has changed in the past three hundred years," he commented.

"What did you expect?" the Czillian asked him curtly. "After all, there were periods in the past histories of many races when they went from primitive barbarism to space in less time than that."

Ortega nodded. "But it would help if I could understand more of the design theory," he said wistfully. It didn't really matter, though; the computers could follow it—and if the computers could follow it in Czill, then the computers of, say, Agitar or Lamotien or a half-dozen others could, too.

"They made the sectional cuts in just the right places," Vardia noted. "The pieces were barely large enough for the Zone Gates, but they all fit—and we could hardly stop them by rights anyway."

"Or force, either," he pointed out. "No wars in Zone, eh?" He looked again at the printout collection. "So the power plant is the only thing we couldn't manage here? They're sure now? Wonder why?"

"You know the answer," Vardia responded. "The plant is scaled and works off principles we don't know. We could create a power plant, of course, but almost certainly not with sufficient thrust to clear the adjacent nontech hexes before they caused shutdown. You know what a miserable failure even our little attempts with cameras have been. Moving a mass this size is, I think, beyond us. It's built into the Well to keep us here. But the size of those engines must indicate power. *They* could do it, if trajectory at launch was nearly straight up."

Ortega admitted the possibility. He had to—it was sitting there in mathematically precise black and white in front of him. "But to make it work they'll need the programming," he objected. "That means the Yaxa or nothing."

"Bullshit, and you know it!" the Czillian shot back, displaying uncharacteristic emotion. "So maybe it takes the Agitar a couple of years to jury-rig a replacement. More likely they'll either deal or steal what's needed. You of all people should know what politics and espionage on the Well World is like. You have Yaxa agents, Dasheen agents, Makiem agents, Agitar agents—probably agents of half the races on the planet."

Ortega didn't reply. Being true, it wasn't worthy of a retort. He just smiled, but it was not a satisfied smile. All of his old friends, all of those who owed him or were in his pay, had provided a great deal of information. But no results. More, he was well aware that the Yaxa would cheerfully double-cross their own parents to get in on the deal, and the Lamotien were as trustworthy as rats in a cheese factory. Whoever got the power supply would, politically, be able to put all the pieces together, he felt sure. He wasn't the only competent backstabbing puppet-master politician on the Well World, only the oldest and most experienced.

But the Czillian printouts indicated the worst from a technical standpoint: the sections had separated intact. They had landed, for the most part, in reasonably good shape. Disassembly where necessary had been professional, knowledgeable, and at the right points.

"What's the war news?" Vardia asked apprehensively.

He sighed. "The Djukasis were tough, but they were whipped. Klusid doesn't have a module, but it does have atmospheric problems for them. It's a fight going around, but there's a very heavy ultraviolet radiation in the Klusidian atmosphere. It's what makes things so pretty and yet so strange there. Their atmosphere has protected them from the Zhonzorp. But, I think the Makiem have managed a deal with the Klusidians through an alliance with the Zhonzorp. The need for passive radiation shielding will slow them down, but the Klusidians aren't able to withstand the alliance from the west and those two-legged crocodiles from the east. They'll give in, since it's only free passage they're seeking. With Zhonzorp having both a module and a key position, they'll be natural allies. The Agitar don't like them, but the Makiem and Cebu are interested because the crocs are another high-tech hex, and can help see that the goat-folk don't do any double-crossing themselves. I'd say the whole force of them will be at the borders of Olborn within ten days at the outside, with Zhonzorp handling most of the resupply problems."

Vardia looked at the map. "Only two hexes from Gedemondas. What about the Yaxa?"

Ortega sniffed in such a manner that it was evident that there was more bad news.

"While the Yaxa got the Porigol module back, the Lamotien infiltrated Qasada. It only takes six Lamotien to create an exact duplicate of those little rodents. Sabotage, false information—and really effective, since the Lamotien are high-tech themselves and knew where to throw everything out of gear. The Dasheen cow army wasn't a big help, but it caused additional confusion, and its Yaxa advisors had done their jobs well. There's still hard fighting there, though; it may be a week or even two before they get through. The Yaxa will deal with the Palim—they're great at that. Another five, six days to move through Palim with their stuff, maybe one more to get the Palim module out, and they're on the Gedemondas border."

"So the Yaxa will get there first," the Czillian concluded, staring again at the map.

"Maybe, maybe not," Ortega said. "Depends for one thing on the strength of the Qasada resistance, and on whether the others listen to the Zhonzorp. I'd fly over Alestol ferrying everybody in a continuous airlift. The air is uncomfortable, and it stinks, but the Alestoli are barrel-shaped moving plants that emit a variety of nasty noxious gasses. You can't talk to them—but they have no air capability whatsoever. If the Makiem-Agitar-whatever alliance can push through Olborn, I'd say that it might be a dead heat."

Vardia looked at Olborn. "What do you know about the place?" it asked curiously.

The big snake-man shook his head. "Not much. No ambassador I ever knew about. Sealed itself off from the outside world. Anybody who tries to go in never comes out. They're mammals there, air's okay, and my stuff says that they're a semitech hex with light magic capabilities, whatever that means. You gotta watch those magic types. All sons of bitches or fanatics—if there's a difference. Even Zhonzorp goes around them, but I can't imagine the most powerful hex on this planet standing against the kind of combination roaring in there. A magic hex tends to rely on its magic too much for its defense; a good bullet stops a good spell every time when you're outnumbered four to one by now well-seasoned troops."

"So either one has a crack at being first to Gedemondas," the Czillian mused. "And what about them? Anything?"

Ortega shook his head. "Nothing. Very high mountains, cold, and snowy mostly. They live high up. They're big—Dillians have seen them, but only briefly. Big suckers, three meters, all covered in snow-white fur, almost invisible against a snow field. Big four-toed clawed feet. They shun all contact, but if you go in too far, they'll drop an avalanche on your head."

The relief map showed a mild plain at the Alestol-Palim-Gedemondas border, then tremendously high, faulted mountains, four to five thousand meters many of them. Rough, cold country.

"Any idea where in Gedemondas the engine module fell?" Vardia asked the snake-man.

Serge Ortega shook his head. "No, not really, and neither do they. Not on the plains area, though." He hesitated. "Wait a minute! Maybe I do!" He rummaged through a bunch of papers, cursing and fussing. Papers went everywhere, until he finally came across a tattered yellow sheet of lined notepad. "Here it is. The Agitar plotted the mass and shape of the mod from the pieces they already recovered, checked climatological data and such, and came up with the probable location. About sixty to a hundred kilometers inside the northeast border, give or take ten. In the mountains, but still a needle in a smaller haystack."

"How in the world did you get hold of—" the Czillian started, then decided questioning Ortega wasn't worth it. He'd only lie, anyway. "Then there's not only the possibility of a search, but, if they find it, there's a fifty-fifty chance that the Gedemondas will either let them take it out or try to destroy them. That's not a body to be deterred that easily in the latter case."

Ortega nodded. "They're funny people, but we just don't know. That's the problem. We need to know. We need to send somebody in there to try and talk to the Gedemondas, ahead of the armies, if possible. Maybe they'll run away, maybe they'll try to kill them, but we have to try. Warn them ahead of time. Offer to—"

Vardia turned and faced him. "To take the engines off their hands, perhaps?"

Ortega shrugged. "Or, failing that, to try and destroy them."

Vardia would have sighed if it could. Instead, the

264

Czillian asked, "Who do you have in mind for this suicide mission to the frozen wastes? Count me out. I go dormant under two or three degrees centigrade."

He chuckled. "No, you had your fun once. Or one of you did, anyway. No, I don't like what I'm thinking, but it keeps coming up the same answer. There's only one person qualified to inspect the engines, decide if they can be moved, or, failing that, know how to destroy them beyond repairing."

Vardia nodded. "Mavra Chang. But you said she was too valuable to risk!"

"And so she is," Ortega admitted. "It's a calculated risk, I agree. But she's the only one who can do the technical end of the job for us. We'll try and minimize the risk, of course. Send some other people along with her for protection, not expose her to any needless risks."

"From what you've said of her, I doubt that sincerely," the Czillian replied skeptically. "But, all right. It's come down to this. We have been passive observers, and we'll continue to be passive observers watching the Trelig or Yulin bunch blast off for the satellite unless we do something. I agree action is called for. I only wish we'd done something sooner."

"Sooner, none of us thought either side had a prayer of actually making it," Ortega reminded the plant-creature. "Now we know it's possible. It's now or never."

The Czillian turned. "I'll notify my population and our friends as discreetly as possible. You will assemble the personnel, I assume?"

Ortega smiled. "Of course—subject to Czillian Crisis Center's approval, of course."

"Of course," Vardia echoed, not at all certain it made any difference.

Ortega went back to his maps and was soon talking to himself. Xoda was out; the Yaxa would be there. That left Olborn. Damn! . . .

Lata

HE'D TAKEN TWO DAYS TO GET TO THE LATA BORDER, although Doma could have gotten him there in one. The great horse would never let on, but it was almost worn out, and Renard had set down as soon as they'd cleared the storm and he felt far enough away from the war to be safe.

He had no provisions, nor did this land provide any. Doma could eat the leaves of trees and the tops of tall grasses, though, and there was water, so he felt she could survive. Lata was the only idea in his mind; he would wait to eat there. Agitar were omnivores, too; if Mavra Chang could exist there, so could he.

He had a couple of close shaves before he made the border. Some of the hives had left skeleton guard forces, and he was occasionally called upon to fight, but such action was scattered and usually broke off when he turned to avoid combat. There were too few of them to get drawn far from the hives.

Still, he was feeling mentally and physically exhausted, drained. His internal charge was down to a mere pop, and he wondered if a certain amount of stored energy was necessary for his body. Probably; it filled some need in his now alien biochemistry or it wouldn't be there. He stopped several times to run and thereby get a little back into him, and it *did* help, although he was otherwise so physically washed out that the running, prancing, and turning soon had him winded.

But now here it was—the goal in sight from five hundred meters. He had not yet gotten over the incredible sight of a hex border. It shimmered a little from the effect of the two different atmospheric compositions —not terribly different, but enough, like some odd clear plastic curtain. At the border, the life and terrain, often weather, stopped and was replaced by a dramatically different scene. Only the landforms and water bodies were constant; rivers flowed through without notice, seas of one washed on beaches of another, and foothills like those below continued on unbroken.

Djukasis was a dry hex; the thunderstorm was a rarity this time of year, and yet such sudden and violent storms provided most of the hex's rainfall. The grass was yellowish, the trees tough and spindly.

Now, at the Lata border, there suddenly started a deep-green carpet of rich grass, and tall, thick trees with great green leaf-covered branches reaching up for the sky, broken here and there by pools, meadows, and rolling glens. There was no sign of roads and, in the bright sunlight, no sign of people, either.

He wished he knew what kind of people lived there.

About a thousand meters into the hex, when he was still feeling the effects of a quadrupling of the humidity and a ten-degree temperature rise at least, he found out.

Multicolored energy bursts outlined Doma, who reacted nervously but had no place to go but back.

They're shooting at me! he thought in panic, then realized that the bursts were intended to discourage, not kill. Not yet, anyway.

He took the hint and made a 180-degree turn, crossing back into Djukasis. The moisture-hungry air of the bee's home started to dry his perspiration-soaked upper torso under his combat jacket, which he hadn't yet shed.

He set Doma down as close to the border as possible and jumped off, looking warily just across the line, wondering who or what was looking back at him. He took off his uniform jacket and tossed it away, leaving just the standard military blue briefs. Taking Doma's reins, he cautiously proceeded back to the border, leading the horse on the ground.

This time, only ten or fifteen paces inside the border, he was challenged. The trouble was, it sounded like a lot of angry bells; he couldn't understand a word of it.

He stopped, looking out at the silent forest. The bells stopped, too, waiting. He pointed to himself. "Renard!"

he shouted. "Entry!" That second word was different in most languages, though, he realized. It might not be understood here. "Mavra Chang!" he called out. "Mavra Chang!"

That set off more discussion. Finally, the universal rules set themselves in motion. When in doubt, pass the buck.

He put up his hands in what he hoped was a recognizable sign of surrender, hoping they, too, had hands and could understand his meaning.

They did. Suddenly a whole host of them erupted from the trees, armed with nasty-looking energy rifles. As a Djukasis veteran, he also immediately noticed the pretty but obvious stingers.

Pixies! he thought in surprise. Little flying girls. A high-tech hex, though; those rifles looked plenty effective, and whether that antiaircraft fire was automatic or them shooting, they could hit anything they wanted, of that he had no doubt.

They surrounded him, looked wonderingly at Doma, and made unmistakable gestures that he was to move ahead. He saw that they all wore goggles and seemed very uncomfortable. He suspected that they were nocturnal creatures. They led him to a clearing a few thousand meters farther on; one of them made a lot of sign-language gestures that gave no doubt as to their meaning. He was to stay there and make no move, and he would be covered, so no funny business, or else.

That suited him. He was used to waiting now. Doma grazed on the rich new grass, and he stretched out and went to sleep.

Vistaru came into Mavra Chang's ground-level quarters in a hurry.

"Mavra?"

She had been lying there on a specially constructed bed, looking over Well World maps and geographies, mostly children's picture books. You didn't learn a complex language in a few weeks, particularly one established for a vocal system you couldn't imitate.

"Yes, Vistaru?" she responded, weary and bored from doing nothing.

"Mavra, there is one of the creatures involved in the

268

war who came in from the Djukasis border a few minutes ago. We just got a radio report."

The news was mildly interesting, but didn't change
her situation at all. "So?"

"He came in on a huge flying horse! You won't believe it! Gigantic, pale green. And, Mavra—he kept
calling for you! Over and over! By name!"

She was on her feet in a moment. "What did this
creature look like?"

The Lata shrugged. "An Agitar, they say. Bigger
than Lata, smaller than you. All dark blue and fuzzy
at the bottom."

She shook her head. "That's a new one on me. What
do you think? A trick?"

"If it is, it's misfired," the Lata responded firmly.
"Anything funny and he'll never leave Lata alive. They
asked whether you'd talk to him."

"If I can," she replied, and walked out.

There was no problem getting her there quickly. Although the Lata flew and hence had no need for roads
or aircraft, they did have to move freight and foodstuffs
all over. They just diverted a large, crate-laden truck
on government authority and much to the driver's disgust. Mavra Chang and three thousand crates of apples
sped south to the border in a flatbed dual-rotor helicopter, skimming the treetops. The trip took about
three hours, and the sun was into late afternoon when
they arrived. With a straight axial tilt, all hexes had
equal amounts of daylight, a little over fourteen standard hours each.

The pegasus was really as grand and beautiful as
had been described, and its rider was as short, squat,
and ugly.

"Cute little devil," Mavra muttered mostly to herself
—and that's what the face looked like. An old Tradi-
tionist's view of the devil in dark-blue and black hair.
The creature had awakened when the helicopter approached, and stood and walked around. The thick
body and the terribly thin legs looked almost impossible; he moved as if on tiptoe, and reminded Mavra of
a costumed ballet dancer.

Guards armed with energy pistols motioned him to
a cleared area and flanked him on all sides. He won-

269

dered idly what bigwig had come to see this new intrusion, but then he looked again and there was no mistake.

"Mavra!" he cried, and started to move toward her. The guards were quick, no doubt about it. He stopped cold. He pointed to himself. "Renard, Mavra! Renard!"

She was more than surprised. Although she knew the system of the Well—it had been explained at length to her—this was the first time it really hit her in the face. She chuckled, then turned to Vistaru. "This translator —can I talk to him?"

She nodded. "You have a translator," the Lata reminded her.

"Renard?" she called out. "Is that really *you?*"

He beamed. "It's me, all right! A little changed, but still me inside! I traded sponge for goat!" he called back.

She laughed. Communication worked fine. He understood her Confederation, the translator took care of the Agitar.

"Are you sure it's really Renard?" one of the border guards asked her. "Somebody you know? A lot of folks have claimed to be a lot of other folks lately."

She nodded, thinking it over. Then she yelled, "Renard! They need proof that you're you. And, to tell the truth, so do I. And there's only one question I can think of that only our side would know, so forgive me." He nodded, and she went on. "Renard, who was the last old-type human being you made love to?"

He frowned, embarrassed by the question even as he saw the logic of it. Only Mavra, he himself, and the person involved would know the answer, and she would have no reason for deception. "Nikki Zinder," he replied.

She nodded. "It's Renard. Not only the answer but the way he made it sound so terrible convinces me. Let him come to me or me to him."

The guards still weren't all that certain. "But he's an Agitar!" one growled. "One of *them.*"

"He's Renard, no matter what," she responded, and walked briskly out to him. The guards kept at the ready, but appeared resigned.

She was taller than he, now—maybe ten centimeters

with her boots on, three or four without. He was ugly as sin and smelled like a goat, but she hugged him and kissed him lightly on the forehead, laughing.

"Renard! Let me look at you! They *told* me this would happen, but somehow I couldn't really believe it!"

He was slightly embarrassed again, from his strange new form and, oddly, because the Agitar part of his brain didn't really react to her as a woman, but as another, alien creature. He began to realize just how much he'd changed.

Mavra turned to Doma, who looked up as she cautiously approached. "He's beautiful!" she breathed. "Can I—touch him? Will he mind?"

"She," Renard corrected. "Her name is Doma. Let her look you over for a moment and then rub the spot between her ears when her head droops. She likes that."

Mavra did as instructed, and found the great pegasus friendly, curious, and responsive.

She walked around, looking at the saddle between the great, now-folded wings and the neck. It was a sophisticated device—altimeter, air-speed and ground-speed indicator, everything.

She turned to him. "You'll have to take me up on her sometime," she said longingly. "I'd love to see her fly. But, tell me everything that's happened, first."

"If you'll get me some food—any fruits or meats will do that you can eat," he replied lightly. "I'm starving to death!"

They sat there in the glen until the sun was down and the pixie people were out in force. He told her of waking up in Agitar, of Trelig, of being drafted, and of the war and his experiences. She sympathized, while secretly wishing to be in the thick of what he had escaped from, and told him a simplified version of how they'd been hypnotized to minimize the sponge effects, of their capture by the Teliagin, their Latan rescue, and how they'd gotten to Zone.

"What about Nikki?" he asked. "Do you know where she got to? I haven't really stopped thinking about her. She's so young and so naïve—tough to be out cold on this world. *I* know."

Mavra looked at her shadow, Vistaru, who'd joined them. Vistaru shook her head. "Nothing on either Zinder. That's curious. It's not impossible to remain undetected here, of course, but doing so *is* rare. The old politicians have somebody in their pocket in half the South." She spoke in Lata, and Mavra translated. "So we might lose track of one—but both? It's very strange. We would like to know where they are.

"It's as if the Well opened and swallowed them up."

Several days passed, happy ones for Renard, diverting ones for Mavra, whose boredom was at least slightly relieved by the man. He taught her to fly Doma; it was easy for her, she found, although some of the maneuvers required more muscle power than she could easily manage. She decided that she would never be mistress of that great horse, but it was still a great feeling to fly.

And then the Southern alliance reached Olborn. It was ahead of schedule by several days; Zhonzorp, whose people the books said looked like crocodiles standing erect and who wore turbans, cloaks, and all sorts of strangely exotic stuff, had been invaluable. A high-tech hex, it gained them both time and a rest by moving them across the terrain by rail.

That's when Vistaru came to them, with a visitor, an older male-mode Lata.

"This is Ambassador Siduthur," she introduced the newcomer. At Mavra's insistence they had fitted Renard with a translator, which helped immensely, made him feel more in command of himself again.

Mavra and Renard nodded courteously.

"As you know, both wars are going well," Siduthur began, "which means that they are going badly for us. Our friends in other hexes tell me that one or the other of the alliances will surely win, that it is in fact possible to reassemble the ship, and that, if nothing is done, we will face a space-capable Well alliance that could gain control of the satellite and its computer. We can no longer sit idly by and let this happen."

At last! Mavra thought, but she kept silent as the Latan ambassador continued.

"The only possibility we have is the hope that Gedemondas can be talked into either turning the engines over to us or destroying them." He told them about the silence and reticence of the Gedemondas. "So, you see, we need to get someone in there. Explain things to the Gedemondas if such is possible. Get their cooperation if that first is achieved, and— whether we get cooperation or not—if we can not get those engines, make certain that they are destroyed beyond any means of reconstruction!"

Mavra leaped on it. "I'm the only one who can make sure of that," she pointed out. "None of the rest of you know the power plant from the cargo hold, and none of you would be able to tell if the thing were damaged or destroyed."

"We're aware of that," the ambassador replied. "We should have liked to have a few more days to gather together some better people to go with you. The trouble is, the best-qualified help is too distant, and the more local help is either conquered, under siege, or unwilling to get involved, the fools. The best we can do is have an expert Dillian get around and meet you near the Gedemondas border. They are neighbors, good in cold weather, and know about as much of the Gedemondans as anybody. At least, you're not as likely to be ambushed by the Gedemondans with a nonthreatening life form they at least know accompanying you."

"I'll go, too," Renard volunteered. "Doma can carry Mavra as well as me, and that should speed things up."

The ambassador nodded. "We had planned on it. We're not a hundred percent trusting of you, Agitar, but we believe sincerely in your attachment for Mavra Chang. That is enough. Vistaru and Hosuru, another Entry and former pilot, will also go with you."

"Another Entry?" Mavra asked. "I thought they were scarce and that Vistaru, here, was the only one of my kind—"

"That is true," the ambassador cut in. "Hosuru was *not* one of your kind before."

It may have been racial pride, or ego, or just chauvinism, but it was the first time either Renard or

Mavra Chang had even considered a spacefaring race other than their own.

"What was this Hosuru?" Mavra asked. "And how many other spacefaring races are there that wound up here?"

"Sixty-one at last count, in the South. Nobody knows about the North," the ambassador replied. "Certainly as many. She was once one of what we call the Ghlmones, which one of your people long ago described as little green fire-breathing dinosaurs, whatever that means."

Hosuru wasn't a fire-breathing dinosaur anymore. Still in the female mode, she looked absolutely identical to Vistaru except for being a deep brown in contrast to the other Lata's passionate pink.

The ambassador opened a map. "We are here," he told them, pointing to a hex. "To our east is the Sea of Storms. As you can see, the best route would be over Tuliga and Galidon to Palim, which has to be crossed sooner or later anyway. However, the Galidon are fierce carnivores and the atmosphere above the waters is not conducive to flying, so that's out. That means crossing Tuliga to this point here, landing in Olborn. The Tuliga are rather nasty giant sea slugs, but they shouldn't bother you if you don't bother them."

"Doma's good for about four hundred kilometers if pushed," Renard said, "but that's a good deal farther."

"It is," the ambassador agreed. "There are, however, a few small islands along the way, so you can set down to rest. On no account must you go into the water! It is also brackish, not good for drinking, but the islands are volcanic and should have small crater lakes. Pick your camp spot well."

"Anything living on the islands we should know about?" Mavra asked cautiously.

The ambassador shook his head. "Nothing but birds, perhaps a few crustaceans of no importance. No, the problem will be when you reach land again—with the Porigol supporting the Yaxa, there is simply no way around Olborn."

"But this Olborn—isn't it the next target of the Makiem, Cebu, and Agitar?" Renard asked worriedly. "Won't they be likely to confuse us with their enemy?"

"Truthfully, we haven't the slightest idea," the ambassador admitted. "They are in many ways as unknown as the Gedemondas. Catlike creatures, I understand, with semitech capabilities and, it says in the references, limited magic, although I don't quite know what that means. Even so, you need only cross it at the top. The attack from Zhonzorp to the extreme south might actually help you by drawing off whatever fighters and major power the Olbornians have."

"We hope," sighed the worried Renard. "Then what?"

"By air over Palim, as close to the border as you can in order to avoid as much as possible meeting the Yaxa alliance that might well be marching through at about the same time. *Don't* cut south into Alestol, though, whatever you have to do! They are fast-moving plants that can direct poisonous gases that have effects that are sometimes fatal and always bad. They are carnivores who could digest any of you. Leave them to the Makiem and their cohorts to deal with. *You must get to Gedemondas ahead of the others at all costs!* Our only hopes rest with you. Can you do it?"

Mavra Chang wanted action so badly she could taste it. "With a little luck, and occasional help, I've never failed a commission yet," she said confidently. "This is the sort of mission I've been waiting for!"

The ambassador looked at her warily. "This is not the Com," he reminded her. "The rules change quickly here."

The Tuliga-Galidon-Olborn Triangle, Dusk

THEIR CROSSING, WHILE UNEVENTFUL, TOOK THREE precious days. They flew over choppy seas in Tuliga, and the wind was against them most of the way. On the few daylight hours of relative calm they were able to spot coral reefs teeming with great numbers of multicolored fish, and, then and there, shadowy black bulks of great size.

They kept at a safe altitude, not wanting to risk any chance that one of those dark shapes might somehow rise out of the water and bring them down. It was more peaceful when they reached the Galidon border, but the atmosphere looked a little strange over there, and they headed in toward the point of land that marked one of Olborn's six points on the Tuligan side.

Olborn itself seemed a welcome relief—solid-looking, mostly coastal plain, a little chilly, but they had brought protective clothing with them. Nothing in the place looked grim, foreboding, or threatening.

They waited until darkness fell before making a landfall on the beach. They had decided to camp there, within easy reach of a quick getaway and with the great Doma as concealed as she could be.

No roads had led down to the coast, they'd been certain of that. With watery neighbors like the Galidon, they didn't find this the least bit unusual.

It was a clear night; above, the spectacular sky of the Well World was displayed in all its glory, and, off to the north, a silvery disk covered part of the horizon.

It was the first time they had been in the right position with the right weather at the right moment to see New Pompeii. They stared at it in silence, thinking.

"So close, so damned close," Mavra Chang whispered under her breath. It looked like you could reach out and touch it. She thought of the poor people who had almost certainly died there by now, and of the kindly, near-human computer, Obie, who had helped her escape. She wanted to get back to that place, and she swore to herself that she would, someday.

They turned in. Although the Lata were nocturnal, the trip had been a long and tiring one, the daytime travel taking more out of them, and they, too, slept. A watch was established, of course.

Mavra had second watch; the Lata would take the later ones, when they'd be at their peak. She sat there, looking out at the slightly rough sea, hearing the roar of the surf, and watching the skies.

They were glorious skies, she thought. Her element, the place to which she'd been born, the place for which she's done everything, even sold herself, to attain. She looked at the others sleeping. The Lata were perfect here. Flying on those tiny wings would be fun, and there were no political or sexual pressures in their land to shape what happened. Even being short didn't matter; they all looked alike. But their world was 355 kilometers on each of its six sides. Such a minute place, a stiflingly small area when you looked at those skies.

Renard, too, was better off here. The Well World was certainly bigger than New Pompeii, and more stimulating than new Muscovy. He was a walking dead man in the old life; here he had some power, a future, and, if things worked out, could possibly rise high in Agitar if they lost the war. From what he'd said of the people's sentiments, a defeat would bring down the government, and one who helped end the war rather than press it would be more hero than, as he was now, traitor.

But not Mavra Chang. The Well World was an adventure, a challenge, but it was not her element. To go through the Well someday and come out something else—it wouldn't matter. The Well didn't change

277

you inside, only physiologically. She would still want the stars.

Her reflections were broken by subtle sounds not far off. She wasn't sure she heard anything for a short time, and she listened intently as her ears strained for them. She had just decided that she was imagining things, when she heard the noise again, off to the northwest, there, not very far—and closer.

She considered waking the others, but then thought better of it. The sounds had stopped. Still, she decided, a little investigation might be in order. A yell from her would rouse the others in a hurry anyway, and there was no use waking them for nothing.

Silently, softly, she crept toward where she'd last heard the sounds. There was a thin clump of trees near a marshland river mouth just up from the sounds; she decided that whatever made them had to be there. Slowly, carefully, she moved into the thin line of trees.

She heard a sound again to her right, and headed for it. Crouching behind a bush, she peered out.

There was a strange, large bird there. Its body was something like a peacock's, its head a round ball, out of which came a beak that looked almost like a tiny air horn. Its eyes were round and yellow, reflecting the starlight. It was nocturnal, then. She breathed a sigh of relief, and the bird must have heard her. It turned and said, rather loudly and a little rudely, "*Bwock wok!*"

"Bwock wok, yourself," Mavra whispered, and turned to go back to the nearby camp.

The trees exploded. Large bodies dropped all around her, one on top of her. "*Renard!*" she screamed. "*Vistaru!*" But that was all she had time for. Something seemed to cover her head, blotting out all consciousness.

Doma started, and all three of the others snapped awake at the two cut-short screams.

Renard saw them as the Lata took off; large shapes rushing them from the nearby trees. He almost made it to Doma, when one of them, much taller and furrier than he and with glowing yellow-black eyes, got a hand on him.

That was a mistake.

There was a crackle, the Olbornian screamed, and there was the odor of burning hair and flesh. Another one was trying for Doma's reins, but the horse backed away as Renard leaped aboard. The Olbornian snarled and turned to reach out for Renard.

The Agitar got the vision of a great black cat's face, with terribly luminous slit cat's eyes, and he touched a hairy, clawed hand with three fingers and a thumb.

Which sent the Olbornian to cat heaven.

Doma didn't need any cuing. Knowing its rider was aboard, the great winged horse thundered down the beach, knocking over black shapes not lucky enough to get out of the way, and it was airborne.

The Lata, whose stingers had helped clear the way, flew to him.

"We have to find Mavra!" Renard screamed. "They have her!"

"Stay in this area!" Hosuru shouted. "We don't know what they have and we can't afford to lose Doma! We'll go after her, and if we can't free her one of us will stay with her while the other comes back for you!"

It wasn't what he wanted to do, but he had no choice. Neither Doma nor he had exceptional night vision, and if the Lata lit up they'd all make perfect targets.

The two Lata, however, saw best in the dark. Just beyond the river there was a coach of some sort; a finely wrought piece of woodwork moving on great wooden wagon wheels pulled by a team of eight tiny burrolike animals. Four Olbornians, armed with projectile pistols, stood on running boards around it; two more drove it, one controlling the little mules and the other holding a sleek, effective-looking rifle. The doors and windows to the coach were sealed with hinged wooden panels. From the way the driver cracked the whip on the poor little animals, they knew what the coach's cargo had to be.

"We can't do anything but follow the damned

thing," Vistaru swore. "Renard can take care of himself."

That was more than heartfelt sentiments. In all his time in Lata, he'd not discharged. They knew he carried a lot of static electricity, but until the brief fight they'd not realized how much or how lethal.

The coach beat down the grass until it reached a smooth, tar-paved road, and sped along it to the east. It was not terribly fast, and the Lata had no trouble keeping just behind and above it, out of sight.

"We could sting them to death," Vistaru said wistfully.

"How much you got left?" Hosuru snapped. "I used mine three times. I'm nearly dry."

The odds weren't that good.

They studied the Olbornians and their coach. The creatures were about 180 centimeters high; they were all completely covered in black fur, but they also wore some sort of clothing, baggy dark trousers of some sort and sleeveless shirts with a light border and woven insignia in the center. They had long, black, apparently functionless tails, and sleek cat's bodies, but their arms and legs were muscular, and they obviously walked upright on two legs naturally.

The little mules were something else. They looked somehow sad, pathetic, and *wrong*. Their hind legs were taller by perhaps twenty percent than their forelegs; they were a little over a meter high, and they had long necks curving upward so they looked ahead instead of down. Their long ears were large in proportion to their heads, and they had no tails. They were covered in a soft, uniform gray fur.

They were being badly pushed and mercilessly whipped; they were certainly too small and too few for the weight they were being asked to pull, but they managed it, their short, trotting-horse gait getting the wagon there, helped somewhat by the smoothness of the road.

Finally, they turned in at a magnificent estate—a truly grand-looking palace whose horseshoe-shaped driveway was lit by torches; more torches flanked the doors, and there were rifle-armed guards dressed in the same way as those on the coach. The coach pulled to a halt and the Olbornians jumped off efficiently. A door facing the estate was opened, and two more of the creatures emerged, then turned and carefully removed a large black object from the coach.

It was Mavra Chang, and she looked stiff as a board.

"Is she dead?" Hosuru worried.

Vistaru shook her head. "No, they're being too careful for that. Drugged, probably."

"Now what?" the other Lata asked.

Vistaru thought a moment. "First, go back, tell Renard what happened, where we are—describe the place. Then help him find some place to sit down for a while. I'll keep watch here, try to find where in this palace they've put her. Tomorrow, when Renard's at his peak, we'll come get her no matter what."

Mavra Chang regained consciousness slowly, and it took some time for her to get her bearings. She looked around, finding she couldn't move her head, only her eyes. She couldn't move anything.

She was standing up, propped slightly against a wall. She thought that her hands and feet were securely tied, but she couldn't be sure.

The place was a stable. It stank of animal excrement and rotted straw, and on the walls were odd-shaped harnesses.

She strained to look around, but whatever they had drugged her with held her securely. She did see one of the animals, though, briefly. A queer-looking thing. No, that wasn't right, everything on this cockeyed world was queer-looking, she told herself. But because the creature looked so much like draft animals that she'd known back in the human worlds, "queer-looking" was the only way to describe it.

They looked for all the world like miniature mules. Black nose, big, squared-off snout, but with jackass-type ears that seemed too large for that head. A very long neck, almost too long, attached to a small body supported at an angle, the slender front legs shorter than the rear ones, which had the characteristic large upper calf and almost incredibly thin lower.

And sad, large brown eyes.

281

They also bore scars; some from whips, some from other unknown sources.

Three Olbornians entered the room, two in the black-and-gold livery, the third wearing some sort of crown and a long gold chain from which was suspended a hexagonal pendant. His own livery was scarlet, with baggy golden trousers. Somebody important. He was also old—he walked slowly, and there were tinges of gray in his black fur.

He walked into the doorway, almost running into the little minimule. He snarled and swatted it cruelly, claws extended. The thing gave no sound, but there was obvious pain and Mavra could see a set of bleeding scratches. It jumped and moved away.

These were a cruel, callous people.

The old one looked at her. "So, spy! Awake, eh? Good!" He turned to the others. "See to it. We'd best be off. Her companions may try some sort of rescue, so we have to move fast."

Mavra felt relief at these words; the other three had escaped! And, somehow, they would get her out of there, she felt sure. She was necessary to them.

She felt like a puppet with lead wires in it so it could be bent in any shape and would stay there. They put her on top one of the little mules, in a basic saddle. The big man led it down a back path from the rear of the house, into a dark grove of trees. The two guards held her firmly on, but she was powerless to do anything anyway.

Overhead, Vistaru almost missed the departure. There was just a glimpse of the woman and her three catlike captors going out the back and heading into the woods. She followed and tried to guess ahead.

About two thousand meters down, the woods parted for a clearing where there was a large stone structure seemingly carved out of the small hillside. Two other guards were there, having just lit torches on either side of a hexagonal entranceway. Not a Zone Gate, she decided. That stuff had been built by somebody here.

She strained to think what the place reminded her of, and, all at once, she had it. An ancient temple. An altar. Sacrifice?

She sped directly back to Renard and Hosuru. There was no time to lose.

They lifted her off when they came to the hexagonal opening and carried her gently inside. There was a chamber there, an enlargement of a natural cave of limestone or something similar. Torches had been lit along the fairly broad passageway, which opened quickly into the main chamber.

It was a temple, no question about it. There was an area for supplicants to stand, a rail, and then tables set on either side of a large yellow stone that seemed to be protruding out of the natural rock in back. It was multifaceted; millions of them, from all evidence, reflecting the torchlight as if it had a strange, eerie life of its own. Mounted on the both walls, in solid gold, were outlines of the hexagon symbol.

The high priest, for by now it was evident what he was, preceded them, lighting small candles in ceremonial holders, six per holder. Then he went behind the rail. Satisfied all was in readiness, he nodded to the guards to bring her forward. They did, placing her facing the strange yellow stone.

"Undress it," the priest snapped, and the guards removed her black cloth shirt, black pants, and boots. It was suddenly chilly.

She was nude.

The guards tossed the clothing in a heap outside the altar rail. She longed to be able to use some of the things in those boots or the belt, or even to try the nail venom on them. But she was held motionless by something she could not control.

The priest moved toward her, motioning for them to turn her a little bit toward him. His yellow cat's eyes glowed weirdly in the torchlight.

"Spy," he said, his voice crisp, businesslike, and without a trace of mercy or compassion in it, "you have been judged guilty by the High Priestly Council of the Blessed Well," he intoned, bowing his head slightly when pronouncing the last two words. He made a horizontal motion with his right hand, and she felt control return to her head. She moistened her lips, but knew she could talk.

"I didn't even have a trial and you know it!" she protested hoarsely. "I haven't had a chance to say anything!"

"I did not say you were *tried*," the priest pointed out, "only that you were *judged*. There are no mitigating factors. Heathen knock on our door to the north, worse heathen wantonly and horribly kill tens of thousands of the Chosen of the Well to the south. Now, you come. You are not of the Olborn, certainly. Nor are you here by invitation or permission of the High Priestly Council of the Blessed Well." Again the slight nod. "A spy you are, and so I ask you, is there any way for you to conclusively prove your innocence?"

What a loaded question! she thought. Prove you didn't smile. Prove you didn't kill your mother whom the court never knew or heard of. "You know no one can prove they *aren't* something," she retorted.

He nodded. "Of course. But there is a final arbiter of justice."

"You're going to kill me," she said more than asked.

The priest looked genuinely shocked. Mavra wondered why she'd always liked cats in the past.

"Of course we do not kill, except in self-defense. All life is from the Blessed Well, and cannot be taken lightly. As you took no other life, unlike your companions, we could not take yours."

Both parts of that observation cheered her a little. Alive meant hope, and the news that the others had sent some of these religious fanatics to an early grave was just as satisfying.

"The Well, in Its infinite wisdom and mercy," the priest explained, as if in a liturgy, "established among the Olbornians a more equitable means of final judgment—final, absolute, and conclusive. The stone that is before you is one of six, located near the six corners of Olborn. It is proof of the favored status of the Olbornians with the Blessed Well. Its power comes from the Well Itself. What it does has never been undone."

This tack started unnerving her again. She thought of Renard, changed into a different creature. What the hell did this thing do?

"The Well, in Its infinite wisdom," continued the priest, "saw that Its Chosen People were in a harsh land, rich but without beasts of burden to help Its Chosen People till the good soil, pull its burdens, turn its water wheels. Thus we have the Sacred Stones. When a transgressor, whether alien or Olbornian, is accused, he is brought before one of the High Priests of the Blessed Well, and thence in his company to the Sacred Stone. Should you be innocent, then nothing will happen to you. You will be free to go on your way, unmolested, protected by the Seal of the Blessed Well. But, should you be guilty, it will mete out the most wonderful of justices." He paused. "You saw the detik upon which you were carried here?"

She thought a moment. The little mules with the big ears and sad eyes. "Yes," she replied, curious and apprehensive. Where the hell were the Lata and Renard?

"They are sexless, joyless. Totally placid, they are incapable of harming anything, and are forced to obey our commands. Should you be guilty, you will turn to a detik, a beast of the fields, condemned to serve the Olbornians in silent labor the rest of your life."

She was appalled, unbelieving. "You mean the mules—all of them—were once *people?*"

The priest nodded. "It is so." He turned to the guards. "Hold her arms tight," he cautioned. Then he turned back to Mavra. She felt strong hands holding her arms just behind the wrist. The priest waved his arms again, and she felt movement return to her whole body. As she suspected, her legs were tied.

"Touch her hands to the Sacret Stone!" the priest commanded, his voice echoing through the damp cavern. The two powerful arms ignored her twisting and pushed her unwilling hands to the faceted yellow orb.

Something like a strong, burning electric shock went through her arms to her shoulders. The effect was so strong and so painful that she screamed and actually pulled away from the wretched thing despite the strength of her two captors.

"That was Mavra!" Vistaru yelled. "Come on! Hurry!" she called to Hosuru and Renard, who rushed ahead. Neither cared any more if there was a whole army ahead; they were going in *now*.

Inside the chamber, the priest seemed to smile and intoned, "Again!" This time the terrible shock and pain went from her hips to her toes, and, strangely, wound up in her ears. Again she screamed and fought to pull away.

"Again!" the priest commanded, but at that moment the onrushing Lata and Agitar charged, Renard yelling bloodcurdling screams that echoed terrifyingly off the cavern walls.

The priest turned, looking stunned and surprised. Like most fanatics, the concept that anybody would invade his holiest of places had simply never occurred to him, and he couldn't handle it. He stood there petrified. Not the two guards. They dropped Mavra and whirled. They had no pistols, which was fortunate, but they bore ceremonial steel swords, which they drew.

Keeping all their attention on the guards and priest, Renard and Vistaru both yelled, "Run, Mavra! Get out of here! We'll handle this!"

The first guard took advantage of this distraction to advance on Renard, sword poised, saberlike, in front of him.

Renard smiled grimly, and moved his tast out in a similar manner, as if preparing to duel. The guard looked at the thin, snaky cooper-clad whip and chuckled. He moved with his sword, and Renard brought the tast up, touching the sword.

Sparks flew, and the guard screamed and dropped to the floor of the cavern, the point where his hand gripped the hilt actually smoking slightly.

Vistaru, who still had some venom left, swooped at the other one, suddenly turning on her internal light to catch the foe off-guard. He was too good for that, and he stabbed in with his sword.

And missed.

She did an aerial backflip and plunged her stinger into his stomach, then pushed off him. The guard yowled, then seemed to stiffen, as he dropped to the floor, limp, lying eyes wide-open and unseeing.

Marva felt the guards release their grip on her and felt the cold stone as they dropped her. Her whole body was tingling and her mind wouldn't clear, but she had enough sense to hear Renard's shout to run, and take that advice. A naked, stunned Mavra Chang wasn't going to be much good in a fight.

She was dizzy, and couldn't seem to get up, so she took off on all fours. Her head seemed heavy; she couldn't lift it, but she could see enough to head for the exit and did so, almost knocking over the guard just now meeting his end from Renard's tast. She wanted to crawl fast, but she couldn't lift her head up far enough; a nerve in the back of it was killing her, and her hair was hanging down in front, further obscuring her vision. But she made the steps and scampered out, passing the now-dead guards slumped under their still burning torches. Out ahead, she could see, was blackness, and that was where she wanted to be.

She crawled into the bushes before she stopped, chest heaving, and tried to clear her head. She looked back at the entrance, but she couldn't get her head up quite far enough, or hold it even far enough to see out of the tops of her eyes without that nerve pinching and hurting.

With the return of her wind came a clearer head. She was still on all fours. Why, she began to wonder. It was dark, but Obie had given her night vision, and she put her head chin against chest, essentially upside down, and looked back at herself. Her hair fell straight down.

Her thin, lithe body was unchanged, her two small breasts hanging down and tugging slightly as a result of being dead weight.

My arms! she suddenly thought in panic. *What did they do?*

She also felt two long bending sensations with her head that way.

She no longer had arms. She now had forelegs—thin and with a knee joint that bent only one way, locking the other way. It led down to a perfectly formed, fairly thick hoof of some whitish-gray substance like fingernails. There was no hair; the legs were still the same flesh color as the rest of her, the skin still looked human. But they were the legs of the little mule.

Looking farther back, she saw what she expected to see, and sighed. Now she understood why she couldn't get off all fours, and why she couldn't seem to get her head up properly. The forelegs were a good twenty percent shorter than the hind legs. In the mule, the long neck compensated; a human head and neck wasn't designed to go that far.

Renard and the two Lata came out of the cave. She heard them more than saw them, and, after a moment's hesitation, called to them. They were there in a flash.

"Mavra, you ought to have seen that old boy's face when—" Renard started cheerfully, when she walked out of the brush into the torchlight. They all three gasped, mouths agape. For the first time they could see and know what the Olbornians had done to Mavra Chang.

First, take the arms and legs off a woman's torso. Then turn it face down, the hips about a meter high, the shoulders about eighty centimeters. Now put a perfectly proportioned pair of mule's hind legs on the hips, so that the base of the body kind of melds into it. Now put two mule's legs on the shoulders, long enough to reach the ground but shorter because of the angle of the body. But don't add an animal's hair or skin—keep it all human, perfectly matched to the torso, except for hard, naillike hooves on all four feet, and, as a final touch, remove the human ears from her head and replace them with large, almost meter-long jackass ears, still out of the same human skin material. Then continue the woman's hair down across the back a bit into a thicker mane of the same color hair, extending along the spine to about where the breasts hung down on the underside. And, since the torso hasn't been otherwise altered, remember to put Mavra's horse's tail growing out of the waist at the base of the spinal column, above the hips, actually starting slightly in front of the hind legs, and drape it crudely over the rectum.

The others felt tears of pity rise within them. "Oh, my god!" was all Renard could say, and he felt bad about it as soon as it was out.

She shifted slightly, then turned her head to one side, almost far enough to look directly at him. Her hair hung down well below her face, crazily. Her voice was the same; even, level, and rich, but her eyes, when she turned her head to one side to look at them, said something else was inside her.

"I know," she told them. "I figured it out. Those little mules they have—they make them with that stone in there, from people. I touched it twice, then got away when you arrived. Tell me—is anything else changed?"

Choking back tears, Renard sat beside her and gently described her to herself, including the ears and misplaced tail.

The odd thing was, they all thought, she looked strange and exotic, to Renard almost erotic, a curious and not unattractive little creature that engendered affection with the pity. But it was still an impractical, misdesigned creature, a one-of-a-kind on a world with 1560 races.

"Maybe I should go back in and complete the process," she suggested, hoping the hoarseness and thickness in her speech would not betray how she really felt.

"I wouldn't," Vistaru said softly, sympathetically. Mavra was already beginning to hate that tone. "You saw how they treated those mules? The thing does something to the mind, too. You'd be an animal, as good as dead."

Renard had a sudden thought. "Look!" he said excitely. "It isn't forever!"

"The priest said it was irreversible," Mavra responded. "He said it so joyfully I believed him."

"No! No!" the Agitar protested. "You haven't been through the Well Gate yet!"

"The priest said the stone's power was from the Well," she retorted.

"That's true," Vistaru put in, "but so is everything

else on the Well World. Why that stone is there and why it does what it does we'll probably never know—it's a substitute for something they would have to handle on their own planet, that's all. Like the magic hexes here, which really mean they can tap a limited part of the Well to compensate for something in their designed homes. You still haven't been classified and added to the Well's input, so whatever changes the stone made won't affect that."

Mavra felt renewed hope. "Not forever," she almost breathed, and seemed to relax. Suddenly she was upset that she'd let something show through the armor, and she took a deep breath.

"Not forever," Renard agreed. "Look, want to head for a Zone Gate now? Not Olborn's certainly, but we can get in somewhere, I'm sure. We can run you through like you ran me through."

Mavra shook her head violently. "No, no, not yet. Later, yes. As soon as possible. But the surrounding hexes are in the war. *This* hex is in the war. That's for normal times. We have to get to Gedemondas."

"I can do that!" Vistaru protested.

Mavra shook her head again. "No, you can't. You won't know what the engine module looks like, nor how it's destroyed. Besides, I have never ever backed out on a commission yet once I've accepted it. They wanted me along and I said yes. After—a Zone Gate —maybe in Gedemondas, if they'll talk to us at all, or in Dillia next door."

"Be reasonable, Mavra!" Renard protested. "Look at you! You can't see three meters ahead of you. You can't feed yourself, you're stark naked with no protection against the elements, in the middle of territory whose natives would take you back to the stone and finish the job in an instant." He got up, looked down on her, and gently moved the horse's tail aside. "You're even going to have bathroom trouble. Your vagina's where your ass should be, and the ass is farther up. The human anatomy is designed for sitting or squatting. Those legs are not designed for your body. You *can't* go on!"

She tried to look at him squarely, failed. It hurt too much. "I'm going," she maintained stubbornly. "With you if you'll have me. Without you if not. If you want, you can be my guide and aide when I have to see far or eat, and clean me off when I shit. If not, I'll go anyway, and I'll make it. When you were sucking your thumb on sponge, and I didn't know where I was, I didn't let you go, and I didn't quit. This won't stop me, either."

"She's right, you know," Hosuru said quietly. "At least, about completing the mission first. The whole world is at stake in Gedemondas. She's needed there. If we can get her there, it's our duty to try."

"Okay," Vistaru said dubiously, trying to see the flaw in the other Lata's logic. "If you're going to be stubborn, we'll all go. But I think a day or two in that new condition may cure you of this bravado. If it does, don't feel ashamed, weak, or a failure to ask us to get you to a Zone Gate. *I* wouldn't."

Mavra chuckled mirthlessly. "Shame and weakness don't scare me, but I die when I'm a failure to myself." She shifted again. "Did anybody get my clothes? I might still manage some of them, with Renard's soldier's kit. And we ought to get out of here. Sooner or later somebody's going to notice the high priest didn't come back and raise a hue and cry. We'd best be well away."

Renard threw up his hands. "I have your clothes. We'll see, later. Now, let's move! This way!" There was resignation and a total lack of understanding in his voice.

He wouldn't understand, Mavra thought. None of them would.

Apparently the shock of the slayings was too much for the Olbornians. There was no pursuit that they ever knew about.

Mavra found that she could trot, like the little mules. Left legs out, *push,* right legs out, *push,* and again, faster and faster. She had no feeling at all in the hoofs, which helped, but all of the exposed skin area was just like normal exposed skin area. The Lata helped, flying alongside or just in front, telling her what was ahead so she didn't run into trees or hurt her neck, and could make some speed.

Morning had them some distance away. Renard mounted Doma, whom he'd been leading, and they scouted the terrain. It was clear that things were not going to be as difficult as they feared from the Olbornian score.

For the "Well's Chosen Ones," they were quite obviously getting the hell beat out of them. They had run afoul of a coast watch set around the Sacred Stones areas; it had been sheer bad luck to pick that spot to camp. The rest of the country was wide open, with the telltale signs of a war going badly all over: military carts drawn by teams of mules hauling supplies and large cannon and mortars south; a steady stream of aimless refugees north.

They stuck to open country, which was mostly deserted now, everyone down south into the fight or guarding the Sacred Stones and Zone Gate. They were able to relax and straighten out their situation.

Because of the precariousness of the camp, Doma's packs had never been unloaded, so they still had their supplies. They ate first; to Mavra, it was a humiliating type of experience she would have to get used to. They'd started to spoon-feed her, but she'd resisted that. They opened a tin of meat which Renard warmed, then broke up some small fruit, and put it in a wooden bowl. By standing on her hind legs and kneeling on her forelegs, she could eat, like a dog or cat. It was hard; the thin legs were even thinner at the ankles, and the legs moved forward, not back, and the damned bowl kept moving, but she managed it and the food tasted good. Water she drank by two methods: lapping, like an animal, and sticking her face in the pan and drinking the top half down.

But it worked, and that was enough for her.

Vistaru tied her hair up between and in back of her enormous ears with an elastic band, which kept it out of her face and food. She could even see level in front of her, by standing on her forelegs while kneeling on the hind ones. That position, too, was uncomfortable, but she didn't mind. It gave her neck some relief, and allowed her to see.

The clothing was more of a problem, though she'd

need it. It was slightly chilly in Olborn, and it would be frigid in the upper reaches of Gedemondas.

They cut the sleeves off her shirt and managed to get it on. The pants were a bigger problem, and they didn't quite reach all the way, but Vistaru buckled the wide belt around her bare midsection and that helped. It looked wrong and stupid, and felt wrong, too, and the pants kept slipping, but it was something and it felt better. The long coat tailored for Gedemondas would possibly do what was needed, covering that impossible tail, they hoped. Some cut-off gloves *might* help protect the exposed skin in Gedemondas snow. Maybe.

Oddly, Mavra felt better now. Obstacles were to be surmounted; that was part of the joy of it all. They noticed a pickup in her spirits they couldn't comprehend.

Sleeping was the worst compromise; the animal's legs were designed for sleeping standing up, but the human torso was not, and sleeping on her stomach was no longer possible. She managed lying on her side.

In the meantime, the war was going from bad to worse for those of Olborn. Occasionally they'd meet some frightened refugees, not looking as fierce or confident as those back in the priest's lair. Their world was coming apart, and with it their world-view and their notions of their place in it. No longer sure of anything, they were somehow sad and pathetic. People they ran into kept trying to surrender to them.

Roving military patrols caused worse problems; most were composed of deserters with the social restraint imposed on them by their life's conditioning and faith in their favored status with the Well all gone; they brutalized the refugees, they tried brutalizing the alien party, but renewed Lata venom and Renard's highly charged personality soon dealt effectively with them.

Mavra also found it interesting that no one gave her a second glance. To these insular people, she was just one more weird alien creature.

But progress was slow, and they turned their attention to trying to find some way to get Mavra *and* Renard on Doma. The problem was the great wings, which needed to be unimpeded, and which came down most of the length of the great animal's body.

Finally, experimentation achieved a compromise that Doma and practicality could accept. Nonessential supplies were jettisoned, and the Lata took as much as they could in their pouches. The weight would slow them, but Doma would also be slowed and impeded. With the instruments tossed out—Renard insisted he never used them anyway—she could sit, legs astraddle, on the lower neck of the pegasus, while he sat just behind, body pressed into hers. Straps from some of the excess saddlebags would hold her, and Doma, while uncomfortable with the extra weight on her neck, managed. The only problem was that it took all three of the others and some cooperation and kneeling from Doma to get her up there in the first place.

Finally, though, they could fly, and the distance sped by. They ducked south of the hex corner, avoiding any more priestly fanatics, and crossed barely into Palim.

The inhabitants of the hex eyed them nervously, but did not interfere or challenge them. The Palim resembled nothing so much as giant long-haired elephants. Their form was deceptive, though; they were a high-technology people, with carefully managed groves of food trees and grain, and a criss-cross of a large electric rail system and odd, gumdrop-shaped city buildings in clusters linked by ramps. They stayed clear; the Palim seemed too unconcerned by the nearby violence. It indicated that they had elected to sit out the war, and that meant the Yaxa-Lamotien-Dasheen alliance was probably making good use of that rail system in the east.

Even slowed, they made the border of Gedemondas in under two days. There was no doubt where they were; the great mountains of the frigid hex were visible from the flat plain, like some intrusive wall, a great distance before they reached it. With a few hours to scout around by air, they found the relatively small plains area that was in Gedemondas itself. It was the logical point for the two advancing armies to head for, and it was empty of all but some minor wildlife when they arrived.

They were first, but by how much?

They studied the maps. It was obvious that the Makiem would airlift over Alestol, probably to near the point where they now were. The Yaxa would move from Palim at the rail terminus, then about thirty kilometers overland to the northern edge of the plain. Renard wondered idly if there would be room for both forces.

"There will be quite a battle," Mavra predicted grimly. "If one gets here first the other will have to dislodge them if it can. If they get here at the same time, the clash will just be more immediate, with this a no man's land. Either way, this nice little plain is going to be littered with the dead and dying before long."

"According to the hex map, here, there's a little shelter over near that cleft in the rocks," Vistaru noted. "That's where we're supposed to meet our guide, if anyone's still there."

Mavra tried to look to where the Lata pointed, but her head wouldn't come up enough. Two or three meters, that was the limit. She swore in frustration, but there was determination on her face as well.

It was about fifteen degrees centigrade on the plain, which was comfortable, but that wouldn't last long, either. The air cooled almost two degrees for every three hundred meters in altitude, and some of those passes were over three thousand meters high.

They walked leisurely to the shelter, and almost missed it. It was a low cabin of old stone and wood set back against the rocks, so old and weatherbeaten that it almost looked a part of the natural formations. It looked deserted, and they approached cautiously, uncertain of what surprises might be around for them.

Suddenly the big door, almost as high as the shack itself, creaked open, and a creature came out.

It looked like a human woman, almost. Long hair tied back in a sort of ponytail, an attractive, oval face and long slender arms. But she had little pointed ears, and from the waist down, below her light jacket, she had the body of a white-and-black spotted horse.

A centaur, the classicist Renard thought, no longer

surprised. Meeting such a creature was no longer strange; in fact, it was almost to be expected.

The woman smiled when she saw them, and waved. "Hello!" she called, in a pleasant soprano. "Come on up! I'd almost given you up!"

Vistaru approached. "You are the Dillian guide?" she said, almost unbelievingly. The Dillian was no more than a girl, perhaps in her mid-teens.

The centaur nodded. "I'm Tael. Come on in and I'll start a small fire."

They entered; Tael gave the strange-looking Mavra an odd look, but said nothing. Doma waited outside, placidly munching grass.

The place was built for Dillians, certainly—there were stall-like compartments for four of them, a lot of straw on the floor, and, up on brick blocks a small wood-burning stove and scuttle filled with chopped wood. Tael threw a couple of pieces in the stove and lit a small piece of paper with a very long safety match, throwing it into the cast-iron belly of the stove.

Dillians never sat; their bodies couldn't stand the weight. So everybody else sat on the straw, Mavra reclining on her side. There was plenty of room.

After some small talk, Renard voiced what they all were thinking.

"Ah, excuse me, Tael, but—aren't you a little young for all this?" he tried, as diplomatically as possible.

The woman didn't take it badly. "Well, I admit I'm only fifteen, but I was born in the uplake mountain country of Dillia; my family has hunted and trapped on both sides of the border for a long time. I know every trail and pathway between here and Dillia, and that's a pretty good ways."

"And the Gedemondas?" Mavra prompted.

The Dillian shrugged. "They've never bothered me. You see them every once in a while—big white shapes against the snow. Never close—they're always gone when you get there. You hear them, too, sometimes, growling and roaring and making all sorts of weird sounds that echo between the mountains."

"Is it their speech?" Vistaru asked.

"I don't think so," Tael replied. "I used to, but

when they asked me to do this guide job for you they fitted me with a translator, and I didn't hear any difference. I've wondered sometimes whether they have any speech as we know it at all."

"That could be bad," Renard put in. "How can you talk to somebody who can't talk back?"

She nodded. "I'm still excited about all this. We've tried off and on to communicate with them for the longest time; I'd like to be there when it's done."

"*If* it's done," Hosuru added pessimistically.

"I'm worried about the smoke from that thing," Mavra said, cocking her head a little bit toward the stove. "Not the Gedemondas. The war parties. They have to be close by."

The girl looked uncomfortable. "I've seen them already, but they just took a close look at me and went on. A few flying horses like yours, and some really strange, beautiful things that must have had orange and brown butterflylike wings three or more meters across. None of them landed."

Vistaru looked concerned. "Yaxa and Agitar both. Advance scouts. We can't stay here long."

"We won't," Tael told them. "We'll leave at first light up the Intermountain Trail in back of the base here. With any luck we'll make Camp 43 shortly after noon, and from there we start getting into snow country—and the air thins."

"How high is this camp?" Renard asked.

"Fifteen hundred sixty-two meters," Tael responded. "But you're already almost four hundred meters up. You wouldn't know it, but the plain's a slope."

"We could fly up that far," Vistaru noted. "We're good to about eighteen hundred meters, and I think you said, Renard, that Doma's good to about that."

He nodded. "But that doesn't help our guide, here. No wings for her."

Tael laughed. "That's all right. I told you I was mountain-born. Even better if we have a head start, but beyond Camp 43, flying will be difficult. I can start up this evening, and be there to meet you in the morning. That way we move even faster." Her face darkened, and she looked at Mavra. "But you will

297

have to be dressed far better than that. All of you, in fact. Frostbite will be a big problem."

"We have some winter things," Hosuru told her. "And I understood you were supposed to bring some stuff."

She nodded, went over to a stall, and hauled out some tough fabric knapsacks. They were heavy, but she managed them without strain. Maybe she couldn't fly, but she did add the muscle power that was their most conspicuous lack.

She sorted things out. Special form-fitting thermal wear to suit Latan contours, including transparent but tough and rigid shielding for the wings, appeared, and a heavy coat and gloves that sealed with an elastic of some kind fitted Renard. "You'll also find these useful," she said, tossing him some small objects which proved to be wrappings for his hooves, with a flat, spiked, disklike sole that would give him not only protection but better footing. She brought out some more clothes, also of the Latan model but larger and without the wing flaps. She looked a little puzzled. They were obviously for a biped with hands and feet.

Hastily, Mavra explained what had happened. The girl nodded sympathetically, but was plainly concerned.

"I don't see how these can be cut down," she said. "Your feet should do all right in the snow, like mine, but you should have some kind of wrapping. You haven't got my protective skin layers and hair," she pointed out.

"We'll do whatever we can," Mavra responded. "Renard will have to lead Doma once we get up there; I'll ride her as long as possible. That should help."

Tael was doubtful, but she was the guide, not the mission leader.

Renard went over to the door, peering out at the sky. No sign of strange or hostile creatures now; a few lazy birds, no more. But soon—who knew?

He wondered just how far off the driving forces were.

At the Palim-Gedemondas Border

THE YAXA CAME IN FOR A LANDING WITH A GREAT beating of its tremendous wings. Coming down, it saw the large number of troops and matériel now massed at the border. It looked good. Convincing.

It had been a long trip, and almost a fatal one. The creature touched the ground gently and went down on all eight tentacles toward the portable command center, a huge circuslike tent established just inside Palim. The Yaxa were born to the air; on the ground they looked awkward and lumbering, never quite properly balanced because of the long folded wings along their back. In the air, however, they were the graceful masters.

The Yaxa entered the big tent, its huge death's head, impassive as always, searching out someone of rank, finally spotting someone who would do over by the big situation map.

Communication between Yaxa was by a complex combination of noises from the thoracic regions and odd sounds made by antennae and slight wing rustles. Their names were untranslatable, so, when dealing with other races, they adopted nicknames that often were nonsense, ironic, or just plain crazy, and stuck to them for multiracial operations.

"Marker reporting in, Section Leader," the newcomer said.

The section leader nodded. "Glad to see you back, Marker. We had begun to think that the enemy had gotten you."

"It was close," the advance scout said. "Those damned little blue men with their electricity and their flying horses. The Cebu are too clumsy to worry about, but even though the horses are slow and awkward, it only needs a touch to get you."

The section leader knew this. She knew, in fact, as much about the physical, mental, and technological characteristics of the Makiem alliance as anyone could. The other side had had a much rougher trip than they; any force that could hammer its way through that much resistance so quickly was a force to be reckoned with.

"How far off are they?" the military commander inquired.

"Down the other side," Marker responded. That meant at least three hundred kilometers, a good distance, and the plain that was the logical camp for the final campaign was only a hundred or so kilometers south of their present position. They would be first. "They're a little slow with their airlift over Alestol, too. After all, they have to move everything they need a fair distance nonstop—more than either the flying horses or Cebu can normally fly. A lot of them are into exhaustion now; the ones who land soon find themselves put to sleep by those big, fat plants and then eaten. Don't sell those Alestolians short, either— some of them have *translators,* would you believe, and they have a hypnotic gas as well. If one of those ones with a translator gets an Agitar or a Cebu, they're sent back against their own people!"

The section leader chuckled dryly. "Oh, yes, I can believe that. A rather large amount was transferred in Zone to get them those translators. I'm happy to see that the expenditure is paying for itself." The tone changed, became more businesslike. "So how soon before they have a sufficient force to start the march?"

Marker was uncertain. "Two, three days at least. And maybe two more to move up to the plain. Call it five days."

The Yaxa leader considered this. "You're sure? As you know, we will be moving this afternoon; we should be in and mostly established on the plain by dark tomorrow. The advance party leaves at dawn by air. With luck we can hold it while our friends go after the engines."

"Who's going?" Marker asked, genuinely curious.
"Some of the Lamotien, of course. Who else?" She
knew that nobody would trust the Lamotien by themselves. They didn't even trust them now.

"Only Yulin can assess the engines once located,"
the section leader pointed out. "So we'll send the
Dasheen up. They're better equipped for a nontech
hex and narrow trails anyway, and they're almost as
big as the Gedemondas."

"None of *us?*" Marker responded, appalled. "But
how will we—?"

"We removed the guidance boxes from the bridge,"
the Yaxa reminded her counterpart. "We'll control it
from the other end. But, no, up there there is no protection for the wings in the cold, and snow provides
little traction. I think the Dasheen and Lamotien will
keep each other honest. We'll hold the plain for them."

"But is it safe risking Yulin like that?" Marker wondered. "I mean, he's the whole game, isn't he?"

"No, the engines are. The only part of the ship that
can't be duplicated. If he gets us the engines, fine. If
he doesn't, what good is he to us anyway? To tell you
the truth, I wouldn't feel a bit sorry if some of those
Dasheen bulls died."

Marker nodded sympathetically. "Their system is
not a logical one, and it grates to see them treated like
that."

"Unfortunately," the section leader sighed, "that
place is really a male's paradise. You know that scientific study they're always throwing up at everybody
to prove male superiority? Well, *we* made the study,
and they're right. Evolutionary-speaking, those cows
are mentally and physically designed to be dull-
minded, willing slaves."

"Well, at least we have better material to send into
the cold mountains than the Makiem," Marker said,
changing the subject to something more pleasant. "The
Cebu could walk up there, but never fly, and they're
terrible on the ground. The Makiem grow semi-
dormant in extreme cold, and the Agitar's flying horses
are valueless at those altitudes."

"But those Agitar can move well," the Yaxa com-

301

mander pointed out. "And there are protective coverings for Makiem. Don't sell them short. They've gotten far already. It's going to be the roughest battle yet for both sides in a few days."

Another Part of the Field

ANTOR TRELIG WAS BOTH CONFIDENT AND OPTIMISTIC. The war had gone well; they were in Gedemondas, and after all they'd been through, not a single one of the soldiers, commanders, and politicians believed they could be stopped.

An Agitar general came into the command tent and bowed slightly, handing him a report. He looked at it with interest, and the Makiem equivalent of a grin spread on his face.

"Has anyone else seen this?" he asked.

The Agitar shook her goatlike head. "No, sir. From the recon man who took it to the General Staff to you."

It was a photograph; a big black-and-white glossy. It was fuzzy and grainy, taken through a very long lens from far away, and it still wasn't *quite* close enough, but it showed the most important thing.

Most of the picture was white; more had been cropped in the blow-up. But there, on a rocky ledge, was a sleek, U-shaped object reflecting the sunlight, and there were not quite legible markings on the side.

He didn't need to read them. He knew it had a symbol of a rising sun with a human face flanked by fourteen stars, and the huge legend NH-CF-1000-1 on the side, and, in smaller letters underneath, the words PEOPLE'S VICTORY.

It was the engine pod.

"How did you *get* this?" he asked, amazed. "I thought nobody could fly that high."

"One of the Cebu scouts pushed himself to the limit," the general replied. "On his third try he man-

302

aged to get over the second string of mountains and found a deep, U-shaped glacial valley there. His eyes are good; he saw the reflection, above him, but knew that it was beyond his reach and range, so he fitted his longest lens and snapped as many pictures as he could with the glare filter on. This was the best."

He had a sudden thought. "What about the Yaxa? Can't they or those little imitator bastards find this, too?"

"Not a chance," the general assured him. "The Yaxa can't possibly fly high enough to clear that second range. I would have said no Cebu could, either, and the scout is half-dead as it is. He'll be a hero if he survives. As for the Lamotien, remember they can only *simulate* other forms, not become them. They have a flying mode, yes, based on the Yaxa, but it's highly modified to their form and requirements, and the wings are as thick as our own mounts', far too heavy to clear that altitude. No, I think we have the advantage here."

Trelig nodded, satisfied. "But they will get to the plain first," he noted. "And our reports say that the Lamotien can neutralize an Agitar shock, and the Yaxa can fly rings around any of us."

"It's about even, all told," the general admitted. "They'll be dug in by the time we get there, well fortified, and they have to play only for time, nothing more. I suggest we do it a little differently."

Trelig's huge eyes enlarged in surprise. "Something new?"

The general nodded, and spread out a commercial-looking map on the table in front of them. It was a relief map of both Gedemondas and Dilla next door to the east, and it showed great relief and, more important, it had a lot of little dotted lines all over it. Trelig couldn't read a word on it, though.

"It's a Dillian guide and trail map," the Agitar explained. "They sell them to interested people. There are rodents and other animals in that wilderness, and they trap them. The Gedemondas don't seem to mind or bother them, although our Dillian sources say they don't know much more about the creatures than we do. They don't overdo the hunting, and that's been the balance."

Trelig nodded, understanding. "So these little dotted lines are hunting trails?" he guessed.

"Exactly," acknowledged the goat-woman. "And those little rectangles are Dillian shelters set up along the trails. The trails are mostly Gedemondan, not Dillian. I understand that too many Dillians get the locals upset, and they push a ton or two of snow down on them."

That was an unpleasant prospect. He let it pass.

"Now, we're here," the Agitar continued, pointing to an area in the southwest corner. "The Yaxa will be here," now pointing to the small plains area about two hundred kilometers north and slightly east, "and, if you look closely at the map, you'll see something interesting."

Trelig was ahead of her. At least three trails came within two kilometers of where they now sat, east of them a bit. One seemed fairly low.

"Twelve hundred sixty-three meters," the Agitar told him. "Low enough for an unobtrusive air drop."

"Then we might not have to fight at all" he exclaimed, excited. "We can beat them by going in with a small force and heading straight for the engines, while they have to poke and hunt!"

The Agitar shook her head slowly in the negative. "No, there will have to be a battle, if only to cover you. They are not dumb. If we didn't move as predicted they would smell a rat and they would have you. No, the battle goes on, everything as planned. The only difference will be that we will not have any rush to win it, or take needless risks. When you secure the engines, others can be sent to try and disassemble them, if that's possible, or figure out how to move them, anyway. By the time whatever force the Yaxa sends gets there, we'll have already won the objective, no matter how the battle goes."

Trelig liked the plan. "Okay, so it's me and some Agitar males. But what protects me from the cold? I shut down below freezing, you know. Can't help it."

The general got up and walked out of the tent, then came back in with a large carton. She opened the carton and pulled out a strange, silvery costume with a huge dark globe.

"You didn't know we have had five Makiem Entries in the past century, then?" she said, satisfied. "And we don't need the mechanical stuff, either. Air you've got."

He grinned again. Things were going his way now, as they had always done. The Obie computer, New Pompeii, the Well World itself—all were within his grasp.

The general excused herself, and he sat there a minute or two, alone, looking at the map. Then he sighed, got up, and slow-hopped to a curtained-off passage between this tent and his portable living quarters. He pulled it aside. There was a flash of movement, and an object landed on the bed in the far corner.

She could hop quickly, she could, he thought admiringly.

It had been a marriage of convenience, of course. *All* Makiem marriages were marriages of convenience in a race that had no sex except one week a year, underwater, when they had nothing but. The convenience of the scoundrels that ran Makiem, the inconvenience of himself, naturally. She was the good minister's daughter, and, if anything, she was slicker and nastier than her father.

What a team we'd make, he sighed once again, *if only we could be on the same side!*

"You needn't pretend, my dear. You know everything and I know it, so what's the difference? You can't go this time."

"I go where you go," she responded. "It is law and custom. And you cannot stop me!"

He chuckled. "But it's *cold* up there, baby! What good would you be as a sleeping beauty?"

She reached over, opened a wicker basket, and removed something. It was a slightly different design, but unmistakably a spacesuit.

He gaped. "How long have you had that thing?" he asked.

"Since Makiem," she replied smugly.

Camp 43, Gedemondas

THE TRAILS WEREN'T BAD. GEDEMONDANS, IT WAS known, were large creatures, and limited but steady use by the horselike Dillians had made them even more comfortable, on the whole around two meters wide.

It was a strange party that set off from the chilly shack into the snow cover: Tael, the Dillian guide, was in the lead, then the two Lata, occasionally walking but more often riding on Tael's back, then Renard leading the winged pegasus, Doma, with the strange figure of Mavra Chang tied between wings and neck. The air was becoming cold; there was little conversation between them, nor was much possible without yelling, for blowing wind howled through the rocky clefts as if it, too, were a strange and living creature of this strangest of worlds.

It was only on the occasional breaks, done mostly for Renard's benefit, that they could say anything. The plain was far behind; the twists and turns that the switchbacked trail forced upon them had all but the confident Tael totally lost, and the bright snow reflecting the glare of the sun, even when cut with sun goggles, made distance impossible to judge. They were tiny figures moving in a sea of white.

The trail itself seemed often lost in the snow, yet Tael went on as if it were a paved and marked highway, never hesitating in the slightest—and the footing was always there.

After they had been climbing for what seemed like a full day, they rounded one more mountain curve and, suddenly, the plain was spread out below them once more.

"Wait!" Mavra called to them. "Look! They've arrived!"

They stopped, and saw immediately what she

306

meant. Tiny puffs of orange seemed everywhere in the air, and large numbers of creatures could be seen erecting tents and digging into the rock that was the start of the mountains. The cabin was invisible, but they all knew that, if it was there at all, it was being converted into a fort.

"Look at them!" Tael breathed. This was her first taste of armies and war. "There must be *thousands* of them!"

"The Yaxa," Vistaru said flatly. "They will be coming up only a day or so behind us. This is not good."

Tael laughed confidently. "Let them try and find the trail!" she boasted. "Without a guide they haven't a prayer!"

Mavra turned and looked out at the sky. There were thin, wispy clouds and an occasional big, fat cumulus puff, but it was basically crystal clear.

"They'll follow our own tracks," she told them. "There's no snow, nothing to cover them. They might mistake them for animal tracks, or Dillians alone, but where a four-footed animal or Dillian can go, so can they."

The centaur frowned. A good snow guide, Mavra thought, but naïve as hell. Dillia must be a very peaceful place.

"We could lay a false trail," Tael suggested. "Run tracks off a cliff. It's not that hard. The powder here could be brushed for a few hundred meters."

Mavra considered it. "All right, do it," she told them. "But it won't do much. Slow them up, get a couple, that's all. Better than nothing, though."

They rigged the deception fairly simply. The Dillian girl picked a point, walked out to where there seemed to be continuous snow, then stopped. Renard removed his small snowshoes and followed gingerly behind in her tracks, then guided her feet as she backed up into her old tracks.

Mavra surveyed the results. "A little too deep," she said critically. "An experienced tracker would catch on, but I think it'll work. Does that snow fall off there and I just can't see it, or what?"

Tael laughed. "This is the edge of what we call Makorn Glacier. A river of slowly moving ice with a snow-cover on top. There is a crevasse there at least three hundred meters down and a good ten meters wide. I could almost feel the edge of it."

The small Lata then went back after they went around another bend with Tael's fur hat and used it to fill in the tracks. Not an expert job, but they weren't trying to fool experts.

They went on, into the hex and up at the same time. More frequent rest periods were called for. The air was becoming thin.

During one of these stops, Mavra said, "Still no sign of the Gedemondans. Hell, if they're big bastards there must be awfully few of them to be this invisible."

Tael shrugged. "Who knows how many there are? Sometimes there seem to be a hundred sneaking around the mountain tops; sometimes you will go completely through the hex without seeing one. That is not the trouble here, though."

"Huh?" they all said at once.

She nodded. "We're being watched. I can feel it. I'm not sure where they are, but there is certainly more than one. I could barely hear some intermittent deep breathing."

They looked around, suddenly nervous. No one could see anything.

"Where?" Renard pressed.

Tael shook her head. "I don't know. Mountain sounds are deceptive. Close, though. They have networks of trails they, ah, discourage us from using."

"They'd have to," Mavra said dryly. She strained but could hear nothing but the howling wind. The working part of her ears was still the same as ever, good but not fantastic; all the bigger ears had done was to give her a little better localization and add a slightly hollow sound to everything, which the wind magnified.

She was freezing to death, too, despite being covered by an amazingly resourceful patchwork set of clothes. Her face and particularly her ears were killing her; still, it was no worse on her than on the others, and they didn't complain.

"Let's keep going," Hosuru said after a moment's

listening. "If they're shadowing us, they'll either make a move or they won't. Just keep listening and looking."

"Don't strain too hard," Tael warned. "If they don't want to be seen, they won't be. All bright white like the snow, they could be ten meters away and out in the open and you'd never know it."

They pressed on.

They reached Camp 43 before sundown, but Tael insisted that this would be their stop for the night. "We couldn't possibly make the next camp before nightfall, and you don't want to be out here after dark."

"I hope those Yaxa or whatever feel the same way," Renard worried.

"I hope they don't," Mavra responded. "That'll kill a lot more of them a lot quicker. Vistaru? Hosuru? You're nocturnals. You want to try this trail in the dark?"

Vistaru laughed. "Not in the dark, not in the daylight, not anytime without a guide who knows what she's doing!" she responded.

The crude shelter was built for two Dillians; the stalls were fine for Tael and Doma, and the others just sort of scrunched in as best they could. With the supplies, it was hard to close the door, and the old iron fireplace was so close to them they had to choose freezing or burning. But, it would do.

It had been a trying day; they were all dead tired, half-snowblind, and ready for a rest. There seemed little point in setting a guard; if the Gedemondans wanted to do them in, they could do it any time. If they wanted contact, well and good. And if the Yaxa coalition party somehow managed to close in on them, they had little means to fight it anyway. As the fire burnt down, they slept.

There was a wrongness somewhere. It disturbed her in her sleep, and her mind fought for it, tried to seize on it, and it seemed somehow elusive yet present and growing more and more ominous.

Mavra Chang awoke, lying motionless. She looked quickly around. They were all there; not only Tael and Renard, but even Doma snored.

She tried to figure out why she was suddenly wide awake. There was some sense of alarm, something that had her suddenly as clear-headed as ever when danger threatened. She reached for the source with her mind and eyes. It was chilly now, yes; it must be well into the night. But that wasn't it.

Doma suddenly awoke and shook her great head. She snorted nervously. Mavra lifted her head a little, sure now that she wasn't going crazy. The pegasus sensed it, too.

There it was. A noise. *Scrunch-scrunch; scrunch-scrunch,* over and over, a little louder each time.

Someone—or something—was walking rather calmly and steadily up the trail, something confident even in the night and snow.

Scrunch-scrunch, the snow was falling under its feet. It seemed to be big.

And now the noise stopped. Whatever it was was right outside the door, she knew. She started to call out, to warn the others, but somehow she couldn't seem to make a move, only stare at that closed door. Even Doma seemed suddenly calm, but expectant. She was reminded of the Olbornian priest's power over her, but this wasn't like that. It was—something else. Something strange, completely new.

The door opened, surprisingly silently considering its rusting hinges and bad fit. A blast of chilly air hit her, and she felt the others stir uncomfortably.

A huge white furry shape was there. It was tall— tall enough that it had to bend a little to stick its head just inside the door. A face looked in at her, and smiled slightly. It raised a huge hairy white paw and put a huge, clawed index finger to its mouth.

Gedemondas—a Back Trail

ANTOR TRELIG CURSED FOR THE THOUSANDTH TIME. One mishap after another on this damned journey, he thought sourly. Avalances in front of them, the trail undercut—almost as if someone was trying to stop them or slow them down, although no one had been sighted of any kind.

The trail was a lot more obvious on the map than it was in reality; it wasn't well maintained, some of the shelters were in disrepair and obviously had been so for years, and the trail often vanished without visible landmarks, causing the Agitar to have to probe gingerly ahead with their *tasts*. Their party of fourteen —twelve Agitar, he, and his not-so-loyal wife, Burodir —was now nine, still including Burodir, unfortunately.

But the landmarks were reasonably clear; the terrain was not bad, most of the climbing having been at the beginning, and as many times as the trail had vanished it had also been crystal clear, as if tramped down by the soles of many feet.

This had worried him at first, until he was reminded by the Agitar that this was, after all, somebody's hex, and somebody had to live in it.

In a way, that thought was the most disturbing. They had neither seen nor heard a native in all this time, in all this way. It made no sense at all that there shouldn't be *some* creatures somewhere along the way, except the occasional panic-inducing arctic hare, or whatever it was, and a few small weasellike creatures.

And yet—somehow, they'd made it. Somehow they'd kept to this trail. Somehow they were going all the way. He was, anyway. What the others did was up to them.

He studied the maps and aerial photos from the Ccbu scouts. He knew pretty much where he was, although without the prescouting he would have been lost and dead now, he had to admit. The inner ring of mountains, slightly taller than the outer but hidden before now, was clearly ahead. And, just on the other side of that big, glacier-carved peak over there, and over a bit, was a U-shaped valley with a very important large object lying askew on a ledge.

They would not make it today, that was for sure. But sometime tomorrow afternoon, certainly, if nothing else happened.

Along the Intermountain Trail

"IFRIT! MY FIELD GLASSES!" BEN YULIN COM-manded. The cow reached into the pack of her cowife and quickly extracted them.

"Here, Master," she said eagerly, handing them to him. He took them without a word and put them to his eyes.

They were not merely binoculars; they had additional special lenses that helped his nearsightedness. With the already ground prescription snow goggles, they brought anything within their range into sharp, clear focus.

"Trouble?" growled a low voice next to him.

He looked away and over at the thing. It looked like a walking hairy bush, about as tall as he, with no apparent eyes, ears, or other organs. In actuality, it was not a single creature, but a colony of thirty-six Lamotiens, adapted to the cold weather and the snow.

"That shack up there," he pointed suspiciously ahead. "Doesn't look right, somehow. I don't want any more tricks like that fake trail. We lost two good cows there." Neither his, he failed to add.

"We lost thirty brothers, don't forget!" snapped the Lamotien. "We agree it looks strange. What should be done about it?"

Yulin thought a minute, trying to find a good solution without risking his noble neck or his possessions. "Why don't a couple of you go on up? Turn white or something and take a look around."

The Lamotien considered it. "Two each, we think. Arctic hares." The creature seemed to come apart all of a sudden; breaking into small, equal-sized fuzzy masses. Two of the things came off one side and jumped to the snow; two others from the left. Yulin

312

watched, fascinated as always, as the rest of the shaggy creature reformed and readjusted. It looked slightly thinner, but otherwise the same.

Now the two Lamotien in the snow ran together, seemed to blend into one big shaggy lump. The other pair did the same. Slowly, as if there were unseen puppeteer's hands under the shaggy mops, there was a poking here, a wrinkle there, a bend here, a growth there.

Two arctic hares were there in less than two minutes. They scampered off naturally in the direction of the cabin. The rest waited; only the colony leader had a translator, so they'd have to reform before he knew the story. They didn't have vocal communication, that was for sure. He wondered if they talked when they melded, became one being with common mind, or what. He'd asked, but the Lamotien told him not to worry about it, the concept was beyond him anyway.

The hares returned in a little more than ten minutes, disconnected, jumped back into the hairy lump, and melded again. The shape was silent for a minute, talking to the scouts or maybe absorbing the scouts' brief memories.

Finally, it said, "The place is deserted. You're right about it being funny, though. Lots of packs and supplies still there. Somebody was there not long ago, and left—not of their own will, we'll wager. Too much stuff left."

That had him worried. "Think they were the centaurs we've been following?"

"Probably," the Lamotien agreed. "But whoever they are, they're gone now."

"Tracks?"

The Lamotien paused. "That's the funny part. There aren't any. We see their tracks, lots of snow disturbances where they unpacked, and all that. But no other tracks for hundreds of meters in any direction. None."

"Well, they didn't come back *this* way," Yulin said, worried now. "So where did they go?"

They all looked around at the silent mountains.

"And with whom?" responded the Lamotien.

Another Part of the Field

IT SEEMED THAT THEY HAD WALKED FOREVER; THEY had frequent rests—their captors seeming to appreciate their need for more oxygen than the atmosphere now provided—but no conversation. A few grunts and a lot of gestures, none of which the translators would handle, but nothing else.

They were off any trails the Dillians knew, though. Trails so invisible at times that the great Gedemondans leading the way in sometimes crazy patterns seemed to be lost themselves. They weren't, though; they simply knew, somehow, everything that was under the snow.

Doma, carrying both Mavra and Renard, was being led by Tael with the two Lata on her back. In front were four of the giant snow creatures; behind, four more. Others were visible now, here and there, sometimes a large number, sometimes one or two crossing paths.

Mavra still wasn't sure what they were. They didn't really remind her of anything, yet they somehow reminded her of everything. All snow white, not even the dirtiness that such thick hair usually displays so well. Tall—Tael was well over two meters, and they were almost a head taller than she—and very slender. Humanoid, yet their faces appeared doglike, snow white with long, very thin snouts and black button noses, their eyes set back, large but very human-looking, and an intense pale blue. Their hands and feet formed huge circular pads when closed, the palms and soles of a tough, white, pawlike material. But when they spread their fingers, their long, thin fingers, they had three and a thumb—although their hands seemed to be almost without bones. They could bend them any which way and flex them and the whole hand in any direction, as if they were made of some kind of putty. Fingers and toes had long, pink claws, the only nonwhite part of them other than the nose. Even the insides of their saucerlike ears were white.

They filled in the tracks by the simplest method imaginable. They wore flowing white capes of some animal fur, and it dragged behind them as they walked, the light top powder filling in behind them. They didn't sink down into the snow nearly as heavily as they should have; the padlike feet acted almost like snowshoes.

Tracks weren't a problem here; they knew they were being taken into the mainstream of Gedemondan life, whatever that was. This was the part hidden away from all comers, the part they never let you see.

And that made them wonder. Why them? Did the Gedemondans know they were coming? Were they being helped? Or were they prisoners to be interrogated about all these invasions before being tossed over a cliff? There were no answers, only more walking.

Occasionally the great snow-beasts would pop right up out of the snow. It was unsettling at first, until they realized that there must be trap doors of some kind—whether over ice caves, natural or dug, or rock caves, or even artificial dwellings that were covered with snow they didn't know. It was clear, though, that one of the big reasons you never saw the population was that they were living and doing whatever it is they did below the snow cover, the art of camouflage coming naturally to them.

Night came, plunging this wintry world into an eerie glowing darkness. The night sky of the Well World reflected off the snowfields in distorted, twinkling wonder. New Pompeii wasn't visible, but it might not yet have risen, or it might have set, or it might be out of sight behind the distant mountains.

They hadn't had time to take any supplies. The Gedemondans had been gentle but insistent; when they had protested, they had been picked up as easily as Renard picked up a bag of apples, and plopped down on top of the two best able to carry them, Tael and Doma. Tael was too overawed and a little scared to protest much; Doma seemed curiously at home and docile around the strange creatures, as if they had some mysterious power over her.

Or, they hoped, because she could perceive no threat.

Still they didn't go hungry. Just after darkness fell they were led to a large cave they would have never known was there, and other Gedemondans brought familiar fruits and vegetables, from where they couldn't guess, served on broad wood plates, and a fruit punch that tasted quite good.

They even seemed extra concerned about Mavra's problems. Her dish was higher and thicker, the easier to reach it, and the punch was in a deep bowl so she could drink as she wished.

Renard had not used his electrical powers at Mavra's suggestion; they were, after all there to contact the Gedemondans, and this was, if nothing else, contact. But he couldn't resist it, finally, and reached over to a close relative of an apple and applied a small charge that baked it.

The Gedemondans didn't seem impressed. Finally one who was sitting against the cave wall got up and walked over to him, then crouched down across from him, the plate in the middle. A clawed hand reached out, touched the plate. There was a blinding flash lasting only a fraction of a second, and the plate and fruit just weren't there any more. Renard was dumbfounded; he reached over, felt the spot where it had been. It wasn't even warm, yet there were no char marks, debris, or anything but a tiny little odor of ozone or something. The snow-creature snorted in satisfaction, patted him patronizingly on the head, and walked off.

That ended the demonstrations of power.

They were bone-tired and chilled, but they did not spend the night in the cave. Although they didn't run, it was apparent that their captors were on some sort of schedule, and that they had a particular place for their captives to be at a certain time.

It was several more hours before they reached it, and by that point Tael was complaining to the silent leaders loudly that she couldn't go a step farther.

It was a solid rock wall, looming ominously ahead

in the near-darkness. They started for it, expecting to turn any minute, but it didn't happen. Instead the wall opened for them.

To be precise, a huge block of stone moved slowly back, obviously on a muscle-powered pulley, and bright lights shone into the darkness. They went on, into the tunnel.

The light was from some glowing mineral that picked up torchlight and magnified it a hundredfold. It was bright as day inside.

The inside of the mountain was a honeycomb; labyrinthine passages went off in all directions, and they were quickly and completely lost. But it was warm—comfortable, in fact—inside, the heat coming from a source they never did discover, and there were strange noises of a lot of work being done—but what was going on it was impossible to see.

Finally, they were at their destination. It was a comfortable, large room. There were several big beds there, filled with soft cushions of fabric, and a large fur rug that was perfect for Mavra. There was only one entrance, and two Gedemondans stood there, conspicuous yet as unobtrusive as possible. This was it, then.

They were too tired to talk much, to even move, or worry about what was in store for them. They were sound asleep in minutes.

The next day all awoke feeling better, but with some aches and pains. Gedemondans brought more fruits, a different punch, and even a bale of hay which could be used by both Tael and Doma. Where *that* came from there was little mystery; it was a ration at one of the trail cabins.

Mavra stretched all four limbs and groaned. "Oh, wow!" she said. "I must have slept solid and unmoving. I'm stiff as a board."

Renard sympathized. "I'm not feeling too great myself. Overslept, I think. But we're the better for it."

The two Lata, who always slept motionless on their stomachs, still had their own complaints, and Tael said she had a stiff neck. Even Doma snorted and flexed her wings, almost knocking Tael in the face.

The Gedemondans had cleared away the breakfast dishes; now only one was in the room, looking at them with a detached expression.

Vistaru looked at him. Her? No way to tell with them. "I wish they'd say *something*," she muttered, as much to herself as to the others. "This strong, silent treatment gives me the creeps."

"Most people talk too much about too little *now*," said the Gedemondan, in a nice, cultured voice full of warmth. "We prefer not to unless we really have something to say."

They all almost jumped out of their skins.

"You *can* talk!" Horsuru blurted, then covered, "That is, we were wondering . . ."

The Gedemondan nodded, then looked at Mavra, still on her side on the rug. "So you are Mavra Chang. I've wondered what you would look like."

She was surprised. "You know me? Well, I'm pleased to meet you, too. I'm sorry I can't give you my hand."

He shrugged. "We were aware of your problem. As to knowing you, no. We were *aware* of you. That is different."

She accepted that. There were lots of ways of getting information on the Well World.

Tael could not be restrained now. "Why haven't you ever talked to us?" she asked. "I mean, we had the idea that you were some kind of animals or something."

Her lack of subtly did not perturb the Gedemondan. "It's not hard to explain. We work hard at our image. It is—necessary." He sat down on the floor, facing them.

"The best way to explain it is to tell you a little of our own history. You know, all of you, of the Markovians?" That was not the word he used, but he was using a translator and that's the way it came out.

They nodded. Renard was the most ignorant of them; even Tael had had some schooling. But Renard, at least, knew from his own area of space of the dead ruins of that mysterious civilization.

"The Markovians evolved as all plants and animals evolve, from the primitive to the complex. Most races reach a dead end somewhere along the line, but not them. They reached the heights of material attainment. Anything they wished for was theirs. Like the fabled gods, nothing was beyond them," the Gedemondan told them. "But it wasn't enough. When they had it all, they realized that the end of it was stagnancy, which common sense will tell you is the ultimate result of any material utopia."

They nodded, following him. Renard thought there was some argument against that, and that he'd like to try Utopia first, but he let it pass.

"So they created the Well World, and they transformed themselves into new races, and they placed their children on new worlds of their design. The Well is more than the maintenance computer for this world; it is the single stabilizing force for the finite universe," the snow-creature continued. "And why did they commit racial suicide to descend back to the primitive once more? Because they felt cheated, somehow. They felt they had missed something, somewhere. And, the tragedy was, they didn't know what it was. They hoped one of our races could find out. That was the ultimate goal of the project, which still goes on."

"It seems to me they made a sucker play," Mavra responded. "Suppose they weren't missing anything? Suppose that was *it?*"

The Gedemondan shrugged. "In that case, those warring powers below represent the height of attainment, and when the strongest owns the universe—I'm speaking metaphorically, of course, for they are mere reflections of the races of the universe—we'll have the Markovians all over."

"But not Gedemondans?" Vistaru prompted.

He shook his head. "We took a different path. While the rest ran toward materialistic attainment, we decided to accept the challenge of a nontechnological hex for what it was—and not try by ingenuity to make it as technological as we could. What nature provided, we accepted. Hot springs allowed some cultivation in these uniquely lighted caverns, which run through the entire hex. We had food, warmth, shelter and privacy. We turned ourselves not outward, but inward, to the very core of our being, our souls, if you will, and

319

explored what we found there. There were things there no one had ever taken time to dream of. A few Northern hexes are proceeding similarly, but most are not. We feel that this is what the Markovians created us to do, and what so few are doing. We're looking for what they missed."

"And have you found it?" Mavra asked, somewhat cynically. Mystics weren't her style, either.

"After a million years, we are at the point where we perceive that something was indeed missing," the Gedemondan replied. "What it is will take further study and refinement. Unlike those of your worlds, we are in no hurry."

"You've found power," Renard pointed out. "That dish of food was just plain disintegrated."

He chuckled, but there was a certain sadness in it. "Power. Yes, I suppose so. But the true test of awesome power is the ability *not* to use it," he said cryptically. He looked over at Mavra Chang and pointed a clawed, furry finger at her.

"No matter what, Mavra Chang, you remember that!"

She looked puzzled. "You think I'm to have great power?" she responded, skeptical and a little derisively.

"First you must descend into Hell," he warned. "Then, only when hope is gone, will you be lifted up and placed at the pinnacle of attainable power, but whether or not you will be wise enough to know what to do with it or what not to do with it is closed to us."

"How do you know all this?" Vistaru challenged. "Is this just some mystical mumbling or do you really know the future?"

The Gedemondan chuckled again. "No, we read probabilities. You see, we *see*—perceive is a better word—the math of the Well of Souls. We feel the energy flow, the ties and bands, in each and every particle of matter and energy. All reality is mathematics; all existence, past, present, and future, is equations."

"Then you *can* foretell what's to happen," Renard put in. "If you see the math, you can solve the equations."

The Gedemondan sighed. "What is the square root

of minus two?" he asked. "That's something you can see. Solve it."

The point was made in the simplest terms.

"But this doesn't explain why you pretend to be primitive snow apes," Tael persisted.

The Gedemondan looked at her. "To entwine ourselves in the material equations is to lose that which we believe is of greater value. It is really too late for any of your cultures to comprehend this; you are too far along the Markovian path."

"But you broke your act for us," Hosuru pointed out. "Why?"

"The war and the engine mod, of course," Vistaru said flatly, in a tone that indicated she thought her friend a total idiot.

But the Gedemondan shook his head from side to side. "No. It was to meet and speak with one of you, to try and understand the complexity of her equation and perceive its meaning and possible solution."

Renard looked puzzled. "Mavra?" he asked quizzically.

The Gedemondan nodded. "And now that is done, although what can be added is beyond me right now. As to your silly, stupid, petty war and your spaceship, well, if you're up to a short journey I think we will settle that now." He got up, and they did the same, following him out. Another Gedemondan followed with their clothing; they wouldn't need it in the warm caves, but it was obvious that they would not return to that room.

They were left in a junction area for a while, and their talkative guide left them. Soon they were joined by another Gedemondan—or was it the same one?—and they continued off. It was silent-treatment time again, regardless.

Later, after what seemed like several hours' walk, they stood again before a stone wall and were helped getting their cold-weather gear on. Some kind Gedemondan had created a form-fitting fur coat with leggings for Mavra. She was amazed, and wondered how they could have done it in a night.

But it helped. The great door opened with a rumble and revealed a strange scene.

It was a great bowl; a U-shaped valley hung over it, and snow filled it deeply.

And, askew on a ledge, unmistakable even at that distance, was the engine module.

And now the guide spoke. It was a different voice, they thought, but with the same kindness and warmth.

"You spoke of power. Over there, just next to that little promontory there, your Ben Yulin and his associates now stand. We marked the trail as subtly as possible, and they almost lost it several times, but they managed to blunder through."

They strained their eyes, but it was too far away.

Now the Gedemondan pointed to the opposite rim. "Up there," he said, "stand Antor Trelig and his compatriots. Again, their journey was stage-managed so they arrived at their point within minutes of the other. Of course, neither party knows the other is there."

The snow-creature turned back and stared at the engine module, marvelously intact and preserved, the remains of the great braking chutes still entwined in it.

"*This* is power," said the Gedemondan, and pointed at the module.

There was a rumbling sound that shook the entire valley. Snow started to fall all around, and the engine module trembled, then started to move, slowly at first, then more rapidly, off the edge of the hanging valley.

It poised for an instant at the edge, then plunged over the side with a roar. But it didn't just fall—it seemed to break apart, and there was a tremendous rumble and roar. Smoke and flames and white-hot billowing clouds erupted. The thing blew itself up on the way down, and, when it hit the snow below, the explosions continued, making the valley look like a minor volcano for several minutes. When the smoke and roar died away, the last of the echoes gone, there was only a melted, smouldering ruin in the snow, bubbling and hissing.

The Gedemondan nodded in satisfaction. "And so ends the war," he said with a finality that was hard to deny.

"But if you could do this—why did you wait?" Vistaru asked, awed and a little frightened.

"It was necessary that all sides witness it," the

creature explained. "Otherwise they would never have accepted the truth."

"All those dead people . . ." Renard murmured, thinking of his own experiences.

The Gedemondan nodded. "And thousands more now littering the plains. Perhaps this experience will save thousand more in times to come. War is the greatest of teachers, and not all of its lessons are bad. Their cost is just so terribly high."

Mavra had a different thought. "Suppose the engine module hadn't landed here," she asked him. "What then?"

"You misunderstand," replied the Gedemondan. "It landed here because it *had* to land here. It could land nowhere else." He nodded, almost to himself. "A *very* simple equation," he muttered.

They stood there a while in silence, stunned. Finally, Mavra asked, "What happens now? To us? To the warring powers?"

"The warring powers will pack up and go home," the Gedemondan replied matter-of-factly.

"Trelig? Yulin?" Renard pressed.

"Are too devious to have been caught here," the creature replied. "They will do as they always have done and act as they always have acted, until the time comes for their equations to solve. They are much entwined, those two, and with you, Renard, and you, Vistaru, and, most of all, with you, Mavra Chang."

She let it pass. All this talk of her importance seemed ridiculous.

"And us?" she prodded. "What happens to us now? I mean, you've pretty well blown your cover, haven't you?"

"Power is best used judiciously," the Gedemondan replied. "A simple adjustment, really. You never were picked up by us. You followed an old trail that seemed recently used, and discovered this valley. Then you watched as the engine module destroyed itself, jarred perhaps by too many sounds echoing across the valley and hitting just the wrong points as it fell. Then you made your way east, into Dillia, to report. You never ever saw the mysterious Gedemondans."

"That's going to be a hard story to keep to," she pointed out.

"But it is *true,*" the snow-creature told her. "Or, as far as your companions are concerned, it will be, the moment you cross into Dillia. We have picked up your pack and supplies and will provide them before you cross the border."

"You mean," Vistaru said, a little upset, "you're going to make us *forget* all this?"

"All but her," he replied, gesturing toward Mavra. "But she will get sick and tired of trying to convince you of all this fairly quickly."

"Why me?" Mavra responded, still puzzled.

"We *want* you to remember," the Gedemondan said seriously. "You see, while *we* developed here along these lines, our children out there in the stars did not. They are all dead now. All gone. The Gedemondans here may yet solve the Markovian problem, but they will never be in a position to implement that solution."

"And I will?" she asked.

"The square root of minus two," replied the Gedemondan.

South Zone

"BUT IT JUST ISN'T *right,*" VARDIA, THE CZILLIAN, objected. "I mean, after all she did and tried to do." It pointed a tendril at a photograph. "Look at her. A freak. A pretty human girl's body, always facing head downward, supported by four mule's legs. Not even able to look straight ahead. No protective hair or body fat. She's so *vulnerable!* Eating like an animal, face pushed into a dish; eating food she can't even prepare herself. She must have normal sexual urges, yet what will have her, from the ass-end at that? She almost has to wallow in her own excrement just to relieve herself. It's awful! And so easy to cure. Just bring her here and send her through the Well Gate."

Serge Ortega nodded, agreeing with all the other ambassador said. "It *is* sad," he admitted. "There is nothing I have done in my whole foul life that pains me like this. And yet, you know why. The Crisis Center of your own hex came out with the cold facts. Antor Trelig will never forget that there's another ship down on the Well World; neither will Ben Yulin. Both can see New Pompeii on clear nights. And if Yulin settles down, the Yaxa will push him into it. We can't control them or the Makiem—and they can pass through Zone as safely as we. We haven't the right to stop them. Nations that would not lift a finger in the war would act against us if we militarized Zone. I still hold to the idea that the Northern ship is beyond *anybody's* reach, and, Lord knows, both the Czillian computers and I have tried every angle! Some of the Northern races are interested, but the Uchjin are completely opposed, and there's no way to get a pilot there physically, anyway."

He paused, then looked at the plant-creature, eyes sad. "But can we take the chance that it *is* impossible? Your computers say no, and so do my instincts. A Northerner once got South, remember. If we can find how. . . . Trelig won't stop. Yulin won't stop. The Yaxa won't stop. If a solution is possible, no matter how complex and off the wall it may be, even shooting a pilot over the Equatorial Barrier with giant sling shots, somebody will come up with the solution. My channels are pretty good, but so are theirs. If anybody comes up with the answer, we'll all have it, and it's a miniwar all over again. And if we aren't to leave it to Yulin or Trelig, then we'll need somebody who knows how to tell that computer to take off and land and such—and who can reprogram it for the almost impossible launch situation and acceleration that would be required. The Zinders can't—even if we knew where and what they were, and we most definitely do not. Nor can a classical librarian like Renard. None of them ever flew a ship. I can't, either. I'm too out of date. And that ship is still there, still intact, and it'll stay that way because the Uchjin don't even understand what it is but think it's pretty, and because that atmosphere they have is almost a perfect preservative."

"If only we could get somebody in the North to blow it up," Vardia said wistfully.

"I've already tried that," Ortega replied swiftly. "Things are different up there, that's all. So we've got a ship that's a ticking bomb, and maybe, hopefully, it'll never go off—but it just might. And if we run her through the Well of Souls, we might lose track or control of the only pilot we have!"

He shuffled through some papers, coming up with a photograph of New Pompeii.

"Look at that," he told her. "There's a computer there that knows the Well codes and math. It's capacity-limited, but it's self-aware, and so it's another player in the game. Against uncounted billions or trillions of lives in the universe, can the fate of one individual be considered? You know the answer." He slapped the computer printouts angrily, upset himself. "There it is, damn it! Tell me some way around it!"

"Maybe she'll solve her own problem," Vardia mused. "Get to a Zone Gate and get here. Then the Well's the only way out."

He shook his head. "That won't work, and I made sure she knows it. Whatever she is, Zone gates will be guarded day and night. If she makes it here, she'll be locked up in a nice, comfortable one-room office in this complex. No windows, no way out. She'll be an animal in a zoo, unable to smell the flowers or see the stars. That is more horrible to her than death, and she's just not the suicidal type."

"How can you be so damned sure of everything?" the Czillian asked him. "If *I* were her, facing her kind of future, I'm sure I would kill myself."

Ortega reached into his massive, U-shaped desk and pulled out a thick file. "The life history and profile of Mavra Chang," he told the other. "Partly from Renard, partly from some hypno interviews we did in Lata that she's not aware of, and partly from, ah, other sources I'm not ready to reveal now. Her whole life has been a succession of tragedies, but it's also the story of a dramatic, continuing fight against hopeless odds. *She is psychologically incapable of giving up!* Look at that Teliagin business. Even not knowing where she was or what was what, she refused to abandon those people. Even as a freak she still insisted on going to Gedemondas, and she did. No, somehow she'll cope. We'll make it as easy as we can for her." That last was said softly, with a gentleness Vardia would never have suspected of the Machiavellian snake-man and former human pirate.

"Look," he said, trying to soften it, "maybe another Type 41 Entry will come in. Then we'll be able to do something. There's hope."

The Czillian kept staring at the photograph. "You know the figures. One time there were lots of human Entries; what have we had in the last century? Two? And we lost track of both of those."

"One's dead, the other's in a salt-water hex and is the wrong kind of pilot," Ortega mumbled. The plant-creature hardly heard. Once it, too, had been a human female. That was why it was picked as the liaison with Ortega.

"I'd still kill myself," Vardia said softly.

Aboard a Ship
Just off Glathriel

THEY HAD TAKEN HER FIRST SOUTH FROM DILLIA through Kuansa to Shamozan, the land of great spiders. She had no fear of spiders, and found them charming and very human.

The ambassador was very kind, but he explained the situation to her in graphic detail, concluding, "The only thing we can do right now is make it as easy as possible. Understand, *we have no choice.*"

She started to say something, but a needle from

someone behind pierced her skin, and things had blacked out.

They took her to a medical section with a strange machine. The ambassador explained it to Renard and Vistaru, who still accompanied her. Hosuru had gone to report and was home already.

"Basically, it reinforces the effect of a hypno," he explained. "It doesn't work on many races, but she's still Type 41, although modified, and it'll work on them and her. What it does is to do a more or less permanent burn-in of a basic hypno treatment, so it doesn't wear off. We know it works, because we took data on her in Lata using a similar device and then blocked all memory, and it held."

"But what will you tell her?" Vistaru worried. "You won't change her, will you?"

"Only a little," the ambassador replied. "Just enough to make her comfortable, adapt. We can't do anything serious; the whole reason for this is that we must keep her on hand for the skills and qualities she possesses. I think she understands that."

The process began.

"Mavra Chang," said the device, preprogrammed carefully. "When you awake, you will find your memories and personality unchanged. However, while you will remember being human, you will be unable to imagine yourself that way. The way you are now will seem natural and normal to you. This form is how you are comfortable. You cannot conceive of being any other way, even though you know you once were, and you wouldn't want to be any different than you are."

The thing went on for a bit, feeding her various bits of information, methods, skills she would need in order to cope, and then it was over.

She had awakened a few hours later, and felt strangely better, more at ease. She tried to remember why she had felt different before, but it came hard. Something to do with being in this form, she recalled.

She remembered being human. Remembered it, but in a curious, lopsided kind of way. It seemed like she'd always had four legs. She tried to imagine herself walking upright on two legs, or picking up things with hands, and she just couldn't. It was just not *right* somehow. *This* was right.

Vaguely, in the back of her mind, she knew that they'd done something to her, something to create this situation, but it didn't seem important, somehow, and she quickly forgot it.

But she remembered the stars. She knew she belonged there, not here, not in any planetbound existence anywhere. She would sit there, topside on the ship as it crossed the Gulf of Turagin, sometimes by sail, sometimes by steam, depending on the hex, head and forelegs propped up on some crates or a hatch cover, looking at the stars.

She chuckled to herself. *They* thought she wanted to go through the Well. Or maybe they thought she'd settle down and forget in this new existence. But the stars came out every night, and those she would never forget. It went beyond reason and logic; it was a love affair. A love affair now forcibly broken by circumstances, but not beyond repair while both lovers lived.

And now, as the sun came up, there was a shoreline out there. It looked green and pretty and warm; sea birds circled offshore, diving occasionally for fish and clams, then took their catch to rookeries in the hillsides overlooking the beach.

Renard came on deck, stretched and yawned, then went over to her.

"Not an unpleasant looking place for an exile," she said calmly.

He stooped down so his head was level with hers. "Very primitive. A tribal culture, not much else. They're human—what we think of as human. But this wasn't our ancestral home. They had a war with the Ambreza; the big beavers gassed them back into the Stone Age and swapped hexes, so it's a nontech hex."

"Suits me fine," she replied. "Primitive means small population." She looked straight at him, head to one side. "And soon your job will be done, and Vistaru's too. They've built a compound for me to my requirements, with a fresh water spring and everything. Once a month a ship will drop off supplies in little plastic pouches I can open with my teeth holding them between my forelegs. There are hostiles and water all around except on the Ambreza side, and they'll keep Zone Gates 136 and 41 secure. The primitives have been effectively tabooed from the compound. No risk to me, and no chance I'll escape. You and Vistaru can go back through the Zone Gate, tell them all is well, and then try and find new lives or pick up old ones. I understand the Agitar are so pissed off at the war fizzling out that you're some kind of hero."

He was hurt. "Mavra—I—"

She cut him off. "Look, Renard!" she said sharply. "You don't owe me anything and I don't owe you anything. We're even now! I don't need you any more, and it's about time you learned you don't need me, either! Go home, Renard!" She was almost screaming now, and the look she gave him said it even more eloquently.

I'm Mavra Chang, it said. I was orphaned at five and again at thirteen. I was a beggar who became the queen of beggars, a whore when I had to be to buy the stars I craved, and I got them! I was a thief they couldn't catch, the agent who snatched Nikki Zinder off New Pompeii and kept her and you alive until help could come. And against all odds, I reached Gedemondas and saw the destruction of the engines.

I'm Mavra Chang, and no matter what comes along, I will cope.

I'm Mavra Chang, bride only of the stars.

I'm Mavra Chang, and I don't need anybody!

The Wars of the Well will be concluded in *Quest for The Well of Souls.*

Appendix: Races Referred to in Exiles at the Well of Souls

N=Nontechnological hex. S—semitechnological hex. H=high-tech hex. A parenthesis (for example, (N)) denotes a water hex. The addition of an M to the hex designation (i.e. SM) means it has what would be regarded as magical capabilities by those who don't have them. Uchjin, the only hex in the North, has an atmosphere that's mostly helium and other useless stuff.

AGITAR	H	Diurnal	Males satyrlike; females reverse animalism of males but are smarter. Males can store and control electric charges.
ALESTOL	N	Diurnal	Moving, barrel-shaped plants that are carnivores and shoot a variety of noxious gasses.
AMBREZA	H	Diurnal	Resemble giant beavers. Used to be N until they beat the Glathriel in a war and swapped hexes with them.
BOIDOL	NM	Diurnal	Giant sphinxlike creatures. Look fierce but are peaceful herbivores.
CEBU	S	Diurnal	Resemble pterodactyls with prehensile apelike feet.

CZILL	H	Diurnal	Asexual plants who duplicate; mobile by day, root at night. Pacifistic scholars with a huge computer center.
DASHEEN	N	Diurnal	Basically minotaurs. Females are much larger and dumber than the males, but males need their lactose/calcium to live.
DILLIA	S	Diurnal	True classic centaurs. Peaceful folk who hunt, trap, farm. Can eat anything organic but are basically vegetarians.
DJUKASIS	S	Diurnal	Giant beelike colonies where citizens are bred physically and mentally for their jobs.
GALIDON	(N)		Giant, tentacled manta rays who are bad-tempered carnivores.
GEDEMONDAS	N	Diurnal	Large, thin, hairy apelike creatures with round feet and doglike snouts.
GLATHRIEL	N	Diurnal	The ancestors of humanity; very primitive since the Ambreza gassed them back into the Stone Age and swapped hexes.
JIIHU	(H)		Large clamlike creatures with lots of tentacles, but they rarely move once full grown.

KLUSID	N	Diurnal	Thin, delicate birdlike creatures in a land of great beauty. Atmosphere is much too high on the ultraviolet for most others.
KROMM	(S)	Diurnal	Huge flowers that spin across their shallow swamp.
LAMOTIEN	H	Diurnal	Small lumpy creatures who can imitate anything, even by combining to build bigger imitations, but can not change their mass.
LATA	H	Nocturnal	Very small humanoid hermaphroditic pixies who can fly and have nasty stingers. Can also glow by secreting chemicals in the skin.
MAKIEM	N	Diurnal	Large reptiles resembling giant toads who need some water daily though land-dwellers. Cold-blooded and have sex only ten days a year during one period.
NODI	N	Nocturnal	Resemble giant mushrooms; thousands of tendrils drop from their "caps" when needed.
OLBORN	SM	Diurnal	Resemble huge, bipedal pussycats with the ability to create their own beasts of burden.

333

PALIM	H	Diurnal	Resemble great hairy mammoths with remarkably prehensile trunk with fingers all around.
PORIGOL	(HM)		Dolphinlike mammals who can stun or kill with sound.
QASADA	H	Diurnal	Large ratlike creatures with long tails, whiskers, and hivelike communities.
SHAMOZAN	H	Diurnal	These huge, hairy tarantulas like alcohol, melodic music, and games of skill.
TELIAGIN	N	Diurnal	Great cyclopses; carnivores who raise their own sheep to eat and are bullheaded but not dumb.
TULIGA	(S)		Giant, rather repulsive sea slugs, neither nice nor communicative.
UCHJIN	N	Nocturnal	Look like giant paint smears flowing down glass.
ULIK	H	Diurnal	Great six-armed snakemen that live in a desert hex at the Equatorial Barrier.
XODA	NM	Diurnal	Resemble four meters of praying mantis, and have a hypnotic way of inviting you to dinner.
YAXA	S	Diurnal	Females who eat their husbands after sex. Look like giant orange-and-

brown butterflies with
hard shiny black bodies,
eight prehensile tenta-
cles, and a death's head
for a face. Visual system
is quite different from
Southern norm.

ZHONZORP   H   Diurnal   Large, bipedal relatives
of the crocodile given to
dressing up like grand
opera, capes and all, but
are solid technicians.

ABOUT THE AUTHOR

JACK L. CHALKER was born in Norfolk, Virginia, on
December 17, 1944, but was raised and has spent
most of his life in Baltimore, Maryland. He learned
to read almost from the moment of entering school,
and by working odd jobs had amassed a large book
collection by the time he was in junior high school,
a collection now too large for containment in his present quarters. Science fiction, history, and geography
fascinated him early on, interests which continue.

Chalker joined the Washington Science Fiction As-
sociation in 1958 and began publishing an amateur
SF journal, *Mirage,* in 1960. After high school he decided to be a trial lawyer, but money problems and
the lack of a firm caused him to switch to teaching.
He holds B.S. degrees in history and English and an
M.L.A. from the Johns Hopkins University. He
taught history and geography in the Baltimore public
schools between 1966 and 1978, and now makes his
living as a free lance writer. Additionally, out of the
amateur journals he founded a publishing house, The
Mirage Press, Ltd., devoted to nonfiction and biblio-
graphic works on science fiction and fantasy. This
company has produced more than twenty books in
the last nine years. Chalker's hobbies include esoteric
audio, travel, working on science-fiction convention
committees, and guest lecturing on SF to institutions
like the Smithsonian. He is an active conservationist
and National Parks supporter, and he has an inten-
sive love of ferryboats, with the avowed goal of riding
every ferry in the world. He lives and works in Baltimore.

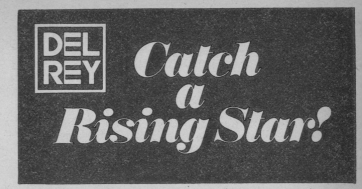

DEL REY *Catch a Rising Star!*

LG-5

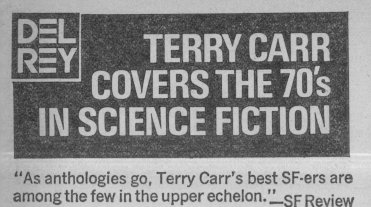

DEL REY *SCIENCE FICTION CLASSICS*
FROM BALLANTINE BOOKS

CHILDHOOD'S END, Arthur C. Clarke	27603	1.95
FAHRENHEIT 451, Ray Bradbury	27431	1.95
HAVE SPACESUIT, WILL TRAVEL, Robert A. Heinlein	26071	1.75
IMPERIAL EARTH, Arthur C. Clarke	25352	1.95
MORE THAN HUMAN, Theodore Sturgeon	24389	1.50
RENDEZVOUS WITH RAMA, Arthur C. Clarke	27344	1.95
RINGWORLD, Larry Niven	27550	1.95
A SCANNER DARKLY, Philip K. Dick	26064	1.95
SPLINTER OF THE MIND'S EYE, Alan Dean Foster	26062	1.95
STAND ON ZANZIBAR, John Brunner	25486	1.95
STAR WARS, George Lucas	26079	1.95
STARMAN JONES, Robert A. Heinlein	27595	1.75
TUNNEL IN THE SKY, Robert A. Heinlein	26065	1.50
UNDER PRESSURE, Frank Herbert	27540	1.75